PRAISE FOR *HE'S GONE*

"Mesmerizing . . ."
—Sarah Addison Allen,
New York Times bestselling author of *The Peach Keeper*

"Thought-provoking and moving."
—Erica Bauermeister,
New York Times bestselling author of *The Lost Art of Mixing*

"Masterful . . . one of the best books I've read all year."
—Barbara O'Neal, author of *The All You Can Dream Buffet*

"Perfectly executed . . . strongly characterized and emotionally complex fiction." —*Kirkus Reviews* (starred review)

"An all-in-one-sitting affair . . . Caletti solves the mystery in the end, but more riveting and of greater depth is her second conclusion, that you bring your same self wherever you go."
—*Publishers Weekly*

"Readers will find themselves swept up . . . by Caletti's believable characters and their raw emotions. As much a gripping emotional thriller as it is a book about love and relationships, Caletti's newest work will please old fans and garner new ones." —*Booklist*

"Readers who appreciate a slow reveal and family drama tied up in their mysteries will appreciate this one." —*Library Journal*

by Deb Caletti

He's Gone
The Secrets She Keeps

the secrets
she keeps

the secrets she keeps

A Novel

Deb Caletti

Bantam Books
New York

A Bantam Books Trade Paperback Original

Copyright © 2015 by Deb Caletti
Reading group guide copyright © 2015 by
Penguin Random House LLC

All rights reserved.

Published in the United States by Bantam Books,
an imprint of Random House, a division of
Penguin Random House LLC, New York.

BANTAM BOOKS and the HOUSE colophon are registered
trademarks of Penguin Random House LLC.
RANDOM HOUSE READER'S CIRCLE & Design is a
registered trademark of Penguin Random House LLC.

Library of Congress Cataloging-in-Publication Data
Caletti, Deb.
The secrets she keeps: a novel / Deb Caletti.
pages ; cm
"Bantam Books Trade Paperback Original."
ISBN 978-0-345-54810-8 (acid-free paper) — ISBN
978-0-345-54811-5 (ebook) 1. Female friendship—Fiction.
2. Ranches—Nevada—Fiction. I. Title.
PS3603.A4386S43 2015
813'.6—dc23
2014029889

Printed in the United States of America on acid-free paper

www.randomhousereaderscircle.com

9 8 7 6 5 4 3 2 1

Book design by Virginia Norey

For my sister

Benedictio: May your trails be crooked, winding, lonesome, dangerous, leading to the most amazing view.

—EDWARD ABBEY, *Desert Solitaire*

Longed for him. Got him. Shit.

—MARGARET ATWOOD, *Six Word Story*

the secrets
she keeps

chapter 1

Nash

She isn't one bit sorry. Not right now. Not when she closes the door of that car and the window is down and there are crickets and millions of stars and miles and miles of open road. For once, she is not the one making the careful, thought-out decisions that make her the practical sister, because there is no question: This is a mistake. This is a doomed mission of the heart, and Veronica May Fontaine says no life worth living is absent a few of those. Of course, Veronica May Fontaine had tipped back more than one Moscow mule before she said it, and Nash's mother had only rolled her eyes. By that time, Alice had heard it all.

But this night, no theory of love matters. No consequences do. There is a thin yellow curve of moon in that big, big desert sky. The night air smells like dry grass and horse manure and summer. Nash is flying down that dirt road with her true love beside her, and she is filled with all the complicated themes of two people bound together by circumstances of fate—rescue and renewal, joy and fear, connection and inevitable loss.

She has made a promise. A vow. She may be only eighteen years old—Jack Waters called her *Peanut* before he stopped seeing her as a child—but you don't grow up on a divorce ranch and not learn to take a vow seriously.

Honestly, though? It may seem terrible to say—horrible, a betrayal—but even the vow, the terrible night of it, the metallic smell of blood and the sound of thunder that wasn't thunder but horse hooves, hundreds of them, has retreated in the face of this. This soaring. This rise in her whole body now, as they pick up speed and the ranch falls away behind them and there is only the sweet catastrophe of what's to come.

chapter 2

Callie

Thomas washed his wallet by accident, and that's what changed my life. He'd left it in his pants. My mother always told Shaye and me never to do a man's laundry, but as I watched him spread out soggy receipts and dollar bills on the foot of our bed, I wished I'd never listened. He looked defeated. He was bent over that small, wrecked pile, and it seemed as if all the annoyances of living had suddenly caught up to him—the cracks in the cement and missed planes and calls to the cable company. Two minutes later, our marriage as we knew it would be hanging in some awful balance, but right then I felt bad for him. I thought maybe he'd lived a life of quiet desperation, only I hadn't known it. My mother—she ended up alone, anyway. She'd say that's how she wanted it, but we were two different people.

It was Saturday morning, and I was still in my robe. I sat cross-legged on the bed. Thomas wore that T-shirt with the sailboat on the back and his favorite old cargo shorts. I always thought he looked cute in those. Thomas was still a very good-looking man, no doubt about that. He was fit and strong, and that dark hair, well, even now it got to me, these many years later, the way it had that slightly mussed mind of its own.

"Did it make it?" I asked him. The wallet looked battered

and soaked but also like it just had the ride of its life. Thomas set it up at an angle on the dresser. It was not any usual old day for that wallet. No flat, dull outing in a back pocket for that adventurous leather accessory.

"I hope so," Thomas said. "It better have."

He seemed to mean it. I was surprised he cared so much about it. It might have been a Christmas gift years ago, and God knew he could do with a new one. He never bought himself the things he needed. He still had coats from his college days, and he could go miles with the sole of a shoe flapping. He was smug about all the things he could do without. It could drive you insane.

"I think it's okay." He exhaled his relief, unfurled a photo from the small stack of wet paper in his hand. There you had it—we'd been talking about two different things, and to that I can only say, *No comment.*

He set the small square of paper on the comforter to dry. It was an awful picture of the four of us from the time of shoulder pads and high-waisted jeans—I'd forgotten how high. My hair was permed for the first and last time, and if you saw it, you'd know why. I did it at home from a box, and the curls were as tight as an Airedale's. Thomas's own hair was long in front, and he was wearing an Alpine sweater that worked so hard at being cheery, your heart went out to it. Amy and Melissa wore the dresses Thomas's mother had bought them just before cancer-scare number one. I made them wear the scratchy lace because we thought she was dying, but naturally she wasn't. Those kinds of people go on forever. I think we had the picture taken for free in the back corner of a J. C. Penney or somewhere like that; at least, we were in front of a cloudy blue background. It was the sort of photo they show on crime programs after someone's been murdered.

"Look at us," I said. Who knew if J. C. Penney even had photo studios anymore.

"I thought it was done for," he said, before moving on, peeling away a sodden ticket stub and a voter-registration card. He held up the damp, noble face of Andrew Jackson, torn in half by the spin cycle. "Great. Terrific."

"A little tape will fix that right up," I said.

"What time is it?" He didn't wait for an answer. He leaned over to look at the clock on the bedside table. "Shit. I'm already late."

He exhaled the frustration of the morning. I felt a curl of guilt for my wifely shortcomings. Thomas was the sort of husband who brought you a cup of coffee and made sure the snow tires had been put on, though maybe, too, you could always feel a sigh in there somewhere. Folding his socks wouldn't have been such a big deal, though he probably would have lost a lot more wallets had I been in charge of the washing.

"How about if I go get her?" Our daughter Amy was at the last Global Citizens meeting before her post-graduation trip to Costa Rica. The group was leaving in the morning. I should also mention what a good father Thomas was. He was even one of the parents who helped at the fundraising car wash. He'd done it for Melissa, too, a few years before. I wanted to be with Amy every chance I could get right then, but I can't truthfully say I minded missing out on the jumping and screaming and sign-waving of the girls on the street corner. T-shirts with glitter could get the better of me. Thomas woke up early, though. He said, *Rise and shine, Sunshines!* and made the rounds of the house, rousing us with the sock of a pillow. He put a baseball cap over his tousled morning hair and even got donuts for the kids on the way.

"I'm going! I'm going right now."

"It's no big deal. She can wait," I said.

He had that look, the one he often had when he came home from work and it was an endless day of weighing what was best for whom, studying zoning laws and park space and the height of bus-stop shelters, making decisions when there were no real right answers. He'd had that look quite a lot lately. Clearly there was a greater thing on his mind. A greater thing that made all other things irritating intrusions.

And that's when it happened. He palmed a sodden business card and crushed it into a ball. This alone did not make me understand that life as I knew it was changing before my very eyes. It was what he did just after that—the way he glanced up to see if he'd been caught. All it takes to unravel or undo is one lost stitch, one tiny tear, and that's what that glance was.

You know way too much about each other when you're married; that's one of the problems. Another is that you know way too little. Still, I'd have recognized that look on anyone. On Shaye when we were kids, or on my own children, or a stranger, for that matter. Even Hugo. He'd had that same look whenever he tried to run off with someone's Kleenex.

Our eyes met. Thomas dropped his away.

"Mack?" I said. It was my love name for him. I felt a little sick inside.

"What?"

"What is that?"

"What?"

"In your hand."

"Garbage."

"Some secret?"

He shook his head, as if I'd been the one to do something disappointing. "Jesus, Callie," he said. A *Je-sus* of disgust, drawn out to two syllables to underscore how irrational I could be.

More than anything, more than *anything*, I wanted my life to stay as it was. I loved my life. I loved Thomas and our daughters. I loved my house. I loved that house so much. Sometimes, you'd put up with almost anything if it meant not losing that brick pathway you'd planted with perennials. It could get confusing. Whether you really did want things to stay as they were, or whether you just didn't want things to change.

Thomas grabbed his license and a credit card and a few still-wet bills and he stormed out of our bedroom. The storming felt like something you'd see on TV. The boat on his back, KAILUA YACHT CLUB, from the last trip we took as a family before the kids got too old for that kind of thing, sailed down the hall in a sitcom huff.

I didn't follow. I didn't ask him questions or demand answers. Not right then, anyway. I kept my suspicions to myself, as if I had a plan. That's the thing about change. Sometimes you think it's something that happens to you, when actually you're right there, acting as its naïve yet diligent assistant.

Late Sunday afternoon, we dropped Amy off at the airport. I wasn't used to seeing her hair so short. She looked even lovelier, changed already, with her eyes shining and that enormous backpack on the floor next to her. *Don't* worry, *Mom*, she'd said. *I'll be* fine. *I'll be great!* The group had all just graduated from high school, but the girls still snuck self-conscious glances into reflective surfaces, and the boys still punched the arms of their friends. We'd known a lot of these kids since kindergarten, and they mostly seemed their same selves, only larger. I remember when Sam lost his lunchbox and cried so hard he threw up, and here he was, with those same vulnerable shoulders. Amy looked back at us and gave a last wave, and for a moment it was like my heart had walked off and I was left with a vacant body. For a second, I wasn't sure what to do. I was at a total loss. Thomas and I stood there together like we were college freshmen just dropped off by their parents and assigned to room together.

We picked up some Thai food and watched a movie Thomas ordered. I had moments where I forgot all about that guilty look he gave me, until the ugly memory butted back in. My head spun, and then the hit of denial kicked in, as helpful and soothing as any sedative. I love denial; I admit it. It's the best drug—plentiful, and free, besides. Thomas, scooping pad kee mao out of a Styrofoam container, looked like old Thomas.

That night, after we turned out the light, the red digital numbers of the bedside clock stared me down. I tried to ignore it, but of all household objects, bedside clocks are the most insistent, more than beeping refrigerators and door alarms, more than kitchen timers and even blaring radios. It's the strong silent types that get you.

"Thomas?"

"Mmm."

"Are you awake?"

"No."

"If you're talking, you're awake."

"I wasn't talking."

"I don't want you to get mad, but I've got to ask you something."

"Cal, what, it's almost midnight."

One of the digital numbers blinked, six to seven, and then stared. Okay, all right! I set my hand on the hill of Thomas's hip. "Yesterday, when you washed your wallet . . . You crumpled something up."

"I don't remember." His voice was clear now. It had lost the muffled quality of near sleep.

"I think you do."

He sat up then. Actually, he didn't just *sit up*; he rose with a pissed-off tussle of blankets, yanked the quilt to cover him. I could see the outline of his face turned to me in the dark, and I knew by the set of his jaw how upset he was. "Jesus, Cal. Really? Why are you going on about that again? Do you think I'm having some *affair*? It was a *piece* of *paper*."

Should I have stopped there? Would that have ended it? Well, I couldn't, because if it were nothing, I'd still be seeing the motionless curve of his body, the hump of him, under the covers. He would not have sat up like this, fuming now. He'd have stayed close to sleep, offering the tired explanation that would finally settle the matter.

"What kind of piece of paper?"

"A business card."

"Whose?"

"Do you think this is in any way reasonable? You wake me up at midnight to interrogate me about a stupid card from some . . . I don't know what his name was, Jarret? Jarret Smith? Some guy who came by the office offering *financial services*. Okay?"

"Okay," I said.

He punched his pillow, made his feelings clear through fist and down feathers, and then dropped his head again. I knew he was awake, though. I had that heightened awareness that speaks of possible danger, the feeling you get after there's been a wrong sound in the house and you wait, just as I was doing then, to see if you might hear it again. After a while, there was the familiar rhythm of his breathing. He'd fallen asleep. But I lay awake for a long time, the glowing red numbers of that clock sending their steadfast message, telling me something I was sure I already knew.

The next day, I was finally alone. It was the kind of alone I hadn't been in a long, long time, with Melissa out on her own and Amy away, and Hugo, my companion and my greatest protector, gone to wherever good dogs go when they die. Denial is never fond of *alone*; it tends to flee then.

The house was eerily quiet. Time loomed before me, too, since I'd recently left my job. I blamed the management change, but, truth be told, I had long ago lost my enthusiasm for photographing kayaks and hiking shoes when I didn't even kayak or hike. My true feelings about Thomas and that crumpled card had apparently been waiting for this most empty and defenseless moment, because they stormed the gates, and I was trampled. I felt queasy and panicked. I poured a cup of coffee and stared out the kitchen window for a while, waiting for the row of mailboxes and the newly mown lawn to send me some courage. Unless Thomas threw that little ball out the window as he sped down the highway to pick up Amy, it was here somewhere.

And Thomas wasn't the type to throw anything out a window, even something he might want to hide. He was the law-abiding sort who was burdened by other people's recklessness—the one who picked up after a neighbor's dog and who trimmed the overgrown trees that impaired visibility next to the stop sign. He always did more than anyone else, including me, and then said he didn't mind. He appeared to mind a great deal, though. There was the huff of overwork, the passive–aggressive complaint of various physical maladies brought on by overexertion, the plain old undercurrent of displeasure, and yet, much to my bewilderment and frustration, he continued on this ever-spinning wheel, being the bothered good citizen and burdened husband and father. It seemed simple: Get off the wheel. Still, those simple things—they're never simple to the poor soul wrestling with them. Think of the energy we spend in our private, raging battles that seem downright ludicrous to everyone else.

I respected that man, more than I can say. Did I mention he was a vegetarian, too? And he always recycled. All that goodness—a lifetime of it—it would get tiring, wouldn't it? Being such a prince of a man would be exhausting. Honestly, I was exhausted by it. Each was a hallmark of moral superiority in Seattle—the good-neighborliness, the abundant vegetables, the reusable bags; we only needed to open a microbrewery or start using the words *farm-to-table* and we could rise to the ranks of religious leadership in the Emerald City, hit the hip, slick pages of *Seattle* magazine. I never confessed my own lapses in judgment, though: the times I'd forgotten a plastic bag for Hugo on our walks, the containers I didn't want to rinse and sort, the beef—the fast-food beef, no less—that I devoured. Here, you could maybe get away with eating beef as long as the cow had a good life and you sent him to college beforehand.

Not that Thomas would have cared about these transgressions. He wouldn't have. He might have edged toward maddening self-sacrifice and a stubborn insistence on being underappreciated, but for the most part, he was also truly generous. I'm not even sure why I couldn't admit my own imperfections, aside from the fact that a person's constant goodness can feel like recrimination. You hide your little failings.

I set my cup in the sink. I had to find out what was going on.

The house was so quiet that I could hear the upstairs hall clock ticking. I knew deep inside, or maybe not so deep at all, right at the surface, that Thomas had given up the grueling goodness and morality. I knew it because it made sense—it made a lot of things clear, because he hadn't been himself for a while. Those long runs he'd been doing, for one. He hadn't run since just after Amy was born, but lately he'd lace up his shoes and put on the kind of loose running shorts people didn't wear any-more, and he'd be gone for hours. *Gotta watch my heart*, he'd say. *What was Dad, fifty-five?* He'd also turn his back to me in bed after saying good night. You get used to that when you've been married awhile, the various meanings of his back. The back that shouted your wrongdoings or that punished with its slightly freckled silence. But this was *more* back. Or, at least, a back that kept its secrets. A back that was a wall.

And I'd hear him wake up in the night. He'd be down in the kitchen. The pantry door would squeak open, and then, next, the cupboard where we keep the glasses. I thought he was de-pressed. His mother had recently passed away, so of course he would be. His eyes welled up during Amy's graduation, too, and in all the time I'd known him, I'd seen him cry only once before, at his mother's funeral. Our friend, Dan Fallon, of Jan and Dan Fallon, told us at a barbecue one night after too much wine that he couldn't even walk past his daughter's room without bawling after she, their youngest, had left for college.

We didn't talk about this, the soundless weight that had moved in, bringing silky jogging shorts and morose stares out sunny windows. We should have, I know. But we didn't. I made a few tries at it, but it was apparently large enough that we had to step around it. It became a *thing*. You know the ones. The particular, unspoken entities you feel at every curt *good night* or aloof *how was your day*. The thing follows the two of you around to every room and breathes down your neck, but you pretend with some degree of frost and unspoken fury that it's not there. Sometimes, marriage is just too intimate for intimacy.

I tried the pockets of the jeans Thomas had worn on Saturday, which were upstairs, neatly folded on a shelf in our bedroom closet. Then I opened his underwear drawer and fished around in there, and felt inside the satin pouches of his suit jackets. I looked in the bathroom garbage can, which Thomas had recently emptied, and then headed back down to the kitchen, straight past that ticking clock. I don't know when it happened, but recently that hallway had begun to slope—the porch off the kitchen, too—and I could feel the unsettling tilt under my feet, a little metaphoric jab. Mike Murphy, from Phinney Contracting, said it was an issue of settling and rot, and that the foundation "needed work." This kept me awake at night. The house I loved suddenly seemed to have a mind of its own, and I pictured it slipping farther until it sped like a toboggan (pages 30–31 of the REI catalog: *ski equipment–sleds*) down into Carkeek Park ravine. Shaye once had a segment of her roof collapse, back when she was married to crazy ex-husband number one, and she still slept in the house that night. I could never do that. As it was, the fact that our house had begun to shift felt like a betrayal. After all I'd given it over the years.

The most obvious places to look for that horrible business card awaited. Of course, I didn't want to actually find it. Outside, summer was starting and the sky was wrongly blue, and I watched the innocent petal of a magnolia blossom drift to the ground like a line in a poem. I turned my back to the window and leaned against the dishwasher and gave a disappointed look to the canisters of flour and sugar, to the cup of pencils next to the pad of paper where we wrote the grocery list, all that orderliness that had not come through for me. I shouldn't even tell what I did next, but I will. I called for Hugo. I called out his name in the high-pitched voice that usually made him come running. I know it sounds nuts, and I didn't expect anything from it, of course. He wasn't going to come trotting around the corner, hoping for a treat. His ghost wouldn't appear holding his orange ball in his mouth. That boy—I just missed him so much, my chest ached. He'd have never let anything happen to me if he could help it, and every FedEx man around knew it. He would have even protected me from this, if it were in his power.

My voice sounded hollow and clanging in all that silence, and I embarrassed myself. Thank God people don't see all the crazy things you do in private. I felt a little out of control, because I knew if that paper was anywhere, it would likely be in one of two remaining places—the trash can outside or, where I looked next, the kitchen garbage. I rooted past a banana peel and a half-filled coffee filter, mad at the cliché it all was, and then my phone rang. I startled, as if I was the one who'd been caught.

I have no excuse for the fact that I answered. Answering right then was unwise. It just added a rainstorm to a bad driver on a curvy mountain road. I loved my mother, but she made my head ache. It was almost instantaneous, like eating ice cream too fast. Still, you go on eating ice cream too fast.

"I'm glad you're there. I have a favor," she said, skipping straight past those pesky hellos.

Headaches, ice cream, mountain roads—none of it mattered. I needed my mother. "Thomas is seeing someone," I told her.

"Like a someone-someone?"

"I think so."

"What do you know."

I crooked the phone against my shoulder, washed the coffee grounds off my hands.

"Jesus, are you standing under a waterfall?"

I shut the faucet off, dried my hands on the legs of my jeans. "Is this where I'm supposed to throw his stuff on the lawn?"

"Are you sure about this? Thomas isn't the affair type. He's as loyal as a pocket watch."

I was surprised she defended him. Men had a thousand ways of disappointing you, according to her, and she was always happy to list them. I was also surprised that the comment stung me a little. He was my pocket watch, after all. Or had been, all these years.

"He would. He did. Is. I don't even know."

"You sound awfully calm about it."

"I do?" I didn't feel calm. I felt like I was holding back an avalanche with the palm of one hand. I opened the fridge and stared inside for answers. Instead of answers, there was a note I hadn't noticed yesterday, inside the butter container. I lifted the little door. *Love you, Mom*, it said. *Don't worry.*

My throat got tight with tears, and I swallowed hard.

"Are you there?" Gloria asked.

"I'm here."

"What did he say about it?"

"Nothing yet."

"Nothing? He hasn't admitted anything?" If it were her, she'd be lighting his favorite record albums on fire by now. At least, that's what happened with her boyfriend, Bob, when I was a kid; I remember a funny smell and the melted faces of Sonny and Cher over the Weber in our backyard.

"I tried to get him to tell me, but he wouldn't."

"Do you have proof? Did you check his email?"

"Not yet."

"You have to check his email! That'll tell you everything."

"I can't. I don't even know if I want proof. It all just seems weirdly *inevitable*." How could it not? There was my mother herself, and Shaye, and that ranch, and the way history could ride along in your bloodstream.

"Nonsense. If anyone can stay married forever, it's you," my mother said.

She sounded like my sister. Shaye had said the same thing to me a million times. Maybe I was overly sensitive, but it always seemed like one of those insults disguised as a compliment. Shaye and Mom were the similar ones, from their romantic histories and Bay Area houses down to their light hair and delicate features. I resembled our father, who left just after Shaye was born, at least according to the three snapshots we had of him, the white-bordered, yellow-hued kind from the days of drive-through Kodak Fotomats. With Shaye and Mom, I was always the one in the backseat, saying, *What? Who?* because I couldn't quite hear back there. Not that I entirely minded— the backseat has its benefits. More space, for one.

"Thanks, I guess," I said.

"That's not a *bad* thing. Anyway, I'm sure there's some kind of mistake."

"I don't think so." I paced the perimeter of the kitchen. *Some kind of mistake.* I never knew how lovely that phrase was.

"Did you hear the news?"

"I don't think I can take any more news."

"Shaye's threatening divorce. Eric bought a sports car."

"Oh, no. It's getting ridiculous over there."

"I told her he should've just painted his dick red."

I always seemed to forget that needing your mother and getting what you needed from your mother were separate but neighboring planets. I considered making brownies and eating the whole pan of them while polishing off a bottle of wine. The urge got worse right after what she said next.

"That's not what I called to tell you, though. I need you to do something for me. Remember Art Harris? Nash's . . . well, I always thought they were lovers, but never mind. He called. He thinks someone should come. Her health isn't the greatest, for one, and apparently she's been doing some bizarre things."

"What kind of bizarre things?" My aunt wasn't one for irrational acts, and it was perhaps the thing I loved most about her. She was practical. Able. Calm when angry. The antithesis of my mother.

"She's been taking off, causing scenes. Letting things go. There's some crisis with the forest service about her property. I have no idea. She's getting senile, probably. It's shitty getting old. You've got to keep active, and what does she do out there? Watch the grass grow? Well, she's always been strong-willed, to put it politely."

This was akin to a tornado insulting a hurricane. "Something's wrong, then," I said. "Because none of that sounds anything like her." I couldn't even fathom senility in an equation involving Nash, with her solidity and sturdy resolve. Likely it all had a purpose, if a cryptic one, though what did I know about being eighty.

"What is she thinking, living out there alone at her age?" my mother went on. "She should have sold that place a long time ago. It's, what, two hundred plus acres? She could've got a nice condo like mine. Can you imagine spending your whole life on that ranch? God, how could you stand it. And, now, Jesus, she's the big eight-oh."

"Well, you're seventy-nine."

"Do you know how shocking that is? If we have to get her into a *home*, it's beyond me how we'll do it. Someone's got to go over there, *assess* the situation. Harris could be completely overreacting. I don't know the guy as far as I can throw him."

"You're her sister. You should be the one. And obviously I've got a lot going on here."

"You know I hate that place. I'm not good in a crisis. I don't want to see her old and crazy. Besides, I can't leave my students." Gloria taught pottery three days a week at the community college near her place in San Rafael, where she and Shaye moved when Shaye married her first husband, Mathew. "You're not working. You could take the girls! They'd love to ride the horses."

"They're not seven, Mom. Amy just left for Costa Rica. Melissa's in college. She's got a *job*."

"*You* don't! We need *someone*! We can't just ignore the guy after he calls, saying there's an emergency."

I gave her my response through gritted teeth and pursed lips.

"Never mind! Fine, forget I asked."

We had a few more minutes of tense, meaningless conversation, which was actually only an opportunity for my mother to display by her tone of voice how I'd let her down and how she would now rise above it. She was old, too, and I was supposed to be nicer. I reminded myself of this a hundred times. You didn't want to have regrets. But she never seemed truly old to me, except in flashes where I noticed a slight imbalance in her walk or an unexpected difficulty when she rose from a chair. She was as large to me as ever; she would always be large, likely, even when she was gone, and after we hung up, I felt a bolt of rage jet through me. It braided together with a strand of unearned but maddeningly persistent guilt. I wouldn't easily shake off Nash's distress, and my mother knew it. Unlike her, I was the type to remember the birthdays of elderly relatives, the one who showed up at the airport two hours before departure, the one who never parked in handicapped spots. Someday I was going to go wild and keep my phone on just before takeoff.

I uncorked that wine, took a swig right from the bottle like a cartoon pirate. And then I finally did it. I dug through the trash can outside.

It was that easy, the white ball nestled up against—yes—some discarded tofu! Fucking tofu! I hated the stuff! I hated those smug gelatinous cubes, and the years of patience I'd given them shoved together and became a burning fury.

I took the business card into the house. I sat down on that helpful bench we'd put next to the door, where a person could remove their shoes or set a stack of mail. A pair of Amy's colorful flats waited on that bench like a hopeful boy at a dance. I didn't want to open that ball of paper, and I did want to. These confused desires made my hands shake. The card had dried, and much of the print had been lost among our joint laundry. But there. You could see it clear enough. *Mary Evans*, it read. *Eastside P*—That was all. No clue what came after the *P*, and much of the phone number was missing. The lost alphabet letters were likely trapped in the suffocating hell of dryer-vent fuzz, and good luck to them.

Jarret Somebody, financial services, eh, Thomas? It wasn't even a good lie! And for God's sake, if you're going to lie, have enough self-respect to make it *believable*. Make it have legs and a backbone, make it *stand up*, instead of pulling some rubbery story out of your childish ass. *Cover your tracks*, at least.

Rage gathered, and it filled me with an energy I never knew I possessed. I could lift a car off a baby. I could strangle Thomas and Mary Evans with my bare hands, if I wasn't already utterly done and finished with this pathetic nonsense. Great! No problem, Thomas. Honestly, after dealing with his moping and moods, what I most felt was *Good. Go.*

The phone call from my mother had actually been a kindness from the fates; I was sure. It wasn't an irritating interruption after all but an offering, an outreached hand. I was a woman who believed in fate. Maybe I even believed that the timing of that call was a reward—*finally!*—for my own goodness. I looked down at that horrible card and truly believed that something was being made easy for me. Likely it was just another hapless move by our old pal coincidence, but there you had it.

The energy turned into a swift plan. No, *a plan* sounded graphed and numbered. This was more a swarming mass that spoke one word: *out.*

It was Thomas and Mary Evans at Eastside P, but not just Thomas and Mary Evans at Eastside P. It was the dog dying, the daughters growing up, the unchanged mother, the floors of the house beginning to slope. It was Thomas's back, and a bad perm from a lifetime ago, and adventures in Costa Rica, and the failed idea that I might find happiness once everything finally got crossed off the list, only now that the list was mostly crossed off, what I was most was crushingly lonely.

I knew there were road maps in the den. Yes, we had a den! I know! Who has a den? Dens were in the television shows of my childhood, the territory of Darrin Stephens and Mike Brady. Forgive me, but it also had paneling. I liked the paneling! It was reassuring! The maps were in a box up in the closet. Who has maps anymore, either, but I wanted one. A real fold-out map, with roads and possibilities you could follow with one finger.

The box was high up, and it fell when I tipped it down. Maps spilled. I found the western states and left the rest on the floor. I packed what I needed. I brought Amy's note from the butter shelf. I didn't leave a note of my own, unless you counted the crumpled business card I left on the kitchen table, the one that once passed from the hand of Mary Evans, Eastside P, to that of my husband, Thomas Bennett.

It had been a long while since I'd been out to the ranch. The last time was when Thomas and I took the kids when they were small. Back then, Nash had been fit enough to get on a horse. Still, I remembered this, even without a map: seven hundred fifty miles, thirteen hours, to Reno. Drive past the Washoe County Courthouse and the Park Chapel, and then head over the bridge. After that, it was just under an hour down the dusty road to the log archway and double gate of Tamarosa Ranch.

What heedless actions would you change if you could read the future? I don't have the answer to that even now. I am still a woman who believes in fate, same as Nash. Kit Covey was also likely *meant*.

I hauled my suitcase down that perfect brick walk and wedged it into the trunk of my car. I slid behind the wheel and buckled my seat belt. But then I unbuckled it again and got out. I went back inside the house. I filled Hugo's water bowl, which still sat in its place on the kitchen floor. And then I jammed the car into reverse and screeched around the corner like Starsky minus Hutch.

chapter 3

Nash

Nash drives past the Washoe County Courthouse and the Park Chapel, and then she heads over the bridge. After that, it is just under an hour down the dusty road to the log archway and double gate of Tamarosa Ranch. She doesn't realize how tightly she's been gripping that steering wheel until they arrive in front of the main house. She unclenches her fingers and rolls her knotted shoulders with relief. The trip felt a day long, going that carefully over the bumps in the road. When they pull up, Jack Waters is waiting on the porch. Oh, Jack—that's how she feels when she looks at him: *Oh, Jack*. He's only a few years older than she is, but he's a man who can carry the world on his shoulders, all the while wearing that grin of his. Not everyone's eyes twinkle, but his do. The ladies always wink at each other about the way he looks on the back of a horse, but that's not the best thing about him. He watches out for a person, and that is.

When he sees them, Jack gives Nash the thumbs-up. He knows her license is only two weeks old, and they both know how Alice feels about that wagon. Nash's mother, a practical woman who still follows the guidelines on the back of the old ration books (IF YOU DON'T NEED IT, DON'T BUY IT.), ponied up two thousand dollars for the Styleline Deluxe, with its natural-wood trim and room for eight passengers. When Alice brought it home two years ago, she was beaming and Gloria was beside herself with joy, but Nash could only see the new car's sad, thoughtful headlight eyes and downturned grille mouth.

Jack opens the car door and holds out his hand. "She kill any jackrabbits on the way, Mrs. Marcel?"

They've had beautiful women at the ranch, tons of them, actresses even—Lola Phillips, from that movie *Two by Sea* with Cary Kramer. They've had expectant mothers before, too—Nash remembers Mrs. Betty Woods, who placed Nash's hand on her hard, round belly so that she could feel the lumps and turns of the baby underneath, which was embarrassing but fascinating. Even after her six weeks and her turn at the courthouse, she still called herself Mrs. Betty Woods. She didn't throw her ring off the bridge or toss it into the full glass vase of them on Alice's piano, either. She kept wearing it, which was probably smart in her condition.

But Lilly Marcel—she's not just beautiful or an actress or an expectant mother; there is something else. Something different. Nash can't put her finger on it. Maybe it's how strong her voice is, even when her wrists are so delicate. "Only a single rabbit," she answers Jack. "But he had it coming. We put him in the back so the cook could roast him for dinner."

Jack catches Nash's eye, drops an impressed jaw. "I thought you were bringing a dude, Miss Nash, not a new ranch hand."

He plays this up for full effect, the them–us, the *ma'am*'s, the threat of snakes in the grass, his thumbs hooked in the waistband of his jeans. He always wears his hat, too, especially when he's the one to drive in and pick up the ladies from the train station or the airport. On that first trip back to the ranch, Alice be damned, he'll drive fifty miles an hour through the desert, spitting rocks under the wheels and flattening plenty of unlucky rabbits, the ones who choose that doomed moment to dart across the road, as the women from New York and Los Angeles and St. Louis squeal with terror. He isn't mocking them, though, or taking advantage of their naïveté. It's not like that. He just says that for a hundred and forty-eight dollars a week, they ought to get more than steak dinners and a divorce, and this is why Nash's mother, Alice, both made him her head dude wrangler and forbade him to drive Stuart Marcel's wife in her absence. Nash's mother is, above all, a good business-woman. No one should end up dead because Mr. Marcel, the great and powerful Hollywood director, tired of his latest wife.

During the drive, Nash gathered this information about Lilly Marcel: the smell of citrus; a soft profile tilted toward passing scenery; a question about desert temperatures spoken in flute notes. Now Nash really looks at her. She is perhaps seven months along but holds herself upright, with only a trace of a waddle, as she walks beside Jack Waters, who carries her suitcase. Her black, shiny hair is crimped and held to one side with a single barrette. Those stockings look hot and uncomfortable. She's probably only a few years older than Nash, though this seems impossible given the places she must have been and the life she must lead.

Jack holds that large suitcase as if it's made of dust and feathers, and he tells Lilly Marcel about the trips into Carson City and where to find extra towels. As they pass the pool, Veronica May Fontaine, who is stretched out on a chaise longue, lifts her sunglasses to watch them, nudging Ellen Parker's calf with her toe. Ellen raises herself on her elbows and watches, too.

"You ever ride? You know, before—" Jack pats his stomach. The riding ring is long behind them, but the barn and stables are up ahead. The horses are turned out into the pasture, and though she can't see Cliff, Nash does see the wet sand and pine chips flying from the end of his fork as they land in the wheelbarrow just outside the door of Zorro's stall.

"No, but I've been taken for one."

Jack laughs too hard, which is irritating, and so is the way he looks pleased with himself just for being in Lilly Marcel's company. "That's why you're here," he says.

"That's why I'm here."

"You're sure you don't want a room in the main house?" Jack says. "We don't like this. It's not right. You shouldn't be in a cabin alone, you know, given that you're . . . in the family way."

"I'm fine," Lilly Marcel says. "I prefer my breathing room."

"Well, I understand that," Nash says. More than just about anything, she loves to be alone in her room, reading. A book gives the best company, the kind that expects nothing in return. Still, Nash feels shy after saying it. There is no way they're the same, and she shouldn't imply it. Lilly Marcel must need so much more from her privacy and retreat. Stuart Marcel has his own airplanes. They say he has a different woman every week just to light his cigarettes. It's strange, come to think of it—Lilly only has a single suitcase. Sometimes, when a guest arrives, the entryway of the main house fills with monogrammed trunks.

"There's not much out this way except breathing room." Jack tilts his chin out, indicating the big sky and the wave of blue-gray Sierras that you can see in the distance, just past the Carson foothills. His love for the place is corny, but it's clear he doesn't care. "Well, Nash here is always around, and I'm down the path a bit if you need me. Look for the place with the large woodpile, just before the lake."

He unlocks the cabin. This one is called Avalon. The sign,

with letters burned into wood, hangs over the door. Next to Avalon is Shangri-La. The windows of that bungalow are open, and Nash can hear the *click-tick-tick* of Hadley Bernal's typewriter.

There are two twin beds with quilt bedspreads, and a wooden nightstand with a reading lamp and an ashtray that someone stole from the Nugget. The mothers with children stay here, and there is a bookshelf with games for them: Easy Money and Raggedy Ann and a Giant Cootie, who doesn't have many legs left. Gloria put some of her old books in here before she left home—*Little Toot* on up to *The Dana Girls*—but Nash would never give away her old books.

"Nothing fancy," Jack says.

"I don't even like fancy," Lilly Marcel says.

Jack tries again. "The main house is much more comfortable."

"Summer camp," Lilly Marcel says.

"With cocktails," Jack says, and they both laugh.

"I've never been to summer camp."

They leave her there to rest up. Sometimes, when they finally close the door, you can hear them burst into tears. Or else there is just the sigh of bedsprings.

"There you go," Jack Waters says to Nash. "You see?"

She hasn't even told him how worried she's been about her mother leaving her in charge, but he knows. Her heart crashes at his knowing. There's the feeling that they've accomplished something together, and this pleases her so much that a warm buzz starts in her chest. After all these years growing up at the ranch, with all the broken hearts and wrongly hopeful ones, she hasn't learned a damn thing.

* * *

It gets so cold here in the evenings. People from the city don't know this about the desert. They expect what they see in the movies: heat and dust and cowboys. Some even think they'll see Indians. Horses! Rifles! Tumbleweeds! It is heat and dust, but not only heat and dust. It is also frigid nights. It is cowboys, yes, but they are the men Nash knows. Danny, who left home when he was fifteen, who rides the fence and can fix a tractor engine just by looking at it. He once screamed when a spider fell in his lap, and they haven't let him hear the end of it since. There's Cliff, too, who's been at the ranch since he was a young man; he delivered both Bluebell and Zorro and buried Little Britches and once drove all the way to San Francisco to pick up a tearful guest too scared to make the trip alone. It is tumbleweeds but also the purple-flowering carpets of verbena, and the scorpion weed, with its horrible smell of body odor and the prickly hair that can cause a rash if you're not careful to keep your distance. It is horses, yes, but each horse: Maggie, who gets depressed in bad weather, and Zorro, who sees your soul when you look in his eyes, and Bluebell, who is high-strung and prefers Jack. The rifle is a real one, the Savage Model 720, an automatic, which Alice keeps under her bed in case of wolves or coyotes. Before he died, Nash's father tried to teach her to use it, but her aim was bad. Instead of hitting the target on a nearby tree, she shot out the porch light of Shangri-La. Her father laughed so hard he could barely stand up straight, but he never let her touch that thing again.

Lilly Marcel might need extra blankets, the way the cold drops down at night, so Nash carries a stack of quilts to her cabin. The evening light is turning pink, and there are these smells: sage, and cooling dry grass, and horse manure, smells Nash loves. Just down the path, though, Nash runs into Lilly as she's coming out of the bungalow where the toilet is.

"Well!" Lilly says, as if she's on the other side of a recent adventure.

"The main house . . ." Nash says.

"I prefer to stay where I am."

But this is when Nash begins to worry. Lilly might speak boldly, but except for her large stomach, she is small, and there are dark crescents under her eyes. She shouldn't be alone in one of the cabins, they shouldn't let her, Nash's mother would insist; and it's possible that this is the beginning of the disaster Nash feared when her mother left the ranch in her care. Lilly Marcel's own insistence seems a symptom of something larger, of a heedlessness that has led her here. Nash had gotten it wrong before—*this* is what distinguishes Lilly Marcel from the rest, because, of course, there is much more that people say about Stuart Marcel. It's not just the airplanes and the women and the film studio and those beautiful clothes and the way people are drawn to him in spite of his almost hideous looks. There is *the* thing: the first wife who leaped (or was pushed? Did he push her? They say he pushed her.) to her death from some high, deserted Topanga Canyon road.

Gloria would say Nash is being stupid, the way her nerves are rubbing and twitching like the legs of a mosquito. But Gloria would never have caught the way Lilly Marcel flinches right now when the door of the main house slams.

"You!" Veronica calls, pointing at Lilly with her elegant finger. She strides toward them, wearing her new shirt with the pearl snaps, a bandanna tied around her neck. Ellen runs to catch up. "You may have swallowed a bowling ball, but you are still coming for cocktail hour."

Lilly has an uncertain smile when she meets Nash's eyes. It's the same look Nash's friend, Louise, gave her when that boy took her hand at the Fireman's Association dance, and she gives the same response in return—a smile and a shrug.

"You must need a drink, your first night here," Ellen says to Lilly. Ellen is as cheery as a daffodil in that yellow dress, and her heels require her to walk cautiously down the dirt path, arms out slightly like new, tentative leaves. Her blond hair is in a perfect curve. She's smiling now, but she cried for her first three days, until Alice insisted she take a trip to Carson City with the girls one night. *She danced with a cowboy!* Veronica said with a wink afterward. There was a great deal of laughing and elbowing one another. *If Bill had seen me, he would've* died, Ellen said. *He would've had me put* away*!*

"I was just going to read in my room," Lilly says.

"Nonsense," Veronica says.

Ellen takes in Veronica and those pearl snaps for the first time. She adjusts Veronica's bandanna just so. "Very chic."

"You like? I couldn't decide if it was hideous or the best thing ever, which is exactly how I felt about Gus on our honeymoon."

"I look like a frump," Ellen says.

"Never." Veronica links her arm with Lilly's. "We don't allow hiding in one's room. We are also coming to get Hadley, who tries to avoid us."

"I guess I'm doomed," Lilly Marcel says.

"We don't bother with You-Know-Who in *the Ritz*." Veronica tosses her head toward the cabin.

"She came with a spare," Ellen says. "So . . ."

"A spare?" Lilly asks.

"The new man. The next one in line," Veronica says

"Busy trading one prison for another, then?" Lilly says.

Hadley comes out of her cabin door, her dress slim and shimmery. "We make our own prison, my dears."

"Oh, please," Veronica groans. "I can't stomach profound observations before a drink."

Nash still holds those blankets as the women change direction and head back toward the house. The quilts made the trip out of the cupboard for nothing. The unease she feels—it stops its ugly whispering as she follows the women inside. There is a yellow dress and shimmery fabric and Jack will be coming with some friends.

"I'm through with you cynics," Ellen says. She waves her hand, and the White Shoulders she dabbed at her wrists spins and flaunts.

"Us cynics are all you have," Hadley says.

"Love is an act of courage," Ellen says. This is not something she would have said when she first arrived, but Nash knows that even a single, uncharacteristic dance can set change in motion.

Boo the dachshund sits straight by the piano, being his best self, and Ellen picks him up, looks in his pointy face. "Oh, you are just waiting for your mind to get read, aren't you?"

Hadley holds out a stack of sheet music. "Nash? Please? If your mother were here, she'd play something."

"You know I tend bar," Nash says. She is secretly proud that she can make a mean martini.

Veronica sets one beautiful finger on Lilly's round stomach and taps. "Come here, and tell us who did this to you," she says, as if they all don't already know.

Jack—he's wrong about *breathing room*. In spite of the ranch's two hundred acres, with its spilling pastures and wide views of Washoe Lake, in spite of the miles and miles of desert beyond that, in spite of the vast sky, where you'll frequently see a single red-tailed hawk or a peregrine falcon soaring in all that space, once you drive underneath the archway with the Tamarosa sign, once the fenced pasture comes into view with the white farmhouse beyond, breathing room, at least the kind that Lilly Marcel means, is just wishful thinking.

Here, there is always someone at your side, especially when you need it most.

And likely, very likely, there will come a time when you need it badly.

chapter 4

Callie

I drove underneath the archway with the Tamarosa sign. The fenced pasture came into view with the white farmhouse beyond, and I got that strange, nearly out-of-body sensation one gets when traveling long distances, when you step out of a plane or a car and you are smacked with startling heat or nighttime or palm trees, when only a few hours before there were cool temperatures and daylight. In front of me was a ranch in horrible disrepair, and it seemed shocking. The disrepair, yes, but more the fact that I had somehow brought myself there. Things can change so quickly, and at your own doing, too.

The night before, I'd gotten a room at a Marriott Hotel in Bend, Oregon, and so I had slept off quite a lot of the anger that had gotten me that far. Anger has grand plans that sometimes look foolish later. It occurred to me that I should turn around and head straight home. I should get the full story at least. Then again, the fact that I had finally stopped driving in Bend, Oregon, was perhaps a sign. A change, a turn in the road, being *driven round the*: It seemed important. So did the three cars piled up in a gruesome accident I tried not to glance at but did. And the fact that every station had cut out once I entered the desert, all except for a radio show with a molasses-voiced marriage guru, Dr. Yabba Yabba Love. *The first rule of marital success: Don't marry crazy and don't be crazy.*

Other important bits of information (though how to read them was another question) were the seven missed calls and various messages from Thomas, who, after seeing all the mess and maps on the floor, had at first worried I'd been abducted, apparently by a kidnapper with a bad sense of direction. Was he really confused as to why I'd left? Did he truly think some harm had befallen me? It seemed to indicate some sort of innocence on his part. One message later, though, he apparently had found the business card, exposed and yet half furled, as if Mary Evans herself was trying to cover her nakedness with her two hands. His questioning, worried voice had turned incensed. *I don't know what you think, but you've got it wrong. This is how you react? You just take off? What has gotten into you?* Oh, the power of the *delete*. It felt fabulous. I wished I could go around deleting like crazy. I'd delete suspicious spots on X-rays and malls at Christmas, car troubles and tragic events in history, the world's and my own. *Try Mary Evans*, I texted him, and then I shut off my phone. The last thing I wanted was to have an actual conversation with Thomas. Talking to him would mean having the facts, and having the facts meant you had to do something about them.

I looked around at where I'd ended up. My first thought was that I'd clearly traded one mess for another, perhaps an even larger one. Not just because of the size of the place and its obvious decrepit condition, but because of how the ranch had mattered over time. My own marriage had twenty-two years' worth of history, but this place had been here for decades, even before my grandparents swapped cattle for divorcées in the late 1930s to make a more lucrative living. Nash herself had lived here her whole life long, and my family maintained some kind of ongoing but mixed loyalty to the place, claiming its unusual, romantic history as ours (it was good dinner-party fodder) but not wanting to face the actual burden of its aging. And then, too, there was the stuff beyond human history, before society women and Hollywood starlets came to establish residency for a quickie divorce when a divorce was a difficult thing to get, before the time, even, when the place had been a true working ranch. The land itself—it had existed for billions of years, transforming era by era as shallow seas lifted and tectonic plates crashed and volcanoes erupted. My mother had a fossil on her coffee table that she'd found there as a child.

The sun had risen on Tamarosa for much longer than on the twenty-two years of my marriage, and now look. It was a significant and monumental mess. I could see the encroaching weeds as I drove up, and the ragged, tumbled fences. A buffalo wandered in the distance. As I reached the house, I saw that the old riding ring had fallen. The house itself, a once-bright white and expansive two-story farmhouse with a wraparound porch, was dim and sagging. The pastures were mowed, at least, probably by old Harris riding that husky, prehistoric tractor, which I saw parked near a tilting mailbox. But the short grass was an odd mess, with strange, deep grooves of dirt and mad gouges. I didn't know what to make of them. They brought to mind crop circles and ancient rituals, some desert mystery I couldn't comprehend.

I couldn't see the pool from where I was, or the barn and the stables, so God knew what state they were in. This was all beyond me. My expertise was along the lines of fixing vacuum cleaners and repainting bedrooms. I lived in the suburbs, first off. I could unclog a toilet with the best of them, but I had just seen a buffalo, an actual huge and woolly buffalo, whose head hung low and who looked capable of bad moods. How do you repair that much damage, damage that has been slowly accumulating for years due to neglect and the passage of time itself? I hadn't even laid eyes on Nash yet. I was afraid what time had done to her.

I got out of the car and was hit with heat. Immediately, my clothes were heavy and I needed my hair up in a ponytail. I was tired, and this all seemed immense, and, clearly, I hadn't thought it through. I was worried what other disasters might be waiting. It looked like the kind of place where you'd find someone dead, with flies buzzing around the corpse, weeks gone by, their absence unnoticed by anyone. It was a place of sour milk and open cans of Chef Boyardee, or so I thought.

My unease about dead bodies wasn't entirely brought on by fallen fences and long hours in hot, flat landscapes—I had repeatedly tried to call Nash's home phone (Nash with a cell? Ha!) to warn her of my imminent arrival, with no luck. I had also tried to call Harris, who had a place a good mile down the road, but he didn't answer, either. The ringing phones left a lot to the imagination, and I was worried about both Nash and Harris. My mother wasn't the only one who thought the two of them had been lovers, but Nash had always been maddeningly tight-lipped about her private life. Harris—he'd been fit enough to get on a horse those years ago when we visited; now that old cowboy was also likely frail and vulnerable, certainly no match for overgrown pastures and large, entitled mammals.

I was fond of Harris. He'd been Nash's right-hand man from way back when Shaye and I were kids, when divorces had become easy to get and the ranch was back to being just a ranch, and we swam in the pool and pretended that one of the empty cabins was our little house. Shaye wanted to be Laura, so I was Almanzo. She cradled babies and made molasses candy, while

I chopped a lot of wood. Harris gave me a pair of steel wedges and a splitting maul I couldn't lift, trying to even out my end of the deal.

I unstuck my sweaty shirt from my back. I carried a bag of fruit that I had bought at a stand on the way. I always brought a gift for the hostess; who knew where I got that. Maybe from a magazine, some well-intentioned *Redbook*; certainly not from my own mother, who'd just as soon skip the party entirely if it meant kissing someone's ass with a box of chocolates.

I opened the screen door and knocked. No answer. I looked out over the property, and I could see the pool then, drained and now filled with a few inches of orange-red desert dirt that had blown inside. There may have been some trash in there, too; I saw a small lump of something that resembled an old boot. The heat felt capable of melting me to that spot on the porch, and I had to use the bathroom, and I wouldn't have minded taking another bend entirely back in Bend. The Marriott, with its cool, bland lobby and toilet paper folded into a triangle, sounded like heaven.

"Nash?" I called. "It's Callie! Your niece Callie!"

A small black dog popped his head out the dog door.

"Hi, Tex," I said. I'd seen pictures of him. He jumped through the small swinging panel, gave a little bark. Then he sniffed my pant legs and stared at me, as if I were a questionable parcel the UPS man had dropped. "Tell me she's not dead in there."

She was not dead. Not at all. I heard the bustle and footsteps that meant someone was coming, and then there she was, still surprisingly tall (though not as tall) with broad shoulders (though not as broad). She had the deep wrinkles and permanent tan of a rancher and a head of glorious gray hair, pulled back into a barely contained ponytail. She was still beautiful.

"Callie! I thought you were that man from the bureau," she

said. The bureau? If she was having delusions about the FBI, I was in trouble.

"It's just me, Nash."

We hugged, and then she let me go to have a good look. "This is you? It's the voice I know, but you've changed some since you came last."

"Don't I know," I said.

"What are you doing here? This is a surprise."

Now that my arrival seemed to be good news, the dog began jumping around on his hind legs, hopping up on our knees. Nash scooped him up and tucked him under one arm. "Tex, enough," she said. "He loves visitors. Except that bureau man. He hears his truck and goes crazy."

I decided to let the bureau comment pass, at least for now. There'd be plenty of time later to *assess*, to use my mother's word. "Well, sure," I said. "Dogs have their own opinions about people." I didn't even want to look at Tex. I didn't pet his velvety little head. His canine self reminded me of Hugo, even though Hugo had been large and sturdy. I didn't want to befriend another animal, let alone love him, knowing what his loss would do to you.

"Come in, Callie. I must say, this is somewhat of a shock."

"I tried to call." I handed her the bag. "Peaches."

She opened the top and gave a long sniff. "Mmm. Summer."

By that time, we were inside the house. We'd walked through the large front room that I remembered, the one with the red and yellow plaid couches and pine-covered walls, with the grand piano in the corner. As far as I could tell, nothing had changed. I followed Nash to the kitchen and dining room, where large wide windows looked out onto the endless acres of ranchland and the Sierra Nevada Mountains beyond. The same long tables were there, with benches on either side, and so were the high shelves displaying horseshoes and miniature cowgirls done in porcelain.

I tried to find the crisis. There were no open cans or molding dishes of cat food. The kitchen was neat, and the plank wood floors covered with carpets were clean. The house smelled a little musty, maybe, but not more than was due. I calculated repairs—fences, that pool, a few phone calls, easily within my abilities. And Nash looked well, if maybe a bit thin in the face. If I looked that good at eighty, I'd be counting my blessings.

Nash set Tex down and took a pitcher of tea out of the refrigerator. Right there, tea in the refrigerator—how much could be wrong? She reached for two glasses, ones that I all at once recalled. They were decorated with strawberries and pink-white flowers, and I no doubt drank out of them when I was eight and eighteen and twenty-eight. She poured us both a drink, and then she looked at me hard.

"Have you run away from home, Callie?"

It must have been something in my eyes, something likely familiar to her, after all the women who'd passed through those doors. But I couldn't admit it. I wasn't sure exactly what I had done.

"Mom called. She asked me to come check in. She was worried about you."

"Worried about me?"

"That's what she said."

"Baloney. Maybe worried about herself having to worry about me." Nash reached for a Mason jar of dog treats. Her hand had a slight tremor, which made the contents chime against the glass. She gave Tex a biscuit, and he crunched vigorously.

"Harris phoned her."

"He did?"

"He did."

"How dare he! You know, I pay that man."

"He was concerned, Nash. Concerned enough that I brought my suitcase." People who bring hostess gifts and visit the sick in hospitals and who ride in to save the day are experts at disguising our own needs behind efficiency and help. You get plenty out of being the giver, beyond being the giver. Thomas may have been better at this game than I was, but we both played it, which was another one of our problems.

"I can't believe those two! The nerve." But I could see something in *her* eyes. I wasn't the only one hiding something. "Maybe the place isn't as shipshape as it used to be. I don't pretend I can keep cattle or even horses anymore. But everything is fine here. *I'm* fine."

"Do you mind if I stay for a day or two anyway?" *Or a week or six?* "It's been so long. We can catch up, at least."

"Thomas will miss you," she said. She cocked one eyebrow. I didn't answer.

"Ah, well." She nodded. "I see. Stay as long as you like. I wasn't prepared for guests, mind you, so don't give those spies a bad report card on account of that. I haven't had visitors in a long while." I couldn't tell if she was glad about this or not. "You can stay in Taj. That was always the favorite."

I retrieved my bag from the car. Tex followed like an incompetent but well-meaning valet. Upstairs and down the hall, I found TAJ MAHAL right next to CASTAWAY—the doors still had the signs on them, with log-shaped letters burned into wood. It was hot in there, and the dust in the curtains made me sneeze when I reached past them to open the windows, but who could blame Nash for not tending to each room? Once the kids hit high school, I barely wanted to cook anymore. Taj was tidy enough, with its large pine bed and quilt spread. I could see why it was a favorite—the view was immense, one that would please any choosy tourist.

I put on a tank top, washed my face in the bathroom across the hall, and then I turned my phone on again to check for messages. Thomas or no Thomas, my daughter was traveling in a foreign country, and I might have to hop on a plane to rescue her from some terrible jail or tropical disease or heartbreak or whatever else might befall her away from the safety of home. I was still trying to hold on to the idea that my children needed me.

There was only one message, though. It wasn't from Thomas or Amy. Surprisingly, it was Melissa who'd called. She was using her bossy-eldest voice, which could make me mad when directed at me, and she was saying something about Thomas and me and Mary Evans. Thomas had used her to relay his side of the story, and the wrongness of this barely registered before I heard what she said next.

"Mary Evans, *PhD*, Mother. He said you thought he was having an affair! For God's sake! *Dad*? She's a *therapist*. He's been seeing her for about six months. . . ."

I sat down on that quilt-covered bed. It wasn't what I had expected, not at all. I felt the slight lift of relief before the anger rolled in. Six months? How many lies and lies and lies does it take to cover weekly appointments for *six months*?

I held my phone in my hand and stared out over all that ranchland, which looked less wrecked than exhausted. I watched a woodpecker *bam-bam-bam* his beak into a beam of rotting wood. All those small lies, the late nights at work, the lengthy errands, maybe even those long runs in the hideous silky shorts ... The fact that he couldn't tell me this basic truth, it felt oddly worse than my original, mistaken conclusion. It felt like the final verdict on the state of our marriage, the kind of vast desert distance that was impassable. Passion, legs entwined with legs, hot mouths and bare desire, found love—it was tangible, even understandable. I could grab hold of that and either choke it to death or let it go on its foolish, temporary way. But unhappiness—an unhappiness deep enough to hide—it seemed like such a larger, untamable enemy.

The Mary Evans of my imaginings was gone. The shimmer of her, the desert mirage, went up in a poof. Why I also felt a small, odd sense of loss over that, why some strange emptiness took her place, I didn't yet ask myself.

Well, I didn't have time, for one. Right then, I heard a tremendous clatter down the hall, a sliding crash. Nash had fallen, I was sure of it. She wasn't as sturdy as she looked. I leaped to my feet. Dear God, she'd probably broken a hip or something. After all that time living alone without incident, the very second I arrived, she had a catastrophe. It was proof how another person's capable presence could turn you incompetent. I hurried to Nash's room, only to find her just fine and upright, looking guilty.

"Shit," she said.

Shit was right, because clearly this was the reason (one of the reasons) for Harris's worried call. Yes, the reason was scattered and splayed out in front of me. What had fallen, what I bent to help Nash with, though she waved me away, were a chair and a stack of books that had been on it. This might have been innocent, except that it was only one small part of the disturbed chaos and bizarre accumulation of paper in that room. There were stacks of it. Stacks and more towering stacks, along with piles of large, fat envelopes and stuffed file folders. I'd been wrong about Nash and senility: She must have lost her mind; this was proof. Her bed was in there somewhere, and in there somewhere, too, was a ringing phone. A cellphone! I heard a jazz riff, but Nash made no move to answer it. Nothing was what it seemed. I felt a sick dread.

"Nash, my God," I said. "What is going on here?"

"What are you talking about?" she said.

"What is all this stuff?"

My eyes caught a label on the end of a box, and then I saw the number everywhere. A folder, a letter, a newspaper: *1951, 1951, 1951.*

She folded her arms, and her eyes blazed. That's when I also noticed a nearly empty glass of beer and an open box of crackers. Nash followed my glance and tried to shove the box into a trash can overflowing with paper. "Last night's snack," she snapped. But then her head tilted, as if there was a sudden noise. "Do you hear that?"

Voices, probably. I was so far over my head that I was sinking fast.

"Yes," she said, and her face lit. She grabbed my arm, hurried me downstairs to those large windows in the dining room. Waves of heat came off the desert like ripples of water, and it was quiet except for an *awwwk!* of a falcon overhead.

But then I also heard it. A sound like thunder; that deep bass roll off in the distance. And then—same as thunder, too—the *boom* was suddenly right there in Nash's very own pasture, a roar of hooves and huffing and wildness; there were manes flying and thick haunches with muscles clenched in forward motion, a blur of brown and satin black. I could not hear or see or feel anything else, not the ringing phone, not the car coming down the drive, not the horrible heaviness in my stomach, not even a sense of inevitability about these horses and my future. There was only this: motion and power and thrill and fear.

"My God," I said.

Nash's fingers gripped my arm.

"They're back," she said.

chapter 5

Nash

Waves of heat come off the desert like ripples of water, and it is quiet except for an *awwwk!* of a falcon overhead. It is You-Know-Who's day in court, Mrs. Daisy Davidson Fletcher, who is some relation to the long-dead James Buchanan Duke of the American Tobacco Company, or so she says. It is also her wedding day to Mr. Jeremy Gunther, who sits with her in the back of the Styleline Deluxe. Mr. Gunther is a poet, Veronica discovered a few weeks ago. She shared this fact after dinner. *He explores the themes of parting rich women from their money*, she cackled, and Nash's mother began to play "I'm Always Chasing Rainbows" on the piano, making everyone laugh.

Maybe the quiet is the silent shouting of second thoughts. Little Jimmy Fletcher sits beside Nash, his hands folded in his lap, staring sullenly out the window. He looks like a miniature businessman in that suit.

When they go into the courthouse to meet Bill Thisby, the attorney, Jimmy waits in the car. It's Nash's first time standing in for Alice. She's accompanied her before, though, so she knows what to do. She rises. The judge asks if Mrs. Fletcher has been a Nevada resident for the required six weeks, and Nash answers, *Yes, Your Honor*, as Mr. Fletcher glares from the other side of the room. He cites three of the nine grounds for divorce, when only one is necessary, though Mrs. Fletcher seems unfazed as her crimes are stated aloud. Adultery, insanity, extreme mental cruelty, and that's only a third of the ways love can go legally wrong. It's over in half an hour.

The poet is dashingly handsome but no physical match for Mr. Fletcher, so Nash is relieved when they are down the courthouse steps, fetching Jimmy from the car. Jimmy spots what Nash guesses is his father's black Mercury parked by the curb, unless he always cranes his neck to look at certain automobiles with obvious longing. Still, they are in a hurry; the second official of the day waits. The newly ex–Mrs. Fletcher yanks the boy's hand, and she laughs as they cross to the other side of the street to enter the Park Chapel.

In ten minutes, it's done. It takes longer to break promises than to make them. From all she's seen, Nash thinks it should be the other way around. The poet's friends arrive to drive them off, and a strange impulse overtakes Nash. She bends and kisses the boy's cheek.

Then Nash spots him. Mr. Fletcher, still sitting in his black Mercury. His head is in his hands. He is weeping. So often it seems that one person's gain in love is another's loss. In the courtroom, she'd been afraid of him, but now her fear turns to pity. Her heart wrenches. He once looked into Mrs. Fletcher's eyes and saw forever. Every single couple who walks up those steps, every woman carrying a purse and smoothing her skirt and fanning herself from the heat, every man who checks for his wallet and admires the shine of his own shoes and removes his hat once indoors—they all once looked into each other's eyes and felt enough passion to overcome their own unspoken uncertainties or the objection of parents or the weight of the future and they *vowed*. What it took to actually fulfill that vow, well, that's where no one seems to have any answers. The distance from the vow to forever seems as long and bumpy as the one from the Park Chapel to the arch of Tamarosa. There's heat, drought, snakes, and your own confusion once you get turned around out there in the dark.

Nash should go back, but in her palm is You-Know-Who's doomed wedding ring, the gold band that the weeping Mr. Fletcher once placed on her finger. Nash walks to the Virginia Street Bridge, the Bridge of Sighs, they call it, over the Truckee River. She intends to complete the ritual that You-Know-Who has left undone. Some women leave their rings in the vase on the piano, but the others fling them off this bridge into the tumbling waters below.

When she gets there, though, Nash sees a familiar figure. Her first instinct is panic; people jump from this bridge, too, and Lilly Marcel is on her watch. But coming closer, she sees that Lilly is only leaning forward to peer down at the bridge's cement double arches and at the river, which flows with some speed, as if heading off to more-important business.

"I thought you might leap." Nash makes it sound like a joke.

"Not with Beanie." Lilly Marcel sets one hand on the round bump under her polka-dotted dress. There's the smell of citrus again. It's the smell of sun and California and good fortune. Lilly Marcel is beautiful, especially set against the turquoise of that river and sky.

"Beanie," Nash says. She smiles.

"No creep is worth losing your life over, anyway," Lilly says. "No mistake is, either."

"Definitely not," Nash says. "How did you get here?"

Lilly hooks her thumb over her shoulder. "Some cowboy," she jokes.

Nash sees Jack, his familiar broad shoulders and thoughtful profile, leaning against a cement pillar on the other side of the bridge, smoking a cigarette. He's wearing her favorite hat, the one that's a small bit too large, which he'll flick from his eyes with his thumb and forefinger. Her heart twists in jealousy, for no good reason. Lilly Marcel—well, look at her, with that ivory skin and those bright blue eyes; she could have anyone she wants, even if she wants some cowboy who's never even cared about going to the movies.

"When is the baby due?" Nash asks.

"Ten weeks."

"Are you scared?"

"Very," Lilly Marcel says. They lock eyes. It's strange—Nash first saw that face ever-so-briefly on a large screen at the River- side Theater, but right now they are two young women on a bridge, and something passes between them.

Jack catches sight of Nash and waves, heads over. There are things she knows about him: His mother died (and he adores Alice); his father drank (he does, too; too much); he was smart enough to go to college (but hated being stuck inside a class- room). She knows his strengths—his charm, his kindness, his loyalty—and his weaknesses. The small lies he tells to get out of things, the flash of hotheaded temper when he's criticized. But there is so much she doesn't know—what as a man he is hungry for. All of that seems like such a mystery. One thing Nash has realized about love, if this is love, is how powerful and powerless it makes you feel at the same time.

"You're ginned up," he says to her.

"Mrs. Fletcher's day in court."

"Six weeks," Lilly Marcel says, and sighs.

"We'll make sure the time flies. You'll want to stay. You won't even miss the green tiled pool or the red plush seats."

The pool, the seats—they are obviously a part of a private discussion Nash had no part of. Jack spins his circle of keys on his finger, as if eager to get the show on the road. There is her and him and her, and it's confusing. Desire and envy skitter past before disappearing underground, same as a zebra-tailed lizard.

Nash doesn't know what is happening, or what is about to. She is naïve to the way wild hooves and forces of nature can destroy orderly pastures and upright fences. Still, she decides not to throw in the wedding ring after all. She tucks it into her handbag. She zips that abandoned circle of gold into a small pocket. She does this with care and even love—the way a mother puts a baby to bed.

"So what's he like? Stuart Marcel," Veronica asks. She's wearing a green satin evening dress with a bow at the hip, and her blond hair is smoothed up into a twist. Her legs are crossed; she swings one ankle in a circle and blows a stream of cigarette smoke up into the air, like a freight train pulling out of the station. When Veronica first arrived, she carried her fur over one arm, until Peg Marx Dunnell (successfully divorced and returned to Chicago) accused her of needing a security blanket. An ashtray was thrown by one and impressively caught by the other.

"Veronica!" Ellen says. "That's hardly our business." Ellen is thrilled by the question, though. She laughs a little but leans forward so she doesn't miss a word. They all want to ask, but only Veronica is bold enough to actually do it.

"Oh, I don't know," Lilly says. She is working out a tune on the piano. Her long fingers plunk wrong keys and then try again. "I don't even know if I remember." But she means the song.

"I saw him at a restaurant once," Hadley says. She leans one hip against the piano, watching. "He was . . ."

"Attractive, oddly. Very attractive," Lilly Marcel says.

"*Magnetic* is what I was going to say."

Nash has seen pictures. She can't imagine what's attractive about that huge head and those fat fingers.

"*The Bird Kings* was brilliant, I must admit. *The Forever When*, too." Veronica adds an *mmm* of remembered pleasure.

"My friend Eve was in *The Bird Kings*," Lilly says. "Eve Ellings? She played the daughter."

"Oh, right," Veronica says, but she's just being polite. Their focus is on Lilly.

"You were the girl in the hotel. In *The Changelings?*" Ellen asks. "At the front desk."

"'Don't interrupt me, Mr. Black.'" Lilly recites her one line. The line isn't what you remember, anyway.

"Did you ever ask him?" They all know what Veronica means. Ellen opens her eyes wide.

"Well, once," Lilly says.

The air is stifling hot. A fan spins on an end table. It might rain. No one speaks, and even the crickets have fallen silent. Anticipation hovers. It's like a gavel in midair, the finger on the trigger, the lips parted for a kiss, but it appears that Lilly is not planning on saying more.

Hadley can't stand it. "And?"

Lilly raises her hands and then slams her fingertips—*bum, dum, dum*—over the deep, ominous notes of the left side of the keyboard.

"You asked only once, I take it," Veronica says.

"He made me feel like I could do anything, until he made me feel like I could do nothing."

"Oh, don't I know about that!" Ellen says. She holds a drink, which she swirls in anger, if you could call it that. Ellen's anger is sighs and tears, and Hadley's is crossed arms and door slams, and Veronica's is a string of curses that could make Jack blush. Nash doesn't even know what her own anger truly looks like yet. It's like the Styleline Deluxe, which can supposedly go as fast as sixty-five miles per hour but no one, not even Jack, has dared try.

"After all the flowers and candy and fancy dinners, the big wedding? I thought he loved me. I thought I'd reached the happy ending. But I don't think Eddie ever really even wanted to be married. Scotty is two. My Bobby is only six months old. I don't know what will become of us." Ellen says this to Lilly, because the rest of them have heard these facts a hundred times by now. "I begged and pleaded with him, but it's like I'm not even there. Like *we're* not there. Eddie walks right out of the room whenever Bobby cries. He says he's fed up."

"That's awful," Lilly says.

"Most of the neighbors think that I'm on vacation and Eddie's on a business trip. I'm too ashamed to say anything. They must think we do a lot of traveling."

"What are you going to tell them when you get home?" Hadley asks.

"I'm going to say he works overseas."

"Gus is a sweetheart. I'm the one who's wicked." Veronica grinds the nub of her cigarette into the ashtray.

Hadley widens her eyes in pretend shock. "No! Wicked, you?"

Veronica lobs a cashew in Hadley's direction. How many objects have been flung in the Fontaine household, Nash can only imagine.

"Sit here," Lilly says to Nash, who is standing over by the

window. Lilly scoots over, pats the bench next to her. "Do you play?"

It's stupid, but she blushes. "A little."

"A very little," Hadley teases. She was there that night Nash made such a mess of Kirchner.

"Do you think it's possible that some women are not meant to be married?" Veronica asks.

"In what way?" Ellen knits her brow.

"I feel murderous when his leg brushes up against mine in bed. I want to scream sometimes when he's just being *alive*, breathing through his mouth. And when he pouts after being rejected in the bedroom—"

"Primitive man pouted when he was rejected in the cave," Hadley says, and they all laugh.

"What kind of a person screams inside when her husband breathes too loud?" Veronica lights another cigarette. Her cupped hand and her bent head are serious.

"The same kind who feels nothing inside when he sobs his heart out," Hadley says quietly. It's the kind of confession that requires hushed tones.

"Why did I even do it, when I knew it was wrong?"

"Well, the day says one thing, and the night another, doesn't it?" Hadley says. "Who wants to listen to what two A.M. says? We think two A.M. can't be trusted, when it's the honest hour."

Boo is disturbed by something he hears outside. He darts around, barks at the window. Maybe it's the heat, or an animal, or an imminent storm. Moths flutter around the yellow light outside, flying figure eights. Beyond that light, it is so dark you'd never even see a coyote prowling right outside the house.

"I wonder what it is." Lilly watches the little dog.

"Just an animal, probably," Nash says.

"Well, maybe I'm fed up, too," Ellen says. "I'm tired of being ignored. And tired of being treated like a child! He takes the kitchen knives from my hand, like I'm not to be trusted with sharp objects." Her eyes shine. She still hasn't learned not to drink those Moscow mules so fast, and each *S* she speaks slides and crashes a little.

"Darling, I saw you with that pair of scissors," Veronica says.

"I don't even know how to drive!"

Veronica dunks her olive into her drink and then slides it off the toothpick into her mouth. "We'll fix that."

"You can teach her, Nash," Hadley says.

Nash looks at Hadley like she's just told a bad joke, but Hadley's actually serious.

"Every woman should know how to drive," Hadley says. "You don't want to be his little girl. Or his mother, either." Hadley's husband is the playwright Joseph Bernal, who wrote that play *The Blue Shoe*, the one with the scandalous scene in the Garden of Eden with supposedly Freudian undertones. It was Hadley's *Golden Butterflies*, though, the labor-union play, that won some award. Hadley has not said much about him or them or why she's here. There have only been small dropped details—something about Jewish guilt, and the effect of bad weather on moods, and how the pages accumulate now, without constant interruption.

"I tell you, ladies, I'm the louse here," Veronica says.

"We don't need any further convincing." Hadley sidesteps the airborne candied-covered almond.

"This," Lilly Marcel decides. She places the sheet music on the stand.

Boo trots back and forth in front of the window. His eyes are focused and intent. There is the squeak-spring sound of the tiny doors of the cuckoo clock as they open and then the call of the little wooden bird.

"A coyote or something, maybe," Lilly Marcel says to Nash. "Ready?"

She *is* ready. When she sees their hands together on the piano keys, Nash is astonished at how alike they look. It makes her get that great feeling, that rare, euphoric one, where all of life and its possibilities rush forward and your arms are wide out, ready to take in every one of them. Of course, there is no room in that feeling for the mixed and messy truth of it. When your arms are out wide, you'll capture love and joy and golden moments but other things, too. Mistrust will sneak in on a wave of that joy, and complications will ride the backs of the golden moments, and there will be both love and the risks of love. That's the way it is. That's the design. The net is wide, if you're brave enough to hold the net at all. Buoyant with hope and goodwill, Nash doesn't even hear the squeak of leather shoes as they rise from a crouch outside the window or the crunch of soles walking down the gravel drive. She shuts her eyes just before she begins to play her heartfelt and imperfect song.

chapter 6

Callie

The mustangs were gone. Tex stopped barking. There was the squeak-spring sound of the tiny doors of the cuckoo clock as they opened and then the call of the little wooden bird, and then it was quiet. If it wasn't for the mess left behind, I might have thought it never happened, which is something my dear sister said about a few of her failed loves, but never mind.

What had happened out that window, the unruly passion of it—it had altered the landscape. First a cloud of dust lingered, thick and red-brown, like the volcanic ash in the Seattle air after Mount St. Helens blew when I was a girl. And then the ground was rutted with fresh grooves, with hunks of dry grass hurled to far-off places. A distant fence post had also been somehow lifted and flung to the road. Even the buffalo had fled in self-protection.

"The forest-service man," I said. I understood now.

"Forest-service man?"

"Mom said a guy's been calling—"

Nash scoffed. "Forest service! *Bureau*. Bureau of Land Management."

"Ah," I said.

"That Kit Covey. He comes over as if he's going to get me to *convert*."

Bureau of Land Management: I imagined a dull, square-shouldered man in a green Smokey the Bear outfit. Oh, how wrong I was.

"Nash, my God. Why are you ignoring them? This isn't some little problem with a . . . with . . ." I didn't know the sort of problems the Bureau of Land Management dealt with.

She shook her head as if I was missing the point. "They are planning to *gather* them."

"Good! Gather away! You need some help with this! Look what just happened. Those horses—there were so *many* of them! They were right *here*. They're going to destroy this place!"

"It doesn't matter."

There was a knock at the door then. Nash folded her arms. "If that's him, I've said all I have to say."

"Let me handle it," I said. Those horses were nothing, *nothing*, I could handle.

"Hello? Anyone home?" Someone was calling through the screen door, all right, and it wasn't a forest-service man.

"Shaye?"

"Callie?"

She looked good. She'd lost weight. I guess weight was something sisters always noticed about each other right off, an unwelcome but permanent reflex of sibling rivalry.

"Holy shit! Those horses! I was in my car. I thought I might die in there." Shaye dropped her suitcase to her feet, held her hand to her chest. "Did that really just happen? I gotta sit for a minute." She grabbed my arm, pulled me down beside her to the hanging porch swing.

"Girls!" Nash said. "Don't—"

Too late. There was a crash and a terrible clatter, and we were up and then we were down. Nash had her hands over her ears. Tex ran inside the house. Something hurt—my leg, my butt. Shaye had splinters in her hair from where the hooks had dislodged from the porch roof. I spit out a piece of sawdust from the 1930s.

"What are you doing here?" we said at the same time.

"Jinx," Shaye said. "I think I broke my tailbone."

"Me, too. Jesus."

"Don't tell me. Mom called you."

I looked at Shaye and she looked at me. I knew those eyes. I'd been looking in those eyes since the day she was born. We both had our mom clothes on. Shaye wore a PTA-parent no-sleeve shirt, shorts, and those white tennis shoes you get at Rite Aid every spring, and I wore one of Amy's hand-me-down tank tops and jeans, and we were a far cry from the girls in summer dresses we were years ago.

"That chain hit me in the shoulder," Shaye said, rubbing her bare arm. I looked over my head. The wood above us was clearly rotted, and two new ragged holes gaped like frightened eyes where the hooks once were.

"Quit whining and help me up," I said.

I don't know what it was, but this made Shaye laugh, which made me laugh. It began as ordinary laughing and then turned to the bent-over stomach-holding variety. The two of us, Laura and Almanzo, back at the prairie in our mom clothes—it was beyond hilarity. What a mess both our lives were, too—I could barely catch my breath with the calamity of it all. "Jesus," Shaye said. "God." And then her little white Rite Aid mom shoe made a farting sound as she tried to get up, and this sent us over the edge again.

"Girls!" Nash barked, as if we were seventeen and had just come home drunk from a party. Poor thing: We'd come uninvited, and now this. It was shocking the amount of trouble well-meaning people could cause.

Tex had trotted out again now that there were no more falling objects. He hopped up on Shaye's lap and went for her face with his fast pink tongue. "Down dog," she said. "Ow, ow, ow. Toenails."

I managed to stand. I reached out my hand and Shaye took it, and I pulled her up. "I heard about Eric's sports car," I said.

"I heard about Thomas's girlfriend," she said.

"How old is this stuff?" Shaye twisted open the cap of some bottle of liquor that looked like it had been in that cupboard for a million years. She took a sniff and reeled. "This could kill you, Nash. You know how they have those places that recycle motor oil? You should bring this."

"I'll keep that in mind," Nash said, as she rooted around in her freezer. I couldn't believe that thing still worked. It was big enough to put a body in, but it was nearly empty save for a few packages wrapped in white paper. "I could make us pork chops," she said. "I wasn't expecting company."

"Oh, Nash. I'm sorry. We descended," Shaye said. "I'm going to get us some Chinese and a bottle. Did you see that new Chinese place *and* a grocery store?" she asked me. Out here, it was practically like getting a mall with a Cineplex.

"It's been there forever," Nash said. "Ten years."

"Maybe in another decade you'll get Thai food," I said. The light was turning yellow-orange, and the hills changed to shades of pink as evening fell. I was starving. I threw a twenty at Shaye.

"If you're going to go, don't dawdle," Nash said. "You shouldn't be out there when it's dark."

I elbowed Shaye. "Yeah, bring your pistol, cowgirl."

"Never met a varmint I couldn't handle," Shaye drawled.

"Girls, don't be smart," Nash said. "You don't know. I've seen plenty."

I watched Shaye drive off in her giant SUV, and then I put sheets on the bed in Castaway for her. I hauled her suitcase to her room and folded down the bedspread like a hotel's. I wished I had a little mint for her pillow, because she'd like that.

"How long does it take to get Chinese?" Nash said after a while. She had the gnarled hands of a woman who once could put an animal twice her size in its place, and her silver hair and gray eyes meant business. But she was eighty, and didn't you get nervous at that age? I didn't know. I just knew that with her skittishness and those horses somewhere out there and that big white moon and the sense that we were all lost together, I was glad when I saw the two beams of Shaye's headlights come down the road.

While Shaye was away, my mind had been weighed down. Images and feelings tossed—my daughter eating gallo pinto in an outdoor restaurant; my husband opening a beer as he took off his shoes and unrolled his socks in an empty house; a hit of grief that Hugo was gone, gone, gone to wherever the dead go. My heart was heavy with fear and despair about Thomas and me and our own wrecked ground, and I could hear coyotes, and there was the kind of dark out there where you could disappear and never be found. But as soon as Shaye showed up with plastic bags filled with white cartons, and a fat grocery sack with the neck of a Jack Daniel's bottle sticking from it, all that disappeared. It just *went* in a comforting, familiar flash, because, damn her, I knew it! I knew she'd eat all the fortune cookies on the way.

* * *

I called Thomas after dinner. Well, I had to. We'd only had a fight this cataclysmic once before, a few years ago, when we'd fought again about his mother. She'd come for a visit, and he accused me of not trying. I hadn't tried, but all that history had left me cold by then. I suppose every marriage has its issue, *the* issue that's been shot at and strangled and drowned and stabbed, and yet its mean little heart still goes on beating. This was ours. June Bennett. Of course, the fights about his mother weren't about his mother. The issue is never the issue. It's about what you need most colliding with what he needs most.

He wanted me to be more generous. I wanted him to *do something*. It was like he'd brought a wild animal into our house and then let it piss on the carpets and rip things up with its teeth while he stood there and smiled indulgently. Or, worse, didn't notice when it drew blood. I tried to handle her various rejections and jabs and green-eyed moves with kindness, with bribery and gifts, with every self-help-ish term from *boundaries* to *detachment*. None of it solved anything, naturally. Thomas was the key here, and he was unwilling or unable to move from our fixed triangle. My hands felt tied—in such situations, if you fight your own battle, you lose, and if you don't fight your own battle, you lose. I wanted him to make me a priority, and he wanted me to make her a priority, until finally, after that argument, I left. It was a short-lived gesture that lacked true courage, though I ate a burger that arrived under a dome of silver and remembered that I was a human being with a life apart from Thomas.

This time, though, June Bennett was dead, and I had run away to the ranch, and there were six months of small lies, but you went on after a fight, after a day or two or a week, didn't you? It got lonely otherwise. Ignoring each other is hard work, and downright awkward in a shared bathroom. He sees you undress. The toilet flush reveals. Your toothbrushes still touch in the cup.

His crimes were small, and so were mine, and this was repairable. And the thing was, I wanted to tell Thomas, more than I wanted to tell anyone, about Nash. About the horses, and Shaye, and how you could really see the face in the moon in the desert. The sheets smelled like someone else's closet and someone else's laundry soap. Thomas was the one I told things to. Isn't it part of why we marry, to have a person to tell your life to? You choose each other and become the principal witness. You begin to require his response to the funny sight, the victory, the trouble, because it completes the experience. Telling your witness sets a small volume or a large one to its place on the shelf. *There*, is what a part of you says.

And while I sometimes could have relayed my day to a large appliance and let it hum back in the right parts—not because Thomas wasn't listening, but because I forgot to really *see* him across from me—for the most part I did see him, and he saw me, and it wasn't about having someone, it was about having Thomas, the way he understood exactly what I meant when I said, *Remember Vegas?* or waved my arms in our private joke, which referred to the time his sister got hysterical at that party but which had come to mean any time a person overreacted.

He wasn't just the one I told things to. He was the one.

I picked up the phone. I'd set the little patches around the injury, as you must; opened myself to the prospect of forgiveness. Likely I'd be heading home soon, maybe in a day or two, after Shaye and I *assessed*.

Thomas was out of breath when he finally picked up. "I was taking out the garbage. I didn't hear the phone."

I didn't know what to say, now that he'd answered. As soon

as I heard his actual voice, the warm balloon of my goodwill seemed to lift off and disappear.

"Callie?"

"I'm here." I picked the tiny balls of fuzz from the quilt and made a small hill.

"You're at the ranch, huh? That old place, Jesus. Melissa told me."

"Yeah, well."

Silence.

"If you're mad about how much the therapy costs, insurance covers it, so don't worry."

"I don't care about the *money*. When have I ever been the one to care about money?" Thomas—he was the one who thought it was an extravagance to throw away a yogurt carton past its due date. I saw his words for what they were, one of those alluring, argument side trails, the sort that you both careen down even when they're so far off the main road, you'll end up walking in circles for hours. He would remind me of the one time he ever bought anything for himself, and I would remind him that when he bought that car, we only had four hundred dollars in the bank. He'd say I was controlling, and I'd say he loved to play the victim. But the main road—this time I was scared where it was headed. The trails have a purpose, which is probably why they're so widely used.

His voice was tight and strained, a thin wire. "I just . . . I needed to talk to someone."

I wondered what it was like. A couch, the requisite box of Kleenex, two people in one intimate, silent space.

"I'm here, you know, as far as someone to talk to. Your wife?"

"There's no need to be threatened."

"I wouldn't be *threatened* if you hadn't kept it a secret. You lied to me, Thomas. And why? How often did I suggest it myself? Remember that Saturday when you barely got out of bed? I said, *Thomas, you've got to call someone. You're clearly depressed.* And what did you say? *I don't believe in paying someone to listen to my troubles.*"

I tried to keep my voice down, so Shaye and Nash wouldn't hear. Things could get so confusing so fast between two people. You wouldn't think it was possible, and every time it happened, it astonished me. In a second, we—lovers, friends, partners—could be two animals thrashing over one carcass. "You lied for *six months*, Thomas. I doubt Mary Evans would think that was burgeoning good health."

"She doesn't know I haven't told you."

"Oh, great. Super. We should be going together, Thomas, if you feel like this. Marriage counseling—"

"Why is this suddenly about you? This is *mine*. I kept this to myself, yes. So sue me! I wanted to figure out my own head first."

Here was the question that had to be asked. It was the boulder that must be dropped from the cliff, and when I shoved it over, I heard the gruesome thud and felt the landing in the pit of my stomach. "And what *is* in your own head?"

There was no sound, just the buzz of phone static. And then I realized something awful. He was crying. Thomas, who never cried. I could hear the *eck eck* of his sobs, the struggle for words.

"I'm wondering. If this . . . is *all*."

"This? Us?" Oh, God. It was awful.

"No!" He blew his nose. From my side of the phone, it sounded like a typhoon gust whipping through a room. "This, all of it." His next word was tiny, which was funny for a word so big. The biggest: "Life."

Damn it, my heart flooded with feeling. Compassion. I wanted to cry, too. For him, and me, and for all of us poor, sorry human beings doing our best in this world. "Jesus, Mack. Maybe you should just buy a sports car."

I meant this to be light and caring, a gentle joke, but it was the wrong thing to say. The minute the words were out of my mouth, I knew it was the most wrong thing, but you'd think by then we could have seen each other's good intentions.

"And you wonder why I didn't tell you? Of course you'd make it trivial! A bothersome setback you could sweep under the rug with all that you *know*—"

He hated my emotional practicality. I hated it sometimes, too. "Thomas, I'm sorry. I didn't mean it like that! But isn't this what *happens*?"

"To men of my age, you mean."

"To people who've . . . Your mother just died. The girls . . ."

"A midlife crisis. A *cliché*."

"An understandable situation! A thing can be clichéd and still be just as devastating."

"Nice, Cal. Terrific."

"There's nothing wrong with it! There's nothing to be ashamed—"

"How can you understand what a man feels? Really? You never even had a *father*."

I crooked the phone between my chin and shoulder. I opened my suitcase, then put the small stack of T-shirts in the musty dresser drawer. Here was another truth, I thought, as I stood in Taj, holding a bathing suit that had seen better days. Thomas didn't fight fair, and I was tired of it. It was something no one would see from the outside or ever suspect. He'd go from zero to sixty on the anger scale, and then all the days of laundry-doing and lawn-mowing and hardworking goodness would be gone. No one would recognize that monster from the way he swept the garage and made chicken with dumplings. He'd fling my most raw failures at me, too, like the excellent weapons they were.

I never liked big emotion. My mother's was big enough during our childhood that high intensity resulted in the urge to flee to the safety of my room. At times like those, when Thomas stomped and fumed, I wanted to either leave home or slip a lethal powder into his chalice, but I'd handle him with distance instead. I'd shove a fat lot of it between us, so his raised voice and the lingering hurt from his words would have to climb a few barriers to reach me. The problem was, distance is a thing that can stack up. Over the years, bits of it gather like sedimentary layers in rock. The little ways you injure each other—they rise and harden.

He barely paused for breath. "Is it any wonder I don't feel heard? This isn't about us, or you, or our family. It's about *me*. Figuring out what I want. When do I ever think about what *I* want?"

Oh, how fast that old jet plane was, the one that went from love to hate. This was just my familiar Thomas after all. The Poor Me Thomas, the I'm Last Thomas, the eater of cereal dust and burnt toast, who only needed to *speak* if he truly wanted to be heard. Frankly, I was sick of all his pointless self-denial. He may have thought it deserved some kind of medal, but I no longer saw anything admirable in it. There were so many ways you could go wrong in a marriage. Being selfish, not being selfish enough. Not being selfish enough and rubbing it in everyone's face.

"Maybe it's good you left for a while," he said. "You know what? I'm glad. I need some time."

I didn't say a word. I bit the inside of my cheek so I'd stay silent. Dear husbands and wives. Sweet, loving people entwined in bed on a Sunday morning, turned to vicious bastards and bitches. The hardest part of being married—why don't they tell you this?—is all the days you hate each other. We'd been together for twenty-two years. We had two daughters. Yet in an instant I could imagine my own small beach house, with white rugs and blue curtains and popcorn for dinner. I was sure right then that freedom was every woman's secret wish.

Thomas was the husband every friend of mine envied. He was sweet and smart and he cooked and worked hard and he was still so damn handsome, with those broad shoulders, and that hair, and those brown eyes that brought to mind softness and suede. He was funny, too. But he could turn into a spiteful child and claim that's what people did when they got mad.

And I, too, was the wife who was admired by his friends, and the wife no one knew, with my own arsenal. My preferred weapons were large and light, nothing sharp or speared or bloody for me. They were powerful, though; make no mistake about it. Silence and distance can drive a person crazy.

I hung up on him.

I could feel the tendrils of change crawling upward, wrapping themselves around everything usual and daily. I could feel them squeeze; at least, I could barely breathe. No one had made the call to fix that rot that made our house slope. He hadn't, but I hadn't, either. It was mystifying (frightening, alluring) the way you could let it all just *go*.

The worst kind of cocktail, fury and fear, roiled in my stomach. I put that old bathing suit in the drawer and slammed it shut.

"Take all the time you need," I said to my empty room.

* * *

"I didn't want to say anything before, but guess who I saw when I went to get dinner? The forest-service guy. He was coming down the road to see us. He stopped and stuck his head out the window. I waved him off, pointed at my wrist like I was in a hurry," Shaye said.

It was late, and Shaye looked exhausted. She lay on the couch, feet up, arms crossed on her chest like a corpse. Her eyes had ashy half-moons beneath them. Thomas and I weren't the only ones fighting long-distance. Just after she arrived, I'd heard her outside, crying and yelling on the phone with Eric. I hated that sound. Other people fighting—it sent me right back to being seven when Mom left Gene. She'd been married to him for a long time, and he felt like a father. Shaye and I had hid in her room, clutching hands.

"Why didn't you talk to him? I mean, clearly we can't just let those horses run around and wreck everything."

"I didn't want to talk to him! I looked awful. I needed to brush my teeth! You should have seen him, Cal. Very Redford-*Out-of-Africa*-y. I mean, wow."

"We'll have to deal with him one way or another," I said, which was true, truer than I knew then. "You can't just go around ignoring government agencies."

"You can when your deodorant gave up an hour ago. Anyway, we should at least get Nash's side of the story first."

"I tried! All she'd say was that she wanted the horses left alone. I'm worried Harris is right. This *is* some kind of emergency. I told you, that stuff in Nash's room? It looked *crazy*. She said it was *ranch business. Closing out the paperwork.* No way all that stuff is ranch business. She doesn't even have a ranch anymore, for starters."

"Maybe she's writing her memoirs."

"She's not writing her memoirs."

"She could be!"

"This might sounds nuts . . . I sound like Mom." Our mother loved a conspiracy. She once became convinced that a garbage bag of couch cushions was the dead wife of our neighbor, the murderous Mr. Fluke, who worked at a garden store. "But I saw a date. I think I did. It all happened so fast."

"What kind of date?"

"A year. On file boxes, on a folder, lots of places. Kind of jumped out at me: 1951."

"You do sound like Mom," Shaye said.

I threw a pillow at her and missed. I was in my pajamas, too, and I lounged in the leather chair. Its seat had a permanent crater from all the time it had spent accommodating demanding asses, something Shaye was pretty familiar with, too, if you asked me. "Well, we'll never know now. She locked her door. I tried to go in there to snoop when she was looking around for an extra bottle of shampoo."

"A bottle of Breck circa 1977. It'll make us go bald."

"It'll make you go bald. I brought my own."

"She'd have a few things to say in a memoir. Didn't some movie star come once? Ava Gardner, a fancy car, and something-something in a bar?"

"Yeah. I feel like we've heard the same three stories over and over."

"Ava Gardner," Shaye counted on her fingers. "Grandma and the drought . . ."

"The time the lady set her room on fire when Mom and Nash were babies."

"So? It'll be a short book." Shaye bit the skin by her fingernail. "Can you believe she never got married? I can't imagine it."

"Sure, *you* can't imagine it." I was joking, but maybe it was a bad time for it, especially after that fight I'd heard. I'd given Shaye a set of glass bowls for her first wedding to the brooding, controlling Mathew, a pair of vases when she briefly moved in with that sweet but chaotic artist from Montana, a knife set for her brief, disastrous union with Quentin, the fuming egomaniac, and nonstick pans when she married Eric.

"Shut up!" she said, but it didn't have much gusto. "Well, she had a few men in her life. There was that one guy for a while."

"She did? What guy?" Tex snored from the corner of the couch, where he probably didn't belong. I could hear the sound of insect applause, the *tick-tick-tick* of moth wings against the glass of the window.

"Hangy ears, backwoodsy name. Hooper? Hopper? Cooper! That was it. You don't remember?"

"I didn't know! No one tells me anything."

"A few years before her mastectomy."

"I didn't know about any Cooper."

"They weren't together that long. It was before Harris."

"Harris? They're together, for sure?"

"Honestly? You can't tell just by the way he looks at her? The man adores her. Oh, Cal, you've never been much of a romantic, have you."

"No, I guess not. You're right." She was. My first childhood crush had been on the Professor from *Gilligan's Island*. He was the practical one, sure, but he was also the only one who might actually save the lost, with his phone made out of a coconut.

"And I'm right about Harris. Trust me."

The ice had long ago diluted the alcohol in my glass, but I sipped it anyway. The radio was on softly. That stupid Dr. Yabba Yabba Love was back, with her easy psycho-relationship BS: *What you think you see, you see.* "God, turn that off," I said.

Shaye sat up, reached over, and pushed the power button. The unit was from the days when bigger was better and laser shows were in. Either the stereo was now off or the captain had just landed the spaceship.

I flipped through another magazine I found under the coffee table, feeling slightly irritated. If Shaye knew so much about Nash, what was I doing here? "It's like the historical museum of magazines down here." I held up a *Woman's Day* from 1960, with a woman and a man beaming over a glossy turkey.

"That one had Reno in it." Shaye pointed, and I reached for a *Look* from 1958, with Jerry Lewis and family on the cover. "No, that one."

"*Confidential*?" The face of some dead movie star beamed up at me, his teeth a row of perfect white Chiclets. "How do you know these things?"

"I saw it when we were kids. It's the same one."

"Your memory is amazing. Ask me what I had for dinner yesterday. No idea."

"Quiz me. I'm answer woman."

"Eric, for starters. Tell me what's going on there."

She rolled her eyes. "I can't. I don't even want to talk about it."

"He doesn't mind running things while you're gone?" Shaye and Eric both did freelance marketing and were making a go of it under one umbrella.

"Mind? He couldn't wait to get rid of me."

"Okay, where are the kids? I'll ask that."

"Eric's girls are home. But, you know, Josh and Emma always spend a month with Mathew in the summer."

"How is it that I sort of forgot about Mathew?"

"Lucky you."

I turned the fragile pages of *Confidential*, trying to find old Reno, then gave up. I tossed it back on the pile. "Tell me why you ate all the fortune cookies, how about that one?"

"Your magnetic personality will bring you a new hobby," she said. "Duane's mother started hoarding, too, when she got Alzheimer's."

Duane, that's right. That was his name, the boyfriend from Montana, whose new girlfriend was probably enjoying those vases. I rose, stretched my legs. Wandered over to that big window that looked out over that bigger night. Tex woke up. He stared at me, alert and watchful.

"Nash isn't hoarding. Look how tidy the rest of the house is. She seems perfectly fine, that's what's strange. Maybe it's a mission of some kind. Wouldn't you need something like that out here? Still, why not just *tell* us? We've got to get into that room."

"Well, she's not fine."

"Those papers, I know. It's not right. It isn't. The room is stuffed."

"Not the papers."

"What do you mean?" It was so dark out that window. Who knew what the snakes and wolves were up to in that darkness? Except for the white beam of the moon, shining down on the pool as if the pool were a silvery baptismal font promising renewal, it was only black and more black out there.

"You didn't know?"

"What?" Why didn't anyone ever tell me anything?

"She's dying."

chapter 7

Nash

The moon shines down on the swimming pool. It makes the water look silvery-black and shimmery, as if a dip in it might save your soul. A leaf floats across, a small, glowing boat, a cupped hand. It hits the edge and spins.

They don't speak, but they are walking close together because of the dark path, and their shoulders nearly touch. Hadley has turned in early; her porch light is already off.

"I'll make a stop here," Lilly Marcel says. The white dots of her dress are illuminated, too, tiny stars, as she heads off to the toilet.

Nash waits. She can see the constellations in the sky. She rubs her arms against the cold. She doesn't feel capable of protecting anyone. She wonders about soldiers and guards, and—wait—men in general, all of the people who are assigned to be strong. They must be just as scared as anyone else.

The door of the shack bangs and Lilly is back. "Now the baby wakes up," she says. "A night owl."

Nash likes this thought—a little swimming life, already equipped with habits and preferences. She follows Lilly to the cottage and up the stairs. Lilly has her hand on the knob of the door when they hear a long, high-pitched scream.

Lilly grabs Nash and shrieks. The noise is the strangled cry of a woman getting her throat slashed, but it is not a woman. It's a sound Nash has never gotten used to.

"A rabbit," Nash says. "It's only a rabbit, caught by a hawk or maybe a coyote."

"Oh, my God. That is the most chilling thing I've ever heard."

It is. You know that fangs are sinking into the soft flesh of a neck. It's horrible.

"Get in here, fast." Lilly grabs Nash's arm and pulls her inside. She turns the lock.

"Are you all right?" Nash asks.

"I don't know." Lilly sets her palm to her chest. "Rabbits have it rough, don't they. Jesus, where's the light switch?"

Their hands hit against each other on the wall, and Nash's shin hits the bookshelf with an audible clunk. It's the darkness and that scream, and now Nash's poor shin, and they both start to laugh. They are holding each other's arms and giggling madly from tension and the shared knowledge of their own false courage. A scream like that will set anyone on edge.

Lilly wipes her eyes. "Oh, God, oh, God. Where is that light?" she sputters.

Nash hits the switch. They squint at each other in the sudden brightness, and this is hysterical, too.

Lilly takes a big breath, exhales. "Whew. There. All is well." Her eyes are bright blue.

The black windows gape at them. Anyone could be out there. "Let's close those curtains," Nash says.

Lilly's suitcase is open on the bed. She follows Nash's eyes to it. A corner of it is stacked with baby clothes. Nash can see a tiny sweater and a tiny pair of socks. "Just in case," Lilly says. She holds up a sock in each hand.

"Oh," Nash says. Her heart feels struck.

"I know," Lilly says. She tucks the socks back into her bag. "Am I going to have to walk *you* back now?" She gives Nash's braid two short tugs.

"Then I'd have to walk you again," Nash says.

"It could go on all night."

"I'm fine. This is practically my backyard. I grew up here."

"If you say so. My God."

"It's okay," Nash says.

"We heard its life ending."

When Nash leaves the cabin, she thinks again about Lilly's choice to stay out here alone. The curtained windows glow with yellow light, but the whole cabin seems like another rabbit out in the open. Nash doesn't understand what leads some people to the edge. The bull riders, for example, with their arced backs and tight, gripping fists, full of bravado but with breakable bones and heads that could smash like overripe gourds. Or those men who walk on the wings of an airplane. Last summer, she and Jack saw one at the air show at Lansing Field, and they stood together and gasped when that tiny figure emerged from the door of the roaring plane. Or the women, even, who come back from Reno with stories of dancing with strangers, who marry men like Stuart Marcel, who drive too fast in cars with the wind blowing their hair.

Lilly shouldn't be there alone, Nash thinks for the hundredth time, but she supposes everyone has their reasons for their rash acts.

Nash hurries back toward the house, past the stables where all the horses are tucked in, past the riding rink and the pastures and the pool with its beam of holy light. Her heart is beating fast because of that rabbit and Lilly Marcel and because it feels darker than usual with her mother gone.

There is the chew and spit of tires against gravel. It makes her think her mother is home, but of course her mother isn't home. Nash recognizes the sound of the truck: It's just Jack, coming in from a night out.

She waits for him. He hops out, tosses Nash the keys. She misses, and they land at her feet.

"Aw, Peanut, it was a bad throw."

She smells the alcohol. He is one handsome man, oh, dear, he is, and that smell of alcohol and his eyes in the night—Nash may understand heedlessness after all. All lovers are bull riders and wing walkers. Every person who risks giving their heart over stands with their feet at the edge of a high, open doorway.

"What are you doing out here?" he asks.

"Waiting for you."

He grins. "Oh, really now."

"Really now."

He takes a pinch of her shirt and playfully pulls her closer. It's an infuriating gesture, closer to him but not *to* him, his hand grazing her skin. She wishes he'd kiss her. "It's getting late. Better head in."

"If you say so."

Nash watches him head away; he'll go down that path that leads right past Lilly Marcel's cabin. She shouldn't think what she's thinking.

He turns around to look at her once more, walking backward as he speaks. "Bob Watson said he saw mustangs on his property."

They came only a few times in a person's lifetime, and Jack knew how she felt about those wild horses. She hoped and hoped she might one day see them. She'd confessed it that afternoon when they sat together next to the lake, after he'd taught her how to smoke a cigarette. *Seeing them changes you*, he'd told her, that's what any cowboy knew, and she was sure it was true, same as seeing any rare event, those comets that came once every hundred years, a blue Mount Charleston butterfly that crossed your path. You would have gotten a singular, extraordinary message from nature then, a message that would leave you transformed.

"You may just get your wish, Peanut," he says.

Veronica is on the telephone. She is wearing her silk robe and sits at the wood table in the kitchen with the phone in front of her. She pokes her finger in each hole of the dial. Her head is bent down, and when Nash comes in, Veronica only glances up at her. It's late, and Veronica's makeup is off, and her eyes look weary and distant. Her real name is Dorothy, she admitted one cocktail hour. Tonight she is Dorothy again. She is saying, *Please, please*, into the phone. That phone has heard plenty— pleadings and apologies and declarations of love and hate. Nash thinks about how much anguish phones have suffered through, especially at late hours. Night has a way of stripping you down and leaving only your true, scared self. At a late-enough hour, we are all rabbits, hiding safely in our warrens, or making mad, dangerous dashes, or trembling in the open.

I'm sorry, Veronica says. She sounds crushed. *I'm so sorry. I never meant to hurt you.*

Nash hears it again and again, the way people hurt each other without meaning to, making decisions based on runaway hearts and dimming passions, past mistakes, and promises of change. In a lifetime, the recipe always needs amending—more of this, a little less of that, what to do now that the cake has fallen. Not many people mean to be cruel, as far as Nash can tell. But there are always those few who do.

It's a different car. When you live out in the middle of nowhere, you know cars. You know the sound of a strange one same as you know a rattle in the grass.

Nash watches from the darkness of the main room. The car is long and low and it comes down the road with its lights off. This is strange. Very, very strange, and she doesn't know what to do but watch. Boo begins to bark in the quiet house. He races down the stairs, and with the late hour and the uncommon speed, he loses traction and skids across the floor.

Nash scoops him up and holds his tense little body. "Shush," she says.

A man gets out of the car. He walks along the road but turns away from the house, down the path to the pool and the cottages. He is a large, walking shadow. He is holding something. His hand grips it against his chest.

Nash feels all-out panic; her heart stomps. There is not time to get Veronica off the phone so that she might call Jack or Cliff or Danny. This man is more dangerous than a wolf or a mountain lion, this seems obvious, and for a moment Nash thinks about getting the shotgun from under her mother's bed. Instead, she is out the door before logic kicks in. She was raised here, and, more than anything else, more than her friends from school or her books or some hazy vision of the future, the ranch and the women who come here are hers. Even though she is barely eighteen years old: *hers*.

She runs down the porch steps. She waves her arms, as if scaring a rabid dog away from chickens. "Get out!" she yells. "Get away from here!"

The man takes off running. His long dark coat flaps behind him, and the camera—she sees it's a camera now—bangs against his chest. He gets in his car. The back wheels of his car spin and swerve in the gravel.

Veronica is out in the yard in her bare feet. "What is going on?"

"A man," she says.

"Who?"

"Someone trying to take pictures, I don't know," Nash says. But she does know; they both do. At least, they know who sent him. He's not a reporter from *Confidential* or *Photoplay*. Only one other person would likely see the pictures the man is after. The photos would be proof of wrongdoing, as if a man like that needed proof. She begins to shake. Veronica puts her hands on Nash's shoulders.

"Some people can't stand the outrage of being left."

"*She* left *him*?" Nash is surprised. She thought it was the usual. It happened so often, a powerful man finding a replacement when he got bored.

"She told Ellen. Of course she told Ellen! Ellen's got that kind of face. A killer would confess to Ellen."

If her mother knew this, she never would have gone running to help Gloria. Gloria's most recent romantic calamity or whatever it was would have had to wait. Alice knew the dangers. Angry men who were left—well, there had been Vic Jones that one year, and then Harv Cullins. Vic waved a gun out on the front lawn, and Harv smashed a car window with his fist.

"Come on. Come inside."

Nash must have set Boo down without realizing it. He stands on the dark porch, looking worried.

"You should have seen yourself," Veronica chuckles. "I never knew you had it in you. Watch out! You're one tough cookie, after all! I'm never going to cross you, Nash McBride, that's for sure."

Veronica has her arm around Nash. She is in that robe and

her bare feet. Her toenails are painted red. Her eyes look smaller without all that makeup, but softer, too. "Let's put this goddamn day to rest."

She squeezes Nash's shoulder. It's almost motherly. Veronica does not have children, but Nash wonders right then if every woman is a mother in one way or another.

chapter 8

Callie

Shaye was painting her toenails red. She looked like she hadn't slept all night. She had Einstein hair and parentheses of frown lines between her brows. "You know it's not just the car," she said.

"Of course it's not just the car. The whole stepfamily thing . . . It sounds like a nightmare. Wait," I said. It hadn't hit me before, not really. You could have arguments and new sports cars and mad leavings to Nevada; you could even use the word *divorce* and not mean it. "Are you actually *leaving* him?"

Shaye stopped the little brush in midair. Her toes were half done; the poor blank ones looked like sad orphans next to their flamboyant friends. "I don't know. I don't know what to do anymore. I mean, we've also got a business together now. I feel like such a failure."

"You're not a failure."

I'd dragged an old vacuum cleaner down the hall, and now it sat beside me, a too-short dance partner, same as David Selby in the seventh grade. I hunted around for a plug. Words like *commitment* and *vow* knocked wrongly around my head and threatened to spill. Failure wasn't an option if you stood behind words like those. But who was I to talk? We were both there at the ranch, and, if I was being honest, there were many times that it was cowardice and cowardice alone that kept me in my marriage, not some superior moral footing. Not some exalted word like *vow*. Honestly? I might have been Shaye, if I'd had more guts.

Because there were these tender and treasured things: his body next to my body, rubbing sore necks, bringing medicine; soft words on bad days, and the fact that he seemed like my only true friend in the world sometimes, my still-laughing sidekick through bills and diagnoses and the triumphs of our children. But there were also these: a wish to be better known after all those years, hearts kept private, a list of past crimes; years that made us companionable roommates, and sometimes not even that. Often, marriage was solitude, with company.

How did one add it up? What conclusion could a person come to? Could anything hold the weight of two lives lived side by side? Or, perhaps even weightier, the lives not lived?

Then again, could you go through a colonoscopy with some-one and not be wedded for life?

"How can you clean at a time like this?" Shaye yelled over the roar of the vacuum cleaner.

"A time like what?"

"How can you just . . . I mean, you, here . . . Thomas . . . Something is wrong, Cal. Telling you to stay out here—it's not like him. He hid going to therapy for half a *year*."

"Move that chair," I shouted.

"You can't keep busy forever," Shaye said.

"Lots of people do," I yelled. "They go from dinner plans with so and so to the kids' birthday party to the roof cleaner."

"You haven't even cried."

"You know I hate to cry."

"You can run, but you can't hide."

"He's just grieving! It's loss. His mother just died! Besides, I wouldn't even know how to imagine . . ." My stupid voice cracked.

"What?"

"Some new life. I don't even know what that could look like."

This shut Shaye up. It shut us both up. There was only the roar of the vacuum and the sound of it knocking against the wall as I maneuvered around furniture.

"How can you clean at a time like this?" Nash yelled from the doorway. I flipped the switch, and the roar silenced.

"I never saw you as the housecoat type, Nash," I said. "Those roses are so sweet."

"I can't believe we're wasting time discussing my attire," Nash said. She crossed the room, flung open the curtains. "Look."

"Brown grass and more brown grass," I said.

"A brand-new day?" Shaye guessed.

"*There*."

"I thought the eyes were supposed to go when you got old," I said. I couldn't see a damn thing except all that wreckage that needed tending to.

"Those two." She tapped the glass with her finger. "They're fighting over a mare."

Ah, a splotch of darkness in the distance. "I see them."

"Wow, they're tall," Shaye said.

"That's a pair of acacias, you idiot," I said, and Shaye socked my arm. "The black spot to your right."

"I hated those horses for years," Nash said. "Dirty, dangerous creatures. A menace. And then a few months ago I saw them again. For the first time in a long while. I was washing dishes. Soapsuds up to my elbows, and there they were. Right out there! And it was the most incredible thing. It changed me. Changed me again. I could see how beautiful they were, in spite of the trouble and the danger. I'd forgotten that."

We huddled around the window like a trio of hostages. Nash's old road-map hands rested on the sill. Her nose was scrunched and her eyes narrow as she squinted to see. I tried to do the same, but the horses still only resembled a moving thumbprint.

"Nash, I get it—why you're ignoring the bureau guy. I do," I said. But I didn't. Not at all. "The grandeur of them . . ."

She turned to me, raised her brows like I'd taken leave of my senses. "*Grandeur?*"

"Whatever you want to call it. But they're destroying your land."

"*My* land?"

"This is an animal-rights issue to you?"

"It's not an issue to me at all. It's a personal matter. I want them left alone anywhere near the property."

The vehemence, it was another thing I thought I suddenly understood. How had we missed it, when it was so obvious? "This is what the papers are about. In your room. You're trying to stop the gather."

"Nonsense. I don't like it, but I can't stop it."

"You're not building some case . . ."

She scoffed. Looked at us like we were a pair of children who'd not yet learned the ways of the world.

"I don't get it," Shaye said. "Sure, they're beautiful, but anyone in your position would want those horses gone. Out of here, and *fast*."

We waited. The silence was a standoff. Finally, she spoke. "It's a sign," she said, almost reluctantly.

"A sign."

"A message."

Shaye scooted her painted foot next to mine and nudged. She made crazy eyes at me behind Nash's back.

"What sort of a message?" My voice was high-pitched. It was the way you talked to the guy with a bomb strapped to his waist.

"It's *meant*."

"Meant," Shaye repeated.

"I never should have said anything. I knew I shouldn't have told you."

"Come on, Nash," Shaye said. "You have to tell us. We can help if we understand. You don't want the horses messed with because the horses are a sign. Okay. Great. So what's all the stuff in your room?"

The black thumbprint got smaller, until it was gone. Nash turned away from the window. "I told you. It's *ranch business*. If I wanted your help, I'd ask for your help. Not every corner of a person's life needs to be *discussed* and *shared* and *passed around*."

"Let's talk about 1951," I ventured.

"The summer of 1951," Shaye said.

I thought I saw a flare of shock cross Nash's eyes. There was no question, though, about her sharp exhale.

"You girls sound just like your mother," she said.

"Thanks a lot," I said.

"And with that, you'll have to tend to your own breakfast. Obviously you saw all the work I have to do, since you keep going on about it. You think this place runs itself?"

"You could tell us if you were writing a book or something, Nash." Shaye, she could be like a dog with a knotted sock when she had an idea. There she was, back on the book thing. Of course Nash wasn't writing a book! There was no possible way she was writing a book!

"I'm not writing a book," Nash said.

I shot Shaye a smug look.

"I'm closing a chapter."

"Summer?" I asked Shaye. "Summer of 1951? Where'd you get that?"

"Things always happen in summer in the movies."

"Did you see it, though? Her eyes got funny."

"I don't know, Cal. Remember when Mom thought we were related to that Civil War general?"

I sighed, rummaged in an old box of nails I'd found in the barn that were now at my feet.

"Was it the bacon? Look at you. Shouldn't you just wait for Harris? He said he'd be by later to do some stuff."

"I can't just sit around all day. Harris is a million years old and it's eighty degrees out already. I don't want him kicking off while we're here," I said. The sky was blue, with skid-mark clouds, and the sun beat down on that hard, rocky ground. Short yellow shrubs, numerous tufts of bad haircuts, dotted the area. Out there, it all looked like one color at first—an endless brown. Looking closer, though, you saw orange-gray rocks and an unexpected purple flower, and a smear of red in the clay earth.

A person just couldn't sit around and *think*. Thinking led to action. I put two nails in the corner of my mouth, like Thomas always did, held another against the wood and hammered it in.

"This place is a disaster. I admire your attitude and all, but in my garden, I pull a couple of weeds and then look around and think, *Jesus, there are so many weeds.*"

"What else can I do with this anger?"

"You talked to Thomas again?"

"He left me a message this morning. He's going on a sailing trip today, with people from the office. They've had those trips every year. When has he ever gone? Oh, that's right. Never. How nice he's in the mood for a sailing trip now that I'm away from home." The hammer made a satisfying *bam, bam, bam,* until there was the disappointing *thwick* as the nail bent.

"You think that's bad? You'll never guess what Eric is doing tonight. Taking his girls to the *theater.*"

"Movie theater or theater theater?"

"Guess. When have we ever gone to the theater? The last time I even went was when Jay took me to see *Grease* at the Moore Egyptian."

Jay was her boyfriend the summer of her junior year of high school. He was the one guy who was actually nice, until Eric. "Remember Jay wore a suit?" I said. "Ha, it even had a vest."

"Eric wouldn't have bought those tickets for *us.*"

"It's Eric's guilt taking them to the theater, not Eric."

"I didn't know guilt could drive."

"Either way, the good news is, the three of them won't fit into the new Porsche." I'd heard about the trouble those girls had caused—the hidden-dagger acts, saying things Shaye could hear but their father couldn't, saying things their father could hear but she couldn't, teenage girls acting like determined mistresses. They sounded a lot like June Bennett. I couldn't even picture Eric at the theater, to tell you the truth. He was the kind of guy who liked his televisions large. He watched loud sports on that large television. Thomas never watched football. I always appreciated that about him. Me, I could watch football if the sound was off and I could read during the game.

"A Porsche, how original. And I hope Thomas falls off the

boat," Shaye said. "You're supposed to hold it down here." She slid my hand down the hammer.

"I know how to hold it."

"You're holding it like a toddler with a fork."

"We took a home-improvement class!" I said.

"You what?" Shaye started to laugh. It pissed me off, but, still, she looked like her six-year-old self, bent over laughing. It reminded me of the two of us and *H. R. Pufnstuf* on Saturday mornings.

"It's one of those things you do. Shared hobby, whatever."

"Try *cooking*?" Shaye said. "Maybe a dance class?"

"You cook however-many meals in your life, and who gives a shit about duck confit in blah-blah sauce."

"But, home *improvement*? I mean, no *wonder*."

"What do you mean by that? Thomas likes home improvement. He's great at that stuff. That man can fix anything."

"You said the house was falling apart."

I ignored her and got that board up. The pasture fences would require new bolts and posts, but the short, simple one that hugged the road, we could do it. Old Harris and I could handle that. No need to be intimidated by a *ranch*. Seattle might have lattes and slugs and damp, mossy ground, whereas this place had black coffee and lizards and grass dry enough to ignite, but at the end of the day, wood and nails were wood and nails. Fences were built and fences fell apart, wherever you went.

"I wish the pool had water," Shaye said. "I even brought my bathing suit."

"Me, too. Hey, we could run through the sprinkler."

"Ha. Do kids even do that anymore? Remember Marco Polo with just us? Talk about an exercise in frustration."

"Mom would never get her hair wet."

"There was that creepy boyfriend who smoked. He got in with us."

"Don't remind me. You know what amazes me? Hold that end." Shaye grabbed the end of the board and held it to the post, which made the job a hundred times easier. "The way she let us fight. Would you ever let your kids fight like that?" I said through the nails in my mouth.

"Oh, my God," Shaye said.

"I can still feel your skin under my fingernails."

"Oh, I know! Rolling around and clawing! If my kids ever even hit each other . . ."

"Yeah, it'd be, *Use your words*!" I singsong. I bent another nail with a good whack. A large part of me wished I hadn't started this project. It was getting hot out there, and I was tired already. "Remember when I broke your glasses?"

"We thought she was going to kill us."

"Mom hit us for hitting each other, and we're so afraid of messing up as parents, we can barely say no when they want to borrow the car to rob a 7-Eleven. No wonder we're unhappy. They should call us the Be Seen and Not Heard Generation. The first half of our lives, we're afraid of our parents, and the second half, we're afraid of our kids."

"No kidding. I forgot Joshie's sharing for kindergarten and I felt awful for days. We're parental pansies." She handed me a few more nails from the box on the ground. Shaye had one of those cute, small noses you see on cheerleaders, and it was getting sunburned.

"Then again, these kids care about building shelters in foreign countries. We never cared about building shelters in foreign countries."

"We never cared about foreign countries. California sounded cool. Cal, look," Shaye said. That buffalo was probably back. I gave a few last powerful blows, and the nail head went in satisfyingly flat. I stood, shielded my eyes, and glanced the way Shaye pointed.

"Forest-service man," we both said.

"You take him, I'll take her," Shaye said.

"I don't want him!" I said.

"You prefer sick and deranged over pre-Sundance Redford? I may have to hold her down forcibly."

"Fine. Go sit on her. Or make her eat something. She needs food."

"Food, nothing. I'm going to create a diversion, then sneak into her room. See what I can find out."

I fanned my shirt in and out. I'm sure I looked just terrific. The screen door slammed shut after Shaye, but at the sound of the truck, Tex bolted outside, a bullet heading for the enemy heart. He bared his tiny, sharp teeth and barked like a superhero.

I tucked him under my arm, but I was still on a canine strike, so I tried to ignore his actual self behind those little black eyes. "Cool it, Rambo," I said. "He looks harmless enough."

The man slammed the door of his truck. He walked over, the gravel crunching under his cowboy boots. He wore jeans and a plain gray T-shirt, and . . . well, Shaye was right. He was fit, and his face was rugged and handsome under a tan suede hat, which covered his light brown-blond hair. "Should I duck?" he said.

"Duck?"

"You're not going to throw something?"

"Not yet," I said. "Did she throw something at you?"

"A boot. I believe it landed in the pool." He smiled. It was a white, white smile against his tan face. Cinematic, but also slightly imperfect, enough to be likable.

"I see," I said. "Well, at least it was just one."

"Look." He gestured with a hook of his thumb.

The other shoe leaned against the tree as if it had passed out after a rough night. "Ah."

"Kit Covey." He held out his hand.

I took it. It was a strong, wide hand. "Callie," I said. "McBride." My hair was a mess, and what had happened to my clothes over the years? Why had I entirely forgotten about how they could make a person feel? "I'm Nash's niece."

"Hey, guy," he said. He reached his hand down to Tex, who'd proven to be a traitor. His tail was going a million miles an hour. Kit scratched his small, disloyal neck.

"I hate to keep bothering you folks, but I saw a new car head out this way and thought I'd come by and try one last time. You may have heard from your aunt that we're doing a gather? Right at the edge of her property. Public land, though—I want to be clear. I'm not sure we ever had a rancher object. Usually it's the horse enthusiasts we deal with. But we're doing what we can to make sure there's adequate public notice and information. We'd like your support."

"I'm afraid I don't know much about this," I said. "My aunt hasn't been well."

"I'm sorry to hear that."

He seemed to mean it. His eyes were kind. Tex sat at his feet like a faithful servant. "What do you need from her?"

"We just want to know that she got the information and that we've answered all her questions to her satisfaction. As the one in charge of the operation . . . well, it can take a while. The setup, first off. The gathers—another three or four weeks. We'll be right in her face, and she'll be in ours. We want her to know that the horses will be looked after. Adopted out, or given permanent care, or returned to the range . . . They'll die of starvation and disease if nothing is done. The population gets too large for their own good."

"You're trying to avoid a lawsuit."

He laughed. His eyes crinkled. "*Another* lawsuit. She used the word."

"*Sue?*"

"*Attorney.*"

"So this is just . . . public relations? You'll go ahead whether she wants it or not."

"Yes."

It was hot out there. And that land was too much for a woman her age. "Hopefully she'll run out of boots," I said.

He laughed again. He took his hat off, wiped his forehead with the back of his hand. He gave me a good look. I felt like I knew him from somewhere. That happens with certain people. You're sure that maybe you went to high school together, but you didn't go to high school together. Anyway, high school was years ago. Kit Covey was a grown man. His broad shoulders and the look in his eyes made that clear. "I think a strong arm runs in the family," he said.

"Yeah?" I smiled.

"It's much improved already."

He meant that fence. I hadn't realized how much progress I'd made. I only needed to do another mile's worth, but it was true. It looked kind of great.

"I might win this battle but not the war. There's a buffalo."

"I saw him. I ran him off with a few choice words, but he'll likely be back."

"Well, thank you. I am trying not to use the expression *hell in a handbasket.*"

He reached into his open truck window with one arm. "My

parents went to Nevada, and all I got was this lousy pamphlet," he said, handing me one.

"I'll pass this to my aunt."

"She's already ripped up one or two. This is for you."

"Thanks."

"We'd rather work with her than against her. Protests and television cameras make for a bad day."

"I'll do what I can," I promised.

"Wait," he said. He reached into his back pocket, took out his wallet. "This, too. My cell, in case that woolly thug makes you nervous."

Kit Covey. Bureau of Land Management.

"I appreciate that."

"My pleasure."

I held the card as he nodded a goodbye. His tires kicked up a storm of dust as he drove off. The spinning column of it disappeared into the distance, and it made me feel a hundred things. Some rumbling desire for far-off places merged with a vague but powerful longing for the young woman I was before I met Thomas. That dust had made me thirsty, too, my throat as dry as a long-forgotten road. Still, I stayed there and watched that truck until I couldn't see it anymore.

"I didn't stare at his ass!"

"I saw you!"

"Shaye. Stop. I did not."

"You stared at his a-ass," she sang. "For-est service a-ass." She stood at the open refrigerator, looked at the expiration dates of a mayonnaise jar and a bottle of mustard.

"Enough." I wished she'd shut her mouth, I really did.

"It was a nice ass! You can *look*."

I wasn't the looking type, for one. Not at all. I was the type who believed you never should go grocery shopping while hungry, first off, because you'd surely go home with a sheet cake you couldn't handle. "I'm going to see what's taking Nash so long, while you remember how to be more appropriate."

"She says she has a ham down there."

"Nash," I called.

"In the cellar!"

I spotted the stoop of her back and the tidy braid against her T-shirt, as she hunted around on a shelf in a dark corner. "How can you see down here?" There were cane chairs and wine barrels and an old radio. There were metal folding cots and yellowing board games. Oh, how we accumulate stuff. A spiderweb snagged my cheek, and I swatted it away.

"I forgot. Harris gave me a ham. He cured it himself."

"What, did it have some disease? Ha-ha."

She turned around, stood upright. She held it in her arms, a package wrapped in newspaper. "I knew it was down here somewhere."

"How long have you had that?"

"It's fine! It's got six more months, at least!"

I took the ham from her. That thing was heavy. She took the stairs back up, pausing at each. I could hear the effort in her breathing. Well, of course there would be signs.

"You okay, Nash?" I said this to her back, because I was too much of a coward to ask while meeting her eyes. I regret that. I should have held her hands and used the real words and showed her I wasn't afraid, even though I was afraid. I was too scared to even call the thing by its name.

"The lungs." She tapped her chest, two thuds. "Turns out

you don't even have to smoke a damn cigarette. I guess something's going to get you."

"You shouldn't be alone out here."

"I'm not alone. Harris is here. And right now I'm fine. This is how it goes. I know it well enough from my own father, my mother, Aunt Geneva, Eve down the road, you name it." She paused, catching her breath. It was a long list. "There's something wrong, and you find out. Then you got time before it gets worse. I'm taking advantage of that time. Nothing more to say."

We reached the top of the stairs. She stared me down in a challenge, and so I nodded. She was right, at the heart of it. This is where we were, and words wouldn't change that. I guess my practicality came from somewhere, because it sure didn't come from my mother. I plunked the meat on the counter. "Harris cured this ham," I told Shaye.

"What of?" She chuckled.

Nash sighed.

Shaye sniffed the mayonnaise, just in case. "Whole or half, Nash?"

"I don't want a sandwich. I am thrilled to see you both, I am. You can stay for the rest of your lives, if you want. But I have my *routines*."

"Here's your *routine*," Harris said as he kicked open the screen door with his boot. He dumped a huge box on one end of the table. "Jesus Christ. Look at this. What're you, writing a book?"

Maybe we all should have moved out there years ago, the way people aged. There was nothing frail or vulnerable about that old cowboy. His gray hair was short and buzzed, matching the stubble on his cheeks, and he was stocky and still ruggedly attractive. When he leaned in to give Shaye and me a hug, he smelled the way an old man should, some mix of heat and motor oil and wood chips.

"Where was that? I've been waiting for it. Hands off," Nash said.

"On the porch! For God's sake, you don't have to shove. Glad to see you're finally digging in to that ham."

"We got a delivery and the darn dog just laid there?"

Tex panted in a bit of shade on the kitchen floor, unoffended by Nash's remark. He looked spent, actually. His tongue lolled out of his mouth, as if it lacked the necessary energy to stay inside where it belonged. We'd interrupted his routine, too.

Nash wrapped her long arms around that box. "Enjoy your lunch, all."

"Give me that," I said. It was too heavy for her to carry, but, more than that, I wanted to see who it was from.

She shot arrows at me with her eyes to set me straight. A ham was one thing. When it came to guarding our secrets, though, we were all titans, if sometimes weary ones.

Shaye set a sandwich in front of Harris, while I poured us iced teas. "Finally, we can talk about her behind her back," Shaye said.

"The mustang guy came by again," I told Harris. "He's worried she's going to sue. He said she threatened. Used the word *attorney*. I thought maybe that's what all the boxes and paper were about, but she denied it."

"She's not gonna sue. There's nothing she can do, and she knows it and they know it. She's just being a crazy old lady, and they're just making nice so she doesn't become a pain in their backsides," Harris said. "They're going to be neighbors for a while. It's starting. I saw the semis coming. Parked out by the lake now."

"Semis?"

"You should see all the stuff. They've got to set up corrals, first off. Takes a few weeks."

"I don't get it," I said. I took a huge, satisfying bite. "I mean, she doesn't want the mustangs gone, but she's hated them for years. And if not the horses, what's all the mess about? What's the big operation?"

"We could *help*, if she didn't insist on all the furtive stuff," Shaye said, hogging the bag of chips. "What's with people your age and all the skeletons in the attic? We keep our skeletons where they belong, right out on the front lawn."

"That's for sure. I don't want to see your damn skeleton." Harris had his phone on the table beside him. Not only were the old people deeply wrinkled and still beautiful here, they were also incredibly technologically current. Thomas's mother had gotten confused when she used the microwave. "All that reality TV, Jesus." Harris shook his head with disgust. "We never had reality TV."

"You never had *TV*," Shaye said, cracking herself up. She rolled the top of the bag of chips shut and slid it my way. "Get these away from me."

"I don't know, girls. It's nice to think she has some plan she's carrying out. I thought so, too, at the start, but I'm not sure anymore. You know what was in that box?"

"You looked?"

"Of course I looked. A box comes from Leonard Petit in Beverly Hills and I don't know any Leonard Petit in Beverly Hills, I'm gonna look. I watch out for her. And apparently Leonard Petit is some weirdo who collects movie stuff. It's a box of pictures. Picture after picture, stills of old black-and-white films. Can you imagine how much she paid for that? Leonard Petit had the sale of his life."

"I didn't know she was a film buff," Shaye said.

"She's not a film buff! That's what I'm saying. She's a reader. TV is barely on. This is exactly why I phoned your mother—the boxes, the packages from places in Montana and Los Angeles when she doesn't know anyone there, and, hell, all the woo-woo stuff about *signs*, and her temper . . . And it's even worse than that. I wouldn't have called otherwise."

"Worse, like how?" Shaye asked.

"I caught her burying something. By the side of the lake."

"What do you mean?" Shaye said. "Burying what?"

"A book," Harris said.

"A book?" I said. I couldn't imagine this. It made no sense, but aside from that, Nash loved books. As Harris said, she was a reader. She had turned one of the rooms, Monte Carlo, into a little library, and I always knew what to get her for her birthday.

"Well, what happened?" Shaye said, and put her foot on mine under the table. This was bigger than both of us.

"You know I come by most every day. See if she wants me to drive her anywhere, pick up whatever she might need. Visit a little."

"How long has it been since she stopped driving?" I asked.

"Oh, years," Harris said. "Maybe she never did. She's always been terrified of it. But I came by that day, and she wasn't here. I looked around, looked everywhere. I thought she'd . . . Well, it gave me a scare, I'll tell you that. I found her by the lake. She seemed *off*, to put it mildly. She had a shovel, and she'd dug a hole. The ground out there . . . It was hard. Middle of winter. The hole was shallow as a beauty queen, but still. There was a book in it. When she saw me, she got mad. She made a huffing sound and said, *Oh, never mind*. She took the book out and wiped it on her jeans."

"What was the book?"

"Damn if I know. Old red leather, some classic, that's all I could tell. I asked her, I said, *What are you doing, sweetheart? What are you burying that for?* And she said, *Same reason anyone buries anything. To say goodbye.*"

"Someone died," I said to Shaye.

"Summer of 1951," Shaye said to me.

"Girls, this is the kind of thing that happens with old-timers. Or maybe it's the cancer. I want this to make sense as much as you. I do, I do." The words sounded like a vow. His eyes filled. Jesus, I couldn't bear to see a tough man cry, I couldn't.

"Oh, Harris." Shaye put her hand over his.

"Some secret mission? Nah. After all these years, I doubt there's much I don't know about that woman. You know what I think? All that *work* she's doing? I think it's like that movie where the guy loses his mind. You know the one." He snaps his fingers.

"*The Shining*?" Shaye said.

"Not *The Shining*!" I said. "She's not stalking around with a kitchen knife."

"Where the guy has notes tacked up everywhere . . ." Harris shook his head, tried to get the name to come loose.

"I don't know," I said. All I could see was a book in a hole out by the lake.

We were quiet. Harris looked sad, and my heart was breaking because so much was ending. I held the cool glass to my cheek.

"*A Beautiful Mind*," Shaye said.

"That's the one. What do you think of this ham, huh? Isn't it great? It's all in the aging." Harris wiped his mouth on a paper napkin.

Shaye got up and propped open the kitchen door with the

flour canister. "It's so hot here, I don't know how you guys can stand it," she said.

I checked out all the features in Shaye's car. Eric liked everything big, not just televisions; that SUV was bigger than Thomas's and my first apartment. The seats were plush leather, and there were dials to warm your seat and set the temperature and shoot off the rockets in the event of a nuclear war. It was a mobile movie theater, too; DVDs were stacked in the center console. "Why don't *you* go out," I said. "I'll just get in the backseat and watch—" I did a quick shuffle through the movies. Action-adventure and more action-adventure. "Never mind."

"Do you think she was trying to get rid of us, or what?" Shaye said. "She slipped me a five-dollar bill and told me to have a good time."

"She slipped me one, too."

"I feel bad staying if she doesn't want us."

"I know. But now we've promised Harris to see what we think. What do we do if we find out he's right?"

"If he's right, there's no way she can live out there alone."

"I hope he's not right," I said.

"Do you really think there's a reasonable explanation for what he told us? Come on, Cal."

I didn't, so I just studied all those buttons and the ways they might improve my life.

Finally Shaye said, "I don't want to go home."

I imagined my own house and felt a hit of longing for the place, the three brick steps to the lovely blue door, the stairwell with its smooth, polished wood railing leading up to the bedrooms. Even with the slope of the upstairs hall, there was still my own room, *our* own room, my own pillow, and the drawer where my pajamas lay folded. *Folded pajamas*—what beautiful words. They beckoned.

I *did* want to go home, to my cave, my hovel, my place of safety and rest, but that's not what it was now with Thomas and not what it had been for a while. I wanted my house minus Thomas, or at least the recent Thomas, the Thomas who stayed in the shower forever, with his head tilted as the spray went on and on at his back. I'd ask him what was wrong, and he'd say, *Nothing!* in the way that meant *something.* Amy would come back from a car ride with him, rolling her eyes and saying, *God!* at his mood. A mood can become an ogre in a house, an ugly creature you must placate and feed. You needed to build a shed for it out back and toss it raw meat.

"Me, either," I said.

"The kids are having the time of their lives. Emma caught a fish. Can I say how much it bugs me when they have the time of their life with their father?"

"Of course you can."

"The official line is how glad you are that they have a good relationship with the other parent, but, really? He does one good thing and it's like he just gave them a million dollars. My good things are bread crumbs. They don't even notice."

"They'll notice later. They'll see all that."

"I don't even want them to see, but I want them to see, you know?" The windows were down. Shaye popped in a CD. Some girl-power music, played loud. "Up yours, sailing trip. Stick it, *theater,*" she yelled out the window to the endless miles of desert.

"I haven't been to a bar in years," I said.

"Well, it's time we changed that."

I met Thomas in a bar. Little Red Hen, in Seattle. We were both barely twenty-one. He was there with a group of friends, and so was I. All these years later, we still got together with Dave and Larissa, who have four kids now, and, of course, with Thomas's oldest friend, Richard, and his husband, André. Richard was ordering a round of beers when I first saw Thomas at the table next to ours. He was the shy one in a plaid shirt; Oh, he was so adorable. My friend Patty had spilled her drink, and Thomas was the one who helped her wipe it up. Her boyfriend didn't even notice. Thomas was so *nice*. He smelled good, too. Sometimes I'll smell that cologne again, drifting over from some stranger, and I'll feel an ache of nostalgia.

Before Thomas, I'd dated Nathan Jarrison, and he once got so mad he left fingerprints on my arm. But that night, a waitress at the Little Red Hen brought French fries instead of onion rings, and Thomas just said, *I don't mind. French fries sound good.* It was an easiness that spoke of maturity, I thought, utterly unaware of love-lesson number one: What draws you is what will make you craziest later. Nathan Jarrison would have refused to eat those fries. My mother would have sent them back and refused to pay the rest of the bill besides. Of course I said yes to Thomas when he asked me to marry him the next summer. He told me I was his best friend, and meant it.

"That bar, the night I met Thomas? Jed Nelson was playing, before he got famous."

"Jed's dog slept by the bass player. Tell me something I don't know. Thomas was nice when they got his order wrong."

Shaye concentrated on the road. I would have, too, if I were driving that thing. I glanced at her profile, which was still lovely and youthful-looking. She'd always had a lot of boyfriends and it was clear why, but what wasn't so clear was why she chose the ones she did. They were dark storm clouds against her blue sky, and their jackets smelled like cigarettes. After Nathan Jarrison, Shaye's and my relationship roads diverged in a yellow wood. Still, we'd both been in that yellow wood, looking for the same thing, likely.

"Thomas drove me home afterward," I said. "And that was that."

"Yeah, and he hit that raccoon, don't forget that part. He wanted to put it in the *car* and take it to the vet. You thought that was so sweet."

"Oh, my God, the raccoon!" I said. "That thing was so scary. His eyes were glowing green out there, and he was baring his teeth."

"How could you have forgotten about the raccoon? That was the best part."

I was so known, by Shaye, by Thomas, by my kids. No wonder Thomas had asked if this was *all*. It was an old story. Familiarity, the liar, convinced us that we already knew everything about each other. Familiarity, the cheat, stole our passion. We'd had it, too. Back then I once told him that I could never imagine lying next to him without wanting to touch him. We were in his bed in that cold house he rented, and it was all hands and skin and hands and skin. It made me ashamed to think of us back then. Not because of our passion, but because of how we were so sure of it.

The city of Reno had grown since Thomas and I were there last. It had sprawled. As the sun set and bold smears of pink and orange brushed the sky, tiny lights twinkled on all around us. In the dark, we passed bright gas stations and fluorescent-lit minimarts, the beacon of golden arches, and the afterglow of curtains in cheap hotels; then the red brake lights of the cars in front of us stacked up, too. Downtown became all busy intersections, with banks and drugstores and government buildings.

After we drove under the curve of the red deco *Reno* sign, there was a greater explosion of lights and motion—casinos, hotels, the sci-fi rise of the Silver Legacy Hotel with its illuminated blue ball dome; garish greens and jolting fuschias, flashing marquees, and tourists making mad dashes across the street. There was a lot that hadn't changed, though. The Riverside Hotel, the courthouse, the beautiful old Virginia Street Bridge, which arced over the river in which the women would throw their wedding bands. Salvage divers had actually found them in there, I remember reading once.

My head suddenly throbbed. There was that city smell of French fries and exhaust, and it was all too much after two days in the delicious sensory deprivation of the desert. My mind was full of Thomas, and of Nash's illness; unraveling minds, and the way things were crumbling. This was all new energy and wrongness. This was life, life, life. The desert had two different selves, devil and saint, introvert and extrovert, the slow passage of time versus now and now. I was always more saint than devil, like it or not. Give me a good novel and a hammock by a lake, same as my failing aunt.

Shaye honked her horn at a couple of kids in a Camaro, who hung out their windows at a green light. "For God's sake, idiots!"

"Watch the road rage, sis. You're driving a lethal weapon."

"I don't know if I'm in the mood for this. I'm sorry, Cal. This is all just . . ."

"I know," I said. "Me, too."

"I feel old all of a sudden."

I'd always been old. I knew that about myself. "Well, I've got five bucks burning a hole in my pocket. Do you think that place we used to go when we were kids is still there?"

"That was back by the ranch. In Carson City."

"I thought it was in Reno."

"Nope. Let's get out of here."

"Fast," I said. "I'm suddenly in the mood for a Shirley Temple and a breaded veal cutlet."

I recognized the big gold urn of the Carson Nugget the minute I saw it. Shaye and I hurried through the casino like a pair of nuns and headed to the restaurant bar for our preferred path of corruption. It was warm and friendly in there, with brick walls decorated with old photos of the place. The Carson Nugget had been here forever. The music was loud, but it was a we're-all-friends-here loud and not a volume that expected things of you. People were smoking, which shocked me. You couldn't smoke a cigarette in a public place in Seattle unless you didn't mind being forcibly escorted out by tattooed vegans, and even outside, smokers risked social shaming and death penalty by glare. Cigarettes right out in the open—my God, we'd practically stumbled on an opium den. Shaye edged toward an open table and snagged it.

I eased to a sitting position. Damn. After that fence, every suburban muscle in my body was lecturing me on my arrogance.

"I'm so sore I can barely move," I said. I peered at the photo above our table, a black-and-white image of two women and two cowboys at a roulette wheel in this very bar.

Shaye studied the plastic-covered menu. "Remember Mom and Nash and their Moscow mules?"

"I wonder what those even were," I said.

"Booze, strong. Well, the breaded veal cutlets are gone." Shaye set down her menu. We ordered margaritas and four different appetizers. The place was crowded, and you could hear the *bing-ching* of the slot machines in the next room. Shaye's blond hair was shiny in the candlelight. Her shoulders had also gotten sunburned; I could see the pink of them yelling silently against the edge of her sleeveless top.

Our drinks arrived, and we clinked glasses, though to what we didn't say. "Now that you mentioned it, I keep thinking about that raccoon," I shouted over the music. "Can you imagine wanting to bring that thing in the car? It probably had rabies. I had to talk Thomas out of it!"

"I always thought that was a little nutty," Shaye admitted. "Can you imagine it leaping over the seat and sticking its teeth in you? But, hey, Mathew had wild eyes and fangs, and I *married* him." She laughed, now that she had a few sips of tequila in her.

"Eric's nothing like Mathew," I said. And he wasn't. I actually liked Eric for the most part. He was good to Josh and Emma, for one thing. He was a big, friendly man, the kind who hugged you a little too hard without realizing it. He once gave me a fancy remote control for my birthday, which was supposed to operate every device in the house. One look at the directions, and my head exploded.

"He's not. He's not at all. He can be so amiable. Such a friend. But, I don't know, Cal. I thought I was done being helpless at the hands of angry men, but now I'm just helpless at the hands of angry stepchildren. Yeah, there's a theme."

"Oh, Sham." It was my childhood nickname for her, short for *Shamu*. I hadn't called her that in years. It started after a trip to SeaWorld with Mom and Gene, and she used to punch me hard when I said it.

"Let me tell you, every stepfamily is an experiment. You've got their foreign country, with its own customs and history and boundaries, and you've got your foreign country. And you know what foreign countries do. They go to war."

"It can't go on forever, can it? Maybe it's just an adjustment period. A very long adjustment period."

"I think it *can* go on forever, Cal. That's the thing. It can. This is who they are. This is who I am. They don't go together. They draw the circle, and I'm outside of it. In my own house! I'm tired of being left out under my own *roof*. Why are step-mothers always the wicked ones, huh? There are two sides to every story. I understand the poison apple, I do. I know that sounds awful, but maybe Snow White sat on her father's lap and stroked his hair and called him *Daddy*."

"It all looked so different on *The Brady Bunch*."

"Yeah, because the exes were *dead*. They weren't behind the scenes, tweaking the little psyches of their offspring. We've been arguing so much, Eric's been sleeping on the couch."

Our food arrived. There was so much of it and it was all so large, I had the obligatory moment of concerned silence for unhealthy Americans and overweight youth, and then I dug in. "I kind of like it when Thomas sleeps on the couch."

"Oh, I know. How can you want him to touch you when you're that angry."

I meant all the room to stretch out and actual, real sleep without the soundtrack of snoring, but it was true. The lack of expectations, the *clarity of intent*, that came with sofa sleeping—they were nice, too. Shaye dove into those potato skins. She folded one right in half and took a big bite. I didn't know how she looked so good, the way she ate.

We weren't the kind of sisters who talked about our sex lives. Maybe this was more my own doing, since even with Anne, who'd been my best friend since high school, there were no clichéd movie scenes of shopping and having lunch and spilling the details of orgasms. But the tequila was working on me, as well. I could feel its warm loosening, and that place, the Carson

Nugget bar, with its encouraging music and curls of cigarette smoke, with those photos of men in fedoras and women in boas—it made me feel more generous and open than I had in a long while. It was possible I could be friends with every single person in there, and with the bartender, too. A round of drinks for all. Maybe this was just what happiness felt like.

"This is going to sound awful, but you know what bugs me?" I said. "How cheerful and positive Thomas gets after we have sex. The resentment, moodiness, whatever—gone. Poof. Blue-birds twitter around his head, just like that."

"Oh, I know. I can be such a bitch, and then we have sex, and he thinks I'm amazing and we're amazing and that life is beautiful. Cue the unicorns."

"I wouldn't want it any different, but still! It's too easy. I don't respect him for it."

Shaye took a drink of her margarita, clutched her temple when the cold hit. "Damn. Headache." And then, after the pain passed, "Why does sex become so *laden*?"

"All of the worst, naked insecurities, probably, literally and otherwise."

"Why is it such a gauge? *The* gauge, for a lot of people."

"Not a very fair gauge. You have kids, it starts getting compli-cated. Of course it does! How could it not? You're so busy and exhausted and your body feels so depleted that if one more person wants something from you, you'll scream. You don't have sex, and then he's mad because you don't have sex, and then you're mad at him for being mad that you don't have sex."

"That was eighteen years ago for you, Cal."

"You're making me regret opening my mouth. I'm just say-ing, it becomes laden because some understandable *no* turns into years of rejection-fueled assumptions."

"You're right; it's a vicious circle." She sighed, stabbed at an errant green onion with her fork. "I love being with Eric. I miss him when we're not close. But when you're *furious*? That's my understandable *no*, except, one, we're angry all the time, and, two, he couldn't care less if he's angry. Doesn't everyone always want sex no matter what? That's how he thinks. It becomes an ongoing nonverbal conversation. Every single night it's *will we or won't we*, without anyone saying a word. He's touching my leg—he wants to have sex. I moved my leg, which means I don't, so now he's pissed. Okay, FINE! We'll do it! And then he sulks for days and avoids me, and I'm like, *He doesn't even find me attractive anymore.*"

I laughed. The music, the drinks, being *away*—who knew a body held a hundred tiny knots, which could then be untied? What a relief it all was.

"*Laden*," I said.

"Still, with Eric, at least it's normal-people problems. One time Mathew told me I wasn't *meeting his needs.*"

"You didn't know he was the sultan of Brunei?"

"It wasn't just that. He said it the day after he'd screamed in my face because dinner had taken too long."

"Oh, honey."

"Somewhere along the line, my appropriate-outrage dial got broken. I didn't know how to be mad enough to protect myself. And now that it's working again, well, how do you *stop* being furious, is what I want to know. Stepchildren, jeez. Does Eric even understand how badly I want to love them? But you can only live so long with people who hate you before you start hating them back." Shaye did a double take. "Oh, my God."

"What?"

"You're not going to believe this. Look."

I squinted. I really needed to get my eyes checked once Thomas left me for good. "I can't see."

"That forest-service guy."

"Really?"

"By that sign for twenty-one."

Yes. There was Kit Covey at the bar, wearing a black shirt this time, the heels of both boots hooked on the low brass rail of his stool. His hands gestured in storytelling mode, as a bald, handsome guy clapped once in appreciation at the punch line, threw his head back, and laughed.

"Cal, what are the odds? This is a movie moment! Two people, ending up at the same place at the same time, in some sort of amazing coincidence. You should buy him a drink."

"I am in no way going to buy him a drink. You're crazy. He's a stranger. I would never do something like that. And just because Thomas and I are having problems doesn't give me an excuse to hit on the first guy I see."

"Hey, a restorative affair with a cowboy was practically mandatory in the old days."

"This isn't the old days."

"Do it for Nash. For forest-service relations." Shaye wiggled her eyebrows. "Your eyeballs practically fell out when you saw that guy."

"Shaye, come on."

"Okay! I was just joking!" she said, but she was laughing loud, drawing attention to us. Jesus! I remembered this maneuver of hers from back in high school, the oversize display of a good time that made everyone turn around and stare.

Of course, Kit Covey turned around. He smiled when he recognized me, and Shaye waved her hand for them to join us. This was exactly how Shaye ended up with the unapproachable Carl Decker (senior year, just after nice Jay with the vest), and with every guy before and after him.

I was nervous. I don't know why. Well, the way he looked,

for one. And I was in a bar. When was the last time I was in a bar? Introductions were made. The other man was Steve Miller, a bureau public-affairs officer. Steve's nose was red from his glass of wine. His head was shiny from heat, but he still wore his suit jacket over his T-shirt.

"What are you guys doing here?" I asked. "Of all places."

"What are you doing here, is more like it. We stay in this hotel whenever we work in the area," Kit said. *Film-moment coincidence, ha.* "Rangers, ranchers, and cowboys. We've been coming here for years."

"*We've* been coming here for years. Or, at least, we came when we were kids," I said.

"Our aunt Nash said they used to bring the *gals* here," Shaye said. "As part of their 'Reno-vation.' The bar was called something else then, I think. Not the Nugget."

Steve Miller gestured with his empty glass, caught the eye of the waitress, and we all ordered more drinks. Shaye joked about him being a musician, and he laughed like he hadn't heard that a million times before. They asked us if it really did rain all the time in Seattle, and we asked if they'd ever been bitten by a rattlesnake. A live band set up on a small stage and started to play. The place had filled with people and I hadn't even noticed. This was what they came for: dust-kicking, boot-stomping music, sung by a man with a voice like a whiskey sour, as a woman played fiddle, her chin down, right arm flying, sweat starting at her temples. Shaye said she couldn't sit still during a certain song, and she and Steve Miller pushed into the crowd to dance.

"You want to?" Kit shouted, but I shook my head. We sat across from each other and leaned in to talk. I could feel his warm breath on my face. I could smell the mixture of beer and an indefinable something else that was just Kit.

"Well, that's a relief," he said. "I always get embarrassed when they clear the dance floor when I get out there."

"Is it that slide you do? Across the floor on your knees?"

"Balancing a beer mug on my forehead? You saw me?"

"On the news, the friendly part of the broadcast at the end, when they show cute kids and people's dogs. That thong was hard to forget, though," I said.

Kit Covey's laugh made nice crinkles by his eyes. He looked at me straight on, turning his glass in a circle in his plain, ringless hands.

"Your eyes are really blue," he said.

"It's the disco lights," I joked.

"No, I mean it. They're startling."

It was strange, but this mention of my eyes made me realize they were another thing I'd forgotten. In college, Will Adams told me he could look at them forever, and even Nathan Jarrison had said he'd never seen a blue like that before. Every day I looked at those eyes and never really noticed them. Kit tipped his beer back and took a long swallow. There was a shy energy between us, an awkward moment, and I felt the old crackle of being seen, the thrill of my own command, my eyes, or the ass in the jeans that might make a man look twice. It occurred to me that maybe I was still beautiful. What a shocking idea, though suddenly I thought it might even be true.

I could never do any of the things Shaye had joked about, but I could do this. I could feel like myself for a night. The weight of Thomas's mood was nowhere near the desert, and, free of that mood, I felt an unfamiliar glee and I heard a friendly murmur, welcoming me back, telling me that it was a good thing to be in my own body. I sipped my drink. I felt sure of myself, in a way I hadn't in a long time. Admittedly, that second margarita was also starting a party inside me. "So, tell me. Is there any truth to all those movies about horse whispering?"

"Well, anyone who works with animals sees the way it is. They're more like us than people want to believe. Horses, all animals. The distance we put between our species—it's just plain arrogance on our part. You treat them with understanding and respect, and there you have it, all the magical BS of horse whispering. Still, the wild ones? They do what they want. I could shout and they wouldn't hear me. They don't listen to anybody."

"I saw them," I said.

"Yeah?"

"They were right in the front pasture of the ranch."

"Bet that was a damn mess."

"You got that right."

"They say it changes a person, though. Seeing them. That's the lore."

I held out my hands, looked them over.

"Not yet, huh?" He grinned. His eyes—they were their own strong blue. A blue with experience, a blue that had managed to hold on to playfulness, even through all those brutal years of adolescence and beyond. "Well, you should come out. We're just past your aunt's lake, setting up. I'll show you what we're doing."

"P.R."

"Leave the attorney at the ranch."

The song ended. It had gotten late, and my head felt strange. We needed to get home. Maybe I'd had too much to drink. I felt a warm buzz, the sense of liftoff. It was the alcohol, and my own sweet power.

The band stopped for a break. Shaye and Steve Miller were finished dancing. Kit Covey downed the last of his beer. Shaye and I gathered our purses and said goodbye. And then we were back in the tomblike quiet of Shaye's suburban tank. New-car smell merged with the liquor on our breath. There was a pair of small soccer cleats in the back and a half-filled water bottle, along with an empty, flattened, snack-sized package of Doritos.

"I can't believe you danced with Steve," I said. I felt like I could stay up all night, talking. Joy and late-hour energy filled me. What was a stupid sailing trip? I took my shoes off. I hadn't been up until—I checked the clock—*1:00 A.M.* in a long, long time.

"I can't believe you *didn't* dance with the forest-service man! It wouldn't have meant anything, Cal. Wasn't that fun?"

It was. It was so much fun, I didn't even feel like myself. And it continued to be fun as Shaye popped another CD into the player. Billy Idol was so right. If I had the chance, I *would* teach the world to dance.

We whispered and giggled as we let ourselves into the ranch house. Tex looked confused at the middle-of-the-night activity. He greeted us at the door with squinting eyes and wobbly, suddenly awake legs.

"Sorry we're past curfew, Dad," Shaye said to him.

"There wasn't any alcohol and the parents were there the whole time," I said, even though I'd never done stuff like that. I wished I had. I wished I'd embraced every possible rebellious moment. I wished I'd grown out my hair and kissed bad boys and danced and danced.

"Hey, Cal, next we're going to be tossing our rings into this."

It was the vase on the piano. It had been there since the days of the divorce ranch, and it was filled with wedding rings. It had been in that spot on the piano for so long that I'd forgotten all about it; I hadn't even really seen it there, either. Not for years.

There it was, the truth of it. Things could vanish, even as they sat right in front of you.

chapter 9

Nash

Lilly Marcel swirls her hand in the gold. She scoops the rings into her palm and holds them close to her face, as if she's taking a drink of water from a creek bed. She studies the bands and then chooses one, holds it in the air.

"Whose was this?" she asks.

"I don't know. There've been so many," Nash says. They've gathered in the main room. Jack should be arriving any minute to drive the women into town for the night. He usually brings another cowboy or two along, men he knows from the Flying W or Washoe Pines. Nash will have to have a quiet night at home. It's disappointing to be left behind. She's forgotten where in her book she left off.

"Make something up," Hadley says. She's the one who is good at that. Her typewriter goes all hours of the night.

"Let me see," Nash says. The ring itself brings back no memories. But, wait: There's an engraving inside. *My beloved Olivia, forever.* "It was Olivia Remington's. She married—"

Veronica interrupts. "Isn't this confidential information? You know, same as a priest?"

They all laugh. "I heard my priest yawn during confession," Ellen says.

"No!" Lilly drops her jaw.

"I did! He's really old, but still! Tell us, Nash."

"Hmm. Olivia was married to . . . I think his name was Oscar. He never had a job after they married. He told her he was just having a spell of bad luck, but it lasted years."

"The old bad-luck story," Veronica said. "The kind of bad luck that makes you lazy."

"I can tell you a story like that without even using my imagination," Hadley said. "I could show you photographs, even."

"This one," Lilly Marcel said. It's a band of gold with a moonstone center.

Nash takes it. She holds it up. Through the ring far off, past the front yard, she sees the brown wood of the barn, where Zorro and Maggie and Starlight and Bluebell are likely settled into their stalls for the night. Jack and Danny would have removed their halters, sponged the saddle marks off their bodies, and checked their feet after the long trek they'd made that day up the Del Mar trail.

"Mrs. Barb Halloway," Nash says. She doesn't know it was hers for sure, but she's getting into the spirit of the game. "Mr. Halloway would measure her hemlines with a tape to make sure they weren't too short. He accused her of flirting with every man she passed—which was not many, since he didn't allow her to leave the house without him. When she came here, she didn't tell him where she was. The first time in years that she wore a bathing suit in public was at our very own pool."

It may not have been Mrs. Halloway's ring, but she remembered Mrs. Halloway and her husband. It seemed to Nash that some marriages were doomed from the get-go; the minute two sets of eyes met across a room, it was done for if one of the people was just plain bad or broken. There were always signs they ignored, the women said—the way he snatched her menu before she could decide, the harsh words to her mother, the way he drank. Nash was sure plenty of men would say the same thing—certainly Mr. Fletcher would think back and recall Mrs. Fletcher's loud laugh, the particular way she languished on a chaise. The husband of Gina Francesca must have certainly seen her dramatic sobs and her endless, mysterious illnesses and noticed the way she clung to his coat whenever he left home. Doc Bolger was summoned to the ranch five times in her six-week stay, and she clung to *his* coat. The themes repeated. That was clear. Drunks, cheaters, bullies, and liars; the helpless, the hungry—for attention and money and more. The ignored signs of the bad and broken, and the men and women who rode in to rescue and nurse so they might be beaten down for their efforts.

It seemed simple enough. Avoid those people if you wanted half a chance at happiness. Flee at the first sign of a big ego and a mean streak. But it apparently wasn't simple in the least. A mean streak could be a magnet.

But then, too, you had the marriages that didn't appear to be doomed at all. The ones between two good but tired people, or the well meaning but mismatched. The ones worn down by terrible circumstances or the persistent drone of daily life. Like poor Mrs. Drake, who still smiled when she talked about Mr. Drake. Their child had died. And Franny Frederick. She talked about Mr. Frederick with pride and respect, but Mr. Frederick had a dream that they should move to the French countryside, and Franny didn't want to move to the French countryside. Still, she spoke wistfully of him buying a house with a thatched roof and making his own sausages. On the last day, right there on the court steps, she changed her mind about leaving him.

Of course, there were also the marriages that lasted, and she shouldn't forget those. No one should. Under thousands of rooftops there were people they'd never see at the ranch, people with marriages like her parents', ones of deep love and faithfulness and friendship, or even just stubbornness, in spite of everything that came their way. Her mother was never the same after her father died. Years after he was gone, Nash saw her father's photo on the bed pillow next to her mother's, moved from its usual place on the nightstand. With all the trips to the Washoe County Courthouse, it was maybe most important to remember those unions above all. *Union*—the word sounded as gentle and resolute as flower petals joined at the same center.

"I didn't even want to get *near* a bathing suit with Stuart," Lilly says.

"Really?" Hadley lights a cigarette.

"He gets furious when other men look, even when most are only staring at the water, trying to decide whether or not to get in."

"For all of that attention, you're meaningless."

"Veronica!" Ellen says.

"I'm not being cruel! I'm only saying, she might as well be an expensive vase on his shelf."

"It's true," Lilly Marcel says. "Since a vase is expected to be pretty and empty, waiting for someone's flowers to fill it." She holds out her palm and Nash drops the ring into it. Lilly Marcel puts it on her own bare finger. She holds out her hand to admire it.

"Get that hideous thing off," Veronica says.

Cook—Irma, who's been with them for years—leaves for the night, and Helena Orlando, who cleans, is long gone. The girls are still waiting for Jack to drive them into Carson City. Nash checks the barn to see what's taking so long, and Danny tells her he just went back to his place to wash up.

Nash returns with the report. "We're not getting any younger!" Veronica says. "You drive us, Nash. Jack can catch up. Join us! We'll slip you a drink."

"Twenty-one," she reminds Veronica. "They're more strict here than anywhere."

"Leave it to me. I promise."

"I can't go like this." She's still in her ranch wear.

"Run and change. You'll be faster than he is."

Her mother wouldn't like this, her taking the ladies out to dance and gamble. Not one bit. Until Nash is of age, that's Jack's job, but Ellen has had her pocketbook tucked under her arm for nearly an hour, and Veronica's tapping her foot, her hands on her hips.

"Come on! This one will need to go to bed and get some rest before long." Veronica hooks her thumb at Lilly, with her round belly in that red and black dress.

Well, her mother did leave her in charge, and Nash isn't expecting her to even call to check up. First and foremost, it's Nash's job to make sure the women are happy and having a good time. If worse comes to worst, she can wait in the car, which would be better than being stuck at home. Nash dashes upstairs to change. She's excited. She once snuck into a bar in Reno with two of her girlfriends from school, and they sipped one drink and confessed their crushes and had the night of their lives. Nash writes a note to Jack and leaves it on the piano.

She is not used to driving in the dark, but her nerves settle after the ranch retreats into the distance. She knows that road, and the chatter of the women makes the night feel full of promise.

"Turn on the radio," Lilly says.

Hadley is in front next to Nash, and she swivels the dial. She's wearing stylish short gloves with a pearl button at the wrist. They can only get one station out here in the desert, and Tex Williams is fast-strumming his guitar, telling them to smoke, smoke, smoke that cigarette. Ellen leans her head out the window and lets the wind rush against her face.

"Roll that up, you're messing my hair!" Veronica says.

"Oh, boo," Ellen says, but does as she's told. She looks happy. Nash spent the day with her and Cliff, their oldest ranch hand, trying to get Ellen up on Jemima, the sweetest little Arabian you'd ever see. Lilly rested by the pool in her shorts and sleeveless top, as the other ladies trekked down the Del Mar Trail and up into High Canyon.

Nash has only seen Broderick's Bar and Casino from the open doorway before. It was one of the places they always took the ladies, there and the Old Corner next door, when they wanted someplace a little quieter. This night, the strip out front is crammed with Plymouths and Chevrolets and DeSotos, all polished up, hoods gleaming with pride under the streetlights. Nash finds a spot by Hudson's Garage and they pile out. The place is packed, and the loud sounds of shouting and high spirits and slot machines spill from it. Nash is nervous, but Veronica takes her arm and says, "Relax. I have this handled."

They find a table. Veronica leaves her fur wrap hanging over a chair as if it's an animal that's just been shot. It's a high-class animal, though, black and silky; mink, Nash guesses—like a skunk without the bristle. Veronica tells the bartender that her daughter would like a mule. The owner, Ella Broderick, stocky and stern-looking, knows full well who Nash is, but she only shakes her head with a little smile at the corner of her mouth.

Everyone has seen how tough Alice can be. Ella's either trying to slip Nash a bit of kindness or she's taken this chance to stick Alice a little behind her back.

"Roulette!" Hadley wiggles her eyebrows up and down. She has to yell to be heard. There's a wheel up by the bar. Two well-dressed men in white hats and a woman in a green dress sit around it, chips piled in front of them, and the wheel spins red-black, red-black. They're probably guests from the Flying W. The woman in the green dress whoops, and one of the men kisses her cheek. "I love a chance to give away my hard-earned bucks, as you all know." Hadley has hinted more than once that Joseph Bernal has cost her plenty.

"There's a free seat next to that lawyer," Veronica shouts.

"How do you know he's a lawyer?" Lilly asks.

"The shoes. Wingtips."

"Where's the music?" Ellen asks. She snaps her fingers.

"One dance with a cowboy, and now look," Veronica says. They've heard about Ellen's dance a hundred times by now. It may end up being the high point of Ellen's life. Her mother never let her go out after ten o'clock, and then her husband never let her go out at all. After her time on the ranch, she will likely marry a successful traveling salesman and have two more children. Nash hopes for this for her.

The brown liquid shoots down Nash's throat and leaves scorched earth. Nash imagines the bare black spikes of incinerated trees after a fire in the valley. How the women drink these things, she'll never know. Lilly gets up to use the bathroom again. It's astonishing how frequently expectant women go. Lilly makes her way through the crowded bar. She looks beautiful in her red and black dress with the high Chinese collar, and Nash worries that, with all the people here, someone will knock into Lilly or harm Beanie. Ella Broderick is watching her, too. Either this is a businesswoman's protective gaze or Ella knows who Lilly is. Word has likely gotten around. After that mobster was gunned down in Las Vegas, there's no telling what might happen on your own doorstep.

The thought makes Nash edgy. Wasn't alcohol supposed to relax you? But with Lilly lost in the herd, she doesn't feel relaxed. She remembers the man with the camera, and she sees another man in a dark suit sitting alone at a table. He's not wearing a hat, and his black hair is slicked back over his head. He wears flashy two-tone Oxfords. He holds his glass in his fingertips, swirls his ice. Nash follows his eyes to a glint of red satin. Who wouldn't look at Lilly Marcel, even in her condition? Still, Nash sees the man with the camera everywhere—in the black coat by the cigarette machine, playing twenty-one next to a blonde, sitting at the bar by a gray-haired man with a lumpy nose that Nash is sure she recognizes, maybe from Nevada Savings and Trust.

And then, thank goodness, there's Jack. His saunter says he owns the place, and every other place, too. His confidence makes Nash feel so good, she practically sighs. Once, he plucked up a desert tarantula with his own bare hands, to stop it from heading toward Mrs. Fitz Greens; Nash should tell the ladies about that. They would love it. Heads turn, because here he comes, with Danny and Ted, too, a rodeo rider and dude wrangler at Washoe Pines. It's Jack's smile that makes people look—a smile that says he's open to a little trouble.

Three cowboys. The ladies make room, and there is squealing as Ted lands on Veronica's lap. The excitement at their table kicks up; it's both animated and expectant, like the rodeo crowd just as the ticket booth opens. Jack sets an arm around Nash's shoulders and gives them a shake.

"What are you doing here?" he whispers. She doesn't answer. She only smiles as if she is capable of mischief, too. She's not, really. She wishes she were. His breath in her ear gives her chills.

"What took you boys so long?" Veronica asks. She holds a cigarette between her fingers, and Ted, a tall man with eyes as black as Zorro's, strikes a match and lights it.

"Had to wrap Starlight's leg. She was hobbling, after you ladies wore her out."

"Did you hear?" Hadley says. "They made us cross the river. We rode straight through!"

"Did I tell you you'd be fine?" Danny says. Danny is small but tough. His size doesn't impair his success with the ladies. Collette Brown-Hastings wrote him letters for months after she left the ranch. She wanted him to join her in Palm Springs. You could never imagine Danny keeping company with men who played golf. The idea was hilarious. Danny needed a dentist, too, but Collette Brown-Hastings apparently didn't notice. "You barely got wet."

"I got wet!" Veronica says. "I was soaked!" She wasn't soaked. Maybe the hems of her trousers were damp when they got back. The river barely has any water in it this time of year.

"Did Miss Ellen make it into the saddle?" Jack teases. Nash wishes he would take her hand under the table, but he doesn't. There was that one time he took her hand, out by the cabins, on a night when he'd had a little too much to drink. He almost kissed her, too, and Nash hasn't forgotten that. She thinks about it so often, the memory is nearly as worn down as those rosary beads Rosemary McNalley left on her bedside table the day she left Tamarosa.

Someone wins at the slot machines and there is a cheer. Nash sees Lilly exit the restroom. The man in the far booth keeps his eyes on her back as she moves across the bar. She slips onto the padded bench next to Jack. He orders her a martini, and Nash notices that he doesn't need to ask the way she likes it.

"I most certainly did! Tell them, Nash," Ellen says.

"Several circles around the ring, and Jemima barely minded the screaming."

Ellen sighs. "I screamed, I admit it. If I never have to get on one of those animals again, it would be fine by me."

"Aw, come on. You just need a little practice," Jack says.

Ted's arm is on the back of the padded bench where Veronica sits, and his thumb grazes the bare skin of her neck. Lilly Marcel's hand briefly touches Jack's as they rest on the table; fingers touch fingers as glasses are passed. Hadley is on her third whiskey. She takes it with her as she finally heads off to lose a large stack of chips at the roulette wheel. Danny brings more drinks. Jack tells that story about the bull. The energy in the bar seems to grow and grow; it's outsize now, a bloodthirsty organism, like in *The Thing from Another World*. Ted pulls Veronica close and whispers something to her. The room seems to shift and sway with noise and bodies and skin. It is hard to know what is what and who is with whom and where each voice is coming from.

A few hours later they all rise to leave, laughing and knocking into one another as they go. Outside, Jack leans against his truck and lights up a cigarette. His cowboy hat is on the hood, and as he exhales, he tilts his head to the night sky.

Veronica says she's driving, since Nash isn't walking straight. Nash's mother will kill her if she ever finds out, but who cares. Veronica drives too fast, and Nash has her nose out the window because she doesn't feel well. Her clothes smell like cigarettes.

"If Eddie could see me now!" Ellen says. She won some

money at craps and is riding high on her victory. "We're better off without him! The children don't need a father like that."

"I told Stuart the baby was someone else's," Lilly says from the backseat.

Even through her nausea, Nash is shocked by the words. Veronica snaps off the radio. Merle Travis abruptly stops singing after *I ain't coming back*.

"What?"

"So he'd let me go. So he wouldn't have anything more to do with us."

Ellen chatters on about Scotty and the birthday gift Eddie never gave him, but Veronica catches Hadley's eyes in the rear-view mirror. Nash feels abruptly sober. She thinks about the man with the camera and the one in that back booth, who paid his tab just as they were leaving. She watches the beam of the headlights behind them in the side mirror. She thinks about Jack, smoking that cigarette. How he'd better be careful, because jealousy can be lethal. She's mad at him, the way he acted all night, how he pretended to read Lilly Marcel's palm, tracing lines with his fingertip. Still, nothing bad had better happen to him. Jack belongs to them, not to Lilly. He thinks he knows so much, but he's an innocent next to Stuart Marcel.

"Shit!" Veronica screeches, and swerves the car.

Lilly lets out a little scream.

"Dear God, Veronica!" Ellen has her hand to her chest.

It was just a stupid rabbit. Nash wouldn't have overreacted if she were driving. Jesus! Sometimes, truly, the ladies could get on your nerves, and on one another's, too.

"If I remember, you don't even know how to drive, so shut your trap," Veronica says.

"Be nice, and keep your eyes on the road," Hadley says, and tosses a bottle cap she must have found deep in the backseat of the Styleline Deluxe. It pings against Veronica's chignon, which doesn't feel a thing.

It comes to Nash then. It's eluded her all night. The gray-haired man with the lumpy nose. He doesn't work at the bank. He's a judge at the Washoe County Courthouse. He's the Honorable Judge Riley, whom Nash stood in front of with the adulterous Mrs. Fletcher.

That night, no one was what or who they seemed. Veronica wasn't, as Ted slipped his tongue into her mouth, and Hadley wasn't, when she opened her pocketbook and handed out more bills to lose, and Lilly wasn't, in her sweet, jeweled hair clip, letting her hand rest, palm up, in Jack's, and that man at the back table wasn't, either. He'd gotten in a different car from the one that has been following them ever since they left Broderick's.

Veronica hits every rut in the road to Tamarosa. Yet they are home safe, Nash thinks. *Home. Safe.* This is what home should be above all else, though Nash knows how often *home* is the secret setting for the darkest troubles.

They tumble from the car. A wind rushes through and shakes the curved branches of the desert willow, and there is a brief shower of purple flower blossoms catching moonlight as they fall. The sky is silvery-black with a salt shake of stars, and Nash thinks she hears thunder in the distance, above the chatter and laughter. *It is going to rain*, she wrongly tells herself, right before she lurches toward the acacia tree and retches up the regrets of the night.

As far as regrets go, she is just getting started.

chapter 10

Callie

"I'm just not happy," Thomas said. "It's been months since I felt happy. Maybe longer." His voice sounded far away, as if he was driving somewhere.

It was looking like a mistake to talk to Thomas so regularly when he needed his "time alone." I had no idea what else to do, though. I felt helpless, as if I were holding someone else's crying baby in my arms, wishing his mother would hurry back. I watched the landscape out the window of my room; a gust of wind blew through and the desert willow shook in protest. Purple blossoms fluttered past, as if fleeing that old cranky tree at last.

"Should I come home?" In Taj Mahal, I walked around the bed and back again, a metaphorically fitting path. Maybe staying at the ranch was foolish. Only a few days had passed, but perhaps this was the time that a wife was supposed to rush in with marriage-saving gestures—sheet-tearing nights of lust, proclamations of love and loyalty, sickbed attention of grilled cheese sandwiches and soup and shoulder rubs.

I felt an odd lack of alarm. Then again, I had always preferred dread to panic. It was quieter. It had an element of the slow burn that panic lacked, the benefits of stalling and denial.

Panic got in there with its fists up. Dread painfully dragged its feet, but at least it bought you time.

"No, don't. Your aunt needs you. It's great. I'm taking it easy. Eating what I want. Doing some self-care."

I couldn't believe he'd just said that. Did he actually use those words? "*Self-care?*" I repeated.

Who was this man? Had I been married to a stranger all these years? None of this was like him at all. Thomas was a happy person. He sometimes even whistled. Who whistled? Small things pleased him—a package of powdered-sugar do-nuts, lumber from the hardware store, a call from Melissa. He deserved my kindness; he was honestly struggling, and I respected the integrity in that, but the man I knew hated a cliché. *Self-care?* Really? Would he be taking lavender-scented baths next, with those plastic blow-up pillows? Dear God, would he start lighting candles?

"Thanks, Cal. I appreciate your sarcasm."

"I'm sorry, but where's my husband? Can we be real here? What do you *want*, Thomas?"

"I want to *know* what I want! I feel . . . empty."

I hadn't had a cup of coffee yet. Tex sat by my bed and stared at me, as if he, too, felt empty and might be full again if I could only read those small, pleading eyes. Down the hall, Shaye was talking to Nash as if Nash had gone deaf. I wished I could lay my head on a pillow scented with lavender oil and *rest*.

"Your mother died! It's only been six months."

"Stop saying that. It's not just her dying."

But grief, I suspected, was a dangerous creature. A person had no idea how menacing it was. It lurked behind rocks, leaping out to take you down the moment you thought it was safe to come out. It was our evil nemesis our whole life long, the enemy we dreaded and avoided and stood right up against as it blew its withering breath on us. It was wily, too. It could make sneak attacks during innocent tasks like cleaning a closet or turning pages in an address book. Small losses could fell you as sure as large ones; they could gang up, thugs on a dark, empty street, taking your valuables and beating you senseless.

"It's like we're buddies," he said. "A couple of roommates."

"Is this about sex?"

"It's about *passion*. It's about giving up some idea . . ."

"Everyone feels this way," I said. "And do you know why? It's not a fair story to put on two real people."

Thomas didn't reply. There was only the hollow-chamber whooshing of him in a moving car.

"Do you want to leave me?" I asked.

Silence. And then a long exhale. "I found myself looking at a woman at work," he said.

My stomach sank. I thought, *Here we go*. "People look, Thomas."

"I don't look. I've never looked."

"Who was it?"

"Doesn't even matter. Someone I can't even stand. It's the idea."

"I want to know."

"You don't." I didn't, not really.

"I do! Who?"

"Fine. Remember that Laura?"

"The one with the—"

"Right."

"Tall? Brown hair? Kind of . . ."

"Yeah, that's the one."

"I know who you mean."

"She's annoying as hell, to be honest. But, still."

"It doesn't mean anything," I said.

Well, that wasn't true; it did, and I knew it.

My mother-in-law, June, once told me that *marriage takes work*. She said it as if she'd thought up this concept herself. She was one of those people who always said obvious, long-accepted truths in a way that implied she was the expert, teaching and enlightening. A person needed to be careful using credit cards. Video games could cause children to be violent. Too much salt could lead to high blood pressure. Who knew.

She cornered me in her kitchen the Thanksgiving before Thomas and I got married. He had sold his Volkswagen Beetle to buy me a ring, and it sparkled on my left hand. I was so proud of it. I actually tried to catch it in beams of sunlight, because I loved the rainbow reflections it made. That ring somehow evened things out with the tight-mouthed woman who was Thomas's mother and me, I thought, but I was wrong.

The house smelled like turkey cooking: sage and thyme and something buttery. June had grabbed my wrist and looked at me sternly as if I'd already made dire mistakes. And I had, in her eyes. Deciding to keep my surname was a rejection of her and her husband, the deceased Mr. William Bennett. *You know, Callie*, she said, *marriage takes work*. With her eyes fixed on mine and her voice as thin and cunning as the silk of a spider, it sounded mean and dark and doomed. It sounded like a prognosis of failure, a pronouncement of her lack of faith in my ability to come through. Instead of Sunday mornings together, and our own children, and a lifetime of each other's birthday cakes, she made Thomas's and my future sound like black lung and canned beans, the Sisyphean hauling of boulders and cold cellars lit by a single lightbulb.

But what kind of work should one do, exactly, when a partner is *not happy*? Or when a partner feels a lack of passion or finds himself *looking at a woman at work?* Does one try to juggle clowns to make him smile? Ride a unicycle in a negligee? Send him off on a tropical vacation involving fruity drinks and girls in small bikinis? Apply the assumed cure-all *couples counseling,* even if half of the couple refuses to go? *Work* implies the application of specific tasks and efforts to get particular results. The problem is, what tasks? Which efforts? This kind of *work* had no job description or employee manual. You couldn't fix life. You could come to accept it; you could modify it and shine it up a bit, but you couldn't change what it was.

I suspected something then, as I held that phone with the silent man on the other end: When it came to us mysterious, complicated, and wayward human beings and our even more mysterious, complicated, and wayward hearts, *work* was a comforting illusion. It was better than nothing, but sometimes it was a downright lie. It was a life preserver with a tear, or a road sign spun the wrong direction by mean boys. Even if two people were working cheerfully beside each other, sharing the same goal, picking up litter on the freeway of life, keeping it beautiful, there was no telling when one might decide to hop into the back of a stranger's pickup. As much as we might wish otherwise, a person had his own thoughts on the matters of life and love and acted of his own accord. Thomas would, Nash would, and so would I. Think of the time and energy we'd save if we got *this* through our thick heads: All of the work and cajoling and manipulating and being good and being kind and being hideous that every one of us partakes in in order to control someone else—well, it is no match for the simple will all humans were given on the day sperm met egg. *Will* was our surest road to ruin, and to glory.

* * *

I wasn't sure if I still knew the way to the lake. I hoped so, otherwise I could get lost out there, and it would be embarrassing when they had to search for me with small planes and infrared lights. I'd have to apply the knowledge I gained when Melissa was (too briefly, it now turned out) in the Girl Scouts. She never liked that uniform, and, brave girl—a girl much bolder and braver than I ever was—she refused to wear it.

I passed the cabins. Old Avalon and Shangri-La and the Ritz and another that no longer had a sign hanging above the door— they had held up well over the years, but they were eerie in their vacancy. When you looked at the spiderwebs everywhere and the windows crusted with dirt, you felt the ghosts of people who must be dead by now. Any kind of animal might have made a home inside there. Bats, even, with their vampire faces and webbed, leathery wings; prehistoric mammals from your worst nightmares.

Across from the cabins was a creepy outhouse—it had a shower stall and a metal sink. I remembered us running in for a quick pee when we were kids, hurrying out as fast as we could, sure we were going to be murdered by a maniac hiding under that rusty showerhead. I remembered Amy and Melissa, too, years later, holding hands and squealing whenever they dashed by.

Past the outhouse, down the gravel path—which I could barely see beneath the weeds—was another cabin, a larger one, made of logs, with a porch and a tilting chimney. The dude wrangler used to live out there, if I had that right. A woodpile leaned against one wall. I wouldn't reach for a stick of that wood without a medic nearby—it had been there so long, the spiders would have evolved to fist-sized brutes. A metal pail sat on the porch, and a frayed rope hung on a rusted hook. A cabin like that, land like this: It would seem like some kind of

Western cliché to us Seattleites, who lived amid vegetarian restaurants and yoga studios, yet here it was.

The path wound through open acres, headed up. Hugo would have loved that walk. A thicket of eucalyptus snagged my memory, and I went that way. I'd told Nash I was taking a nature hike, and she'd looked at me the same way people supposedly looked at the first joggers of the 1970s. In Seattle, if you didn't hike or bike at least once a month, they took away your citizenship and made you live in the suburbs, where people actually used their cars. But here, there were no nature hikes. There was just nature, the plain-faced fact of it. You walked in it to get places.

I felt a little out of breath from altitude, or from my sorry physical condition. My imagination got carried away with me as I tromped across the yellow grass and the rocks of that hill. I tried not to think about snakes and lizards and poisonous things, and so of course I thought about snakes and lizards and poisonous things. I swatted my ankles at every innocent brush of a tall weed. It was one of the reasons you wore boots out here and not the silly sandals I had chosen.

I hiked on. I remembered the rise that came just before you saw Washoe Lake spread out below. But obviously I didn't remember it very well, or maybe that kind of majesty is required to fade and then hit you anew every time, because, when I reached the ridge, the vista shocked me. "Wow," I said out loud, to no one or to the One who might be out there. It felt like something offered, something that required an expression of appreciation, at least—the enormous, rugged expanse carved by ice flows and rivers, the valley of yellow with splays of purple flowers, the deep blue-green of Washoe Lake, and, beyond that, miles and miles and miles of land and land and land. I was a silly, insignificant human with my squabbles with Thomas, with my menial, mortal issues. This vista was reason enough to spend your life out here, as Nash had. Even alone, and with more to handle than was good for you, if you could just stand on that ridge every now and then and witness how large the sky was, it would be worth it.

I breathed it all in. There, I could understand how people used the word *Maker*, a word that sounded preposterous in everyday life. People in Seattle would smirk with superiority at a word like that, but it made sense then. I saw the hand of the One True Great Artist, and let the capital letters fly; I don't care. That's how I felt.

And from there, too, I could see where the semitrucks had gathered. I could see a tiny huddle of men and a tiny pile of something metal. I saw a row of trailers.

I moved on, traveled toward them. From the ridge, the collection of equipment and crew had looked like the slightest muddle on the landscape, but when I arrived, I saw how wrong that first impression was. There was a dusty energy around me, a sense of something large happening. There were hay bales and men unloading things and dropping them with loud clatters, and there was the slam of doors and orders called out and the smell of heat and bodies and horseshit.

I saw him before he saw me. I recognized that tan suede hat, and the shoulders in that heather-blue T-shirt, and something about the way the muscles in his back moved as he rode his horse. The horse was shiny, shiny black with white socks, and it had thick, meaty muscles in its hindquarters. Kit's thighs gripped the horse as he rode down the sections of metal fence going up.

He waved. I felt immediately self-conscious. I had no business being there. A woman in stiff jeans stepped around me as if I was in her way. Seven or eight people were in sight—on horseback, on foot, men in plaid shirts wearing sunglasses under cowboy hats. God, it was hot out there, and I was wearing those sandals, and my own T-shirt seemed too bright and wrongly cheery.

Kit Covey rode my way on his horse, and I didn't know a thing about either of them, and they both terrified me. Even the sound of those hooves clopping on the ground was foreign. This had all seemed like a better idea back at the ranch, just after I had that jolt of caffeine. The *why not* of it was fading fast. You had to be careful with coffee. A few sips, and you could feel like the world was yours.

"You came!" Kit said. "You walked?"

"It's not that far," I said.

"Far enough, in this heat. Come on." He swung off that horse and was on the ground next to me. It was something out of the movies—he was. He was another cliché that wasn't a cliché at all here. In Seattle, we had tech guys and hipster baristas with nose rings, and we thought that life like that—the one going on right here right now, with men in cowboy hats, men with silver belt buckles, men with horses and guns—had been gone for years. But Kit Covey—his face and neck were shiny with sweat, and, dear God, if I didn't imagine him in bed. I'm sorry, but that firm grip, those forearms—anyone would have. What was it about a cowboy? I didn't know; I just saw it there in front of me. He was a lost thing, the antithesis of men you see in city elevators, carrying their cardboard latte cups and their paper bags with a scone inside.

"This is Jasper," Kit said. He set his hand on the horse's neck. The horse gave me an appraising look and then turned away. Who could blame him. He found out all he needed with one glance.

"He's very large," I said. I hoped it sounded like a compliment.

"You don't ride? With a ranch in the family?"

"I've lived in Seattle all my life." All I could think about, aside from Marlboro Men minus the cigarettes, were those stories of horses kicking people in the head. Even Jasper's breathing was powerful. I tried again to get on his good side. "He has very pretty feet," I said. "I like his stockings."

"Jas is my pilot horse." Kit patted Jasper's huge side. "Right, buddy?"

Pilot horse. I didn't have time to ask what that meant. We'd arrived at a trailer next to a truck with a huge barrel tank. "You might call this our lunchroom," Kit said. Several coolers were set outside on a folding table, and he reached inside one, tossed me a cold, wet water bottle. It didn't have a label and was made from thick plastic; filled, I suspected, from the truck, one of many water-hauling vehicles I could see around the site, some with spigots on the side. I was grateful for it. The woman in the jeans stood nearby, eating a slice of watermelon. She wore a purple sweatshirt and had long hair pulled into a barrette, and she was clearly a better woman than I, as neither the long hair nor the sweatshirt seemed remotely doable in this weather.

"Lorraine!" Kit called. "This is Callie. From Tamarosa. I told her I'd show her around."

I didn't miss the way she briefly raised an eyebrow in surprise.

"Visiting niece of the crazy old lady," I confirmed.

"Well, it's nice you came out," Lorraine said. "See for yourself what we're up to. It's good to get the facts. We care about these horses as much as anyone, as I'm sure he told you. They'll get the treatment they need. They'll get adopted out. All the stuff you hear . . . a lot of misinformation."

I nodded. It was the same nod I gave at my friend Anne's poetry readings, just after she finished the last line and slowly shut the book. It was the false gesture of thoughtful under-standing, one that we'd all perfected in Seattle. With the nu-merous art openings and literary readings, it came in handy when facing unsettling childbirth metaphors and confusing canvases. You could throw in a variation by adding a quiet *hmm*. What a surprise to find this useful here.

"Let me show you around," Kit said.

I followed Kit and Jasper to a corral near the trailer, which had temporary stalls and a covered area for shade. There were troughs of water inside, and Kit led Jasper in for a drink and a rest. "This is where we keep our guys on their off-time. That's Cactus, Lorraine's horse." I could only see the back of him; he was brown with a twitchy tail. "You know, I'm glad you're here. I didn't think you'd come."

"I wanted to see what the new neighbors were up to," I said. "Maybe you were really building a strip mall."

"We're building something, all right. Come on."

We walked to the line of semis, where more supplies were being unloaded and stacked. He kicked a pile of plastic netting with the toe of his boot. "Step one."

"That's a lot of plastic."

"And a lot of fencing." Another kick, at a pile of indefinable metal. "When we finally get the delivery that ended up in Cheyenne this morning, we'll have us some large chutes. They'll start way out there." He pointed to an area of land that was still only dirt and scrub. "Picture a well-organized maze leading to a corral. It's a pretty simple setup. The horses are guided through the chutes, and then we mouth them, sort them. Studs, dry mares, mares with colts. The young, the old, any needing medical care."

"Mouth them?" I wasn't even sure I'd heard that right. I had a hundred questions suddenly. It was a whole slice of life I knew nothing about, which makes you realize just how many such slices there are.

"Check their teeth. The size, the shape. It tells us their age."

"Then what?"

"We let them rest for a while. Then we take them to holding facilities—our own BLM stables, not far from here—where they get their freeze brand, vaccinations, blood tests, checkups by a vet. All that good stuff before they go up for adoption."

"And how do you get them to come here?"

"Helicopter. Helicopter and Jasper, mostly. I know what you've probably heard, but it's the most humane way we know. Well, sometimes we do the water traps, which are easier on the horses, sure. But helicopters take much less time, and sometimes time is something you don't have. The chopper starts the horses moving in the right direction, and then the pilot'll back off." He demonstrated with his hand. "We let them move at their own pace until they need to be turned. Jasper and I, a couple of other guys, help down on the ground, lead in the strays. But that won't be for a bit. All this takes a while to set up."

"I can imagine." One of the semitrucks rumbled to a start. The driver yelled something out his open window and then pulled forward, out and away, kicking up dirt and spitting rocks.

We kept walking. "Fuel trucks, water-hauling trailers." Kit hooked his thumb toward them.

"A lot of water-hauling trailers."

"You bet, out here. Some regions hire all this out. An independent contractor comes in and handles everything. Imagine a wedding planner, where all that's required of you is to step in and say, *I do*. We're a little more hands-on. Okay, that and we're cheap. You can't imagine how much this whole damn thing *costs*."

An old guy whistled to get Kit's attention. He had a big belly that pressed against his shirt and a belt buckle the size of a dinner plate, and he and Kit communicated something with arms and hand gestures. I recognized Steve Miller, too, from the other night, riding a brown horse out by what looked like a very large RV.

Then I realized. "You're the boss."

"Well," Kit said. He rubbed his chin, where there was a new patch of stubble. In spite of his command on a horse, Kit could be shy. I'd noticed this at the bar, too. I was also a person who often had to fake my confidence before it actually arrived, and I could spot one of my kind.

I followed Kit's lead, keeping pace next to him, as we headed away from the site. "You said this takes awhile," I asked. "How long? Harris at the ranch said weeks."

"That's about right."

"You stay at the Nugget all that time? Don't you miss home and family, being gone that long?"

"Nevada is home, unless I get transferred again. I have a place in Henderson. It's closer to my daughter in Riverside, California. She's the only family I miss. She lives with her mom there." He shrugged his shoulders.

"That must be tough."

"Tough and still new. I'm trying to adjust to it, being on my own again. But, yeah, this kind of work is hard on people. You get moved a lot—Wyoming, Montana, Nevada. Marriage is hard enough without that."

"No kidding."

"How long you been married?"

"Twenty-two years."

He let out a low whistle. "Wow, that's something. It's too rare anymore."

"He's a good man," I said. "You know, we have our things. But, still."

"That's great," Kit said. "That's good to hear. You deserve a good man. I know we just met, but that's clear."

"I guess good people can have their problems, too."

"Isn't that the truth." We'd arrived at a spot where we could see the whole enterprise stretched out in front of us, and we stopped. "Well, one of our problems, Kate and me, was all this." He swept his arm out to indicate all that land. "My former wife grew up with cities and shopping and good restaurants."

"No sign of a Nordstrom out there."

He grinned. "Nope."

"How'd you meet?"

"Wedding. In Montana. One of her college friends met a BLM guy. It sounds like a romantic life until you're stuck in a small town where a night out is KFC and a blanket under the moon."

"Don't you go knocking KFC." I shook my finger at him.

"Blankets under the moon?"

"Love them," I said.

Now I felt shy. Kit scratched the back of his neck. I looked off in the distance as if studying the big picture. I lived in the city, with good restaurants on every corner, and I shouldn't pretend otherwise. We ate Indian food; we ordered Moroccan. Thomas was a city planner who worked in a high-rise. Still, since the very night I arrived, something had been happening to me in the desert. In spite of the crisis at home, I slept well. I slept hard, as if my tired, wandering spirit recognized home. The heat and the hard work, the no-nonsense approach to a problem, whether that problem was a band of wild horses or a forest-service man—I understood it. I may never have lived there, but that ranch had been in my blood for generations.

"So where are they now? The horses."

"Between you and the old Flying W. They move around. You said you saw them once?"

"Practically in Nash's front yard, if you could call it a yard. She said, *They're back.* I thought it meant they migrated or something."

Kit laughed. "No. They don't migrate. They just travel around very large stretches of land, and that's why you may not see them. For years, even. They're always here, though. Doing what every living thing does—mating, finding food, fighting for what they got. Still, when they happen to make an appearance right near you like that . . ."

"I don't even have words for it."

"None of this means"—he shook his head—"that I don't *get* it. We all do. We have a regard for them, better believe it. We understand why folks get worked up. The mustangs are damn romantic in some respects. I see that. How can you not see that? But you've got your romantic and you've got the truth of the matter. And, to be clear, this isn't about ranchers and cattle. We're not here to help ranchers make money. We're here to protect the land. That's our job. The land and every species on it, including the horses themselves, including the vegetation that gets depleted or even endangered by too much grazing. Those plants are our job, too. We look after the best interests of everything by finding the right balance. You should see what happens to those horses when some of these places wait too long to do a gather, though. The disease—they're dehydrated. They die of thirst or starvation. There just gets to be too damn many of them."

"I understand," I said. "I do." I didn't, not really. I knew nothing about this. "Even Nash . . . I don't think she's acting out of some great love for them."

"I get it. Human interference in the nonhuman world? The natural order, et cetera . . ."

"She's not exactly been clear *what* the boot-throwing has been about."

"Most of these guys? Like Jerry, there? And Neal?" He nodded his head toward the old guy, far away now. "It's the family business. Dad was a rancher or they had a few hundred acres in a town with a rodeo. But you've also got guys like Steve and me, who read Emerson in college, and then that was it. Done. We have the same ideals that the people suing us have, I'll tell you that."

"I can see it," I said. "In you, right now." It was true. His eyes were passionate and locked with mine as he spoke.

He shook his head, laughed at himself. "I guess we spend a lot of time defending ourselves, and you're not even disagreeing. You know what? I don't want to talk about this shit. I don't really care about a tour, to be honest. I was hoping to see you again, is all."

His confession surprised me. I was pleased, more than I should have been. I wasn't sure until then that he wasn't just doing his job.

"I'm glad," I said.

"You asked where they were. I'll show you, if you'd like. I can drive you back, right past them, and then you don't have to walk all that way, either."

"I'd like that."

I rode beside Kit with the windows down. The seat of the truck was hot, so hot it burned the back of my legs. We jostled over the rough ground, and I did some anthropological work, studying his truck for information about him and the life he led. There was a handheld radio in a holster and a compass in a rolling ball on his dashboard; a green knapsack was tossed on the floor, with the cord of a phone charger sticking out. On the seat between us were an open bag of pretzels and the hat he'd just taken off. Not much to go on until he flipped his visor to shield his eyes from the sun. There was a picture clipped to a garage-door opener—a little girl with a big smile and Kit Covey's blond hair, standing at the side of a pool and holding a blow-up shark in the air like a barbell.

"The goddamn AC broke yesterday. Sorry for the heat," Kit said. He put on his sunglasses.

"I don't mind." I was sweating from the temperature and from watching that jawline of his as he drove. I tried to imagine him as a father and what he was like as a husband with a wife. We jounced and jolted around Washoe Lake, past its farthest side, out beyond where I'd ever gone before. I knew the area was spotted with many old divorce ranches; I recalled hearing about the Flying W and Washoe Pines. Harris had worked at Washoe Pines when he was young, if I remembered right, and even for a few years after that, when it, like the rest of those places, became a cattle ranch again after divorce laws began to change.

It looked so dry and desolate out there, you'd think the land was dead or dying. But the desert crackled with life, thriving on that very deception; the animals blended in, the plants looked long gone but were only waiting for the renewal of a rainstorm. I saw a burro, and tumbleweeds, and cacti. This was a place that had lasted, in good part because only certain plants, animals, and people could take the heat.

"Here," Kit Covey said. He yanked the parking brake.

"Here?" I asked. There was only dry brown hills and a single saguaro.

He fished around under his seat, retrieved a leather case that held a pair of binoculars. "Come on."

We got out. I stood beside him, aware of his shoulder next to mine. He looked into the binoculars and then handed them to me. They were unfocused or I was being stupid, because I could only see my own eyelashes.

"Nothing?" Kit asked. He stood behind me. I could feel his chest against my back, and then his arms reached around. He turned the ridged dial and pointed me in the right direction.

"Wait!" I said. "There they are!"

Brown, white, black—a grouping. They were huddled near a small creek bed that looked dry. Some had their heads down, as if for a drink, and some stood nearby, tails flicking.

"Is there even any water in there?" I asked.

"Not much, and that's the problem. We've been monitoring drought conditions since summer started, and it's bad. No water, and decreased vegetation because of it. We've been supplementing the natural seeps and filling tubs and troughs and even giving hay to the horses. Unfortunately, these animals are skittish. They won't drink from the man-made containers. Even with the extra water, the seeps don't provide enough to sustain them."

"You bring them water." It seemed impossible.

"We do. Still, you can bring a horse water, but you can't make him drink. Do you see that black one?"

I did. He stood on a small dirt-and-rock hill, grazing, though there wasn't much to graze. "Yeah. He looks like Jasper."

"He's the stud. That's his harem."

"Every guy's dream, huh?" I said.

"Not mine."

I watched for a while. It felt astonishing to find myself where I was right then. I watched those horses with Kit beside me, and I felt a soaring inside my chest. Life seemed so beautifully large. I spotted a foal, and then another. I thought of the chutes and mazes and what they would mean to these animals.

"They're families." I could see that now. There's where the problem deepened. "You said you try to keep the mares and foals together, though, right?"

"We do our best," he said.

I handed Kit his binoculars. He took the two lens caps from his pocket and replaced them. His head was bent down, and after the extraordinary thing I'd just seen, it was such a familiar, ordinary gesture that I felt like I'd known him for years. I was struck by it. I might have lived this life if my mother had made different choices, or if I myself had. I still could. There were so many possible lives to lead. Every day, you chose your life, even if you could forget that.

"Ready?" he asked.

"Maybe you should let me off here," I said, when we reached the tall arch of Tamarosa.

Kit yanked the brake but left the engine running. "Your aunt knows the sound of my truck, probably."

"She'd send me home packing, sitting here with the likes of you."

"How many boots does the woman have?"

"She has a whole room just for the ones with steel toes."

"I believe it," he said. "Hey, Callie . . ."

I waited. We sat there a minute. Had he shut off that engine, it would have been silent.

"Thanks for not jumping to conclusions. For being interested."

"I think it's fascinating," I said.

"And thanks for the fine company. It's good to remember what that's like."

"For sure," I said.

The wrinkles by his eyes, and the way he smiled, and this quality he possessed, a combination of gentleness and strength—I didn't know what to say for myself. He did a small thing then: He took my wrist. He circled it with his thumb and index finger and gave it a little shake. That was all, and then he let it go.

My wrist kept feeling those fingers around it as I walked back toward the house. Hours later it did. The gesture was a conversation. Something had been acknowledged and agreed upon. I could never hurt Thomas, and that was understood.

Still, I thought about that raccoon, the one Thomas hit on our first date, the one he wanted to bring into the car. I thought about Kit Covey speaking the word *protect*. It was an old word, a powerful word. A word you felt in some deep, ancient part of you.

The thing was, I had lived long enough to know that the ancient places were the ones that kept calling, with the hushed persistence of troubled ghosts.

"How's work going?" I asked.

"Stop trying to change the subject."

"Have you been able to go to Greenlake and do some swimming?"

"Swimming? Really? What does it matter? You should see him, Mom!"

"Melissa," I said. "Calm down." I sat in the kitchen chair near the old wall phone, feeling calm myself, calmer than I had a right to. Actually, what had settled inside me was more likely one of calm's relatives: resoluteness, or maybe surrender. I felt it curling up and tucking down its chin, same as Hugo used to.

"Mom!"

"You need to relax."

"He'd gone through all the cereal bowls. They were stacked in the sink. It was disgusting!"

It was hard for children to understand that there were things about their parents they didn't know. We parents accepted that fact about them much more easily than the other way around. Oh, how I loved my babies; oh, how large was the loss of their growing up, but your children could be such know-it-alls. "He's a grown man. He shouldn't have gotten you involved."

Shaye stood nearby, mouthing *What? What?* as I talked on the phone, which was still attached to the wall by this relic that was once called a cord. You can see them in museums. I couldn't walk away from Shaye if I wanted to, so I waved my hand at her to go away, turned my back.

"*I* was the one who went over there; he didn't invite me. I brought him some brownies, since I knew you were gone. He was freaking out. He said he tried to call you all day and you didn't answer."

"I told you, I was on a nature hike. My battery drained, searching for service. I didn't even know it was dead."

"You always told us it was irresponsible not to keep our phones charged!"

"You were learning to drive. I was trying to make you feel guilty so I wouldn't have to worry you were lying in a ditch somewhere."

Melissa sighed loudly and dramatically. In the moment of silence that followed, I was sure she was considering her options: send me to my room, or ground me. I admit this was slightly thrilling. I really should have rebelled all those years ago; a lack of teen rebellion must guarantee a crisis later in adult life. "Do you know *why* he was in a panic?" she asked.

"Given that he encouraged me to stay out here, not exactly," I said.

"This morning, when you guys talked, you asked him to overnight you your camera."

"Yes? So?"

"You haven't cared about your camera for a long, long time. When was the last time you even wanted to take pictures?"

"There are some things I'm dying to capture out here. It's beautiful, Mel."

"That's what I'm saying, Mom. That's exactly what I'm saying! That kind of stuff doesn't matter to you. No wonder he's freaking out."

"Melissa. You're—" My darling firstborn, with her beautiful shiny hair and ability to dance and her stubborn streak—I loved her more than life itself. They would never know, your children, how full your heart was for them, aching full. They'd never understand the way you saw them all ages at once, from their first day on earth to now. When I looked at Melissa, I saw her newborn eyes asking mine every significant question, and I saw her in that pink apron offering me Play-Doh food, and I saw her as a Disney princess on Halloween. I saw her left-out junior-high self and the first time she was someone's girlfriend. I saw the small daughter and the joyful daughter and the door-slamming daughter and the newly adult daughter with her own tiny refrigerator in her own kitchen. They were all one to me, familiar as my own self. I guess I was a pretty big know-it-all, too.

"I'm what? What, Mom? Tell me."

"There are things you—"

"There are things I what?" she said.

"I know you mean well. But this isn't your business. And your dad can do his own dishes, if he feels like it. Or not."

"You need to come home!"

Who could blame her for her frustration and her outrage? It was our fault, Thomas's and mine. Not for where we were now, but for what we'd abandoned in all the years of her growing up. Our lives were about our children, and now our daughters rested in the power and certainty of that. It was a good thing, a fine thing, as long as no one changed the rules.

"I've got to go. Aunt Shaye is making breaded veal cutlets."

"You and Dad have lost your minds," she said.

"Shaye, do you care if I shut that off? That show just gets to me."

Dr. Yabba Yabba Love had cut to a commercial for J. J.'s Autos and Annabelle's restaurant, but now she was back, shouting from the radio in her silk-gravel, tough-love preacher voice. *A bad childhood is no excuse for being an asshole.*

"Go ahead, but every other station out here is fuzzy," Shaye said. "I'm surprised she can say *asshole* on the air."

"Nash probably has some old records."

"Look around. I have to watch so these don't burn."

I found a stash of albums in the old cabinet under the record player, and I slid an LP from its sleeve. It was a sense memory—holding the disc by its edges, hearing the crackle as the needle hit vinyl. This was four goofy guys in bow ties, not the Earth, Wind & Fire of my youth, but still. Records. Tex stood at the living room window, looking out into the darkness, waiting for Nash's return. I turned up the music, left Tex to his work.

The crooners were going at it. "Sentimental Me." I danced Shaye away from the frying pan, her spatula just over my shoulder. "Dip me, baby," she said, but when I tried, she said, "Oh, shit, ow, that hurts," and I gave up the idea.

I tried to sing along, making up the words. "So in love with you, bring me back my shoe, if you ever do . . ." I belted.

"Set the table, would you," Shaye said.

I made couples out of the knife and spoon, just as I did when I was a child, leaving poor fork out by himself. "She's been gone a long time," I said to Shaye. "Maybe I should go check on her."

"I'm sure she knows the way to her own mailbox. Wait 'til you taste these. Why do people not eat these anymore?"

"Um, you remember what veal is?"

"I'm trying to forget that part. It didn't bother anyone in the old days."

"In the old days, they ate liverwurst. And, oh, man, liver and onions. When I was a kid, I never thought of it as an actual *liver*."

"Tomorrow I'm making stew."

"I remember stew! And biscuits?"

"White bread with margarine. We had that every night. When did every loaf of bread become *artisan*? Don't get me wrong, I love artisan bread. I could live off the stuff."

"I'm going to check on her."

Tex agreed it was a good idea, and about time, too, because he scurried to the door and pushed ahead of me. Outside, the swing was still lying at an angle on the porch, as if it had suddenly needed a rest. I could hear the crooners far away now. It smelled good out there, like warm clay and dry herbs. Still, desert dark was darker than any other, and that old pool looked sad and abandoned in the light of the moon, and I shivered. I wondered what Kit Covey's room looked like at the Carson Nugget.

"Nash?" I called.

No answer. I began to worry. There was a lot of rocky ground and dead-of-night out there. I remembered what Harris had told us. Maybe she took off somewhere. Maybe, not in her right mind, she was wandering out by the lake. We would have to make plans to put her in a home, a care facility, her up-rooted belongings stuffed into one wretched room.

But then I saw her walking back up the road, her back hunched as she sorted through the mail. "I can't see a damn thing out here," she said.

"I told you I'd get it," I said.

"Probably I could get back to the house with my eyes closed," she said.

"Let's not try that."

"Oh, let's do. I'll be Helen and you be Anne Sullivan." Nash cracked up at her own joke, her shoulders moving up and down as she chuckled away. Tex trotted happily ahead, lifted his leg on a creosote bush.

"Safe and sound," I called to Shaye when we were back in. It smelled so good in there. Frying food, and something with garlic.

"I didn't kick the bucket while I was out getting the mail," Nash shouted. "The Ames Brothers! Listen to them. Now, that's music." She snapped her fingers, three jazzy clicks to the beat. "Mmm, that smells delicious."

Nash sat in a kitchen chair, shuffled through bills and ad flyers. "Fix me one of those drinks you girls made the other night, would you?"

I got out the small glasses and the ice-cube tray—one of those kinds from the dark ages, metal, with the little handle you pulled up. I cracked them free, chased one escaping cube across the kitchen counter. With the Ames Brothers and the popping of grease and Shaye shaking the pan against the burner while chatting about the time their mail went missing for three days, I didn't notice that Nash had gone silent until I turned to give her the drink. She sat in that kitchen chair and clutched an envelope. She didn't look well. Her skin had gone slack, and I realized just how old she was.

"Nash?"

"Holy Christ," she whispered.

"What's the matter?"

Was she crying? She was not the crying type. But she wiped her eyes and set the letter in her lap with a shaking hand. The writing on the envelope was spidery. I tried to read it. "Jack?"

Shaye took the pan off the stove, and we looked at each other. I put my arms around Nash. Her shoulders didn't feel broad at all; it'd been my memory that made them so solid. They were small, and they were trembling.

"Nash," I said. "Nash, it's okay."

Of course, it wasn't okay. Not much was okay in that room, for any of us. Tex, maybe, and even he had an uncertain future.

Nash's eyes were sunken and small, and the thin skin of her cheek was wet. "All these years," she said. "A man like that. I wasn't sure if he was even alive."

"Well, see?" I said. "He is." I didn't know what I was saying, what news I was helping to deliver. Maybe someone didn't die after all. Maybe just love had, and now here it was again. I squeezed her hand.

"I've missed that charming bastard for sixty years. I thought for sure he was gone for good."

Summer of '51, Shaye mouthed to me, but it wasn't the time for that now.

"You see?" I said to Nash. "There you go. You never know."

I rubbed my thumb along the smooth tissue-paper skin of her hand. There was the crackle of the needle between songs.

I was right. You never did know. It was what made the whole damn trip so hard, and so worthwhile.

chapter 11

Nash

Nash cracks the ice free from the tray and chases a cube as it skates across the counter. She catches it just before it falls to the floor. She puts it, and a few others, into the copper mugs. In goes a shot of vodka, a few inches of ginger beer, a twist of lime. Nash keeps the vodka to a minimum in Ellen's drink. Three nights ago, she and Veronica and Ted from Washoe Pines went to the Old Corner bar, and Ellen didn't just dance with a cowboy, she kissed one. Her lipstick ended up on the side of her cheek, and her hair had gone as wild as if it had survived an act of God and was still too shocked to speak of it. Mother always said that change had its own clock, but Nash feels it might be best to slow Ellen's down a little. All the late nights and men and alcohol make it seem like change is heating up and rising like boiling water about to spill over on the stove, and although this is how it usually goes, it feels like an imminent disaster now that Nash is in charge.

That morning, Alice phoned to tell her she might be gone another few weeks. A few weeks! There's been the sudden decision to move Gloria in with a friend, since she won't leave California. Something else is going on, Nash is sure of it. It's not just the latest creep, Billy what's-his-name, leaving Gloria. Not many things would keep Alice from the ranch that long.

"Here you go," Nash says, and hands around the drinks.

"She's an ox," Veronica says, and takes her glass. "Her rear end is bigger than Zorro's."

"Oh, you're cruel," Ellen says.

"Correct, but cruel," Hadley says.

"I met her before, you know," Veronica says. "With Gus. At a fundraiser for the Field Museum. The husband looked long-suffering. Like he'd been left outside on a winter night and never let back in."

"She has *children*, poor things," Ellen says.

"Don't worry, they no doubt have a nanny," Hadley says.

Ellen sips her mule. "A nanny! I can't even imagine that."

The ox is Mrs. Morris Shumley, who Nash picked up at the Reno train station that afternoon. After her six weeks are up and she's had her day at the Washoe County Courthouse, Mrs. Morris Shumley will have to reacquaint herself with her own first name. But this is how she introduced herself as she shook Nash's hand with her gloved one as the crowd at the station closed around them. This is how she presented herself to the rest of the girls, too: She politely made their acquaintance and then retreated to her room, as if the introductions were a taw-dry piece of business now concluded.

"She wants nothing to do with us harlots," Lilly Marcel says. Her round stomach has grown so much in one week. She leans back a little when she walks now.

"*I* want nothing to do with you harlots, but I'm stuck with you," Hadley says.

"A nanny." Ellen still can't imagine it.

"I want to see the ox on the back of a horse," Veronica says, which makes them all laugh. "No wonder Mr. Shumley dumped her like a hot potato. He probably hasn't had—"

"Don't even say it, Veronica," Ellen giggles.

Hadley claps her hands over her eyes. "I'm seeing it now. The way he *shudders* for all the wrong reasons."

"Stop!" Ellen says. She is bent over, laughing. She holds her hand up in the air.

Veronica shakes out a cigarette. "She seems to have forgotten that she'll be a divorcée now, too."

"It's an awful word, isn't it?" Ellen says. "*Divorcée*."

"I think it sounds rather glamorous," Veronica says.

"There was a divorcée who lived down our street," Ellen says. "The first one I ever saw. She had beautiful clothes. I watched her house, imagining that strange men would be picking her up in various cars or that her children would set off bombs in the yard, but nothing interesting happened. Her grass turned brown, is all. And then she moved away."

"You must find a way to keep the grass green." Hadley shakes her finger at Ellen. She means it.

"I might have to get a job at a department store," Ellen says. "That divorcée, she sold perfume at the Emporium. I don't know the first thing about selling perfume at the Emporium."

Cook baked a ham for dinner, and there are steaming beans and scalloped potatoes and buttery rolls and peas. As they move to the big table for dinner, there is the swish of chiffon against stockings. Veronica's dress is gold with silver embroidery, and Ellen is in a green formal with netting to fill out the skirt, with a black taffeta jacket over the top. Hadley wears red, with a cut of gown that shows off her bare neck, and Lilly is in pink satin, with a pink wrap off her shoulders. Their hair is perfectly coiffed after a visit to the hairdresser in the city earlier that day; the smell of Lustre-Creme and the bitter-metal odor from Hadley's permanent wave are masked with L'Origan. The meal is hurried, then cut short entirely when Jack and

Danny arrive. They are taking the ladies to Cal Neva Resort in Tahoe, where Johnny Y. Michaels will be performing.

"Don't look so down, Peanut," Jack says. He's wearing his nicest shirt, with the pearl snaps, and he's doused himself with aftershave. "Three more short years, you're free to go anywhere."

They take off. She is left behind with that ham and Boo and Mrs. Morris Shumley, who will likely stay in her room reading novels, same as Nash. The similarity of their evening is humiliating.

Nash helps clean up the dishes, and then Irma unfastens her apron with a sigh and leaves for the night. One time, Nash and Gloria rode in the backseat when Alice picked up the ladies at Cal Neva after Cat Callahan performed. Nash was just a child then. She remembers the tall, flashing lights of the CAL NEVA sign outside the lodge, the crowd spilling out the doors. There was the energy of a party and the smell of alcohol and cigarettes as the women piled into the car. There was high-pitched hilarity, a sense of carelessness and freedom, and it all felt dangerous to her young self, up way too late.

In her room, Nash picks up Boo for a dance. "You look lovely in fur," she says to him, but he's unimpressed. She sets him down, and he eyes her warily from the floor. Nash has Johnny Y. Michaels's record. He is singing into a microphone on the front, his eyes sleepy-looking, his dark hair as shiny as the satin lapels of his jacket. Nash imagines Jack dancing with Lilly Marcel, holding her carefully, the bump of Beanie against him. She imagines Lilly Marcel's neck smelling of Jack's aftershave. There is something lewd about his interest in a girl, a woman, who is in the family way, isn't there? He shouldn't see her as her own, separate self; her body isn't just hers. Nash flings the record and it hits the leg of her desk. She doesn't even like Johnny Y. Michaels all that much.

All of this—the long-ago car ride, the album, Jack's aftershave—circles together and forms a cyclone of feeling even Nash can't understand. It is jealousy, yes, and longing, yes, but for whom and what exactly she can't tell. For all of it, likely. For all of life that's just waiting for her as she stays on that ranch, serving drinks and listening to stories of other people's lives and loves. This is her destiny, and she knows it, and it's pulling her under already. Gloria would have taken the situation with Jack into her own hands, at the least. No. She wouldn't have bothered with a man like Jack at all. She *fled*.

Mrs. Morris Shumley begins to snore. Nash hears her clear down the hall. She sounds like an ox, all right, held down by its throat. Nash is too restless to listen to that for hours on end. She might just go into Mrs. Shumley's room and hold a pillow over her face. She heads downstairs, where Boo watches her without moving from his favorite spot by the fireplace. Like a lot of people she knows, he can say a lot without saying anything.

Nash gets the keys to the Styleline Deluxe, which hang on a hook in the kitchen. She has the urge to do something large and reckless, and the urge rises up and whips around, a bull in the ring, the one in charge, the one that will fling any rider to the ground. She feels as mad and mean as that, too. Peanut, hell. She gets in the car, starts it up. She hits the accelerator hard, and the tires spin and whirl in the gravel, and then she is down that road and into the nearest town of Edwards, if you can call it a town. There's a store and a post office and a gas station. There's the Monte Cristo Motel, and the Ponderosa Café, and that's it.

The flare of fury burns out. It's only sad out here. The lights are on in Copper's. Nash parks in the empty strip in front.

Boxes of cereal and detergent look oddly sunny against the dismal linoleum floor. When she goes in, the bell rings loud. Rusty Harlow is reading a magazine and puts it down. Nash doesn't like the way he looks at her. She buys a roll of Life Savers and a Pepsi-Cola, and this is the extent of the mark she makes on the world tonight.

Rusty clears his throat. He says, "Have a good night, little Miss McBride." His voice says that he's smoked too many cigarettes, and his eyes are smarmy with alcohol. Nash gets the creeps and gets out of there. The feeling of something lurking follows her back to the ranch. Boo stands and stretches when he sees her, sniffs the hand where she has the candy. He decides it's not worth the effort and lies back down, sighing through his nose.

Nash eats the Life Savers in order of preference, leaving the cherry for last. She tries to read. She folds the pillow over her head, as the ox is still dying a slow death in the other room.

She must have fallen asleep, because she awakens when an arc of light fills her room. There's the sound of doors slamming and then laughter, and, inside the house, the toilet flushes. It's very late. People seem to be settling in. Faucets squeak on and off, doors are gently closed, and the house is eventually quiet.

This miserable night appears to be finally over when she hears something else. Voices. The sound of water. Bodies through ripples.

Nash climbs out of bed. She keeps her light off, tries to peer out through the crack between her curtains. The pool is too far from here to see very clearly.

She is acting crazy but can't seem to help what she does next. She gets out of bed, and, still wearing her nightgown, she takes each stair quietly. She turns the handle of the front door without making a sound.

The grass is dewy underfoot. Past the grass, there are rocks and scratchy shrubs and the privacy of the big old trunk of the desert willow. She still can't see, and so she darts to the eucalyptus near the pool, a running apparition in her white nightgown. The tree, with its shaggy, wild bark, is wide enough to hide behind.

It's just as she thought—the lilt of his voice is so familiar to her. She sees Lilly's pale shoulders in the moonlight, and Jack's broad ones. Lilly's arms are out of the water, keeping her balance, and Jack pushes off and swims, popping his head up right in front of her. Lilly holds her hand to her mouth so as not to laugh out loud. He dives again, reappears at the other end. He stretches his arms out like hers and walks toward her. Their arms meet. Their hands entwine. They kiss, and then he takes her whole body in his arms. Her round belly is otherworldly as it rises from the water, and he carries her in a small circle before setting her down again.

They swim and kiss. Nash can't hear what they are saying; she can only hear the tempo of their words, and the tempo is slow and as soft as the gray-green eucalyptus leaves that veil Nash's shoulders. Once again, she thinks she hears the sound of thunder, far off, because she doesn't know what the horses sound like when they're that close. She should warn Jack and Lilly. Storms could move fast across that sky. A guest at the Pines was in their pool when lightning struck, killing him instantly.

She hears this clearly: "Be careful," Jack says. His desire to shelter—it stabs her heart and takes it down, like the vulnerable creature of the pack that it is. Lilly Marcel rises from the water, walks up those steps in the shallow end. Her body is maybe the most beautiful and strange thing Nash has ever seen. She carries a planet, her own weighty earth, which she supports with one arm underneath, the other on the handrail.

Now Jack emerges from the water behind her. Nash cannot avert her eyes from the muscles in his chest, which fall in ridges down his abdomen to his narrow hips and dangling penis. Two white towels are folded on the end of one chair, but they don't reach for them yet. No. Instead, there is one moment where they both stand naked at the pool's edge, a moment where everything is revealed. To Nash, certainly, right here, right now. And in time to other people, as well. People who will consider this private moment in the Tamarosa moonlight their business. Most definitely, this is their business.

There's the flash. White light illuminates the scene briefly, making Nash blink in the sudden brightness. At first, Nash is sure this is lightning. But it's soundless. The whole night is soundless except for the settling water of the pool, until Lilly Marcel shrieks and Jack swears loudly and grabs a towel and takes off running. That photographer is faster than Jack is, though. No wonder—finally he's got something that will make Stuart Marcel happy, or full of rage, which was maybe the same thing to him. Proof of Lilly's betrayal would give him delicious reason to do what he wanted to do anyway—destroy a few people using his fists and his power.

Now there are lots of sounds. Footsteps, people running, Nash's own voice in the night. Her furious, scared voice, yelling. The photographer's car starting up. Hadley's cabin door slamming behind her as she calls, "Is everything all right?"

Mrs. Morris Shumley would complain in the morning that she couldn't sleep one wink, what with all the racket.

chapter 12

Callie

I'm not sure who was happier to see the delivery truck that morning, Tex or me. The sun had barely come up. The light was yellow orange, making the hills yellow orange and the trees and the shrubs yellow orange, too. It was that kind of sweet, magic morning glow you wanted to sip from a cup to start the day.

It was a dangerous thing to do, but after I opened the package, I crept outside, still wearing my nightgown, the one Thomas had given me for my last birthday. I ran and hid behind that big, old shaggy eucalyptus tree. I snapped my first image of Tamarosa—*flash*—a buffalo grazing poolside.

He was a very photogenic buffalo and apparently easygoing about having his picture taken. It felt good, having my camera in my hands again. How long had it been since a camera felt good? No idea. Creativity—an elusive beast anyway, seen only in the wild—had taken off a long time ago. A switch had turned off, the lights had dimmed, the curtains closed, and I only viewed things in the practical way anyone does. A tree was a tree, and rain on windows was just rain on windows, and snow was for skis, sold on pages six to eleven in the winter catalog. For a good long time, I didn't see a buffalo as art, when as a young woman I used to see everything as art. That girl, a lost

version of me, didn't have the necessary passion and where-
withal to make a life as an artist, but she did have the simpler,
daily pleasure of inspiration. Still, something wore even that
down—life, kids, the practicality of pictures of backpacks and
packets of freeze-dried foods. Creativity dies, sure as love does,
when not handled with tenderness and respect and sometimes
firmness.

I ran like hell back to the house. I was excited. I felt giddy,
like a child who'd just galloped down a grassy hill. I didn't end
up mauled for the sake of art, either, and that victory of sur-
vival, the way parts of us endured after all, it called for a celebration of coffee and donuts with Nash and Shaye, who was
heading inside, carrying a large pink box. You had to love a
woman who loved food.

I had my hand on the screen door when I saw a large package sticking up from one of the trash cans by the side of the
house. I walked back down the porch steps to investigate. The
return address was protected with such a sizeable amount of
tape, I was sure I could tell the personality type of the sender—
proprietary and paranoid. The name was clear, though. *Leonard Petit, Beverly Hills.* The box was still full. The black-and-white
photos—men with slicked-back hair, looking dapper, women
gazing off toward the heavens, elegant actors and actresses in
drawing rooms and on balconies—had now been discarded in
a messy heap. Poor Leonard Petit would be destroyed if he saw
this.

I let the screen door slam behind me. I heard Nash and
Shaye chatting in the kitchen. I smelled coffee, that warm rise
of morning joy. "Nash!" I called.

"No need to shout," she shouted.

It all seemed so innocent, and Nash looked strangely well
sitting with Shaye at that table with the checked cloth.

"I'm keeping you girls around, after all," Nash said. She eyed that rectangle of pink cardboard as if it were a chest with a million dollars inside. "I haven't eaten this well since we let the cook go."

"You eat like a bird," Shaye said, as she lifted a square of sticky tissue paper off the top of a maple bar.

"I saw that box out there in the garbage, Nash. The one you just got. The one full of old Hollywood photos."

"Mmm-hmm?" Her mouth was full, cheeks fat as a baby's.

"You're throwing all that away after you ordered it? The entire thing?"

She took a swallow of coffee. "I got what I needed."

"The whole box is in the trash?" Shaye asked.

"I can spend my hard-earned money any way I please. That's why it's called *my* hard-earned money."

"This is the kind of thing that makes us worry," I said.

"Stop it. You're spoiling the morning. Eat a donut. It'll change your outlook."

I didn't know what to make of any of it. She was either crazy or quite sane, which was much the way I felt about myself right then. We skipped the plates and ate off napkins, dropping bits of donut to Tex, who couldn't believe the way his luck had turned. He sat so still to keep the goodness coming that he nearly looked taxidermied. I remembered Hugo's own version of this determined goodness, the way he'd use his soulful eyes to his advantage. My heart cracked whenever I thought of those eyes and the way I missed them.

"Of course," Shaye said. "That's it! Your Jack. He was a Hollywood film star."

Nash snorted.

"No?"

"He was a cowboy. One of our wranglers. Film star," she

scoffed. "I was just reminiscing about the golden age of Hollywood."

The slurp of coffee on her part was unnecessary. No senile person would be that conniving and take such pleasure from it, too.

"Which reminds me. I forgot to ask you about using your computer," Shaye said. She had frosting on her cheek.

"Ha. I don't think so."

"No, seriously. My laptop is useless. I can't sign on here, and I've got to answer mail. And I want to write to Eric. I've got some things to say to him."

"So write a letter."

"Come on, Nash. Me, too," I said. "Amy sent me all these pictures, and they're too small to see on my phone."

"Hack in to Harris's network. Look for *Horndog*."

Shaye cringed. "Oh, that's scary."

"Password, *Stallion*."

"Jesus. I'll never look him in the eyes again," I said.

"Wait," Shaye said. "You know about networks? I don't even know about networks."

"What do you think, I live in the dark ages?"

"Shaye, did you eat the chocolate sprinkle?" I asked.

"I buy the chocolate sprinkle, I eat the chocolate sprinkle. Nash, come *on*."

"I know what you people want. You want to snoop."

Shaye looked at me and shrugged. I shrugged back.

"We could take you to see him," I said.

"Who?" Nash licked maple icing from one old finger.

"Jack!" I said.

"What makes you think I want to see Jack?" she said.

"Nash, really," Shaye said. "You're telling us it's some sort of coincidence you get a letter out of the blue from that guy? All that stuff in your room, it isn't about trying to find him? And now that you have, you can get on with the reunion."

"A reunion? I told you girls. I'm working on the family tree. To leave behind after I'm dead."

"Family tree? You said it was about running the ranch," I said.

"You're trying to tell us he just writes you a letter out of nowhere?" Shaye narrowed her eyes.

"He didn't write me a letter out of nowhere. I wrote to him first. At the last address I had. I didn't know whether he was even alive or not. I wanted to share some news I recently got. About a person we once knew."

"Who?" I said.

"Just a joint acquaintance. Am I on trial here?"

"Sounds like an excuse to get reacquainted, to me," Shaye said. "I wrote Jay a letter like that once, telling him our old math teacher died, just to see if we could start things up again."

"You did?" I asked. "Ha-ha. You loved those vests. All these years later, still thinking about that three-piece."

Shaye ignored me. "It'll be a road trip to see our friend Jack! We could help you, Nash, if you'd stop being so stubborn."

"You're fixing my fence; that's all the help I need. You're bringing me food. You're keeping a nice elderly lady company."

"Uh-huh," Shaye said.

"Who says I'm being stubborn? Family tree, the ranch— what difference does it make? It isn't your business."

It didn't escape my notice that I had said the same thing to Melissa. But this was what happened, wasn't it? The generations just kept on and on, figuring it all out from the start, even if it had been figured out a hundred times before—swapping roles, playing the younger, playing the older, over and again as the sun went up and the sun went down.

"Secrets make you want to find out secrets," Shaye said.

Nash didn't even bother to look at us. I waited for another weak justification, or an outright denial. But she gave us neither.

"Too bad," she said.

I found four new boxes of nails in a paper bag in the storage shed with a receipt from early 2004, and with the energy and determination brought on by fat, sugar, and the lingering kind words from a man I barely knew, I worked outside on that endless fence. The year 2004 seemed like yesterday. With the sun beating on the back of my tank top, I thought about what Thomas had said about the woman at work. I thought about my own body, if I could ever let another man see it. I thought about all of the things I owned, too, the drawers and cupboards full of serving trays and tiny forks for appetizers and miniature plastic corns with spikes to stick in the ends of cobs. There were candleholders that looked like turkeys, and some long-dead relative's embroidered pillowcases; there were yellowing paperback bestsellers and datebooks from 1998. I felt the weight of it all. I wondered how many garbage bags it would take to haul it all out to the curb.

I wiped sweat from my face with the bottom of my shirt. Things could end, whether your body was in any shape for it or not. Things could end, no matter how many platters you had.

Not long ago, Thomas and I were in bed together. The smooth white skin of his back was under my hands and he was breathing heavy in my ear, and it was in out, in out, and he was saying slightly pornographic things in my ear, and I'd never even told him after all these years that I didn't like it when he said slightly pornographic things in my ear. I found it distracting and even disingenuous, to be honest. Can you imagine never admitting a truth like that to the person who saw you give birth and would likely see you die? But I hadn't. More important, the TV was on. A Swiffer commercial was playing. A woman expounded the virtues of throwaway pads and a swivel arm. His breathing quickened while dog hair under a sofa was removed with ease. Daily life had left us vulnerable; that was clear. Daily life snatched things from a couple. Mattress sales stole intrigue; shirts ruined by that damn spot of bleach grabbed desire and wrung its scrawny neck.

The word *husband*, the word *wife*—on a summer day when a ring slipped on a finger, those words shimmered with promise. But they evolved; they turned and changed and turned again, adding facets with each rotation. Sometimes, those words were contentment itself; sometimes, frustration beyond imagining. You spoke them with sarcasm and wrote them on a valentine; you relaxed in those words and were chained to those words and cherished those words. Too, the words could become an item on a list, a thing that must be done, another burdensome object that needed dusting.

Yet that was the beauty of it, wasn't it? The whole complicated mess of two lives, side by side. Love was elusive *and* stubborn. It could hang in there even when you hated his guts. Passion could sometimes feel like a false compliment, but there were the other nights Thomas and I had. The honest and connected ones, which were as close to forever as you got. Neither of us should forget those.

Of course, those thoughts and that heat made the fence a grand impossibility. There was just too much of it. My muscles hurt already, and I was getting a blister where palm met fingers. I really wasn't that great with a hammer, in spite of what Kit Covey had said. Nash would die soon, and the place would be sold, and none of my efforts would matter anyway. But a person did what a person could do against all lost causes.

Shaye sat at the desk in her room. Her laptop was in front of her, and so was a bag of chips. The window was open. She'd found an old iron fan, which sat on the nightstand and blew her hair around. My own hair was still wet from the shower. I twisted it up and took the hair clip from my teeth and secured it there.

"Look at the cord on that. It's going to catch this place on fire."

She looked down at her computer. "What are you talking about? It's brand new. Come here. Wait 'til you see."

I didn't bother to clarify; we could misunderstand each other and that was fine. *We should all—me included—be as generous with our partners as we are with other people*, I thought then.

I looked over Shaye's shoulder. The email said: *Eric—*. Not *Hi, Eric*, or *Dear Eric*. This meant she was being stern. I saw the numbered lines implying conditions.

She minimized the letter, and it disappeared. "Not *that*."

"You wiggled your way into *Horndog*," I said.

"Ick, don't say it like that. But you'd better believe it. Check it out."

"Make it bigger."

"*Jack*," she said.

A black-and-white image zoomed large—a bucking horse barely out of the gate, all four feet off the ground, its mane straight up in the air. The rider on its back wore a plaid shirt and a tall hat, and he leaned forward from sudden motion, held on. A small crowd sat on the adjacent gate and watched. *Jack Waters of Tamarosa, riding Little Britches, Washoe County Roundup, 1950.*

"Wow, 1950? That's awful close, Sham. Nash had good taste. Look at him."

"'*My brother and I were bareback forever. My father had a stable. First time Pop rode a bull, there might have been a little brown bottle involved,' Waters said. Waters, a dude wrangler at the ranch, competed this year in barebacks, saddle broncs, bulls, roping, and bulldogging.* Can you believe it?"

"What the heck is bulldogging?"

"Hey, I'd bulldog that guy."

"It's got to be him. *The* Jack," I said.

"I spent most of the morning looking up *Jack Waters* and *Jack Waters, Nevada*, whatever I could think of. He couldn't have had a more common name, could he? Thanks for that, buddy."

"Now I'm definitely leaning toward not crazy."

"Me, too. Look, we've got 1950, 1951. Jack Waters. And some kind of goodbye happening through the buried book."

"Did you show her this?"

"Why, so she could lie to my face? She's been in her room all day."

"All day?"

"Stop with the tone." It's what our mother used to say. "She lives alone, Cal. She's by herself every day."

"She might need lunch, at least. She's sick, remember?"

"She could hibernate for the winter, with all those donuts she ate. Jesus, Cal, you're bossy. I'm not the little kid you can boss around anymore! Check on her yourself. Stop being such a control freak."

"Only other control freaks accuse you of being a control freak."

Shaye was still hunched forward, looking at that picture, when I started down the hall. Nash's door was closed. "Jack Waters was *hot*," Shaye yelled.

Well, that should have brought Nash out. I tapped on the door with my fingertips. "Nash? You hungry? Can I get you something to eat?"

No answer.

"Nash?" I knocked harder.

Silence.

My chest constricted; my heart squeezed like a fist. I rattled the doorknob. Locked.

"Shaye!" I yelled.

I heard Shaye's desk chair knock over. She was there, fast. "She's not answering. Something's wrong."

Shaye's eyes were wide. "Oh, God, Cal. This is it. This is why we came when we did."

"This isn't why we came when we did. You know why we came when we did." We had come for our own selfish reasons. This wasn't the time for ridiculous metaphysical justifications, much as I loved them myself.

I jiggled the knob some more and shoved. "I think there's something against the door."

"Oh, my God, Cal. Shit! Holy shit! She probably . . ."

A terrible thing happened then. I shouldn't even admit it, but Shaye started to giggle nervously, and so did I. We were slightly hysterical. Her breath smelled like Fritos. Tex was underfoot, seeing what all the excitement was about. "Stop it! Jeez, Shaye. Help me push."

"One, two, three . . ." We threw ourselves against that door. Nothing.

"It's too big to be a body," Shaye said.

This sobered us up. She was right. I thought so, anyway. I had no real idea what deadweight felt like. "Try again." We shoved. There was a scratching sound, wood against wood, and the feeling of something giving. I peered through the small crack we'd made.

"Oh, my God!"

"What?"

"I cannot believe this!"

"What? Let me see."

"She's not in there."

"You're kidding me."

"Nope."

What followed was something too humiliating to recount. It involved Shaye and me running out of the house and trying to climb up into the open window as Tex barked his head off inside. There were a couple of crates nearby, and Shaye had the bright idea to make a platform, and then I attempted that boosting maneuver with the fingers of both hands entwined— nothing I could maintain once I held Shaye's weight. She stopped being pissed sometime after we got up off the ground and then we fetched a spiderweb-laden ladder we found in the barn. I got stuck halfway in the window with my butt hanging out, and Shaye struggled to push me the rest of the way. There was some shrieking involved and some pain. We were exhausted and our hair askew by the time we both flopped into Nash's room.

"We've got to find that letter," Shaye said. She'd turned into Nancy Drew all of a sudden.

"I doubt she's taken off to meet him on their anniversary at the Empire State Building, Shaye. Oh, man, look at this." I had a red railroad-track scrape across my stomach.

"Stop being a baby and help me."

It didn't even hit us at first. A full minute went by before Shaye said, "Oh, hell," and the cleanliness of the room struck us both. There must have been a lot more than a box of photos shoved down into those trash cans. Nash's room was tidy, and all that was left of the mess were a few innocent stacks of books.

"When did she do this?" Shaye asked.

"When you ignored her all day, thinking she was lying around sick in bed."

We ransacked the place anyway, a pair of inept burglars. "Nothing," I said. "No note, no letter, no anything." Shaye stuck her hand under Nash's mattress and felt around. I was on my knees, feeling up her desk, hoping for a secret drawer, when I saw something.

"Wait. Come here."

Shaye knelt beside me. The photo was taped to the underside of the desktop. We craned to look. It was a black-and-white movie still, an image of a woman and a man at the front desk of a hotel, a bellman standing nearby. I plucked the edge of the tape with my finger to see if anything was written on the back. No. I pressed the tape in place again.

"Neither of those guys looks anything like Jack," Shaye said. "This blows our whole story to hell."

We sat on the floor, defeated. "Maybe Harris knew what he was talking about. We're trying too hard to make sense out of . . . pieces. Pieces of senility."

Shaye had a twig in her hair, and her chin sported a bar-code scratch. "I hate to admit it. I think you're right. She's lost it. She could be anywhere."

We shoved the dresser away from the door. It took both of us to budge it; how Nash got it there, I'll never know. We checked the trash cans and found them empty, save for a pile of ashes. She'd burned the lot of it, right under our noses. We called Harris, who wasn't answering his phone. We argued over whether to call our mother.

"What good would that do?" I said. "She's in California. She's terrible in a crisis. I don't want to take care of her while I take care of this."

"You're being mean. We should at least let her know what's going on."

"Fine," I said, which conveniently rehashed every argument we'd ever had on the subject without saying more.

Shaye took off to search the grounds for Nash. The minute she got back, I'd call the police. I stayed by the phone, because someone always stays by the phone in the movies. I nervous-ate my way through the rest of the bag of chips. I thought about fleeing all our family dysfunction and taking the next flight out to Aruba. Being kidnapped by Mexican drug lords sounded kind of nice. Tex had settled into his hairy dog bed, apparently trusting there'd be a good outcome.

I couldn't just wait there. Of course, it's when you stop waiting for the phone to ring that it always rings. I was down the porch steps when I heard it inside. I practically broke my neck trying to get to it in time. I lunged for the receiver and panted my hello.

"Is this Nash McBride's niece?"

"Yes."

Here it was. The phone call. She'd been found on the freeway, maybe. Hit by a semitruck, or who knows what else. My stomach felt sick with dread and with that deep sense of failure that constantly nips at the heels of responsible people.

"My name is Deke Donaldson, and I'm with J. J.'s Autos?"

"J. J.'s Autos?"

"Your aunt is here."

"Thank God! Is she all right?"

"She's just fine."

"Did you find her wandering nearby? Oh, I'm so glad she's safe, I cannot tell you."

"Well, she was wandering in the showroom for quite some time. She liked the Benz with the heated and cooled front seats and the adjustable air bladders for customized back support, but she settled for the Ford Fusion Plus Hybrid with the sunroof."

"Excuse me?"

"Your aunt just bought a car. Problem is, she has no way to get it home."

"What? Is she there? Put her on the phone!"

"She's waving her hand at me. Wait. No . . . She says she's too busy. She says she can't talk right now. Perhaps you can come and get her?"

He sounded a little desperate.

"We'll be right there."

The poor man actually breathed a sigh of relief.

I called Shaye. "Found her," I said.

"Oh, thank God!" Her voice wobbled, near tears. "Is she okay?"

"She bought a car."

"She bought a *car*? Are you kidding me? She went to buy a car without telling us? How'd she get there? Do you know where I am right now? I just left the dude wrangler's cabin!

There was a squirrel corpse in there! The whole bony skeleton was laid out like it was freaking Halloween!"

"Get a move on," I said.

"You cleaned out your whole room. You *burned* stuff. What's that about?"

"I don't keep what I no longer need."

"Well, if you wanted to go into town, you should've just asked. You didn't have to sneak out."

"I can't find how to put this seat back," Nash said. She hunted around down by her feet, near the brand-new floor mats.

"Why did you buy a *car*? We told you. If you want to go somewhere, even if you want to see Jack again, we could just take you!"

"Jack, nothing. I don't care about Jack. Listen to these speakers," she said. She turned the dial, blasting some hip-hop song from the CD still in the player of the showroom model.

"How did you expect to get this home when you don't drive?"

"I thought that nice boy might give me a little refresher. I used to drive, but it was a long, long time ago."

"Well, now we're going to have to go back again to get *my* car. And Shaye may never forgive you. Poor thing. Look at her."

That tractor could go maybe fifteen miles an hour. Shaye looked miserable as she puttered along, pulled as far to the side of the road as possible.

I rolled down my window. "How you doing?"

"You don't have to ask me every five minutes!" Shaye shouted. "I told you, go on ahead!"

It was wrong, I knew it, and I would have to pay for it, but I couldn't resist. "How're the crops looking?"

"Shut up, Cal. I mean it. Shut the hell up."

"Look on the bright side. Your magnetic personality *did* bring you a new hobby."

She shook her head, glared at me. "Damn you!" she yelled from the high black tractor seat. Still, there was the tiniest lift at the corner of her mouth, the barest hint of a smile. It was a good one, and she knew it.

"Wait 'til you see the voice-activated communications system," Nash said.

chapter 13

Nash

"Wait 'til you see the dual-speed windshield wipers," Veronica says.

Nash clears her throat. She tries to sound like she's in charge. "First thing you should locate is the *brake*."

"Look, a heater," Ellen says.

If her mother knew about this, she'd kill her, Nash thinks. She'd kill her *again*. The Styleline Deluxe is only two years old, with all the features. Alice makes Danny wash the desert dust off it every few days. Ellen is behind the wheel. Veronica and Hadley are in on this together. Lilly leans against the porch railing, shading her eyes against the afternoon sun to watch.

"My palms are sweating," Ellen says.

"You cannot keep relying on a man to drive you around," Veronica says.

"Every divorcée needs a set of *these*." Hadley tosses the keys to Ellen, who misses the catch. She hunts around on the floor for them.

"Divorcée," Ellen says, popping her blond head back up. "I can still barely even say the word."

"When life gives you lemons . . ." Hadley says.

"Learn how to *drive*," Veronica says.

Somehow, Nash ends up in the backseat, with Veronica in

front. Clearly, she's losing control of the situation. They are having lesson number one right here in the driveway, and Boo looks out from the front window of the house as if he disapproves. Nash hopes that none of the wranglers see her back there, especially Jack. Danny is stuck taking Mrs. Shumley into town to get her hair done, so Nash is safe from him, and who knows where Jack is, anyway. Every time she shuts her eyes, she sees the flash of that camera and him running, half naked, for that photographer.

The engine is on, chuckling as if in a fine, jovial mood. Ellen checks her lipstick in the rearview mirror. Veronica shows her how to shift into reverse, and down the drive they go in a sudden lurch that makes Nash shriek and causes Hadley to give a round of applause.

"Easy, easy," Veronica says. It's the same thing Jack says to Zorro.

Ellen shifts again, and they go forward and then stop suddenly in telegraph style—dash, dot, dash, dot. Nash's head begins to throb. It is due to last night's lack of sleep, but it is also unexpressed anger, pressing outward against her temples. She is angry at Jack, yes, but she is also angry at her mother for leaving and at her sister for just about everything. When it comes to sisters, it seems that one stays and one goes, one remains bound and the other is set free. She is who she is in good part because of who Gloria isn't. In order to be herself, in order to be different from her sister, she had to take what was left over, the opposite, unchosen road. She is both glad and furious about this.

"The horse was easier!" Ellen says. There is a trickle of sweat by her temple, brought on by nerves and heat, but her eyes are bright and excited. "I never thought I'd say *that*."

"You are doing beautifully. Stay calm. Watch the ditch!

Next, the Grand Prix!" Veronica grips the seat edge. She looks pale.

Veronica may be right about Ellen's next venture, because Ellen hits the accelerator so hard that they go shooting off, and even Veronica screams. "Slow down, slow down!" she says.

Nash prays silently. She asks to be forgiven for all her sins and her uncharitable thoughts, especially about her sister. It's not Gloria's fault that Nash is stuck on the ranch. This is her own choice. This is who she is. She has always been more like Alice than like their father, Carlyle, who was known for his occasional rash acts, a spin of the roulette wheel, a fast ride in bad weather, the buying of a ranch against his wife's better judgment.

"A car is coming!" Ellen squeals. She veers to the side of the road so abruptly, it's only luck that prevents them from barreling into the gully. Nash feels bad for poor Jemima, who has another lesson with Ellen tomorrow; she hopes Ellen shows more calm and restraint with that old girl. Animals are saints, with what they put up with.

The car steadily approaching them—it doesn't belong here; Nash knows immediately that this is serious. She can feel the threat right there in that place under the breastbone, where every living being likely senses a predator. A ditch, a new driver—that's nothing. The car is a shiny black Cadillac convertible, and its top is down. It has white-walled tires and a silver hood ornament in the shape of a flying lady, a goddess with wings. There are red leather seats, too. A man in a suit and a straw fedora is driving, and another man, in casual shirtsleeves and a panama hat, sits in the passenger seat.

Nash looks over her shoulder toward the house, which she can't quite see from here. She sends a silent message to Lilly. *Stay where you are,* she pleads.

"Shut off the engine. Now," Veronica snaps. She's calm but firm. She understands what's happening, too. This car has driven under the tall arch of the Tamarosa sign, and it is on their property, and Veronica and Nash both know who that man is. That's no hired private investigator that can be scared off with a little arm-waving; that's the monster himself.

Nash is out of the car and onto the road. She has her hands on her hips. Later, she'll recognize how silly she must have looked to them, a powerless girl, but right now she realizes she's even more like Alice than she ever thought. Her hands feel like Alice's hands, and her hips feel like Alice's hips.

The Cadillac rolls to a stop. It is so black and shiny and expensive that it has no business being in the desert. It's the same as the minks Veronica wore when she first arrived, and the same as the patent-leather valise of Mr. Jonathan Jakes, one of the few men they'd had at the ranch. Clearly, those things are not from here. Here, the only things that are black and shiny and fast and sleek are the horses, especially the mustangs.

The driver steps out while the second man stays in the car. Of course he stays in the car, and his arm even rests on the window ledge, as if he is enjoying a summer afternoon. The driver walks toward them. He removes his hat and holds it to his chest in some gallant gesture that feels demeaning and hostile. Why this innocent gesture is plainly not innocent is hard to say. Maybe it is the smirk playing about the man's mouth and the self-satisfied gleam of his shoes. His hair is black and greased back. He has a blunt chin and small rodent eyes, but he has large, ring-less hands, with stubby, cigar-like fingers.

"How can we help you?" Veronica asks. She's next to Nash, with her arms folded against her checked shirt, which is tucked tidily into her slacks. This should be Nash's line, but it appears that Veronica has come from her own lineage of women with backbones of iron.

"Looking for a cowboy," the man says. "You got cowboys out here, I take it."

"We've got plenty of cowboys," Nash says. Even her voice sounds like Alice's.

"I only need this one," the man says. He reaches into the breast pocket of his suit jacket and hands over a folded newspaper page. It's Jack riding Little Britches, who died not long after, a terrible death, thrashing and biting at her stomach after she got colic. Little Britches is nearly off the ground in the photo, leaping into the air, and Jack looks cocky on her. It was taken at the Washoe County Roundup last year.

"Never seen him," Nash says.

Veronica lets out a low whistle. "Handsome fella. I'd have remembered that one."

Nash's heart is beating hard in her chest. It feels the way thundering hooves sound.

"It says he works here. Tamarosa Ranch. This *is* Tamarosa Ranch."

"Of course," Nash says. "But we don't have that horse, either."

"Small-town hacks," Veronica says. "With small-town newspapers."

"Right," the man says. He folds the newspaper page again and puts it back into his jacket.

"Let's get out of here," the man in the passenger seat says. "I don't have time for this."

It's over, Nash thinks, a thought that always tempts fate, and this is when she hears the *slap-slap* of shoes behind her, the sound of someone running. It's Lilly, who has wandered up the road to watch Ellen's progress and is now racing toward them—if *racing* is the right word—with her hand under Beanie, her lopsided self lurching forward.

"Stop," she yells. "Stuart, stop!"

Lilly is not close enough to hear or understand what is actually happening, that Stuart and the fat-fingered man are turning back. Her own history interprets what she sees: The man stands too close to Veronica; Nash's hands are on her hips; Stuart removes his arm from the window ledge of the car, disgusted, fed up. What she thinks will happen next is what usually happens next. Only she knows what he's capable of.

Lilly stops, out of breath. She meets Stuart's eyes. There's the *click-clatch* sound of the car door opening, the slam of it shutting. This is all so fast, Nash can only take in image flashes: the flap of Stuart's shirtsleeves, a scream, a hand grabbing the fabric of Lilly's dress, the muscles in Stuart Marcel's arm as he shoves, the sound of Lilly's bottom and the heels of her shoes and her palms skidding backward over gravel.

"Whore," he spits.

Veronica's face has changed. Her eyes are fierce, and her teeth are clenched. She resembles a cat in a fight. "Get out of here!" she snarls.

Stuart Marcel turns to face her. He's so close to Veronica that their noses nearly touch. Nash can hear them both breathing hard. It happens in seconds, too fast for Nash even to act. She will regret this later, the way she just stands and watches in shock. There is no response or plan or move to action on her part. There is only Veronica, holding his eyes, the muscle in her cheek twitching.

"If you lay a fucking hand on me, you will fucking live to regret it," she says.

He laughs.

It's the sort of derisive *heh-heh* that says she's not worth his trouble. With that chuckle and the brief flash of his teeth, Nash's mind finally begins to work, still only offering up wrong, useless ideas, ideas that flail and panic—the Savage Model 720 under the bed; a yell to the boys, who are too far away to hear; a visual plea to Ellen and Hadley, urging them to hit the accelerator and run the bastard down.

But Stuart is backing away from Veronica. *Look at that. He's retreating.* Likely he prefers less of an audience when he uses his muscle against someone half his size. He says, "Come on," to the fat-fingered man, who now watches from the sidelines as if it's just another tiresome playground scuffle. They both get in the Cadillac. Every move drips disdain. The fat-fingered man examines his watch. Stuart Marcel flicks a bit of dust from his shirtfront.

Lilly stays on the ground. No one moves. They watch the car reverse and then turn around. It kicks up all the mean dirt as it leaves. Rocks ping against the hubcaps. Those white-walled tires will be a mess by the time they make it back to Reno.

Nash's hands shake; her legs are shaking, too, as she helps Lilly up. The women look Lilly over. She has scrapes and scratches on the backs of her legs and her palms; there's blood and dirt where the skin has broken.

"Get in! For God's sake, get in!" Hadley shouts from the open window of the car. Ellen's eyes are large. She's still gripping the wheel. Nash can see Ellen's gold ring with the diamond chips on her left hand.

They do get in, Veronica in the front seat next to Ellen, Nash and Lilly in the back with Hadley. "Are you all right?" Hadley asks. "The baby?"

"Yes," Lilly says. "I think so."

"He's your garden-variety bully, that's all," Veronica says. But it's a lie, and they all know it. The first Mrs. Stuart Marcel, the whisper of her sad and furious ghost, is telling them so right now.

"I thought he was directing a film in Africa. Didn't you say he was in the Congo somewhere?" Ellen asks.

"He's supposed to be," Lilly says. Her voice is small. "I am so sorry."

"You're sorry? You're not the one who's supposed to be sorry," Hadley says.

"I am, though. I am."

"Isn't there a cigarette in here somewhere?" Veronica is rooting through her purse. "I need a cigarette." She slams the bag shut, lets out a low whistle of disbelief. It's an all-purpose disbelief, covering missing Chesterfields, as well as vicious men.

Nash's head hurts. She could almost cry. She wants to go into her room and bolt the door. She wants her mother. They sit in stunned silence for a while, watching a cloud of gnats just beyond the windshield. They spin like the neutrons and atoms in Nash's old science book.

"Get us home, Ellen," Veronica says. "Hell with the cigarette, I need a drink."

Ellen sets her glass down on a coaster decorated with a photo of the Cal Neva Resort. Hadley and Lilly have gone back to their cabins together, but Veronica and Ellen are nursing their mules.

"It's all in who you choose, isn't it?" Ellen says.

She's right. It's the bare fact of it. The people who come and go and come and go, all of the many, many people who walk up and back down the steps of the Washoe County Courthouse—they are mostly here because of a wrong move.

They've picked darkness over light, fiery demons over a calm heart. That's the trick: a good choice. It's the most basic thing that draws the line between plain old struggle and utter disaster. Yet there's just something in the way he tips his hat or stares her right in the eyes, something about her weakness or his coldness, that lures, that tugs at some deep, deep place. Some old place, some small piece of a person that makes the danger and darkness feel like a memory.

She keeps seeing that hand on Lilly's chest, shoving. It feels as if Stuart Marcel is still around, hovering. Likely for Lilly, he will always be hovering, her whole life long, even when he's gone for good. She let the monster in, and now only the monster will decide when he leaves.

Can Nash even judge bad choices and wrong love, though? She looks at Jack and none of it matters, the way he drinks too much, the way he held and kissed Lilly Marcel in the pool, even. She disregards the impossibility of it all, the certainty of catastrophe. Something about him compels her. When she sees Jack's hand gripping Zorro's reins, or when he drives too fast in bad weather—it is the ugly unease of danger that lures her, unfamiliar familiarity. This is what her mother would call *against one's better judgment*.

These things are always *against one's better judgment*. Somewhere, the women and the men always know better, but they make their choices anyway. They will tell you this later. They are under a deep, powerful spell that logic cannot begin to conquer. Fate pushes the story forward, and what is a story, anyway, without villains and miscreants, horrible wrong turns, and new days dawning.

The whole thing makes her furious. The women, the men, the court steps. That hand on Lilly's dress, shoving; the lurch, the landing that Beanie surely felt; naked figures in moonlight. The needless risks. Her own stupid heart most of all.

"Excuse me," Nash says.

She leaves Ellen and Veronica to their drinks. She heads outside, passes the Styleline Deluxe, which is now calmly parked in the driveway. She sees Cliff heading into the barn with Jemima, hears the dusky croon of his voice as he leads her. The pool ripples in the tender light of summer and early evening. None of this soothes the red rage she feels, though. She strides down the path, heads straight for Jack's log cabin.

She stomps up the steps, scaring a ground squirrel, which darts into the nearby bitterbrush. Jack's boots are set almost primly outside the door, as if this small, hot place is a temple in the Orient. Nash pounds on the door with her fist. "Open up! Open up this minute!"

"Jesus, Peanut." She hears this through the open window. "Don't flip your wig! Something better be on fire, is all I can say."

He opens the door. Only one button of his shirt is fastened, and he is zipping up his pants. Nash stands on her toes and looks over his shoulder to see if he's alone.

"No one is here, Peanut." His voice is stern. "What is it? I'm not expected at the house for another twenty minutes."

Nash pushes him aside. She's hardly ever even been in his cabin before; she brought him some food when he was sick once, and another time she came in to get a glass of water after helping him carry some firewood. There's a woodstove and a cabinet with a porcelain sink curved into it. His bed is narrow and unmade. Nash's imagination is adding details from another night—a mossy smell, a mix of sweetness and straining muscles—and she thinks she sees the shine of a rhinestone hair clip under the bed. She remembers that clip in Lilly's dark hair. She thinks of the round globe of her, rising from the water.

"What are you looking at with that face?" he asks. He follows her gaze to the spot under the bed, leans over to pick up a small silver money clip with a horseshoe on it, a gift from Alice a few years ago. "I was wondering where that went," he says.

"Stuart Marcel was here, and he was looking for you. What do you think you're doing, Jack?"

"He was here?"

"He drove up in his car. They had that article you were in, from the rodeo! Lilly saw him, and she came running. He shoved her down on the ground! Her and that baby, don't you forget! Right down, and you're lucky that's all he did! He's been checking up on you, obviously. Probably knows every bit about you now, Jack. A little picture of a midnight swim might make a man crazy, don't you think?"

Jack runs his hand through his hair.

"Don't you?"

He takes that money clip and tosses it to the bed, like he's skipping a stone. But when he looks at Nash again, she sees that he's distraught.

"Dear God," he says.

"Yeah, you better start getting on His good side, and fast."

"Stuart Marcel was here."

"Looking for you."

"It makes me think—"

"It's about time, is all I have to say."

"No, it makes me think of the mustangs. Walt over at Bob Watson's? He said there was this stud. Horse walked right up to Bob, gentle as can be, head down with his nose ready for a rub. And the minute Bob reached out, the stud rose on his back legs and lunged for his throat."

"Jesus, Jack."

"He's fine, you know. But, point is, there are all kinds of 'em, I'll tell you that."

This is the most infuriating story Nash has ever heard. She is so mad at him for telling it right now, she could spit. "Why would you get involved with her, Jack? Why? You're pouring gasoline on a fire!"

"Peanut, quit." Jack takes her arms. She hadn't even realized she's been pacing that room until he stops her. She feels like she might cry again. She's been feeling that a lot lately. He looks her deep in the eyes, and for a moment she thinks he might kiss her. "Lilly needs us," he says. "You said he shoved her? That's *nothing*. He loses his temper and goes crazy. Do you know why she was never in another film after *The Changelings*? He broke her arm. It was in a cast. No one would dare hire her. She can't walk down a street without him accusing her of looking at another man."

"Exactly! That is exactly what I am saying! Do you hear yourself? It makes no sense, Jack, that she'd tell him that baby was anyone's but his. She's just asking for trouble! That makes no sense at all. None."

"You're being naïve, Nash. I'm sorry, but you are. This is why I always beat you at backgammon. You don't think far enough ahead. How can she be free of him for good? If he knows that baby is his, he'll be in their lives forever. It's fury now for freedom later. It's a good plan. Better than no plan."

Nash yanks away from him. "And you and her. Is that a good plan?"

"Nash, come on. That's my private business."

"As long as no one ends up killed in the process, it's your private business."

"She's one of ours. She came to us," Jack says.

"You're one of ours. You came to us."

"I'm a grown man. I can take care of myself." He averts his gaze from hers, turns suddenly at a strange noise—but it's only that squirrel, which has now climbed out to the end of a far branch, causing it to dip and scrape against the roof.

Nothing seems clear after all, not good choices or bad ones, not men or horses or even the reasons for her own rage. The only obvious thing is that Jack Waters is in the deep dark heart of his own struggle, pulled toward fragile wrists and delicate cheekbones, drawn to a woman, maybe, but even more to an idea of himself.

She should call Alice. Right this minute. Nash should let her know what is going on, beg her to come back. But she can't and won't call. Nash can feel her own reluctance as strong as an actual hand yanking her back. She is in the deep dark heart of her own struggle.

These are the matters of the heart that have been battling for eons, Nash thinks with spitting fury, as she watches Jack bend his head to finish buttoning his shirt. Ever since the first fierce crash of the atom against atom that created us. Protection and vulnerability. Capability and the luscious descent into another's strength. Yours versus mine. Hunger and reason. Violence and love. This is what Nash understands right now, as Jack Waters loops his belt through his pants and fastens it: All living beings are conceived with some degree of passion and intensity and confused desires, and then are left to figure it all out from there, using their own sorry devices.

"Your stupid boots are outside," she says to him, as he hunts under the bed.

chapter 14

Callie

Clearly, my car was not meant for the kinds of roads out there. It hit a rut in the ground, and I could see the hood bounce. That car was a pampered urban vehicle, familiar only with the occasional city pothole and my own inept reversing up the curb of the Victrola Café. I couldn't explain my presence out in that dry, vast wilderness right then, even to myself. But I felt my own keenness as strong as an actual hand pushing me forward.

Out there were gopher holes and grouse. I bumped past several Joshua trees, and barrel cactuses dotted the ground like sharp, unpleasant little ottomans. At home, there were tall, sulky evergreens and clouds fat with rain, roofs still slick and green from winter, and crows on telephone lines.

The air conditioner blasted. My camera rode in the passenger seat. I wasn't sure exactly how I'd gotten so far from home or why I'd done what I just did—left my own message to Thomas, an answer to his now tense and worried ones. I was the one who needed time to think.

My reasons for staying at the ranch were becoming both more steadfast and further away. Nearly two weeks ago now, I'd tossed my clothes in a bag and filled Hugo's water bowl. The leftovers that had been in the fridge had certainly gone bad, if Thomas hadn't already thrown them away. The mail would be stacking up. My pots of flowers would need watering. I had bought a new pair of sandals that I hadn't even worn yet, and they were likely still where I'd left them on the floor of the closet.

Maybe Thomas and his crisis had just made me weary, but I wasn't sure I cared about any of it. It all made me tired. The sloping floor did, and the laundry Amy left behind before she went on her trip, and the yard, and our neighbors (especially the spying Mrs. Radish), and the garbage collection on Wednesdays. Christmas—right there: It seemed more than I could bear. How weighty was a tree with its wet needles dragged across the carpet, and a search for a parking space in the crowded mall lot, and a stout, frozen turkey in the shopping cart.

The same holiday recipes, the same high-thread-count sheets I'd bought years ago, the same arguments with the same words, the same creak in the same spot in the hall, which I heard every day—well, I was never one to read a book twice or watch a movie more than once, but somewhere along the line, my personal-life button had gotten stuck on rewind. I was the one-woman version of the poor old Rolling Stones, who had to sing "Gimme Shelter" over and over again.

I didn't know how long I'd felt this way or even that I felt this way at all. But now it made me wonder if I had made an actual choice about the way I lived or if I had only drifted to it, riding along like a seed on a gust of wind. Settling into the ground where it landed because that's simply where it ended up.

I have a confession, Shaye said the other night. *Do you remember when Mom was with Gene and we used to go get McDonald's and eat it in the back of the car?*

Yeah.

I used to eat my fries really slowly, just so you wouldn't have any left and I would.

I know.

You knew that?

Of course. Why do you think I read all the time? So I could ignore you.

You always ate yours so fast, she said.

It sounds crazy, I realize, but moments of clarity can arrive like this, through French fries or a song or a heel broken from a shoe.

Shaye?

What?

How many French fries have we eaten without even tasting them?

Thank God, I had a sister who understood me. *Too many, Cal,* she said. *Way, way too many.*

I turned on my car radio, but the only station I could get was that damn KEXP with Dr. Yabba Yabba Love. *You wanna be someone's nurse, work in a hospital.* I snapped it off. I suppose it was a good thing I'd never been that great at following directions involving street numbers and roads going east or west and that I'd always needed a Shell station, or some billboard landmark, because it was fairly easy to find the place where we'd last seen the horses. I remembered the saguaro that looked like a frightening, lethal penis and the two hills that formed a perfect *M*.

I parked way back from the area, same as Kit Covey had, but there were no horses to be seen. Of course, they wouldn't have just been waiting there, the same broad neck leaning to take the same drink, as if we'd never left. Things don't wait for you. Kit had said that the mustangs traveled over miles and miles of land. Still, I was rewarded. A large tortoise ambled wearily past, as if he carried the entire weight of history and human error on his wrinkled shoulders.

I doubted my phone would work out there, but I reached into my purse anyway and unzipped the pocket where I had placed Kit Covey's business card. He picked up on the second ring. I had plenty of faulty ideas about the desert.

"Callie?"

"Hey! How did you know?"

"Unfamiliar area code. It was either you or some credit-card company. You're not offering me a special zero percent interest for six months, are you?"

"Do you need it? I can't give you that, but I could lend you a twenty."

He laughed. "I think I've got it covered."

"I was actually calling to ask if you knew where the mustangs are. I was going to take a few pictures."

It was loud where he was—there was clanging, and someone shouted something I couldn't quite hear. "Just a minute!" he said, not to me. It was muffled, his hand over the receiver.

"You're busy," I said.

"That headache is not going anywhere, trust me," he said. "The horses . . . Well, this is where I give the public-safety announcement. Promise me you'll keep your distance. You don't want to spook them. They can be dangerous."

"Okay."

"Remember where they were when we saw them?"

"I'm there now."

"Okay, great. Do you see that cactus? The one that looks like a giant . . ."

I started laughing. "Yeah. Hard to miss."

"From there, head toward town. Maybe three, four miles. You'll see a ravine that'll stop you from going farther. Drive south, and they'll likely be right around there. You've got to be careful, though, right? Sometimes those studs—they can be unpredictable."

"That's what all the foxy chicks say," I said. I thought the word *stud* had vanished along with Chevy vans and crocheted ponchos, but here it was, alive all along in this world.

He tossed me a *pretty mama*, and I flung him a *boogie on down*, and then we hung up.

The ravine was deep and clearly visible, and I drove alongside it until I saw the horses. Even though I'd set out for that purpose, their presence was startling. I took Kit's warning to heart, because they were larger than I remembered and there were so many of them, and the whole idea of me there alone, without Kit, seemed like folly. They were stunning and romantic, yes, but I had that uneasy animal feeling, the one you get at the zoo after you've just turned your back to that gorilla, whose watchful eyes had let you know he could break your neck with a single Naugahyde hand. The horses didn't look at me, but their own eyes were manic and their tails stringy. They were an entire street corner of scary men shouting that the end of the world was coming. They were beautiful and dirty, alluring and repelling, a reminder that nothing is ever one thing, as much as you wish it.

I stayed in my car and took pictures from my half-open window; I focused on thick haunches and muscular necks, knobby knees that didn't look capable of supporting the weight they carried. From there, I could hear snorts and the thrum in their throats and the scrape of hooves on ground. Two foals hung by their mothers' sides like shy kindergartners on the first day of school. The truth was, they were wild animals, and I was invading their privacy.

I was about to head back to where I belonged, when my

phone rang. "If I don't get myself a cheeseburger soon, I may just fire my gun at the next innocent cholla I see," Kit Covey said.

"That is not the kind of land management we're looking for," I said.

"Can you meet me at Rudy's?"

"If onion rings are part of this plan, then yes."

"I can assure you, Ms. McBride, I never met an onion ring I didn't very nearly propose to."

I'd reached the paved road when something odd happened. My tires slid sideways. It felt like no mechanical failure I'd ever experienced—more like a mysterious magnetic force, a god or alien yanking the tablecloth but leaving the place settings in-tact. I wished for another motorist, someone to lock eyes with to confirm what just happened, but no one else was on the road. If some glowing disc appeared in the sky to haul me off to another planet, it'd be my good fortune. I could use a story to sell, what with my daughters' college tuitions.

"Did you feel the earthquake?" Kit Covey asked, after we'd handed back the plastic-covered menus to the waitress. This was the second time I'd sat across a table from him, though this time the lights were bright and the seats a squeaky red vinyl. Someone's lost napkin was down by my foot, and I kicked it away.

"So that's what that was. I've felt them in Seattle, but every-thing shakes. Here, the whole ground seemed to shift."

"We've got fault lines all over. The Pacific plates meet the North American plates here." He placed the edges of his hands together, creating a flat surface. "Geological accommodation zone."

It was funny how familiar he was beginning to seem. I was getting used to his face, the wrinkles around his bright-blue eyes, and the tousle of his brownish-blond hair, sprinkled with gray. He was familiar but not enough to quell my nerves. Every word out of my mouth or out of his, every gesture, even a sip from my Coke, had a pitched awareness, an energy. "I'm a geological accommodation zone," I said.

"Yeah?"

"Lately, yeah. Shifting with the tremors that come along."

"Shifting gets exhausting. Let me tell you."

"It does."

"Sometimes, though . . . what else is there to do but shift, right?"

"Right."

"You have to."

"Yep." I twisted my purse strap around my finger.

Kit turned the saltshaker in a small circle. Out beyond the window was the tall sign, Rudy's, that rose high above the desert, and across the street there was an old Mobil station, which still had the winged horse riding its roof. I wanted to cry. I don't know why, except that something seemed wholly decided, decided by me, and my heart felt crushed. It wasn't just those wide strong shoulders in that soft denim shirt or those hands—and, dear God, I'm sorry, how much I wanted them on me—but it was also the *way* I wanted. I hadn't wanted anything like that in a long, long time. As the waitress topped off our barely touched water glasses, I felt I was saying no to much more than Kit Covey—I was saying no to something that had been exposed when I was cracked open out here, maybe from that first moment I thought I heard thunder. Still. Thomas deserved my loyalty. And I deserved to be the kind of person who would give it. He might yank that quilt over his half of the bed when he was angry, but, most often, that quilt covered us both.

Our food arrived. The onion rings were fried heaven, and I polished off that burger. There was something in the desert atmosphere that made you so, so hungry. Kit passed me the napkins and talked about his daughter and laughingly admitted a joke that Steve Miller and Lorraine had played on him. I told him about Shaye and that tractor and about the April Fools' Day when Amy put every stuffed animal they ever owned in Melissa's car in the high school parking lot. We discussed whether anyone ever needed to really wait for anything anymore. He confessed a fear of dying young and told me about his old horse, Mack, who got ill and bucked him. I told me about Hugo. He asked if I had a picture, and I showed him, and my eyes misted up when he said what a fine dog he was.

"Do you know where we are?" he asked.

"Rudy's? Is this a trick question?"

He smiled. "No. Out here. It's called Dog Valley."

This pleased me to no end. We paid our bill and stood by our cars; a truck whipped past, and the noise roared in my ears and blew my hair around. Kit looked at me, and I looked back. He pulled a strand of my hair from my mouth, where it had caught.

"You have one more minute?"

"Sure. I've got nothing but minutes." It was a lie. Lately I'd realized just how many had passed and how few I had left.

"Follow me."

We climbed through a hedge of sage behind Rudy's, and Kit trotted off. I kept up, running behind him, though it was hot and I could feel that heat pressing right through the cotton of my shirt. Everywhere you looked, there was only desert and more desert. You could get so lost out there.

"Right up here," he called over his shoulder. Shaye would have accused me of watching his ass, but anyone would have watched.

I saw where we were heading, what he wanted to show me. It was a deep scar in the ground, a long, endless crack that looked nothing if not purposeful. It was two or three feet across and many yards down, exposing strata, layers of color.

"Wow," I said.

"This is a small fault. Can you believe it? It doesn't even have a name. These things? Some of 'em go for miles. Some are fifty to sixty million years old."

"It goes on forever!"

"Miles and miles."

It was shocking and dramatic, and I felt a childlike delight at seeing it. "So far down!"

"The ruptures, they almost always follow preexisting lines. Zones of weakness, they're called. Stress and strain is basically what it is."

"Damn! My camera is in the car."

"Think you'll be able to remember it without a picture? Here?" He tapped his temple with his finger, grinned.

We stood very close together, hard rock beneath our feet, heat bearing down.

"When I close my eyes," I said. And I closed them then. I felt sixteen again, soaring, that way you do when your whole life is ahead of you. He might kiss me. But when I opened my eyes, he was only looking at me, happy.

"Incredible?"

"Incredible." Incredible and majestic. Dramatic and unreal. You knew logically that the earth was a living thing, but the very ground beneath your feet, the ground you counted on for stability and structure—it was beautifully and terrifyingly temperamental. It could break apart even as it held you in place, and here was proof.

"Look what I got!" Shaye called from the stairs, before appearing in the living room, wearing a new denim skirt and a sleeveless Western top with pearl buttons. She had a new pair of boots on, too. She turned so we could admire her.

"I see what you've been doing all day. Nice shopping, little buckaroo," I said. She looked adorable in her ponytail. I got comfy in the leather chair by the piano. Tex settled by my feet.

Nash, who was stretched out on the couch, smiled. "That's just what the girls used to do. We'd take them into Reno. Get them outfitted in Western wear."

"The women who came to the ranch?" I asked.

"They loved the getups! A lot of them thought there'd be Indians out here, like in the movies," she chuckled. "It was the first time many of them had even been out West. Most of them were thrilled! Some hated it, of course—they'd leave early, in a huff, as if we'd planned the dust and what the heat did to their hair, just to make them miserable. But the rest, they came to love it. The slowed pace, the fun, the companionship. The food! After their six weeks were up, when they told the judge they were residents and planned to stay in Nevada, well, they were sincere. They never did stay, not a one I knew of. But I do believe that when they said it, most of them meant it."

"What would they do all that time?" I asked. "Six weeks out here . . ."

"Oh, sit by the pool, ride horses, dance, drink, gamble. Sometimes we'd take them on an overnight trail ride or to the rodeo. In the early days, they liked to ride on the old steam train, the Virginia and Truckee—it looked straight out of the movies. Winters, we'd play a lot of backgammon or take them skiing. Trips to Reno, shopping, the bars. Meetings with lawyers. We'd go to Tahoe, see a show. Talked! God, how everyone talked and gossiped! Though some kept to themselves. Some brought their mothers."

Shaye poured us drinks as a pot roast simmered in the oven, and Nash took a sip and then crunched a melting ice cube. Honestly, it was way too hot for a pot roast and I'd had a week's worth of beef for lunch, but Shaye was determined to use that old cookbook she'd found.

"I can't believe how we never hear about any of this," Shaye said. "Why don't you guys ever talk about it? Mom barely says anything about that time."

"Well, your mother left when she was young. She hated it out here. I left, too, but only for a short while. To go to school. I couldn't stay away, though. Anyway, who wants to hear their parents' old stories? I didn't want to hear mine. And in many ways, it was a painful time. Divorce wasn't like it is now. Women were ashamed. People were hurting. Every kind of hurt. Absent husbands, mental cruelty, meddling in-laws, brutality. Some women never left their rooms. Some went a little wild, wearing casual clothes for the first time, tasting alcohol—"

"Sleeping with cowboys," Shaye said.

Nash rolled her eyes. "In spite of the fun we had—and, God, did we—it was still heartbreaking. Every trip to the courthouse. Every one."

"We still feel ashamed when we get divorced," Shaye said. "I do. Did. Really ashamed."

"Not that kind of shame."

"Like a failure," Shaye said.

"Not that kind of a failure. A woman back then? *He* was what she *was*. It was all *him, him, him*. If you lost him? Couldn't keep him? If he treated you bad? It said everything about you. What you were worth." She shook her head. "We had the occasional career girl but not many. Hollywood types. A playwright, once. We couldn't imagine a life like that. She was a curiosity to us."

"Jack Waters. He's the one I'm still curious about," Shaye said. We were both holding out hope that Nash's actions had a purpose, in spite of the evidence to the contrary. We were still wishing for old, broken love, love lost, instead of so much else gone.

"Jack, Jack, Jack," Nash said. "All you two talk about."

"Well, you got pretty emotional when his letter came," I said.

"He was our head wrangler, that's all. I didn't get emotional because I heard from Jack. I got emotional because I heard from the *past*."

The phone rang. Nash sat up. "Is that my cell?"

"Kitchen phone," I said. "Want me to get it?"

But she'd already risen and was heading out, bringing her drink with her. She'd become awfully fond of the stuff since we'd arrived.

"Think we should cut her back on the booze?" Shaye asked, reading my mind. "She hasn't been that chatty since we got here."

"Probably not the best thing for her, but at this point she should be able to do what she wants, don't you think?"

"I tried to get her in that car today."

"You didn't tell me."

"Didn't have the chance. You should have seen her, Cal. It was weird. It reminded me of Joshie when he went through his fear-of-dogs phase. He wanted to like them so badly, but they scared him to death. She wanted me to teach her, but she was practically shaking. She wouldn't even get behind the wheel."

"If you hadn't driven in sixty years, you'd be scared, too."

"It was more than that. I'm telling you, it was strange."

Being eighty would be strange. Being eighty and learning how to drive again, even stranger. From my place in the living room, even without being able to distinguish what was being said, I could tell Nash was talking to our mother. Gloria probably felt left out with all of us there. Nash's voice had turned snappish. There were bites and edges in her tone, the hills and valleys of pitch that meant long-held grudges and reluctant devotion.

"She's talking to Mom," I said.

Shaye ignored this. "It's *still* about *him*, Cal. Too often, it still is."

"*Him. Her.*"

"I guess so. I guess we all do it. Don't you think women still do it more, though, as much as we don't want to admit it? What about all those successful women you see, married to some loser they have to take care of? Some pothead who can't keep a job? I drank this too fast," she said. She was a tipsy little cowgirl. Neither of us ever drank much in our real lives. The occasional glass of wine was it for me.

"I tend to think people are people, I guess," I said.

"You know what? I'm coming to the conclusion that this place has done its job for me. I gotta go home."

"*Home?*" My voice betrayed me. It was shrill and panicked, relaying things I'd rather not have anyone know, not even Shaye.

"I don't want to go. I'm dreading it. But I can't stay away forever. We may never know the shame those women felt, but

I tell you, I have a good lot of my own. I mean, Cal, I've been divorced twice. *Twice.* I can't even tell people that. I erase the marriage in the middle! Isn't that horrible?"

"Quentin," I said, as if his name alone told the whole story. "I swear, he put a spell on you and took you captive."

"That's exactly what it felt like, but it doesn't matter. Eric's daughters—God, it's so hard. But this time I've picked a mostly good guy, you know? Finally. It's actually *possible* to make it. This is my last chance at relationship redemption."

"I hate to tell you, but redemption is a lousy reason to stay."

"Believe me, I've stayed before for way worse reasons. That one sounds pretty good."

I could hear Nash in the kitchen, her voice sounding as high-pitched and effortful as a chain saw cutting through stubborn wood. Both of us were shrill, with matched anxiety ratcheting up. I don't know what I expected. Of course Shaye and I couldn't remain at the ranch forever, cradled by the past, held in our limbo by the force of days gone by. "If you go home, I think I have to go home."

"That's ridiculous," Shaye said. "You can stay however long you want. But I can't justify it anymore. We're going to have to come back, too, when her health gets worse. I mean, she's got Harris. She's not acting right, but she doesn't seem like a danger to herself. We probably don't need to do anything yet."

"She bought a car she can't drive! She rode a tractor all the way into town!"

I was being selfish, and I was fully aware of that. I just didn't want Shaye to go. I was the one who walked her to school on her first day, who gave her my lunch when hers got stolen, and who helped her pick a dress for a dance I didn't even go to. She stayed on our couch after her first divorce, with Joshie and Emma on blow-up mattresses in the girls' rooms. But I needed her now.

"I feel like we have unfinished business here," I said. It was the best I could do.

"I'm not ready to go home, either. But business is always unfinished, Cal."

I sat silent, but she was right. Our real lives waited. It was time to face Thomas.

"What is that noise?" Shaye said.

"What noise?" It was hard to hear much of anything over the roiling of my own confusion.

"Sounds like rustling."

"Maybe it's the mustangs again."

"Man, I hope not. Those things are terrifying. Have you noticed how dark it is out here? Darker than regular dark. It makes me nervous."

"You're just feeling weird after that earthquake. Pull the curtains," I said.

"She always leaves them open! Why does she do that? It gives me the creeps. I feel like someone's staring in."

"Then close them. She won't mind."

Shaye wedged herself behind the piano, reached up to yank the drapes shut. And then she screamed. A glass-shard, high-altitude cry of fear that caused Tex to fly to his feet and bark like mad.

"Shaye!" I was on my feet, too. Whatever it was, I wanted the nearest exit.

Nash had ditched our mother on the phone and was now in the living room, looking fierce enough to tackle an intruder. "Is everyone all right?"

Shaye's hand was to her chest. "Oh, my God." Her voice quavered.

"Tex, *shush*!" He was whining with urgency, his nose to the glass. I tucked him under my arm. Someone had to handle this. I was afraid to look out that window, but I knew I had to. When I did, I saw two green glowing eyes looking right into mine, and I screamed, too.

"Girls!" Nash said. "Stop! My goodness! That's just Rob!"

Who knew the buffalo had a name? "Rob?"

"He's completely harmless. Shoo, Rob," she yelled. She clapped her hands and waved her arms. "He's just a busybody, same as the two of you."

Shaye cowered in a corner of the room. She clutched a pillow from the couch, proving that we McBride sisters both feared the wrong things and always looked to useless places for protection. "Jesus, he almost gave me a heart attack! Get him away from here."

"Go on, Rob," Nash yelled.

"Git, Rob," I said. I pounded on the glass, but that window was even closer than I wanted to be to the creature. "We don't want you here."

He turned, large and slow, and then ambled away. That old buffalo seemed as dejected as big Tommy DelFonso in the second grade, when April Barker and I told him he couldn't play with us.

Nash sighed and rubbed her temple with her fingertips. She didn't look very well. Her skin seemed the wrong color, the yellow of a healing bruise. "Are you all right, Nash?" I asked.

"I'm just exhausted. I think I might go lie down."

"Everything okay with Gloria?" Shaye said.

"She's trying to talk me into a condo in California."

Nash made her way down the hall and up the stairs oh so slowly, holding that bannister with a tight grip.

"Dinner will be ready soon," Shaye called after her. "Will you join us, or should I bring you a plate?"

"I need a little rest. I'll eat later."

In the kitchen, Shaye shut the curtains. She pulled out that pot roast with an oven mitt that had seen better days. We sat at the large wood table, just Shaye and me, with enough food to feed several ranch hands and divorcées. The pot roast was delicious, and handsome enough to make the cover of any *Good Housekeeping* magazine from the childhood we never had.

"Neapolitan ice cream for dessert," she said. "Dibs on the chocolate."

I'd eaten so much, I could barely move. I had started to clear the dishes when Nash appeared in the doorway. She held the frame with one hand. In the other, she held a blood-soaked towel.

"Something's wrong," she said.

chapter 15

Nash

"Something's wrong," Hadley says.

Nash stops stroking Bluebell's nose, and although Bluebell nudges her hand so she'll start again, Nash jumps down from the ring fence, where she's been waiting for Mrs. Shumley. The old ox probably can't get her stockings over her fat legs, and now they're going to be late for her appointment with Fred Cox, the Reno lawyer Nash dislikes the most. He has yellow teeth and calls her "sweetheart." Every time Nash has been there, half of a pastrami sandwich sits on his desk on a square of waxed paper, making the room smell like tired meat and mustard.

"Plumbing problems again?" This is always a safe guess when something is amiss. Bluebell gives up on the idea of more nuzzling and begins to trot. She's in a good mood, unusually relaxed and happy. Her tail bounces as she prances in a circle, her feet *clip-clopping*.

"It's Lilly."

There's a slam in Nash's chest. "What's happened?"

"We need to call a doctor. There's been a little . . ." Hadley is reluctant to say it. The word is indelicate. "Bleeding."

"Oh, no," Nash says. "That fall?" It's been days since Stuart Marcel was at the ranch, but this is her first thought.

"No, no. Not likely from that, not now. I don't think this is even any cause for alarm, but we best be sure."

Nash is already jogging ahead. Hadley tries to keep up with her, urging her to slow down, suggesting that this is likely nothing, but this is no time to take chances. Nash races up the porch steps and into the kitchen. She calls Doc Henry Bolger, who promises he will be on his way after he is finished with Mrs. May Sortie over at Flying W, who's having palpitations. Dr. Bolger has been at the ranch many times, when Gloria was sure her appendix had burst after a particularly spicy meal and when Mrs. Lee Gilvey broke her leg after falling from old Stormy. They saw him frequently when Gina Francesca was a guest, since she was perpetually injured or dying for attention. But Alice has always been there during a medical emergency.

Alice will not be there every time Nash needs her, she reminds herself. Alice is there every time Gloria does, but Nash does not want to be Gloria. Gloria dreams of men who lean down to cup a hand around hers when lighting her cigarettes, men who shout out compliments across a busy city street. Gloria thinks that sucking the alcohol from the maraschino cherry in her drink and checking her reflection in her compact is bigger than this, bigger than acting as a desert midwife, bringing women from one life to another.

"I'm sure it's just . . . I don't know," Hadley confesses, as they now hurry toward the cabins. "What would I know about having a baby."

The poolside is empty. The door to Avalon is open. Nash can hear the clatter of voices before they reach the steps. Veronica is in there already, and Ellen, too.

"Ellen's arrived," Veronica announces when they walk in.

"Doc Bolger is coming," Nash says.

"Ellen says this isn't unusual in the later weeks."

"She should just rest a little with her legs up." Ellen has finally found her area of expertise. Her chin is raised, and her voice is clipped with authority. She pats Lilly's suitcase, which has been covered in towels and is now under Lilly's knees.

"Everything seems fine," Lilly says. "And Beanie is turning circles like an Olympic gymnast." Her hands are folded sweetly above the covers. She wears a lilac satin nightgown. Right there—those are the delicate, feminine things that Jack wants, things fragile enough to protect. With Nash's strong shoulders and stubborn head, her own capability—lilac satin pajamas would seem ludicrous on her.

"It's not uncommon for this to happen when there's been . . . a little too much . . ." Ellen's hands are suddenly busy, loose in the air around her as she searches for the right word. "Excitement."

Veronica snickers.

"Things sometimes . . ." Ellen tidies up the nightstand, arranging the water glass and the box of Kleenex. She makes the cloth Little Lulu doll sit upright again against the wall. "Become more . . . delicate. In the later weeks. Womanly . . . parts."

Nash has no idea what becomes more delicate and how, but she knows by the look on Veronica's face that this has to do with Jack and sex and Lilly's round, ripe body. She's upset all over again. First there was that swim and those pictures, and now this. How could they take such risks with the baby? She can't imagine anything like what they're suggesting while Beanie is right there, practically watching.

"Sometimes there's just too much said," Lilly says. She sets her hand on Nash's arm. The gesture asks forgiveness. Lilly is as pretty as a note of music, with her eyes especially vivid against the hue of that satin nightgown, and her cheeks flushed pink under the sheet Ellen has insisted she be tucked under even in this heat. Lilly's softness and that curved lump of her—it does Nash right in. Lilly is too lovely to be mad at. Nash's anger collapses in on itself, like a poorly made cake, and relief takes its place. If Lilly and Beanie are all right, as Ellen says, that's all that matters.

"Too much unsaid, I think," Hadley says. "It's positively Victorian."

"You're such a modern woman," Veronica teases. Thanks to Ellen's expert prognosis, they're all feeling it—the giddiness that comes after a false alarm.

"Don't get wise with me, sweetie," Hadley says.

"I am going to spank the both of you right here in public if you keep up this bickering," Ellen says.

"Please," Veronica says, winking.

When Dr. Bolger comes, they all leave and gather by the side of the pool, waiting for him to finish with Lilly. Nash should make sure that Danny got the message she left with Cook about driving Mrs. Shumley to Reno, but there's no way she'll chance missing the doctor.

Veronica pulls several deck chairs together, and they scrape against the cement in a way that makes Hadley's palms fly to her ears. Ellen sits down on one and sighs, as if she's had a hard day's work. Hadley slips off her shoes and rolls up the cuffs of her trousers to her knees. She sits at the edge of the pool and puts her feet in. "I can't stand the sight of blood," she says. She swirls one foot in a circle.

"Weren't you a nurse before the whole writing thing?" Veronica asks.

"A nurse! I could never be a nurse."

"During the war."

"I was wife to a creative genius during the war. That was my contribution."

"You're thinking of Mrs. Loughton. She left just after you and Hadley came," Nash says. Veronica is remembering the story Mrs. Loughton told, of being in the Philippines and hiding under the surgery bench when a bomb dropped. Mrs. Loughton had made the whistling noise of the bomb with her teeth, but Veronica had already had a couple of mules by then.

"Well, I guess I was a nurse of sorts," Hadley says.

Nash listens to the *shlump-ump* of the pool-filter door opening and closing.

They wait for Hadley to say more, but Nash doesn't expect her to. Hadley is curiously protective of the great Joseph Bernal, even if Nash has heard her occasionally say that he stole her best lines.

But then she does say more. "Every day, when he'd just lie in bed, I was a nurse. I'd coax him up. I'd feed him soup. I bandaged his wrists myself when he tried to slice them open with a letter opener."

Ellen, in the chair next to Nash, covers her mouth with her hand. They are all silent until Veronica finally says, "A letter opener? Was he intent on failing?"

Hadley's back is still to them. Beside her, her sandals point in opposite directions. She nods, as if it is she and the pool that are having the conversation. "Better believe it," she says. "He was always intent on failing! Of course, by then I'd hidden all the real knives."

Ellen lets out the kind of sound that an animal makes when injured. Nash feels the same—as if she's been suddenly bruised.

"I loved his archness. He was so witty and sharp-tongued! To the point of cruelty sometimes. But cynicism was just ego masking insecurity."

"Nothing makes a person meaner," Veronica says.

"I am feeling mighty lucky that all I had was a plain old philanderer," Ellen says. She doesn't mean to be funny, but it is somehow perfect and hilarious. They are all laughing. Nash, too, and even Hadley herself. Veronica is chortling so hard, she holds up her hand as if to say, *Stop, no more*, and Hadley has faced them again and her eyes are watering. "Oh, darlings," she manages to say.

Nash carries Lilly's suitcase. Veronica has gathered a few loose items, shoes and a cardigan and a book, *Under the Volcano*, which Lilly had on the dresser. This is more proof that Lilly is the sort of woman Nash wishes she was but could never be— Nash tried to read that book but couldn't manage it.

Ellen decides Little Lulu is coming along, and her tight black curls and red dress flop under Ellen's arm as they accompany Lilly back to the house. Dr. Bolger has announced that Lilly is fine, that she should just rest a little with her feet up, that this sometimes happens when there's been too much . . . excitement. Their shared diagnosis will cause Ellen to be nearly intolerable for the rest of the day.

As she carries that suitcase, Nash's insides crawl with guilt and failure. Dr. Bolger had made himself clear—how anyone ever allowed a woman in Lilly's delicate condition to reside in one of the cabins was beyond him. It shouldn't have mattered how much she insisted. Alice was going to be furious that Nash let her have her way. She watches Lilly, the curved profile that is Beanie. If anything happened to the baby, she would never forgive herself.

Lilly shakes off Ellen, who tries to take her elbow. Instead, she links her fingers with Nash's; they are cool and thin and soft. It's another gesture that fells her. Lilly and Beanie—they take her right down. Who could fault Lilly, really, for seeking

refuge with Jack? Jack has taken on mad bulls with red murderous eyes, and what a comfort that would be. *She's one of
ours*, he said. Yes. She and Beanie both are, yet neither Nash
nor Jack has done the right thing to keep them safe. She made
a bad decision about the cabin, but Jack made a much worse
and more selfish one.

"If you hadn't let me have my way, I would have threatened
to leave," Lilly says. Like most people who've lived with villains, she can read every expression and guess every thought.

"Nash, I'm a stubborn girl, you know that," Lilly tries again,
teasing with the care and sweetness of friendship.

Of course, it makes Nash smile. The fingers are like a butterfly that drops into your palm and then flutters away. Jack is
up ahead. Lilly's focus changes. Nash can feel the beam of light
turn away from her.

"Riding lessons began ten minutes ago. I didn't know there
was a party," Jack jokes. His tone, the lightness—he is so un-
troubled that Nash could smack him.

"We all need a little rest today," Ellen says.

"Too much excitement." Veronica winks.

"Well, that's a darn shame. I know how much Jemima was
looking forward to taking Miss Ellen for a loop around the
ring." He ambles. He does. As if he hasn't a care in the world.
The word *excitement* works its way under Nash's skin and
prickles there.

Hadley stops. "Uh-oh. Guns from your holsters, ladies."

It's that ox, Mrs. Shumley, who rises from her place on the
porch swing. She stands with her hands on her ham-hock hips.

Oh, terrific. Nash pulls on Jack's arm in alarm, holds him
back to whisper privately, "Where's Danny?"

"He tried to find you. The Mrs. refuses to drive alone in the car with him after yesterday. She says he reeked of tobacco. And that three-eyed snake is still waiting for her."

This is more than Nash can take. She has no idea how her mother does it. The ranch is so much weightier than horses and cowboys and cocktails, and the job just feels too large for her. She wants to go to her room and shut the door, to disappear into the understanding silence and faithful comfort of a book, but Mrs. Shumley's eyes are nearly bulging from her head. Nash is so angry with Jack that she doesn't even want to ask, but she can't help it. "Three-eyed snake?"

"That attorney, Cox. One eye at the back of his head." Jack grins.

Oh, what that grin could do to her. Yet it leaves her cold right now. It's odd. Something has shifted. Maybe loyalty. Maybe even love.

"You hurt her," Nash snaps.

"He was chewing tobacco in my company. It was hideous! I smelled it on him. It made me light-headed."

"It's probably the altitude. It takes some getting used to."

Nash keeps her eyes on the road. A rabbit jets across, and Mrs. Shumley gasps. She leans forward from the backseat. Nash can feel Mrs. Shumley's hot, sour breath on her cheek, and her gloved hands squeak as they grip the leather of the Styleline Deluxe.

"It's the tobacco. He doesn't have the decency to smoke a proper cigarette. And those women! Let's not call them ladies. Barely ever out of trousers!"

"It must be very different for you here, compared to Chicago."

"How I will ever tell a soul I was in a place like this is beyond me."

Every single day will be over, Nash tells herself, even ones so hard and terrible. She tries to stay composed. The Mrs. Shumleys are rare. Nash hopes Mr. Shumley has fallen in love with a showgirl, who loves him back madly.

"And don't think I don't know what's going on after hours. That young woman in her condition!"

Mrs. Shumley's perfume is choking Nash. Her fat face falls, forming two jowls, same as a bloodhound. Danny is one thing. Nash couldn't care less what Mrs. Shumley thinks about him. He couldn't care less, either, knowing Danny.

"We respect the privacy of our guests," Nash says. She speaks with more bite than she intends, but Mrs. Shumley's words poke at her, a finger jabbing an injury.

"It's her business that the baby isn't even her husband's? The blonde told me. The aging socialite."

For God's sake! And can't Veronica keep her mouth shut? Nash forgets that Veronica is smart. Veronica knows a big, fat gossip when she sees one. A gossip can be very useful.

"You should be more careful about who you allow in, before it becomes a house of ill-repute. A married woman with another man's child. She ought to be put away."

Nash has had enough. Her pride blazes, and so does her desire to protect, and it is all much showier and easier to recognize than the quiet envy she will wonder about only later. Jack is right: Nash is naïve. She doesn't think far enough ahead. She's still young enough to react to what's on the surface, trusting whatever feelings arise, not looking above or beneath or beyond them to their impact or even to her own soundless but lurking motivations. She's the impetuous gambler, putting every chip on red and letting the wheel fly, even if the game is rigged.

"Stuart Marcel is that baby's father, and I'll swear on a Bible to that fact," Nash snaps, as the stunned Mrs. Shumley finally sits back in her seat and huffs through her nose.

The one who is hurt, the one who hurts—it's a tangled story, always, and every human being can be small and mean and can do bigger harm than they intend. Nash reminds herself often: We all make mistakes. She has to tell herself this again and again. In acts large or small, with outcomes, too, that are large or small—we step forward with our imperfect choices; we set the timer ticking for sometimes terrible and often inevitable conclusions. How could she have known what a small world it really was when it seemed so very large to her, living her whole life on that ranch?

Still. What she said that day in the car with Mrs. Shumley's hot breath on her neck—it's something she will never, her whole life long, forgive herself for.

Mrs. Shumley waits until Nash gets out and opens the door for her. Now she's some kind of chauffeur? Fine. She will wait by the car with her arms folded, same as the chauffeurs at the Riverside Hotel. Mrs. Shumley can make her own way into Mr. Cox's office. Good luck to her. Better luck, please dear God, to Mr. Shumley. May the showgirl have a headdress of feathers and a leotard of sequins and an undying love for the man. And, most of all, may someone save the poor children of that bitter woman. This is another problem of divorce, as far as Nash can tell. The spouse gets to flee the crazy husband or wife, but the children will be stuck with them for the rest of their unlucky days.

Nash waits and waits. She's wearing a suit, as they always do for trips to see an attorney, and the suit is hot. Her girdle is hotter still. She unpins her hat. It is boring, standing there like a chauffeur. She strolls down the street until she gets to the Wigwam Café, and then returns. She strolls a bit farther, and each time farther still, like a toddler from its mother. She passes Union Federal Savings and Orchid Florist, then the new Eldorado Club, and Harold's. She is nearly all the way to the Riverside Hotel when she sees a livestock truck. It's parked along the street. It's a strange sight, especially there. It has wood slats and a canvas top and a mean-nosed cab in front. Union Stockyards is written on the side in white curled letters. Something else brings her attention to the truck. There is a fluid dripping and gathering from the back, and a bad smell.

She knows that's the smell of blood, and yet somehow she can't help herself. She's in her nice suit, but she sets her hat and her handbag on the curb and climbs up one large tire and peers in. What she sees there—it's beyond horror. Nash is not squeamish, not after growing up on a ranch. She has seen foals being born and bad wounds in flesh that has battled wire fence, but this is so far beyond that, she might be sick. Mangled bodies, torn hooves. Hides ragged and in ribbons from bullets. A foal, still alive, his eyes full of fear.

She has heard about the hunters who use airplanes to run the mustangs into pens. There, they shoot them, haul them away, and then sell their bodies to companies that make dog food. She's also heard of the government bounty hunters, who trap and kill the horses because they think of them as vermin, feral vermin, grazing on land that rightly belongs to cattle. And now she is seeing the evidence with her own eyes. How can this be? These are the very same horses held in high esteem in stories and lore and songs. Locations are named after them—Mustang Ridge and Wild Horse Canyon. How can you viciously destroy something so revered? They say that if you see those mustangs, you will never be the same, and now it's true that Nash will never be the same.

She hurries away from that truck. She is crushed at the wreckage. Her stomach turns, from what she's seen and also with a dread that's becoming insistent. She retrieves her hat and handbag and returns to the white building where the attorney's office is. Strangely, it is not Mrs. Shumley who appears but Mr. Cox himself. He holds a pocket watch in one hand, looking ever so much like the white rabbit in *Alice in Wonderland*.

"Mrs. Shumley will be moving to the Riverside Hotel." He speaks quickly, obviously in a hurry. *Late, late, for a very important date*. "She find the conditions at Tamarosa unsuitable." He holds his hands toward the sky as if he is giving up. Nash is grateful for that small act of generosity. "You can tell one of your boys to deliver her things."

He doesn't wait for a reply. His shoes *scuff-scuff-scuff* up the stairs. Her mother would have offered Mrs. Shumley the hotel before she'd even asked. Alice didn't over-tend to the fussy and miserable. She washed her hands of them, for her own sake and for the sake of the other guests. Nash's mother had always believed that some folks relished their unhappiness, preferring to stay right where bitterness met envy, and she had no patience for those kinds of people. Nash remembers what happened after Mrs. Abigail Coldicott, who found the meals too heavy and the company tawdry, left. Alice had sat on the sofa, reading but not reading a *National Geographic*, flipping through the pages in irritation before tossing it to the pile with the others. *Let her stew in her own juices somewhere else*, she said.

So Nash should perhaps be celebrating on the drive home, being rid of that ox. When she gets back, she should suggest that they all raise their glasses in a toast, to freedom from hypocritical acrimony. But she won't. This is not the mood riding with her now as she heads back to the ranch, following the banks of the Truckee River out of the city of Reno. There was that trickle of blood from that trailer, and those terrified eyes. There are hunters and the hunted, cruelties both small and large, trickles of guilt, too.

Mrs. Shumley, still in Fred Cox's office, is already likely brimming with glee, though Nash doesn't know this yet. In only a few days, the Whittakers will be visiting Reno, and if anyone will be interested to hear the latest about Stuart Marcel and that dreadful ranch, it's Phyllis. What a delicious little nugget Mrs. Shumley will have to bring when they meet for dinner!

Nash heads down River Road, past the last Chevron. The turn signal *click-click-clicks*. Right then she's unaware of Mrs. Shumley's twitch of eagerness, unaware of the Whittakers, unaware of just who knows whom. It's no wonder, though, that she can't shake the dark sense that things are going terribly, terribly wrong.

chapter 16

Callie

We'd been sitting there for a good hour, waiting for the nurses to roll Nash back into her room. It was her second day in the hospital. The cancer often invaded the walls of blood vessels, we were told, which could cause these kinds of symptoms. All they could do was give us a status report with various scans and make her comfortable. Cells multiplied, expertly tending to their evil business as we fumbled daily life. I was hungry. Shaye was getting cranky. She tossed the *National Geographic* onto the stack of magazines on the green padded bench, after flipping through the pages in irritation. "Same old volcanoes," she said. "Remember Grandma Shiny? She had piles of these things, going back centuries."

Grandma Shiny was Gene's mother. She was our grandmother for the six years Gene and our mother were married, and then we never heard from her again. There were so many people who made a crucial appearance in your life and then disappeared. How did we let that happen? I suppose we couldn't keep everyone who showed up or our lives would become as stuffed as my closets back home, but Grandma Shiny put up Christmas stockings with our names on them. She'd embroidered those names. We called her Grandma Shiny because she wore lots of sparkly jewelry. She even let us play in her jewelry box, where there were rings too large for our fingers and a charm bracelet with a tiny carriage with wheels that turned. Tucked in the bottom of that box was a small envelope with a creepy but awe-inspiring lock of Gene's baby hair, much blonder and silkier than the bristly brown hair we knew.

"Yeah. We'd hunt through them for pictures of naked tribesmen."

"Who cared about Aztecs and maps of how the Pompeii water system worked."

"Really. Just give us some droopy boobs and bare butts in loincloths. My God, it felt so dirty and wrong and thrilling."

"Kids today wouldn't even care. Big deal. You see more than that in a PG movie."

"We sound like old people again."

"Rock 'n' roll will destroy our youth," Shaye said, shaking one fist in the air.

"It makes me sad, thinking about Grandma Shiny."

"Me, too."

"She's probably dead."

"Jeez, Cal."

"What? It's true."

"Well, you don't have to say it like that."

"She has probably passed on to her eternal rest."

Shaye made a face at me. "I hate hospitals. Why does time pass so slowly in hospitals? Every sick minute is sixty real-life minutes."

"You'd think being so close to the end would speed time up."

"Really." She was looking around in the drawers of the nightstand, the way you do in boring motels.

"You're not going to find anything in there, believe me. I

spent enough time in hospitals when Thomas's mother was sick, and when Thomas's mother wasn't sick."

"Aha!" Shaye said. She held up a small packet, happy to prove me wrong.

"Gauze? Okay, good for you, Shaye, you won the gauze lottery."

The hospital was not bringing out the best in us. We both heard the wheels coming down the hall and straightened up, ready to be on good behavior, but there was only the squeak of shoes on linoleum as the mound of a body under blankets passed.

"I'm scared of what I'll see every time," Shaye said.

"Me, too. You know, we're going to be spending a lot of time here in the not-too-distant future," I said.

"Thanks for that. Thanks so much for another cheery news flash of something I already knew."

"I wonder if our real father is dead yet. Probably."

"I'm sure he is. Men don't live as long. Do you think about it often? It was too bad we never knew him."

"I think it would have been a worse too bad if we did."

"Yeah. No doubt he was better in my imagination."

The next time, the sound of wheels and the squeak of shoes really did bring Nash. The nurse banged the poor woman and her gurney into the door and then into the wall, all the while talking in a voice used on toddlers. "Okay, Mrs. McBride! That wasn't so bad! Let's get ourselves settled back in! We'll see what the doctor says about getting you home!"

Then again, we weren't any better. What was it about certain places that brought out your inner A-student? Hospitals and government buildings, churches—well, a person started speaking in sunny, functional exclamation points. You suddenly wanted to look like the kind of woman who baked pies.

"Look what came while you were gone!" I said. I held up the flower arrangement. Daisies and carnations, a limp rose or two, all splayed against a fern-frond background.

"Someone has a new admirer!" Shaye said.

Nash narrowed her eyes at us. "Stop being so damn cheery. Who are they from?"

I slipped the tiny card from the tiny envelope to show her. Nash didn't quite look like herself in that blue gown with the white paisley teardrops, but she looked better. She'd had a shower and her hair was pulled back in her usual strong, steely braid, and she had color in her cheeks again. She wanted to get out of there. "Deke Donaldson," I said. "J. J.'s Autos."

"Word gets around," Shaye said.

"That Harris has a big mouth. Deke Donaldson only wants to sell me the long-term auto-protection plan, and there's no long-term anything in this picture."

"Oh, Nash," I said.

"We've got to get out of this place. I don't have a lot of time left, and I need driving lessons."

I scooted the heavy green vinyl chair next to her. "Say we teach you to drive. What about a license? You'll have to take the test."

"Yeah. And that eye exam . . ." Shaye said from over by the window.

"I have a license. Everyone needs a license. Just because I don't use it, doesn't mean I don't have one. I go in and get my eyes checked and get my picture taken every few years. I've got eyes like a hawk. I'm surprised you didn't see it in my dresser drawer, with all the snooping you must be doing since I'm not there."

"Why bother snooping now that your room is sparse as a

nun's? And how have we had time for snooping? We've been right here with you almost this whole time."

I studied my fingernails, but Shaye told the lie right to Nash's face without even blinking. She'd found that envelope from Jack Waters in Nash's room the night before, taped to the bottom of the floor lamp, and she'd opened it. And when she did, she found a blank piece of paper inside, with one word on it in Nash's distinctive handwriting: *Gotcha*. Shaye had bolted from the room, waving that paper in my face, but she didn't go back in. She told me that getting caught made her feel like Nash was watching, even as she lay in a bed in room 222 at Saint Mary's Regional Medical Center, being pumped full of fluids because that's about all they could do for her. That, and a few hits of pain medicine. Her bones were beginning to ache now, too.

"You going to drive somewhere with those pain pills in you?" I said. "We'll take you where you want to go. We've told you a million times."

"It's a trip I need to make alone. Of course I'm not going to drive under the influence. But, fine. All right. I'll tell you what the big secret is. Might as well have it out." She crooked her finger to Shaye and me. It was a dramatic, deathbed-ish gesture. We should have known better. We got in close, just as she wished, fools and eternal optimists that we were.

"I'm writing a book," she said.

"Oh, for God's sake," I said.

"You're a barrel of laughs," Shaye said.

Maybe it was the drugs singing through her, but Nash was having a whole lot more fun right then than we were.

* * *

"That's good news, Cal," Thomas said. "I'm glad she's back home again where she belongs. I think maybe you need to come back home where you belong, too, right? I mean, it's getting to be a long time. We need to talk."

When we took Nash in to Saint Mary's, we'd phoned Gloria, and Gloria phoned Thomas, and Thomas phoned me, and there you had it. As Nash said, word gets around, and in a family, I supposed that's how it should be.

"You don't need time alone anymore? What happened? I don't want to come back to the way things were."

"I know you're pissed, and I'm sorry. I was wrong not to tell you about the therapist. I was," Thomas said. "But I miss you. I do. I want you home."

My silence wasn't some sort of revenge for his. I had nothing to say. A wind was blowing through me. Inside, I echoed.

"Cal, I don't like how close we're getting. To some . . . edge." Thomas was talking fast, and I could feel his panic. I heard its rattle, even louder against the steel girders of my emptiness. "It's scaring me. It's a dangerous game we're playing. Our whole marriage, all these years, it could fall in if we're not careful."

I had an image of a wagon train on a very long trail, high atop a canyon. A wagon train that had been traveling for months, its members emaciated from starvation and drought, the only remaining objects a gun without bullets and a hollow tin cup.

"Twenty-two years," he said. "You don't just toss that. We've got to try to understand what's going on. Get past it."

I could tell you exactly when things under our roof changed, the very moment that Thomas took his true first step away from me, a permanent and meant step, not the small, annoyed retreats of a marriage, the two steps back, the one step forward that can eventually lead to a deficit of steps. It happened a few months before June died. We'd brought her home from the hospital, same as Shaye and I had just done with Nash. June was finally back at her own house, the house with the past-tense florals and breakable, too-cherished belongings and the perfect draperies, draperies the children used to brush up against, making her wince. You had to be careful in there, that's for sure. The house had grown too large for her, with its three empty bedrooms. Table surfaces and the tops of picture frames gathered dust. Something smelled musty. Thomas's sister, Bailey, who wisely lived far enough away to be absolved of regular involvement, had flown in to be with her. As we were leaving, Bailey was making grilled cheese sandwiches in a frying pan with peeling Teflon. June chatted cheerfully from the couch. This was the illness attention she had always longed for, and in spite of how sick she was, her cheeks glowed with pleasure.

In the car, though, I could see Thomas's tight-jawed profile. Amy was in the backseat, talking about wanting to run a marathon. It was an involved plan, the sort of complicated idea that Melissa and Amy were fond of in their teen years; there would be training sessions, and new shoes, and a certain number of days before the big event, and friends who wanted to join in. Damn if she didn't actually run that thing and finish, too. But right then her voice bubbled over my shoulder; she was saying something about strength and building endurance, and Thomas's eyes, his usually warm and friendly eyes, got that coldness I was familiar with from when we argued.

Two people can have a silent conversation when you've been together a long time. Maybe you're wrong about who says what, but I doubt it. When we got home, he didn't speak to me, and he yanked his arm from mine when I reached out.

"Thomas?" I asked, as he changed into his old jeans and

went outside and started the lawn mower. The lawn mower shouted. It told me what a disappointment I was. It told me that his mother would die soon, without him ever giving her what she wanted, what Bailey was right then giving her, some easy, doting care, free of undercurrents. It blamed me for the way our children were stiff and overpolite with June and for the way Amy right then cared more about her marathon than about his mother, and it even blamed me for the fact that June would be gone for good, as if I'd been a factor in her demise. The person next to you is the large mirror you look into, a mirror that reflects your own failings. Sometimes, that person is also a soft, easy target, an unknowing and ever-deficient receptacle for your expectations.

The distant eyes stayed distant. Thomas left and a mood took his place. The mood had a place at the dinner table. At first I tried to tame it with kindness, and then I stepped around it when I encountered it in the hall. I let it have the first shower so it didn't run out of hot water and tiptoed so as not to wake it. When June died, I stood beside Thomas and held his arm in that black suit, but he was truly off somewhere, standing alone. I hadn't shared his love, and so I couldn't share his loss, and he made sure not to meet my eyes to remind me of this.

Yes. That's when it had begun.

And when had I stepped away from Thomas? Was it when I was so sick of the mood I could have held a pillow over its puffy, dark face? Was it when he merely patted my hand after Hugo's own eyes had gone blank, just after he sighed his last breath? Or was it an accumulation of farther backs, times I felt despair and was met with his chirpy optimism? When he hadn't *seen* me? When that chirpy optimism in the face of despair told me I wasn't known? That's all we want much of the time, to be seen and known.

Or was he my own soft target, the one who hadn't met my expectations? Maybe it went all the way back to that first meeting with his mother, and the times since, when he'd let her say and do to me whatever she wanted. Or to the times when I was the one to call the police because the teen boys next door were having a party so loud it woke the baby. Or when I was the one to confront a vicious coach, or the insurance company, or that nasty female accountant, because he couldn't stand to be the bad guy. He couldn't stand to be the bad guy, but when I called the police, or confronted the coach, or dealt with the accountant, or pushed away the spiteful mother, I was a person he disliked, and I knew it. I was a person he disapproved of, then. Maybe this went all the way back to that raccoon. To the thing I most longed for since Shaye and I were children, protection against a raging storm, something much too heavy to set upon Thomas's very real shoulders.

You hold a story about your husband or wife in your head—who they are and who they aren't. What they have and haven't done. The catalog of their wrongdoings. You want them to be this somebody who fills this something and they aren't and can't. It was all ancient fault lines, some with names, some without. Cracks and crevices you could barely see the bottom of, going on for miles. You could get so tired of that story. The wagon train could go over the cliff finally, and maybe it would be a relief, that last tin cup bouncing against the rocks before hitting bottom.

"This is the life we have," Thomas said. "This is the life we made."

"This is the life we've had so far," I said.

"I'm coming out there," Thomas said.

"I need some time alone. I need some *self-care*."

It sounded angrier than I felt.

* * *

"Tex, please!"

I recognized the sound of that truck, too. I was glad Nash was napping in her room but dismayed at my own disheveled state. I'd only had a quick shower that morning, and my hair was up; I wore an old pair of shorts I often gardened in and a tank top with frayed seams. I think it might have once been Amy's. I managed to locate my purse in a hurry before he rapped on the door, and I popped a white square of mint gum into my mouth.

Kit Covey held out a gold-wrapped box of chocolates, and for a moment I thought it was old-fashioned courting. Flowers would be next, a nervous interview with the father I never had, but Kit set me straight. "We heard your aunt had been in the hospital," he said. "A little something from all of us."

"P.R.," I said.

"No," he said, and seemed to mean it.

"Thank you." I set the box on the table near the door. If Nash knew where those chocolates came from, she'd never touch them, but Shaye and I would. You'd better believe it.

Kit looked around the room as if he was in a museum, which in a way he was. He tilted his head as he looked at the cuckoo clock. I followed his eyes and then his slid to mine and held. He cleared his throat. "I was wondering," he said.

My heart thumped around. I was nervous, because I felt the crackle between us, and because I could smell him, some warm outside smell mixed with skin and leather.

"We're done for the day, and there's this place, about an hour from here. You might like to see it. If you haven't already. That old resort, the Cal Neva?"

"I haven't."

"You've heard of it?"

"Mmm, afraid not."

He smiled. "Oh, you'll like this. Beautiful place, on the lake. Tahoe. Full of history. The first casino, way back in the thirties. The gangsters used to run it. Guys with names like Pretty Boy and Baby Face. Sinatra owned it in the early sixties. Think Rat Pack and Marilyn Monroe, and toss in a few Kennedys and haunted tunnels, gangsters, and crooners . . ."

"Crooners—I'm in."

"I thought you might appreciate a different view of what it's like out here. The topography . . ."

"The topography."

He laughed.

"A field trip," I said.

"Dinner, maybe?"

"Great." I wasn't sure if it was great. Something inside apparently felt so, though, because this is what I answered without thinking. "After two days of hospital food, that sounds amazing. Let me make sure my sister's got this under control."

Upstairs, Shaye's arms were crossed and she was doing that great trick where she raised one eyebrow. I could never do that. "More like, does *my* sister have this under control," she said.

"You were listening."

"Of course I was listening."

"Well, then, of course I have this under control."

"For God's sake, change your clothes," she said. "And don't do anything I wouldn't do."

"I won't do anything you would do."

"Oh, thanks a lot." She gave me a little shove. "Well, I guess if anyone needs to get *Renovated*, it's you. But forest-service men, you know . . . Only YOU can prevent forest fires. Better hold on to your matches, sister."

* * *

The highway from the ranch to Lake Tahoe climbed steadily up, up from the desert. Before I knew it, the terrain had changed drastically. We were high in the mountains, with views over the Washoe Valley, and then the vegetation changed again, becoming thick and green with tall pines on either side.

"This is more like home," I said. "All the trees. And mountains. I make fun of Seattle, with all its effortful outdoorsyness, but I love it there. It's so beautiful, like this. Whenever I leave and come back, I'm always shocked by how beautiful. Water everywhere. Boats, seaplanes. Clean, clean air. You ever been?"

"I was in Seattle maybe a year ago." Kit flicked on his turn signal, checked the mirror, then passed a slow-moving RV, with a license-plate holder that said Captain Ed. "Giving a paper on 'The Public Response to Designated Wilderness and Roadless Areas.' Exciting, huh?"

"Sorry I missed it." I sort of was.

"I saw the inside of the Hilton, which I could give you a narrated tour of someday, if you'd like."

"Let me guess. The Rainier Room, which opened to the Cascade Ballroom, something along those lines."

"That was about it."

"Well, the next time you come, I'll show you around properly." It was one of those things you say. I couldn't imagine Kit Covey in my world, any more than I could imagine myself back home right then. We were there in his truck, and he shifted gears as the truck climbed, and it was everywhere else that felt imagined. His fingers tapping the steering wheel—they felt real, and so did his profile as he drove.

"It even smells more like home here," I said.

"Smells like green."

It did smell like green, and as we got closer to the lake and you could see the solemn, snowy peaks of the Sierras and the lake itself in the deep basin, it smelled like white and then blue.

We walked under the welcoming awning of the Cal Neva Resort and opened the doors of the main building, with its Alpine-chalet, high-peaked roof. The place was empty; it looked closed, but we could still get in. The Indian Room was locked, so we peeked inside. It had log walls and wagon-wheel chandeliers, elk heads and hides on the walls. I imagined mobsters and mistresses, the blare of saxophones, glasses clinking, and the kind of swagger and glamour that'd been long gone, replaced with us pecking at our phones in athletic attire.

Outside, Kit pointed to the small cabins on a ridge. Number three was where Marilyn slept, he said, likely with Kennedys, plural. Number five was Sinatra's. They looked smaller than you'd think. Not too different from the cabins at Tamarosa, although when we looked in, there were shiny gold bedspreads and wicker chairs. I expected larger and grander, though I guess in those days things were both grander and smaller. We have closets the size of bedrooms now, but they're absent of satin and crinoline.

"Ghosts," I said.

"Everywhere," Kit said.

"Look how beautiful." The lake was a glassy mirror reflecting mountains and trees and the resort itself, turned liquid. I wished my girls could see it. We had plenty of gorgeous lakes in the Northwest; right in the city itself there were four, two very large ones. Lake Washington was stunning, with its large, tech-bought houses hugging the bank and fresh, deep aquamarines, and Lake Union was a quirky cornucopia of floating homes and seaplanes and sailboats. But this huge lake looked almost eerie and cold and even mystical, maybe because I could feel the history there. I could sense the ghosts of movie stars and gamblers and the FBI, betrayers in cement shoes.

"Beautiful," Kit said. He grinned and squeezed my arm. "You, too. You are."

It was a casual, easy compliment, devoid of deep import. It seemed merely refreshingly sincere, and so I smiled. "It's the good air and good company," I said. But I felt beautiful, even in my hurried-on sundress and hair pulled from its ponytail. I felt young, and light, and myself. And Kit—he matched the place; he fit. Even in his jeans and T-shirt, he had an air about him, something lasting. Maybe he was another person who had always been old.

"The sky's as amazing as the water," I said. It was dotted with white quotation-mark clouds.

"I could watch a sky like a movie," he said. "But that water makes me want to be *in* that water."

We walked and explored until hunger hit. At the Crystal Bay Café, we ordered steaks and baked potatoes, which arrived wrapped in tinfoil. It was another thing to love about this place—at home, food was soy-filled, gluten-free, everything-free; here, people ate gravy and enjoyed it. Evening fell. A country-western band was playing. A woman in a hip-hugging black dress and cowboy boots sang into a microphone, as if she'd loved that thing her whole life long. A few people were dancing. We were now on our second time in a bar with a band. Things had changed since our first, and I don't even know how it happened. Change was sneaky like that.

Kit pushed his plate away. He tipped the last of his drink down his throat, grabbed my hand, and I went with him. It was a slow song, and his cheek was next to mine. He smelled like alcohol and warm skin and our mouths were close. I wanted him bad then, I admit it. His shirt was soft where I touched his shoulder. It was the shortest song ever, and we parted and applauded the singer. She bent her head forward in a bow, and her dark hair fell down straight over her face. I wondered whom she went home to—maybe the drummer, with his aviator glasses and wild hair and wet rings under the arms of his black shirt.

"You're a dancer after all," he said.

"I was going to say the same thing about you," I said.

"Only in the delirium of high altitude."

I insisted on splitting the bill, a gesture Shaye would surely mock. Still, I knew what this was and wasn't and would never be. Outside, the air had grown cold and crisp; it was the kind you want to take a bite out of. The night had fallen in earnest, and small points of light had begun to twinkle around us. By the time we'd started down the mountain, night had gotten serious, and the curves felt treacherous.

"It's all right," Kit said. He looked over at me, but I wished he'd keep his eyes on the road. "I've got it. I know this road."

"Ah, that obvious?"

"It was these." He loosened my fingers from the seat edge. You can hold so much tension in your body and not even realize it, until you roll your neck or take a deep breath and suddenly it's as if the wrongly accused prisoner has made his joyous escape.

"I'm sorry," I said.

"For what?"

"It implies something. About your capability. I didn't mean anything by it."

"I know that. No offense taken."

"Well, good."

"I think you're confusing me with someone else."

He glanced at me again and grinned. He did know that road. His own shoulders were easy and his face relaxed. I wanted that drive to last and last after that. Even on those dark and twisty roads, I could have driven all night and into the next day and the next, but we were back at the ranch so fast. Time is so mean, the way it quickens and slows opposite to your desires. I suppose if your only task were to stretch on to infinity, you'd need to play some games, too, but how cruel.

We arrived. Kit turned off the truck, and I could hear crickets. There was that same dilapidated fence and the empty pool and the tractor, which Shaye had abandoned in the driveway, but now Nash's new car sat shiny in the light of the moon. "This was a treat," Kit said.

"It was. Thank you."

"Thank *you*. I needed that, I'll tell you that much."

I leaned in to hug him goodbye and our cheeks set against each other again. I shut my eyes, took in his smell and his warm skin. "Ahh," he said, as we separated. I opened my door and got out. Leaned in through the window.

"Thank you again," I said.

"My pleasure, ma'am. Truly."

The ground slid under my feet. The earth cracked open and left a gash, and I had no idea how deep it was or for how many miles it went.

I was startled when I opened the front door. Nash and Shaye were both up late, sitting in the living room, which was dark except for the light of that stereo. Dr. Yabba Yabba Love's molasses-and-ginger voice poured from it. *Every apple's got its seeds*. Nash's feet were up on the sofa. She was still wearing those socks with the nubs on the bottom they gave her in the hospital.

"Eric bought plane tickets. He's taking the girls on a cruise,"

Shaye said. Even in the dim light, I could see that her face was puffy from crying.

I had barely set my purse down before Nash spoke, too.

"If there's one thing I know, it's that love is complicated. But, Callie . . ."

I'd disappointed her, but I wasn't sure I cared. I'd spent too much of my life not disappointing people. "What, Nash?"

"When the horses are gathered . . . I've seen it. Terrible, life-altering things can happen."

"Life-altering things aren't always terrible."

"That's true, of course."

"It isn't the old days anymore," I said.

"I was going to tell you the same thing," she said.

But we were both wrong. The present was ever-changing, but the past lasted.

chapter 17

Nash

In her room, the curtain drifts like an afterthought, and, outside, Nash hears the *thunk* of a heavy knapsack dropped to the ground. Jack and Danny are taking the gals on a pack trip, and even Ellen is going, in spite of the fact that they'll be on horseback for hours. Veronica and Hadley got her a little tipsy last night and made her sign a promise on a cocktail napkin.

Cook has prepared fried chicken, and the smell lingers. Nash should help her wrap the food and bring it out to Danny, and she should make sure that Ellen is calm and that Veronica has brought more than just a fashionable hat. But Nash stays where she is, in Lilly's room, where they've been chatting and laughing. Lilly told her how she used to collect ants in a relish jar when she was a girl, and Nash told Lilly about Oscar, the old dog they had before Boo, how he used to catch flies in his snapping jaw. In the light of Castaway, Lilly's eyes are the color of larkspur, and they are talking like real friends, and Nash is having fun. Who cares about chicken and nerves and sunburn—everyone can look after themselves for once. Alice would be disappointed in her, but she isn't sure she cares. She's spent too much of her life not disappointing people.

Jack's voice rises and enters through the window, on the same gust that moves the curtain. That's another thing she must do, and soon. She badly needs to talk to him about what she saw in that horse trailer. He can explain it, in some way where she'll stop seeing those images when she shuts her eyes. "Oh, what a beautiful Zorro!" Jack sings, to the tune of "Oh, What a Beautiful Mornin'." He's a terrible singer, and Lilly rolls her eyes.

"Boys," she says.

"Boys," Nash agrees. Honestly, she doesn't know much about them. There's Jack, of course, and then there was Vincent Henry, from school. They went to a dance once, and he told her the entire plot of a film he'd seen, as sweat poured from his underarms. These are her two experiences, and . . . well, she couldn't exactly come to any conclusions.

Lilly is on the bed, where, earlier, Nash had set down a tray. There is tea and toast and the dewy curve of a melon slice. Nash wrapped the silverware in a napkin, and she found a shot glass in her mother's cupboard, in which she set a white flower, a desert evening primrose, that she cut near the acacia.

Lilly is wearing a yellow smock dress with white dots, and her hair is back again in a pearl clip. Her feet are bare, and one leg is tucked underneath her. She raises the last triangle of buttered toast and bites. "After they go, we'll have the place to ourselves," she says. "We should raid Hadley's candy dish."

"The gold ones are caramels," Nash says. She'd never do such a thing but plays along. Hadley keeps a saucer of foil-wrapped confections by her typewriter. She says it helps tempt the muse.

Lilly lifts her eyebrows with delight, as if she and Nash are in on something together. "Caramels are my favorites. We should do it."

Under the Volcano is open on the bed, set up like a tent to hold Lilly's place. Nash taps the book. "Do you like it?"

"Honestly, it bores me to tears. I can't finish." Lilly has dispensed with all manners. She's picked up the melon and is eating it straight off the rind.

Nash laughs. She's happy. She's so happy that it takes her by surprise. In spite of Stuart Marcel, those horses she saw, Gloria and their mother off somewhere—it's just her and Lilly, talking like girls, like real sisters. "I couldn't finish it, either," Nash admits.

"I am so glad you said that! Stuart gave it to me. Do you think *he* read it? Of course not! He can barely read the Sunday comics."

"Really?"

"His lips move!"

"That's awful!"

"And slowly, too. How can a person be so afraid of a man who can't even read *Blondie?*"

They are snickering, but this quiets them both. This: the word *afraid*. Danny heard from Ella Broderick at the casino that Stuart Marcel was still in town, staying at the Riverside, driving around in that car and asking people what they knew about his wife and a cowboy.

"My father was the same way," Lilly finally says.

"Slow reader?"

"Mean. I got out of there first chance I could. Changed my name, even. To Lilly Edwards, my mother's maiden name. Two years later, my father was hit by a train."

"Oh, my God. That's awful," Nash says.

"For the train."

"What about your mother?"

"She got sick. But she gave me things I still have. She liked to read. She liked to tell stories using all the voices."

"She was an actress," Nash says.

"Exactly. Stuart gave me things, too, so many things! But nothing I needed. Jewelry! I gave some to Eve; she's a true friend. And then I left the rest behind."

"Good."

"You should have seen how much jewelry."

"Wait right here," Nash says. She dashes to her own room. There's a pile of books by her bed that's rapidly becoming a nightstand. She wants to be a good book matchmaker, and she thinks she knows just the one. Something joyful and light, for both Lilly and Beanie. It may not be the best choice, really, but it's the best she can do in a pinch. The whole pile slides over as she takes the book from the center. She doesn't even bother setting them right again.

She holds the book out to Lilly. "For you." *The Egg and I.* "It's silly," Nash promises.

"I like silly."

"You do? Well, you should get rid of this thing, then." Nash grabs Stuart Marcel's book and hurls it like a boomerang right out Lilly's open window.

Lilly bursts out laughing. Then it hits the ground with a smack and they both giggle like mad. "I can't believe you did that!" Lilly's eyes are wide and delighted. Nash can't quite believe she just did that, either, but it feels marvelous.

"Gone, like the jewels," Nash says.

"*The Egg and I*," Lilly reads. "Like me and Beanie. My little egg."

"It's about a newly married woman who follows her husband to the Seattle wilderness to start a chicken farm. You will laugh so hard, your stomach will ache."

"Oh, dear, I don't know how much more Beanie can take. He's going to get seasick."

Nash loves this thought—that inside Lilly, Beanie rides the watery swells of laughter.

"You'll hate the husband." Nash has almost forgotten this part.

Lilly turns her dark brows down in a scowl. "If you say so, I already do."

"But don't worry," Nash says. "It has a happy ending."

"She leaves him?"

Nash clamps her lips shut, lifts her chin as if she'll never tell.

"Those are such beautiful words, aren't they? Happy ending?" Lilly says.

They are. They so are. But after all she's seen, Nash doesn't know if she believes in those particular words. She believes in something more intricate and thorny, she thinks then. What she believes is that the story goes on.

Nash's trousers are rolled to the knee, and she sits on a large, flat stone on the bank of Washoe Lake. She dangles her feet in. She'd like nothing more than to take off her clothes and jump in, same as Lilly and Jack had done that night in the pool, but she'd never do that. She wishes she could, but there are just some things we'll never be and never do no matter how much we wish.

It is cool by the lake. The sun dapples the water through the leaves of the trees. Nash watches the light prance and speckle. Silence is her favorite sound, she thinks. She feels a blessed moment of peace. Lilly is at the house, where she belongs, under the watch of Cook, and the ladies right now will be nearing Treetop Ridge, where they will turn and set out for home.

She could almost sleep, and she shuts her eyes, loops her arms around her knees. It's not sleep but that sweet, contemplative place of wakeful rest, where thoughts drift to dreams.

The whistle startles her. It's not a shrill whistle, the kind that Cliff might make when he calls to Danny, but a playful one. A whistle pretending to be birdsong.

"What are you doing here?" Nash asks.

"I can't stay cooped up all day. I'll go mad."

Lilly shouldn't have walked all the way out here, let alone by herself. There was that bleeding, and that private investigator, and the cuckolded Stuart Marcel. "I shouldn't have left you."

"Nonsense," Lilly says. "I brought you something."

She brings her hands around from behind her back. She has a book. It's an old one, red leather, with gold writing on the cover, the title set inside a gilt square. *Sense and Sensibility*. "This is for *you*," she says. "It's one of my favorites."

Nash is speechless. She has never gotten something like this from one of the women before, a gift that gives her the thing she loves best. She will keep this book forever to remember Lilly by, she thinks, and this is true. She'll do just that.

"Wait 'til you meet them. The Dashwood sisters," Lilly says. She wiggles her eyebrows. It's a promise of romance and intrigue.

"I'll give it back in perfect condition."

"Oh, no. A good book should be well loved, not pristine. Keep it as long as you need it."

Nash knows what it means to give your favorite books—it's like handing over a part of yourself and asking the person to understand it, maybe even treasure it. She holds the book close to her chest. "Thank you," she says.

"Don't you wish you could live inside a book sometimes?"

"All the time."

"I'd live in this one."

"Does it have a happy ending?"

"Very." Lilly slips off her flat shoes and steps toward the bank of the lake, where small rocks lead to the water.

"Be careful," Nash says.

Lilly reaches out her hand. Nash sets the book down and takes it, providing the balance. Lilly steps in. "Ahh," she says. "I wish I grew up here. I could be you right now." She bends her big belly forward, splashes her face and neck. Nash holds her fingertips, keeping her steady on the rocks. Lilly stands straight. She moves Nash's hand to Beanie. She unfolds Nash's fingers so that they lay flat.

"Feel what a clown he is," Lilly says. "A swimming baby."

Something rounded orbits under Nash's hand. It is hard, with the curve of an elbow or a heel. It juts out and rolls. Nash sets her other hand there, too. Her heart fills. She feels so much. For Lilly, and for that tumbling baby, for herself, even, and for the way hopeful things keep happening, no matter what. A yearning overtakes her, though for what exactly she couldn't say. With her hands on Lilly like that, on Beanie, a life at its most elemental, she simply *wants*. She wants so much. Passion, flesh, beating hearts, pain, beauty, love, everything under her hands, she wants it all. She and Lilly stand in the water like that, as the hem of Lilly's dress soaks.

That evening, Ellen walks around with pretend bowlegs and complains that every part of her aches. But Veronica and Hadley have a surprise—a certificate they've made on one of Hadley's pieces of parchment paper, awarding Ellen the Riding Prowess Prize. They bestow it upon her during cocktails, along with a jeweled pin in the shape of a galloping horse that Veronica bought in town. Ellen beams and even gets misty-eyed. Veronica gives her a hug and actually lifts her a half inch off the ground while Hadley shouts, *All for one, and one for all!* and pops a bottle of champagne, lifting the cork with an expert thumb.

Later that night, the house is quiet again, except for Boo's occasional exhale and the ticking of the clock. Nash can't sleep. When she closes her eyes, she sees those horses in that trailer again. Every time she closes them, there they are. This time, though, the image clicks between other pictures—men in airplanes, Jack and Lilly in the pool, a dying mother, a champagne cork flying. She feels too much life, and not nearly enough of it her own. The restlessness burns through her body, tangles the sheets. She gets out of bed and tosses on her clothes and sets her ear against Lilly's door. Yes, she hears the quiet in-and-out of her breaths, and so Nash takes the stairs oh-so-quietly and goes outside. She is hit with the cool slap of night air and the sharp smell of sage and wet earth. Someone has set *Under the Volcano* on the porch swing, which rocks gently in a gust of wind. It is raining.

She runs, because it is coming down, a rare summer downpour. Now she is thinking of her hands on Lilly's round stomach, and that longing overtakes her again, a deep, confused longing, because she wishes so badly to be Lilly that she'd even take Lilly's terrible history, the father, that train, the terrible husband, and the jewels. She wants to be a woman who is desired, a woman who needs a lover to save her, who has frail wrists and a tortured past, and, dear God, yes, with a being moving inside her. She wants so many things she never wanted before.

She needs to talk to Jack. She's been so angry with him, but she can only feel the words *need, talk.* She has to tell him about what she saw in that trailer, because he'll help her understand it. This is why she's here at this hour; this is what she tells herself, even if she feels the half-truth of it like knuckles rapping on a door.

The path is already getting muddy. She hopes Hadley will not need the bathroom on this night. Jack's light is still on. She knocks. She's at his cabin for the second time in only a few days. Her life is so different with Alice gone. It's her own, for once; that's the thing. It may be exactly what the women who come here feel.

"Nash?"

He looks tired, and his face has grown dark bristles since the morning. But it's a striking, familiar face. "I'm sorry," she says.

"What's the matter?"

"I have to talk to you."

"What?"

"I saw something. Something horrible. When I was in town."

"What? Come in. You're soaked."

There is a towel by the basin, and when she sits at the edge of the bed, he stands over her and dries her hair. It is such a gentle, caring gesture that Nash feels like she could weep. "Tell me," he says.

No matter how angry he's made her, he's still Jack, their Jack, the man who jokes around to horses as if they can joke back, the man who can trade his natural firm grip for a tender one, as he does with Zorro, as he does with her right now. "I saw some mustangs, in a trailer in Reno. It was horrible, Jack." She lets it out, all the images she's been holding in. There's been so much she's been holding back. "They were mangled, and there was blood everywhere. . . . I saw bare bone. Their skin . . . Jack, it was shredded."

"It's the horse runners. The mustangers. They've been running them down with planes."

"There was a colt . . ."

"They sell them to the stockyards."

"The blood was dripping from the back, a river of it, into the gutter." She can barely speak. She remembers the flow of that blood, and the young animal's half-dead eyes, and the way the fences they'd been run into had cut and gashed their hides. She can't help herself. The sorrow of it, no, the disbelief—her throat constricts. Her eyes fill.

"Oh, girl," he said. "Oh, don't cry."

"How could they?"

His arms are around her.

"I don't understand this, Jack. How?"

She smells the alcohol coming off him. She sees a bottle on the table and the empty glass. She shouldn't like that smell, but it draws her, she wants it, wants *in* it. It speaks of the dark and unapproachable layers of him. "You said . . ." She is crying hard now, into his shirt, into his dusky smell.

"What? I said what?"

"You said it would change me when I saw them. I'm afraid it's changed me."

"No, no," he says. "No." He strokes the back of her head. "When you see them alive and running. The way they're supposed to be. That's what I meant. That's all."

"How can I see anything but all that pain?"

"You will. I promise, you will. There will always be men with guns, Nash. There'll always be . . . I don't know. Ugliness? But one day you'll see how beautiful those horses are. Jesus, those crazy animals! You'll see them, and the beauty of 'em will be bigger than anything awful. Beauty trumps the bad every damn time, Nash, I swear."

His thumb caresses her cheek. She feels the shift in him. And this is the man she wants, the one she saw in the pool in the light of the moon. He is a different Jack because she is a different Nash. She is not the strong, horsey girl, the girl who can flip a saddle onto a mare, the girl who stands with her arms crossed in front of a long, dark car, even though her heart is beating hard in her chest. She is a girl who is crushed, who needs, who is right then leaning and crying, and so much of it, too much of it—love, two people together—seems not about love at all but about weakness and strength, power and powerlessness, the yearning to be small and needy or large and needed, the movement of various pieces by two people, whatever it takes to fill out some idea of yourself, but none of that matters now.

"Those horses . . ." His voice is husky and low. She doesn't want to talk about horses anymore. She turns her face and her mouth meets his. There are his lips, and there is the warm taste of alcohol on his breath, and there is his tongue and hers.

"Nash. We can't . . ." His body says otherwise. "You know I care about you, but Alice'll—"

She shuts him up with her mouth. There are tongues and heat and he grips her hair. She is down on the bed, and he is over her, his stubble is against her cheek, and he is heavy and she shifts him ever so, and his hands are fast and rough. She is not afraid, even though she has not known exactly how to imagine what comes next. She does not think about the rightness or wrongness of what he does, either. Who he is, who he really is, the way he's a contradiction—caring and crass, selfless and selfish, it doesn't matter yet. Nor does the complicated question of who exactly is using whom. Every mistaken idea— none of them matter. He was over Lilly like this, his hands were fast and rough on her, and this strange thought fuels her own heat and desire.

She lets him unbutton her blouse, and she lets him pull her pants down over her hips. She is someone now who is vulnerable and taken, who has small wrists under large hands, a borrowed someone, a someone who is made to feel the one thing everyone wants to feel: protected in the face of danger. It is a someone who will not be there in the morning or in the days that follow. It's powerful, that weakness; who knew? There is the subterranean rumble of triumph. Her secret self is both whole and unmoored, but, most of all, that self is maddeningly fleeting, and this knowledge fills her with urgency. She wants more and more of him and her and them, now.

As Jack's mouth presses on Nash's, as his hands cup the curve of her breasts, Mrs. Shumley, that ox, settles in for the night at the Riverside Hotel. She unrolls her stockings, unsnaps that huge pink girdle. At least, this is how Nash imagines it later, when she finds out what's happened: The ox sighs as she eases into bed, just after dining with Raymond and Phyllis Whittaker, old friends visiting from Chicago. How shocked Phyllis was to hear about the goings-on at Tamarosa, particularly about the despicable ruse played on the great Stuart Marcel by his strumpet of a wife. Mrs. Shumley whispered Nash's own words to Phyllis over oysters Rockefeller, as Raymond chatted with the waiter about the wine. That actress—an *extra*, really—she probably wanted to run off with her cowboy, make a pretty new family without the bother of the baby's father. As if Stuart would stand for that.

The rest of the story will be pieced together with the help of Lilly's friend Eve, but it is also easy to envision: Upon arriving home, Phyllis Whittaker rushes to call her sister Wilma, wife of the great Mr. George Greatstone, *Visions of Africa* producer and longtime business partner of Stuart Marcel. Greatstone's niece, Mary Ann Madrid, even has a small role in the film, thanks to him. In fact, on the other side of the world right then, Mary Ann Madrid is being eaten alive by mosquitos in that costume (a short jungle-print toga, with a palm-frond plume in her hair), as she waits to be taken captive by drum-pounding natives. For two weeks, Harvey Patch, the assistant director, has been promising that Mr. Marcel will be arriving at any moment to finish what's supposed to be his most important film yet. Truthfully, Harvey Patch has no idea where the hell Stuart Marcel is. In spite of the huge amounts of alcohol he's been consuming, Patch has lost a good ten pounds from nerves and dysentery, from blood flukes, and from running around with a shovel to protect himself against another wild-boar attack.

In the desert, though, in a creaky bed in a cabin at Tamarosa Ranch just days before Greatstone gets a call from his wife at the bug-infested front desk of Hotel Misery, Jack's hands are so hot that he is nearly burning Nash's skin. He is right—there will always be men with guns, and, too, there will always be vicious gossips and bad mistakes.

He parts the cleft between her legs, and he enters her, and small choices become large outcomes as the rain falls on the roof and on the dry desert ground, and as Mrs. Shumley shuts off the light.

chapter 18

Callie

Shaye turned off the movie when my phone rang. It was a silly film, an old black-and-white that made you wonder what in the world people were thinking in those days. Right then, a woman in a short jungle-print toga with a palm-frond plume in her hair was being taken captive by drum-pounding natives. We'd been in our pajamas far too long, and it was time to get moving anyway. I went upstairs to talk to Amy, who was phoning from an old, ragged hotel near the bottom of an active volcano. There was a rain forest surrounding it, she told me. She and Hannah saw two capuchin monkeys. They had a view of the volcano from their room. Why had I been gone from home for so long, she wanted to know? Melissa told her I'd been at the ranch. I should go back to Seattle, she said, because Dad needed me. He was the kind of person who'd leave his coffee cup on the top of the car before driving off.

Whether it was distance or Amy's own ever-laid-back temperament, she was less concerned about my absence than Melissa was. It made me think of the two of them, their small, distinct selves, getting ready for school. While Melissa organized her little blue backpack, Amy shoved everything into her orange one and hoped for the best. Back then, I'd have never thought I'd actually miss the days of buying school supplies, but there you have it.

I hung up from Amy and called Melissa to check in. It seemed she'd decided to ignore her parents' bad behavior, which is a trick we used to try, too. She asked if we still had that blow-up raft we had when they were kids. She and Thomas had hunted around in the garage and couldn't find it, but they were sure it was there somewhere. She and Kelly and Jess wanted to float it down the Sammamish River.

This is what we looked like: a trip out in a raft, Thomas making scrambled eggs, dinner with Richard and André or maybe our neighbors Lawrence and his wife, Sienna, at that great Italian place. Amy on the phone with a new love, her voice filling the house; Hugo barking his head off every time he heard the latch of the front gate. Thomas asking if I saw that thing on the news about the art heist; Thomas and me, lying on the couch together and laughing so hard at some comedian on TV. A trip to the Asian market, a meal gone wrong that we all made fun of, filling Easter baskets the kids had since they were babies. A sore throat; an opossum in the yard; the three of us plus Melissa's new boyfriend sitting in a row at Amy's violin concert. The poor guy clapped at the wrong place, because who ever knows when to clap at those things, and we kidded him hard about it. We could, because each and every one of us had done it over the years. Our marriage was us, but our marriage was also a family and a life. Lives entwined.

If I went home, and the mood came back and Thomas looked at me and said it was over, I didn't know what I'd do. If I went home and I looked at Thomas and said it was over, I didn't know what I'd do, either. I'd be destroyed, flattened. I'd be desolate. I'd be the desert. I'd be what the desert looks like at first glance. When you look further, though, when you look close enough to see it all, it is teeming with life. I'd be that old, desert old, and I'd be young as I once was, too.

"Are the horses afraid?" I asked. "Because I think I'd be afraid if a helicopter was chasing me."

The corrals had grown in numbers and size. There were five large holding pens, and the fencing that created the chute now reached out toward the open land of the desert. Lorraine eyed me from the stables, but then she looked up toward the sky. I saw it, too, a dark cloud moving fast. A fat drop of water fell on my cheek and I wiped it away. The rain began to patter down, pinging against metal and plastic.

"Come on," Kit Covey said. He grabbed my sleeve and we ran. We took the two wobbly stairs up into the trailer, where Kit exhaled. "Whew! It's really coming down."

"I've never seen it do this."

"The desert," he said, as explanation. "It won't last long, which is a shame for those horses. They sure as hell need it. You're soaked." He handed me a towel from the padded bench, and I patted my hair dry.

"That came fast. Out of nowhere. The cold, too."

"Sit," he said. He went to a stove and turned on the burner under a pot of coffee. "Cup?"

"Please."

The coffee was bitter and thick from sitting too long, but it was warm, at least, as the rain hit the roof. That day, I could tell that the energy was different at the site. The movement was faster, the voices louder. The chute that reached toward the desert had large, wide arms, arms that beckoned to the animals. I had seen new road-closure signs on the drive.

Kit Covey rubbed the side of his face with one hand. "You

asked if they're afraid? I won't lie to you. Yeah, they are, and in part that's why it works. The noise of the helicopter sets them running. And the pilot has to get pretty low to drive them toward the trap."

"How low?"

"Low enough to get them going the right direction. He'll back off a little after that, depending on the distance, so they don't get as stressed. Then they'll usually follow the Judas horse right on in. There may be a few stragglers for the wranglers to deal with, but it's the helicopter that does most of the work. So, yeah, they're afraid."

"The Judas horse." The name sounded awful. Tricked, trapped.

"The Judas horse, the Prada. The pilot. Called a lot of things."

"Jasper."

"Jasper, too." He smiled. This was the Kit that was familiar to me, the one who drove his truck and danced with me, ever so briefly. The Kit out here, though, he reminded me that there was much I didn't know about this man. How he felt about his mother, what he was like when he was angry. What his daughter sounded like, laughing.

I tried to imagine it: Something overhead. The frightening *whick-whick-whick* of helicopter blades, a huge object lowering itself above you. Running. Fearing for your life and the lives of your offspring. "This is the way it has to be done?"

"There are other ways. I told you about the water traps, right? Fire crews'll bring water to an existing spring to lure them. That means three thousand gallons every few days, and I can tell you, that's a lot of water. Then you wait. You can gather maybe twenty-five, thirty horses at a time that way. But it'd take too long, and it'd be too expensive here. We aim to gather eight hundred."

"Eight hundred!"

"Well, Nevada's got maybe twenty thousand wild horses and burros. Half the entire wild-horse population of the West. This land out here can't sustain them."

The rain stopped, just like that. One of the men yelled, "Damn sandwich is wet," and the others laughed.

"Trevor Tompkins," Kit said. "Our helicopter pilot. And that man's gotta have his food. You need to come and watch."

"I can watch?"

"Anyone can. You call the BLM, tell 'em you want to. Meet at the assigned place of the day, and there you go. And you, Miss McBride, can skip the call to the office."

"P.R.," I said.

"I want you to see."

"I want to see."

"I'll let you know. The first one will probably be in a few days. We can't always tell. Conditions change."

"A few days. So it's happening."

"It's happening."

"My aunt, she said she saw a gather before. She told me last night. She said . . . Well, it wasn't what she said exactly. She just indicated that something bad happened. I think that's the reason for the boot-throwing." I shrugged. I didn't know how I felt about this, or about much else, truthfully.

"Around here? Recently?"

"I think she meant a long time ago."

"Well, that explains it. It was brutal then. It was. Even the early gathers the BLM did. And before that? Damn mustangers did whatever the hell they wanted. It was a free-for-all. They sold the corpses for cash. Dog-food companies . . . Jesus." He shook his head in disgust. "We've got the same pieces, sure— horses, land, humans—but we have a different mindset and different problems. Overburdened land, first off. Depleted vegetation. Vanishing species of it, even. We've got to think about the health of the wildlife, all of it, and how the horses themselves are doing. It's not a perfect answer, but it's the most gentle, humane one we have. Are they afraid? Yeah. Are they sometimes hurt? Yeah. But we give them our care and our respect. We're as thoughtful as we can reasonably be. Some things don't change, right? They gathered back then. We still do it today. They used airplanes. We use helicopters. But we understand more as time goes on, and we try to do better. We try to be a damn sight more kind."

I nodded. "That's all anyone can ask for."

"That's all anyone can do." He put his hand briefly on mine. "Callie, I promise you. I will personally make sure they're as all right as possible."

All right. Couldn't you just lay your head right down on those words and rest? I wanted those words for my own. No matter how much things changed or how time passed, every single earthly creature pursued the promise of *all right*, and I was no different. We sought it in the shelter of caves and underground hollows and in successful husbands and suburban neighborhoods with gates. We fought for it, and manipulated others to get it, and tried to buy it in our organic food and cars with every safety feature, and tried to fake it with tough exteriors, and camouflage, and false hopes. We could want a sense of shelter, real shelter, so badly that we could lose air until the panic of not having it was over, or we could ditch our lives in an instant. The desire for *all right* was perhaps the only thing we all—every human, every animal—truly had in common, even though the relentless drive for it could make us both stand against one another and seek out one another's warm and flawed company. And yet, fleeing it, even briefly, also gave us the thrill of our lives.

Kit removed his hand from mine. He lifted that cup to his lips. "Damn," he said. "Why didn't you say something? This coffee is *awful*."

Shaye's rear end stuck out of the Ford Fusion Hybrid, and she was screeching. "Get out of there this minute!"

"I am not one of your misbehaving toddlers!"

"My misbehaving toddlers aren't toddlers anymore!"

There was the push–pull of arms, and Shaye banged her head backing out. "Shit!" she yelled.

They both looked like toddlers, if you asked me. They reminded me of Amy and Melissa, fighting over a single garish-pink plastic pony.

"People!" I clapped my hands. "Quiet down, and listen up!" The girls' classroom teachers flashed before my eyes, from Mrs. Benjamin to Mr. Clymer, all the way on up to Doug Longman, Ravenna High's orchestra conductor. I wasn't sure which one of them I'd stolen that line from. "What is going on here? You two should see yourselves!"

Clearly, Shaye had won. She held a key ring on her index finger and gave it a triumphant twirl. Her face blazed with righteousness. "She was just going to take off! First she's too scared to get in the damn thing to learn, and then she's heading out like nothing! Luckily, Tex started barking when he heard the car start."

Tex lay on the porch, his chin on his paws. At the mention of his name, his ear twitched. He looked bored with the whole affair, actually, and maybe even a tad disgusted. How humans even managed in the world, well, it was beyond him.

"I got my courage up, is all! Have I suddenly turned into a baby? What would I do right now if you girls weren't here? I'd be getting in the car I just bought and driving it, and neither of you would be the wiser." She got out and slammed the door hard, and the car gave a terrified shiver. I hoped I was that strong when I was her age.

"Well, we're here now."

"Whoop-de-doo."

It was sad, because she'd even dressed up for the trip. She had a red blouse on, tucked into tan slacks. I didn't even know she had slacks, let alone a blouse. Her hair was loose from her braid, and I could see a bit of color painted onto her lips and brushed onto her cheekbones. Honestly, the lipstick broke my heart. I saw her teenage self then, those glimpses you got of people sometimes when the lonely adolescent crept out from the adult exterior. I could only imagine the way she and my mother must have fought. They seemed so different on the surface. My mother was girlish and self-centered, needful of attention, while Nash puttered along on her own merits, defying interference. Still, they were sisters. They had the same downturn of eyes and a stubborn streak. A determination flowed through their blood like defeat flows through the blood of some others. Nash could gaze out a window and I'd see my mother's profile. Then again, Shaye could gaze out a window and I'd see mine.

"We are not here to thwart you," I said. Nash looked up to the sky, then rolled her eyes at the heavens, which surely understood her better than we did. "We care about you. We don't want anything to happen to you. Getting in a car and taking off who knows where—you're not well. You haven't driven in years. It's dangerous."

"Yeah!" Shaye said. It was a two-against-one *yeah*, a proven-right *yeah*. As a little sister, she'd had a lot of years to perfect it.

"And what's going to happen? Tell me that. I'm going to *die*?"

She had us there. Shaye rubbed the back of her neck and sighed.

I looked up at the rambunctious clouds, which had lined up across the sky, ready to march. One slid over the sun, and shade slunk past, like the villain in a melodrama, before brightness returned. "Please," Shaye said. "Just let us help you. My friend Janey? Her grandmother reunited with a man she knew in *high school*. They got married! They were both eighty-something. I saw the pictures. They were so cute! Janey even bought her a garter, but thankfully there were no pictures of that."

"Cute?" Nash said.

"I'm sorry," Shaye said. "I didn't mean it like that. Just tell us where he lives. I mean, look at you. You're all dressed up. We can go right now! What do we have to do here anyway, watch the deer and the antelope play?"

"This is not about Jack," Nash said. She threw her hands in the air, huffed toward the house. She'd had enough of us.

"Come on, Nash," Shaye called after her. In spite of every-thing, this was the story she was sticking with. Shaye was a romantic, which was probably what had gotten her into so much trouble.

"It wasn't Jack who I loved," Nash said, as the screen door slammed shut behind her.

chapter 19

Nash

"Come on, Veronica," Ellen calls from the porch. "We'd better hurry. We've got to get changed! This might be the very night you meet the man of your dreams." Ellen is a romantic, which is probably what's gotten her into so much trouble.

"I'm through with that nonsense," Veronica says, as the screen door slams shut behind her.

Nash collects her purse and a forgotten shopping bag of Veronica's in the trunk. Veronica has bought so many new clothes over her six weeks that they'll have to buy another suitcase before taking her to the airport. Nash is sad that Veronica is leaving. She doesn't feel that way about everyone. Some, she's glad to see go—after they drive away, the ranch fills back up with air and space. Others are quickly forgotten. She might remember their blond hair, a vague story about an inheritance. But every now and then there's a woman like Veronica. A person Nash actually cares about, and who cares about her. Six weeks could feel like you were just getting started. At least, it feels like something real.

Veronica pops her head back outside. "My bag," she says.

Nash holds it up.

"I think I'll wear the green one. I should celebrate."

"You may just meet the man of your dreams," Nash teases.

"I'd be the man of my dreams' worst nightmare," Veronica says.

Boo has been set outside on the porch. Poor dogs, doomed to feel any human emotion a hundred times over; horses, too. Boo knows there's excitement in the air, so he's beside himself. He's like a faulty Fourth of July rocket, spinning circles and making a high-pitched whine.

Helena, the maid, has cleaned everything, including the piano. The rugs have been rolled up, and the floors gleam and smell of polish. Without your shoes, you might fall and break an ankle. All the furniture has been pushed to the edge of the room. Cook has set up the large table where the couch used to be, and she's draping the best cloth over it, the one with the crocheted edge. Next to it, Danny's already unfolded the legs of the card table. He's hauling out bottles from the bar, carrying six at a time, a lock of dark hair falling over his forehead from where it had been slicked back.

"We'll need the glasses from the basement," Nash tells him, though he knows that full well. Mostly she just wants him to turn her way, so that she can see what he knows about her and Jack. *If* he knows.

"Righto," Danny says. But he looks the same as ever. His shirt is coming untucked, and he shoves one hand down his pants to make it right.

Nash looks the same, too; she studied herself in the bathroom mirror that morning. She doesn't know what she expected from the night before, but her hair is still brown and her eyes are still gray, and her nose is still plain. She's crossed over from here to there, regardless, and while this is shocking and shameful, there's part of her that's relieved. All the whispers and jokes and nudges and talk over the years—well, the mystery is over. At least her eyes aren't completely shut anymore.

The band arrives, sets up. It's their usual group, the Ned Night Trio, which comes in from Carson City. Ned works at Brumswick Drug, and Hank Pollard, the saxophone player, is a doorman at the Apache Hotel; Earl on bass rides fences for the Diamond S.

Nash retrieves Boo so that he won't be underfoot as the equipment is set up. Out on the porch, she sees waves of heat rise from the pool. There is a plane overhead. It is close to their property, flying too low. Jesus, the sound. Nash claps her hands over her ears. Idiot pilots—she hates them. They have no idea what that does to the cattle and horses, who may even go off their food tonight after a scare like that.

Nash tucks Boo under her arm. As she heads upstairs to change out of her trousers, a burst of saxophone notes follow, trying to tell her something important in C's and F sharps.

"You'll get to go home," Ellen says with longing. When she shifts her weight to cross one leg over the other, there is the shushing of taffeta against crinoline against nylon stockings. "I'm missing my babies so much. I'm worried little Bobby will forget who I am."

"He'll never forget who you are. When I was a baby? My mother took a voyage on the *Britannic*, before it sank in the First War. Believe me, I never forgot her. Heavens, no," Hadley said. "Shame, too, because she was the sort to chase us with the soup ladle and then cry in bed at her own wrongdoing until we comforted her." Hadley shimmers in blue, her skirt cinched at the waist, making her figure an hourglass.

"Home," Veronica says. Her new green dress has gold trim around the accentuated bust, and she wears a coiled-braid hairpiece that makes her look like a movie star. "I don't even know where that will be now after Gus."

"You'll miss the boring sod," Hadley said.

Nash hands their drinks around. Lilly smiles and says thank you when Nash hands her a glass of champagne. A going-away party is always a celebration. Lilly pats the seat beside her. There is so much to do, but Nash sits anyway. She'll have to greet the visitors who will be arriving at any moment, as Alice usually does. Jack plays host, too, though he hasn't shown up yet.

"Oh, stop," Veronica says. "You'll make me sad."

"You loved him," Ellen says.

"I was supposed to love him. I should have loved him. But I didn't love him. I care about him, as a person. I'm not totally heartless. Did I tell you how we met?"

"The taxi," Ellen says.

"The taxi?" Lilly asks. She's the only one who hasn't heard this.

"I was in New York, visiting Nora, my mother. It was raining. I had shopping bags."

"That, I can't imagine," Hadley says.

"Suddenly there was this handsome gentleman calling a taxi for me. The taxi pulls to the curb. I look at him, and he looks at me, and I say, *Going my way?*"

"You didn't!" Lilly's eyes are wide.

"I did! He was so gallant. He seemed impetuous and interesting. Not a half hour before, Nora had been harping at me again to find a husband before it was too late. I'd turned too many suitors away, she said. I liked being a single gal, living on my own. No one to answer to! It was glorious."

"Glorious," Ellen says. She doesn't sound too sure.

"The fear for my future would keep her up at night, Mother told me. Over tea and sandwiches, she said I was *drying up*. Isn't that awful? I still think about that. I looked over at this man, a man who just *appeared*—right outside Nora's Upper East Side apartment! Like an *answer*. He seemed worldly. He had the most elegant overcoat. . . ."

"You liked him because of his overcoat?" This is a part of the story they haven't heard. Hadley strikes a match, lights her own damn cigarette.

"I did, actually! I saw him in his unusual chic coat, and he saw me hopelessly drenched in the rain, and that was that. We each married a person who never was. And then . . ."

"The overcoat was borrowed," Hadley says.

"No, the overcoat wasn't borrowed!" Veronica swats Hadley's arm. "But I'd been blinded by it. I didn't see the important thing that day. Because the taxi-hailing turned to opening doors to making breakfast to serving me eggs on a plate, and this turned to asking why I was troubled and fetching me a doctor for my headache. And why did I have one headache after another? Because he buttered my biscuits and fretted when I was out alone at night and took my arm when I crossed the street. He hung up my garments and rubbed my shoulders and felt my forehead for fever, and I paced like a tiger. He and Nora began to talk. They were *worried*. We should be thinking about *conceiving*. I picked at him unfairly. I was snappish and irritable."

"You're always snappish and irritable," Hadley says.

"More snappish, let me tell you, Miss Playwright. The slow, sad scuff of his shoes down the hall, the sound of his breathing next to me in the bed, this heavy breathing, a snoring on the exhale . . ." Veronica demonstrates.

Ellen giggles.

"I am a horrible person. I didn't deserve him."

"You're not," Hadley says firmly. "He didn't let *you* breathe. It sounds ghastly."

"We went to a party, and there was a young thing, a lovely frail girl, who laughed at his jokes and batted her eyelashes at him. I watched it all across the room. He brought her a drink and picked up the cocktail napkin she dropped, and I asked our hostess who she was. Genevieve Morley, the younger sister of Arthur Morley, the decorator."

"Jealousy and revenge," Lilly guesses. She raises her eyebrows at Nash, and Nash nods conspiratorially.

"Not at all!" Veronica says. "I was hoping they might meet again! When I began planning a dinner where they might be seated next to each other, I knew our marriage was over. I couldn't tell him for months. His eyes were so sweet when he slept on the pillow."

Hadley snores, same as Veronica had, and they all laugh.

"After I finally told him I wanted a divorce, he and Nora set up an appointment for me with a psychiatrist. I was afraid they might commit me. I overheard them talking."

"You never told us this before," Hadley says.

"Oh, Veronica." Ellen looks stunned.

"That's awful," Lilly says.

"I fled to the apartment in San Francisco that my father left me and then here. Home? I've only lived in that place for three weeks."

"Be glad you're not telling this story to some doctor in McLean," Hadley said. "You could be in there still."

"You were brave to leave," Ellen says.

"Brave," Veronica says, and sighs.

"You were," Hadley says.

"I never loved Stuart, either," Lilly says.

The front door is open, so Nash can tell that cars are arriving. These will be the guests from the Flying W and Washoe Pines, but Nash wants to hear this.

"Never?" Ellen asks.

"I didn't even really like him. I don't know how it happened. He says I flirted with him. At this party. I went with my friend Eve. It was at Lyle Johnson's house. The producer? He gave me the role in *The Changelings*."

"Eddie adored *The Changelings*. For weeks after, he'd jump out from behind the furniture, screaming, *Nevermore*! It scared me half to death." Ellen sips her champagne.

"Joseph couldn't sleep after watching it," Hadley says. "He said it disturbed his dreams."

"You flirted with him?" Nash asks. She can't imagine it. Being that bold or that foolhardy.

"No! At least, not that I remember. He was strangely attractive. Very much so! But he seemed old to me. Like the way you imagine fathers. Not mine, but the kind of fathers with cigars and libraries, who give ponies for birthdays."

"The kind of fathers with mistresses and henchmen, maybe," Hadley says.

"I said it was what he *seemed* like. At first."

"My father gave crisp bills in an envelope and forbade smoking in his home," Veronica says, and searches for her own cigarettes. "But the mistresses . . ."

"Crisp bills," Ellen sighs.

Lilly adjusts her weight in the chair. "He kept giving me drinks. It all seemed to be a wrong turn I couldn't back out of. He kissed me, and I was . . . I don't know how to describe it. I was *repelled*."

"So you married him," Hadley says.

"I can't explain it. He turned up again, at the after-party of *His Last Wish*. Our friend Jeannie had a part. And the same thing happened. He took me outside, and he kissed me, and I was horrified at myself, and yet it seemed beyond my control to stop it. I am still horrified. His thick sausage fingers and big stomach . . ." She shudders. "He just had this *grip* on my arm. It made me feel safe."

"A grip like that can be used against you, if it can be used for you," Hadley says.

"Who would ever do something so inexplicable and stupid?" Lilly says. "Me. I'm the only one."

Veronica stands and smooths her skirt. She briefly takes Lilly's hand. "No," she says. It's one word, but it's enough.

There it is again. How often Nash has seen it—the critical pieces of every couple's plotline, present from the very start. But this isn't the time to ponder the hidden desires that can cause more harm than an out-of-control car you don't see coming. The party is starting. And why hasn't it occurred to her before now that this gathering is a huge and noisy invitation to Stuart Marcel? He's the type of man who'd think this gathering mocks him. It's always best to walk softly and keep quiet around people like that, and there's nothing quiet about what's happening now. Nash thinks about the gravel in Lilly's palms after she was shoved and the crisscross of red scrapes on the back of her legs. She thinks of Lilly's thin arm in a cast after it was twisted and cracked.

The bass player begins to *thumb-thumb-do-do-thumb*, and Dolly Leeds and her gals come inside, laughing and talking. One of them trips on the door ledge, tipsy already, and another clings to the arm of a spare—you can always spot a spare, with his dapper suit and gaze that looks like a compliment. Still, Nash is relieved to see the matronly Dolly, who's been handling men and women and love, with all its mess and pain and fallout, for years. Dolly's wranglers follow behind—cowboys and bull riders and desert men, men who know how to handle a man with a temper. Stuart Marcel would be outnumbered here. She wishes Lilly had never walked into the room where she met him. She wishes Lilly had never placed her mouth against his thick, despicable lips. It is so much harder to undo than to do. Lilly and Beanie deserve so much better.

Here is Bertha Gray now, from Washoe Pines. There is a swirl of dresses and it all begins. Plates and glasses clink against plates and glasses, and the saxophone player, Hank Pollard, surely sweats more heavily than he does carrying monogrammed trunks to the highest floors and down the longest hallways of the Apache. He plays every moment between love and heartbreak, and people start to dance, and Nash pretends she is Alice. She shakes Dolly Leeds's solid hand and brings her a plate of eggs pickled in beet juice, browned-butter mushrooms, and a slice of tarred Swiss premium ham. She wonders again where Jack is, and it's a good thing she isn't Alice right this minute or his job would be in jeopardy. She wants to keep loving him, but he makes it so darn hard.

Someone has tucked a primrose into Veronica's coiled braid. She dances with Ted from Washoe Pines, who has found her in the crowd again. Ted is more handsome than smart, but he once saved all the horses when the stable caught fire that bad year of drought. Veronica catches Nash's eye and winks. Nash is glad Veronica's having fun on her last night, but her frustration at Jack grows to concern. He's never late for these parties. He's always right on time, playing host at the door, slapping backs and kissing the hands of the matrons. Hadley lingers at the food table; she has found the Berne's Gold Label chocolates that Alice has Cook order for special occasions, and she's also snitching the greengage plums packed in sugar-sweetened brandy. Hadley licks the sticky liquid off one finger and points out the delicacy to Harold Ferrill, also from the Pines. Like all the wranglers there, though, Harold would no doubt rather have a pork sandwich and a whiskey.

There is a shortage of men, and the ladies from the Flying W dance together in a circle, bumping into everyone else, causing Bertha to spill her drink. Napkins appear, and so do apologies, but the dancing continues and the noise gets louder. Nash checks on Lilly, who is still in that chair, but before Nash can ask if Lilly needs anything, Ellen appears in front of them. She is in high spirits, and she takes both of their hands and urges Nash and Lilly toward the piano. Lilly protests but then gives in, and the three of them sway as Ned leans over his flying hands on that keyboard and sings about moonlight.

Lewis, a new dude wrangler at the Flying W, cuts in. He whisks Ellen away, while she holds one hand out to Nash and Lilly as if she is drowning and they should save her. They won't save her, as clearly she is thrilled.

"Ellen's found a boy," Lilly shouts above the noise. She sets her hand on Beanie. She looks tired. "I need to sit."

"We'll go sit," Nash says.

But as they head for the sofa, Jack finally appears. He smiles at both of them, but there is something wrong. He is still in his denim pants and his work shirt. He bows to Lilly. "Excuse me, ma'am," he says. He drawls with all his usual sweet charm, but the verve and lightness are gone. He grips Nash's elbow and ushers her away. He's clearly upset. He doesn't even realize he's hurting her.

All day long, Nash has been waiting to see Jack again after their night together. She's imagined this reunion a thousand ways. Their eyes might meet; he'd notice the dress Veronica had insisted she wear, a red satin beauty with soft, round shoulders and a nipped waist and a bust they took in using safety pins. He'd secretly try to kiss her. He'd look at her with the same gaze he's given Lilly. Nash knows better, she does, but she even imagined being his girl now. None of those things are happening, though. He rushes her through the crowd, smiling and greeting people along the way, heading the both of them toward the bar, where Danny opens another bottle of champagne. The cork pops like a gun blast, and Jack flinches.

"Whiskey," he says to Danny.

"What the hell happened to you?" Danny says. He pours. He hands Jack the drink.

"The truck," Jack says. He isn't smiling anymore. "The bastard shot out the truck."

Nash's stomach drops. It's a sudden, sick thud.

"I was in Carson City. We needed some fly spray and I wanted to get an ice boot for Maggie, 'cause she's been limping. I park in front of H and J's, and I'm in there, and there's this *pow-pow-pow* outside, and I know what that sound is. I know good and well what that sound is. We go runnin' out, Al Johns and me, and this car's squealing away, and my tires are all shot out. There's a bullet hole right in the windshield, driver's side. Glass everywhere! We gotta call the sheriff, wait for him to come. Al Johns let me borrow one of his pickups. Jesus. Alice is gonna kill me. The truck's a damn mess."

"*Alice* is going to kill you? Christ, Jack. Sounds like someone else might get you first," Danny says. "A gun, Jack. When a man gets a gun involved . . ."

Nash is shocked into silence. Her body is iron, weighted to the ground.

"It's just a warning. I know a warning when I see one. Okay," he says. He puts both his hands up, palms out, warding off. "Okay, I got it."

"The sheriff—" Nash says.

"Couldn't do a damn thing. Bet you anything, the fucker and his sidekick hopped on their little plane over at Lansing Field. Probably already in Los Angeles by now."

The sense of safety Nash felt here at Tamarosa, surrounded by their own people—it's gone. She looks out over the room. A terror presses down, as Ellen leans in and kisses that cowboy right on the mouth, and as Veronica lifts a glass of champagne and toasts her imminent freedom.

Nash excuses herself. The din of the party falls back as she heads upstairs. Boo scratches at her bedroom door, where he is being held captive. He's made marks. He's never done this before. Mother would die. Nash edges inside so the little dog doesn't make a run for it. She doesn't take the time to scold him, even though the door is deeply gouged in manic, knee-high scratches. Instead, she hurries to retrieve a scrap of paper, used as a bookmark now in *Sense and Sensibility*. On it is the number her mother gave her the last time they spoke, the number at Gloria's friend's apartment, where they're staying. It was all a little unclear, what was happening with Gloria. A boy, a broken heart—who knew. Some new drama fit for the big screen at the Granada.

Nash shuts Boo back in and crosses the hall to her mother's room. The photo of her father stares at her from the nightstand, and the room still smells like the rose-scented toilet water Alice uses. Downstairs, there is a loud round of applause as the trio ends a set. Nash dials, and her heart beats hard while the phone only rings and rings and rings. It feels like such failure to be making this call at all, though that is no longer important.

It is less important than she even knows right then, because that evening George Greatstone will pick up a phone, too. He won't get through, either; not at first. Marcel is probably on a plane or fucking some girl or taking a crap. He'll want to hear this, though, so Greatstone will try again the next day, when he'll finally find Stu poolside at his spread in L.A. The connection is awful at that godforsaken jungle hotel. All Greatstone will hear is the buzz of a bloodsucking mosquito near his ear and the crackle of the word *cunt*.

chapter 20

Callie

The phone rang and rang and rang. I was sleeping hard, and the real-life sound folded into my dream. In it, a phone was ringing, but I didn't want to answer right then, because Hugo had returned. He was there, large and healthy, and he was so overjoyed to be home that he did a fast and furious lap around the living room, causing the rugs to slide around, just like he always used to. He got in his *let's play* stance, with his front paws together, his head low to the ground, and his butt high. He barked, and I clapped my hands twice, like I always did. I said, *Gonna get you*, the same thing I'd say to the kids when they were small, words that kicked off a game of chase.

What a relief it was that he'd come back! My heart shot upward, a rocket of joy. Such happiness. Thank God, he wasn't dead after all.

And then I woke, and the phone rang one more time before stopping. The truth hit. A rush of grief started behind my eyes and went to my chest, crushing everything in its path. Oh, Hugo. I missed him more than I could say. He'd been my friend and my companion, and the loss of him had left me bereft. Dead was so wrong. Dead was so sad and terribly wrong.

* * *

Nash seemed well that morning. She was dressed in her jeans and a red T-shirt, and she looked cheery. She had parked herself at the table, and Shaye scooped scrambled eggs onto her plate.

"I have a little surprise for you girls," Nash said.

"Hmm," Shaye said. "Surprises can go either way."

"I've come around to your point of view. No more taking off in the car."

"Wonderful," I said. I poured myself a cup of coffee.

"You're going to teach me to drive today."

Shaye and I looked at each other. "Oh, super," Shaye said.

"I've come to my senses." She was shoveling in those eggs.

"Sausages?" Shaye asked.

"Keep the spirits up!" Nash said. She patted her stomach.

"I'll have what she's having," I said.

Shaye sat down with us. Her plate was nearly empty. "You okay, Sham?"

"You bet," she said.

"Perhaps we should go over some of the rules of the road first," I said.

"Nonsense. Rules, rules, rules. We eat and get cracking," Nash said.

"Well, I'm thrilled to see you're in such a fine mood, Nash. Because I've been meaning to ask you something." Shaye shoved her chair back, disappeared into the living room.

"What does she want?" Nash said.

"Don't ask me."

Shaye reappeared with the *Confidential* magazine that had been under the coffee table. She folded the cover back to a photo that she put under Nash's nose. "What is *this*?"

"No idea," Nash said, but her brows had turned down into a scowl.

"Let me see," I said.

"June of 1951!" Shaye said, and handed it to me. "We looked right at it, Cal. It was right in front of us." Blame our bad eyes or fate's own timing, but, yes, there was the date in small white print, on the cover. There was a bridge in the photo, and a car in the water under that bridge. The car was upside down, wheels wrongly in the air. *"Director dead in Reno,"* I read the caption aloud. "Hey, that's the bridge in town. The main one, over the river."

"That's where bridges usually are," Shaye said. "Over a body of water."

"Shut up, Sham." I gave the magazine back. "I don't get it. I'm sure there's been plenty of stuff like this over the years."

"I'm sure there's been plenty of stuff like this over the years," Nash repeated. She shoved her plate away. The joy in her eyes was gone.

"Who was he?" Shaye asked.

"Who?"

"You know who. This Stuart Marcel guy."

"You never heard of him?" Nash's jaw nearly dropped.

"No," Shaye said.

"I've never heard of him, either," I said.

Nash shook her head as if there were things she'd never understand. "Big important forgotten man. Well, well, well."

"Who was he?" Shaye asked.

"Some big Hollywood type. How do I know. I live out in the middle of nowhere."

"Nice try," Shaye said. "I saw this before, but I didn't understand then, because we hadn't heard the name yet. But look who's here. Our old friend Jack. *Dude wrangler Jack Waters, who witnessed the crash, said Marcel was 'easily going eighty, ninety.*

Car suddenly veered off. Flew up and then angled down, like a one-winged condor.'"

"Where did you get that?" Nash asked. Her face turned red. Her eyes blazed.

"It was right there in the living room!"

"That was not right there in the living room."

"It was! Under the coffee table. It's been there for years. I saw that thing when I was a *kid*."

"It was under the coffee table, Nash," I said. "Where it's been forever. You sit right in front of it every day."

Nash shook her head. She rubbed one eye with her finger-tips. "I don't believe it. It can't be true."

"You probably stopped seeing it," I said.

"Summer of 1951. Jack Waters. This Hollywood guy. We were right, Cal, and I for one would like some answers."

"The answers don't belong to you, nor do the questions." Nash set her mouth in a grim line. "I've lost my will. I'm in no mood to drive."

She pushed her chair back. She snatched that magazine from Shaye's hand, and a moment later we heard the rattle of the fireplace damper. There was the *schwick* of a match before all evidence of a car, a bridge, and Stuart Marcel went up in smoke.

"Jesus, Shaye, what were you thinking? I mean, first off, a picture of a car crash before we go out for a driving lesson? And why didn't you tell me about this, anyway?"

"I don't have to check everything I do with you, for starters."

"It's just, she was in such a good mood. How about *timing*?"

"How about *your* timing?"

"What do you mean?"

"Ragging on me, right here right now. Can't you see that it isn't the best moment to get on my case?"

"I'm sorry, okay? What? What's going on?"

"I've got an appointment later today."

"What kind of an appointment?"

"With a lawyer."

"Oh, no. Really?"

She turned away, folded her arms. She was crying. I tore off a paper towel and handed it to her. She blew her nose. "You know. Might as well, while I'm here."

I hung my camera around my neck. There was no sign of Rob the buffalo, so I walked slowly as I took in the entirety of that dilapidated place. I lingered at the pasture and the stables, and I stood for a while by the empty pool. I snapped a photo of the blue-and-white tiles that circled its center and one of the long cracks in the cement deck, where Shaye and I had run in bare feet before our mother told us to slow down. Through the dirty windows of the small pool house, I could see lounge chairs piled up like sarcophagi in a crypt.

Avalon and Shangri-La and the Ritz and the one that was now nameless—I tried to really see them in a deep, permanent way, a way that might let me hold on to them when this place was gone, which would surely be soon. A fast, elusive creature scurried under a porch. The tar roofs of the cottages had gone brittle. The signs with the letters burned into wood spoke of cheer and old, good times. I took photos of each so that I could keep those cabins forever, in some form, anyway.

The lake seemed still, until something leaped out and made ripples that made more ripples. Sun played on the water, and I captured this, too. I sat on a rock and ringed my arms around my knees. I also remembered Shaye and me here as girls, trying to skip stones, managing only to fling them across, where they'd sink with a deep *clunk*. Then, Shaye's braids were golden and mine were brown. We were Snow White and Rose Red, one who liked to dance in peaceful meadows and one who liked to stay home with Mother, meeting evil dwarves and the son of a king disguised as a fierce bear.

There, I was hit again with a feeling I'd had rather frequently as of late. Deep in the night, or even in broad daylight, a sense of the transitory would abruptly arise, shocking me, slapping my clueless self with the truth of my own age and of how much time had already passed, and so suddenly, too, it seemed. It would hit hard. And it made me want to keep hold of everything and to toss it all away. How could you even talk about this? What were the words for it? I just didn't know where it all went and how it went that fast. What we lost over a lifetime seemed so great.

I reached my hand down, splashed my face with cool water. I walked on after that; headed to the place I knew I was heading all along. I needed to see the view from that ridge, feel the jolt of majesty, take in the grandeur of the timeworn tapestry made of orange and tan and yellow threads.

There. Ah, yes. Blue threads, and white, and brown, and somewhere, too, though I couldn't make them out, the threads of those horses with their velvet noses, and the threads of ranchers and cowboys and women and men and animals all through the years.

And, too, I could see a new pattern in the living fabric, the finished picture of those splayed wings, the long chutes, the circles of holding pens. There was motion below, ants dashing and darting about, tiny figures scurrying with their own purpose, looking the way we must look to God. The ring of my phone startled me.

"I was just seeing if I could find you," I said to Kit Covey. "I'm standing on the ridge right now."

"Are you? Look for a guy riding a horse. I'm waving."

"Well, I can imagine it, but in truth I'm too far away."

"Jasper's waving now."

"Ha."

"I called with some news," Kit said.

"Tell me."

"The first gather."

"It's time?"

"Tomorrow."

I couldn't stand the sound of Dr. Yabba Yabba Love's voice on that radio show, but Nash and Shaye seemed to like it, so I kept my mouth shut for once. That night's episode: *You seek what you know, so you'd better know what you seek.* Shudder. From my spot on the couch with Tex at my feet, I could hear Nash's old message machine whir on in the kitchen. It made a series of strange clicks and cheeps, like birdcalls. One ancient device, anyway, had bitten the dust. Still, it made me think of the beautiful time before message machines. It was lovely, really, not to know who'd called. To wonder, and maybe even be surprised. To not be able to be found, even if only by a distant and insistent voice wondering where you were.

It got cool there in the desert in the evenings but not cool enough to require the crocheted blanket that was over Nash's knees. She had a hot-water bottle tucked behind her back, too, and was giving us the silent treatment. Shaye had tried to talk her into taking some pills for pain, but she just frowned and shook her head. We all knew the time was coming when she wouldn't have that option, which is likely why she decided not to take them.

I was about to suggest we all watch another old movie, when a noise drowned out Dr. Love. It was the sound of a helicopter, the *thwacka thwacka* of blades, low and close. I knew what it was. I even knew *who* it was: Bureau of Land Management pilot Trevor Tompkins, the man with the wet sandwich yesterday. That helicopter would be taking off again at 7:00 A.M., bright and early, and I would be on the south hill near the site, watching the gather below.

"Listen to that!" Nash said. She looked at Shaye and then at me, and her eyes had changed. They spit sparks, same as a fire when the wood is seasoned and almost too ready to be burned.

We kept quiet. Tex sat up on alert, and I stroked him with my foot to calm him.

"I know what that is," she said.

"Nash," I said.

"Don't *Nash* me. Do you hear how low they're flying? Do you know what that does? I can't just sit here and do nothing!"

A glass on the table rattled from the din. Nash threw off that blanket; someone somewhere had made this careful pattern of chain stitches and slipknots with their own patient hands, but now the thing went flying, and so did the fat red water bottle. It went airborne before landing with a big plop on the floor, which caused Tex to leap to his feet and hide by my legs.

Before I knew it, Nash was out of that room, and there was the *thud, thud, thud* of her determined feet hurrying up the stairs. And then there were Shaye's, running up after her. "Nash, come here! Stop this!" she said.

I picked up poor Tex, who was cowering, and I crooned into

his little triangle ear. There was a crash upstairs and the sound of rooting around, and Shaye's voice, talking in a calm way I'd never heard before.

I needed to help my sister, but before I could even move, Nash came barreling back down. She took the stairs so fast, she was lucky she didn't break her neck. "We'll see who's scared now. Those bastards!"

I blinked. I didn't believe what I saw, frankly. It was all so sudden, and what was in her hands didn't make sense. She was holding a rifle. An actual rifle. It wasn't the kind of life I led, one that involved guns and people who had lost their minds holding those guns.

Shaye raced after her. The calm voice was gone; it had turned into a shriek of panic and fear, one that shook me out of my disbelief. My sister and I had always turned to each other to understand—no, to *witness* and make *real*—the shared crazy experiences of our lives, and right then was no different. "Jesus, Nash! What are you doing? What do you think this is, some action movie, some shoot-out? They won't even see you down here. We're the only ones you're scaring."

"Oh, they'll see me, all right," she said. She headed for the front door.

"Dear God, tell me that thing isn't loaded," I said.

"What am I, an idiot?" Nash replied.

"Give me that," Shaye said.

And that's when my sister lunged for the old woman. They stumbled; now she'd break a hip for sure. There was an explosive crack, and the sound of something actually zipping through the air, and the boom and shatter as the roof of that damn cuckoo clock blew right off.

Shaye held the gun. I'd want that girl by my side in a crisis any day. Even if what she did next was to open the door and run like hell and throw that thing as if it were on fire to the dirt-filled bottom of the pool, where it would lay alongside the boot and who knew what else.

Nash was on the floor. She put her head in her hands.

"Nash?" I whispered.

Shaye was back. Her face was red and she was breathing hard. We'd just experienced something traumatic, a natural disaster arising from an old fracture, buried deep. That helicopter—it was long gone. A whoosh of cool air came through the open front door, and there was only the sound of crickets.

"All right," Nash said. "All right. Fine." We needed to call an ambulance. That's what had to happen. This was the woman Harris had warned us about, the one who'd tried to bury a book by the lake.

She began to crawl on all fours. Oh, dear God, it was too strange and dreadful to take in. It was terrible, that sight, this old woman on hands and knees. She inched along the floor toward the piano.

"Okay," she said.

"What are you doing?" I tried to stay calm, but inside I felt anything but calm. "Nash, get up."

"Get out from there!" Shaye yelled.

Nash had reached the piano now. She crouched there, as if seeking shelter. But this was the thing. This was always the thing: Inexplicable actions are not so inexplicable at all when you know what's underneath.

There was an envelope taped to the old ribs and bones of the bottom of the soundboard, where Shaye and I would surely never have looked. Nash crawled back out, and she reached her hand toward me to help her up. She handed over the package.

"Here," she said.

"What is this?" I asked.

"Open it."

My fingers were on the clasp when there was the stomp of boots and then Harris's blocky frame in the doorway. He was out of breath. "Nash!" he cried. "Girls! I heard a shot."

My God, the old people there—their excellent sight and hearing. His shirt was buttoned wrong and his pants were half zipped, but the concern in his eyes was as solid as it came. He put his arm around Nash. He knew as well as we did that what was happening was significant, because Nash looked both defeated and defiant, and there was still the smell of the gunshot in the air. "Are you all right?" he said.

"Well, this is perfect, isn't it?" Nash said. "Fine. I give up! I'll tell all of you at once! How can I keep it a secret any longer, anyway? I can't. I just can't. I'm too tired. I've been looking for months. Only thing I had was a date of birth. The correspondence and records and research, the phone books! Well, I finally found him. Right when the mustangs arrived. Like I said, they're a *sign*."

I was mistaken about Trevor Tompkins being long gone. There was the sound of that helicopter again, coming in close. Shaye stood next to me, and Harris gripped Nash's elbow as I slipped the papers out. *Missoula County Department of Human Services*, the letterhead read. An old black-and-white photo was attached, the small, slightly yellowed image of an infant, swaddled tight in a blanket, showing only a tiny bit of a sleeping face.

"Damn," Harris said. There were still things to be discovered about her after all.

"You gave up a baby," I said.

"Yes, I did," Nash said. "That's exactly what I did."

chapter 21

Nash

There is the sound of that airplane again, coming in close. Ellen stands next to Nash, and so does Hadley, and the airplane is so low, it kicks up wind and sends their dresses blowing around their knees and their hair around their faces. Ellen puts her hand on her hat.

"Looks like a crop duster. They do the grapes not far from our house," she says.

"No crops here," Nash says, and as soon as she does, she finally realizes what that plane is. It is not a crop duster or some stunt plane, like the one she and Jack watched at the air show last summer. This plane has to do with those horses she saw in that truck, with the gaping wounds and dull, dead eyes.

"It's awfully low," Ellen says.

"Veronica!" Hadley shouts toward the house. "Come on! My God, she'd be late to her own funeral."

Ellen and Hadley are also going to court with Veronica. It was decided the night before, and it was Ellen who said it that time: *All for one, and one for all!* Now they wait in the driveway next to the Styleline Deluxe. Its doors are open to cool it down before they have to get in. Lilly will stay behind to rest. Cook and Jack and the boys will be there with her.

"There's the party girl," Ellen calls.

Veronica is in a smart pink suit with a jacket that flares at the waist. She's wearing a large-brimmed pancake hat, white, set at a jaunty tilt. "What's the hurry, ladies?" she says. "They won't start the divorce without the bride!"

Nash sits in the front of the courtroom. A fan blows overhead, creaking and tilting in such a way that Nash envisions it spinning madly off its fixture and crashing down, beheading a few of them along the way. She picks at her fingernails from nerves. This morning, there's still been no word from Alice, and now she'll have to stand and speak again. When the hearing begins and they are called forward, she will be required to say only three words—*Yes, Your Honor*—but without those three words confirming residency, Veronica will remain in a state of holy matrimony.

The lawyer is on one side of Veronica, and Nash is on the other. Ellen and Hadley whisper behind them, and Nash can't hear what they say, but Veronica can. At least, that must be why she gives a little snort just then. What has been said is easy to guess, though. Gus is wearing a stylish suit the color of new hay, with a bow tie of blue and white. His hat is on his lap. He is dashingly handsome. Yes, *dashingly*. His dark hair is parted at the side, and his long nose points down to a straight mouth. He turns the brim of his hat in his hands and tries to peer at Veronica as Nash and Ellen and Hadley try to peer at him, and as his attorney, a man as plump as a summer peach, shuffles papers in the briefcase open on his lap. But the snort isn't about Gus, exactly. The snort is about the young woman who sits behind Gus, a woman not much older than Nash. Her hair is as dark and shiny as Stuart Marcel's Cadillac, and she twists a handkerchief in her hands while keeping her eyes fixed on the back of Gus's head.

"Genevieve Morley," Veronica whispers to Nash.

"Well, that's good," Nash says. "Isn't that good?"

"Oh, I don't know," Veronica says. "He'll never be happy unless he's miserable. And she's likely to make him happy."

The judge enters. It is the Honorable Rice Clay, who has his own cattle ranch in Washoe. The divorce business is lucrative. They all rise. Genevieve Morley cries softly but still loud enough for them all to hear.

They stand on the Bridge of Sighs.

"This is it," Hadley says. "The start of your new life."

"My new life," Veronica says. "You know, I want to bathe without someone checking to see if I've slipped on a bar of soap. Feel an empty bed without bare legs brushing against mine, legs that are asking, asking, asking something of me. I just want to be *alone*."

It sounds shocking, and Ellen's eyebrows are arched, but Veronica seems to mean it. Strangely, Nash can see the sense in it. The idea appeals to her, too. She has lived with the press of her sister's moods and her mother's expectations, and all at once she cannot imagine a lifetime of someone else's needs. Neither can she imagine choosing the drama of heartbreak or the passion of love over the steady deliciousness of peace. That choice, to be alone—it has never even occurred to her before. It doesn't seem like a real option. No one chooses that on purpose, as far as she knows, and too bad.

Veronica twists the ring off her finger.

"Wait," Ellen says.

Veronica stops.

"Wouldn't you rather keep it in the vase at the ranch? It will be there forever that way."

"Get rid of it," Hadley says. "That man would have put you in an asylum, one way or another."

There is a moment of indecision. Veronica holds up the ring to the sky and lines it up so that the sun shines through.

"Nash?" she asks. "You're the deciding vote."

She would love to keep a part of Veronica at the ranch forever. But she wants Veronica to be entirely free. She wants to see that ring fly.

"Throw it," she says, and Veronica does, and the ring is airborne, sailing up, up, and then down, disappearing into the great Truckee River as they all cheer.

"I'm going to miss you," Ellen says. She leans forward from the backseat, pops her head right next to Veronica's.

"I'm going to miss all of you silly girls, I am," Veronica says. "I thought I'd be happy when I saw the last of this place." Her window is rolled down and her hat is off. Nash can't wait to get home and be rid of her own suit and stockings.

"Boohoo. You're all breaking my heart," Hadley says. "We're mooning like sad old cows. Let's have a drink and celebrate before you have to leave. Life goes on, and that's worth toasting. Nash can make us a mule."

"A last mule," Ellen says. For some reason this sounds funny, and they all laugh.

They drive down County Road, jarring and knocking, kicking up dust. They take the turnoff to Tamarosa, right by the old Joshua tree, with its spear-like leaves, spiky hands reaching for the sky. Now, in summer, its ripe green-brown fruit has fallen and is rotting on the ground below, a feast for weasels and foxes and ladder-backed woodpeckers.

"Home again, home again," Ellen says, as they drive under the arch. "Tamarosa."

They appear just to her left, as sudden and unexpected as a train on an unused track. She hits the brakes. Ellen screams.

"Shush!" Hadley orders.

Ellen quiets. What fills the car now—it could be the sound of a train, too. It's that loud, that rhythmic, hooves hitting earth and hitting earth, so many hooves, so many horses; it is one thundering train. They are right there on Tamarosa, flying past the mailbox, sleek black and brown, bursts of white. There are flashes from savage eyes and a sudden show of teeth. The car rocks. There is dust and more dust and haunches and knees working like steel axles, and there is huffing and the high-pitched *wheee* that sounds like brakes on metal, but there is nothing man-made here.

The women are speechless, as is appropriate when witnessing an act of God. Veronica grips Nash's hand. Hadley's face is pressed to her window, and Ellen rolls hers up madly. It is over so fast. Nash might think she imagined it if it wasn't for the sudden smell of sweat in the car and the realization that she's been holding her breath. The horses have crossed the road and are now disappearing. Hadley leans her head out, to see if she can watch them farther, but Ellen pulls her back.

"Get in, dear God," Ellen says. Her voice trembles.

"That was the most magnificent thing I have ever seen," Hadley says.

Magnificent—it seems like such a small word. Nash feels as if she's been struck by lightning.

"Christ, I need a cigarette," Veronica says.

"Tell me that won't ever happen again," Ellen says. "I thought we were going to be killed."

"They were right *here*. What were they doing right *here*?" Nash asks.

"That's what I want to know," Ellen says.

Then Nash realizes. "It was probably that airplane."

"Well, it scared them!" Hadley says.

"You're lucky if you ever see them," Nash says. She can barely breathe. Everything Jack has said makes sense now. "Once in a life, maybe. If."

Hadley reaches and shakes Veronica's shoulder. "You see? It's a sign. Today is your lucky day, my dear."

"Get me and thee to a mule, fast," Veronica says.

"I feel lucky, all right. Lucky to be alive," Ellen says.

Nash lets go of the wheel. Her foot has been pressed so hard to the brake that the Styleline Deluxe lurches and stalls when she removes it. She feels changed at the sight of those horses, she does, but that's the nasty yet crucial thing about change: It's not a permanent condition. It marches forward, hand in hand with time itself, transforming, adjusting, altering the view in small ways and large. If you could hold it and keep it in place, it might make everything a damn sight easier.

In Nash's mind's eye, the horses are still galloping past, and there is still the boom and rumble of them in her head. But as she drives farther onto the ranch, she takes in other pieces, wrong pieces. A section of fence by the front pasture has been destroyed, and ground is ripped up. There's a scar in the land, a torrid mark that extends beyond the farthest acacias of Tamarosa. She parks. She has a bad, bad feeling. Something else is wrong. The front door has been flung open. There is a bridle dropped on the walkway, and Bluebell is in the ring, running in mad, distressed circles. Boo is outside. He does not even look up from a dark spot he is sniffing and licking on the ground.

"Holy hell," Veronica says.

Nash yanks the brake, and the minute she does, she sees it—a long line of drops, bright-red drops, and they start near the ring where Bluebell is, and they work their way past Al Johns's borrowed truck in the driveway and into the house. She is out of that car, fast. "Stop! Stop that!" she yells at Boo. She flings her arm at him as she rushes inside, and the women are somewhere behind her. They clearly are, because she hears Ellen whispering, "Dear Mary, Mother of God," just before there's a terrible noise, a sound like a rabbit dying, the cry that comes as a coyote bites into the flesh of its neck.

Lilly lies on the floor near the piano. They've tried to prop some pillows beneath her; her knees are raised, and her yellow dress is soaked with blood. She is up on her elbows, and her eyes are panicked, same as the eyes of those horses. Jack and Danny kneel beside her, and Danny's face is white and scared. Jack holds her hand.

"Thank the Lord you're here," Danny says.

"Where is Irma? Or Cliff? What's happened?" Nash drops to her knees, too, beside Lilly. There are bath towels around, from upstairs where they keep them for the guests.

"Irma left to do the shopping, and Cliff, hell, I don't know. Lilly, she was out by the ring. The horses came through. The mustangs. They're out there! That airplane . . . flying so low! She started running. And the blood . . . I could see it. I could see it on her legs! I came after her," Jack says.

"Ambulance," Ellen says. "You've called the ambulance?"

"No ambulance out here. Washoe's supposed to get one next year," Danny says. "I tried to call Doc Bolger, but no one's answering. There's no way to tell where he might be. He's maybe with Mrs. Grosvenor, she's dying of—"

"Go! Danny, go look for him! Find him!" Nash says.

Lilly makes a strange huffing sound. It is not so strange, really, because Nash and Jack and Danny, too, they've seen this before; they were there, each of them, when Rosie gave birth to Maggie, and when Lady foaled Little Britches. There was not this much blood, though. This is a lot of blood, so much, too much, and Nash's shoes are wet, and so are her knees and her hands. She wipes one on her skirt, before she brushes Lilly's hair from her face.

"Help me," Lilly says.

"We're here. It's all right." This doesn't seem to be Nash's own voice, and this is not all right, but she just keeps smoothing Lilly's hair and looking into her eyes, which Lilly shuts tight before crying out again.

"Ellen, what do we do?" Hadley asks. But this is clearly beyond Ellen's expertise. Ellen's wayward husband, Eddie, likely brought her to the hospital and waited in a room with cigars in his pocket, as nurses in crisp white slipped a mask over Ellen's mouth and nose. She would have drifted off, only to wake up later with a bundle in her arms.

"We . . ." Ellen says. "We . . ."

Nash hears Veronica on the phone in the kitchen. She is shouting. There are the words *early* and *hurry* and *you bastards*.

Lilly squeezes Nash's hand. She squeezes so hard, and then she bears down. Ellen is down at Lilly's feet. "I am just going to . . ." She lifts Lilly's dress and gasps. "Remain calm."

"It's fine, Lilly," Nash says. "We're here."

"You hang on," Jack says. "You be strong. Danny will be right here with the doctor."

There is no way to know if this is true. The desert is a big place, and Doc Bolger could be anywhere.

"The baby," Lilly says. She bears down. Her mouth opens and twists in a scream, but this time, no sound comes out.

"There's a head," Ellen says.

Lilly is shivering. Her bare legs tremble. Her arms tremble. Her skin is cool to the touch.

"Blankets," Ellen says. Hadley heads for the stairs.

Lilly thrashes her head to the side, and she looks at Nash. She looks at her straight on. "Promise," she says.

"Anything."

"He can't know."

"All right," Nash says. She doesn't know what she is promising, only that right then she would promise Lilly anything.

"Ever."

"Okay."

"Beanie, either." She breathes hard. "Too much—" She bears down. "Shame."

"Don't worry, Lilly. You're going to be all right."

"Vow," she says.

Nash takes both of Lilly's hands. "I do. I promise. I give you my vow."

Lilly bears down.

"Your baby is coming," Ellen says. "Your baby has black hair."

"My," Lilly says. She puts her hand to her chest.

"Your heart," Jack says. Nash sets her own hand there. Lilly's heart is beating so fast that it gallops and thunders. It's wild and frightening. Nash thinks she hears the sound of it right here in the living room. No, that sound is just outside, matching the beat and the force of the heart under her palm.

Lilly bears down, but it doesn't seem like enough. It feels weak, and there is no logical way Nash should know this. It is instinct. Animal instinct, and Jack must know it, too.

"Put your hands in," he says to Ellen. "Both your hands. Pull the head. This is going on too long." He keeps his voice measured, but it's a command.

Nash and Jack look at each other, and she can see how afraid he is. It seems like so much time has passed since they came home, and she can see that this is partly true. The sky is turning shades of burning orange and red.

"Yes," Ellen says. "Yes, I will," as if she is at a party, accepting an hors d'oeuvre from a tray.

Hadley runs down the stairs with a blanket yanked off Alice's bed, and she covers the upper half of Lilly's shaking body. "He is almost . . . Dear God, he is almost . . ."

Lilly shudders. "Get him away," she says. "Tell him to go!"

"It's all right, Lilly," Nash croons.

"It's all right, darling," Jack says.

"Make him go away!" she cries.

"The baby's coming," Ellen says. "He's coming! I feel him!"

"Oh, my God," Hadley says. "Look at him." Veronica has her arms around Hadley. They are both crying.

Ellen is crying now, too. Tears are rolling down her face between Lilly's knees. "You have a son, Lilly. You have a beautiful son."

There is so much blood, and Lilly is breathing so fast. Fast and hard. She is hyperventilating. Her skin is so cold.

Nash leans down and sets her cheek on Lilly's. "He's here. Beanie is here."

There is all that blood everywhere, and the baby finally cries out, and Jack says, "Thank you, Jesus," when he hears it. Lilly's skin is white. It is white as the moon the night she stepped from the swimming pool. Something is wrong with her eyes. Nash has never seen anyone die before.

Nash trembles. She is so, so cold, even with Harris's arm around her. Her niece Callie takes her hand. It is so dark out. Near the leg of that piano, there is a mark in the floor; it is still there, the place where Nash gouged in her nails in grief.

"Do you understand? I kept my vow for all these years, but I can't anymore. I have to find him. I must see him. That baby, that *man*—he has a right to know his story, before I'm gone," Nash says.

Nash's other niece, Shaye, kneels beside her, too. "He will, Nash. He will. We'll make sure of it," she says.

chapter 22

Callie

It was so dark out. Before I left, I set down my thermos of coffee and my camera. Near the leg of that piano, there was a mark in the floor; it was still there, the place Nash gouged in her nails in grief. I knelt down and ran my fingers across it. My own life, my story, my time at the ranch, even—it all seemed so ordinary compared to this.

"Oh, you," I said to Tex. He wanted to come along. He told me that with his eyes and the way he sat, especially well behaved, by the door. Hugo could manage this sort of thing only for a few moments before he'd turn big circles of excitement. He was a bit of a bull in a china shop, the beast, but that's who he was, and you loved him for it. "You have to stay," I said to Tex. "I'm sorry. I apologize."

The ranch and the entire valley looked so different before the sun came up. It stretched out and beyond into darkness and more darkness. It could make you afraid of falling, and wisely so. Falling should be feared, or at least done with caution.

I followed the directions to the Flat Creek Trailhead, where we visitors would meet before driving up in the bureau truck to the designated viewing site. That was the plan. When I arrived, the truck was already there, parked with its headlights still on. A man leaned against the door and sipped from a travel mug.

"Morning!" he said. His breath made puffs in the cool pre-dawn air. He cupped his hands around his mouth and nose and huffed briefly to warm them. I'd have recognized that shiny head anywhere.

"Steve Miller," I said. "Cowboy and musician."

"I can play the fool, that's about it."

"Where is everybody?"

"You're it. Had a tourist couple from Colorado coming, but she's not feeling well. Drinking and losing too much money gambling can bring on a case of the flu."

"Too bad," I said, though I was glad to be on my own. I was never good at making morning small talk. Bed-and-breakfast weekends were something Thomas and I avoided. We both needed more coffee before listening to stories about the other guests' children and their recent bike trip to Santa Fe.

"We were supposed to go to this nice, safe little spot a good half mile away. That's so no one runs out to take a photo and gets trampled by wild animals. Or so that no protesters leap in front of the chute and get themselves killed, let alone jeopardize weeks of work and tens of thousands of dollars. But you don't strike me as a runner or a leaper, in spite of that camera you got."

I held my hand up in a promise. "I am not a runner or a leaper."

"Then follow me," he said.

"Where are we going?"

"As close as you can get without a horse and a hat."

Morning dawned, casting a golden glow over the rangeland. The tenderness of the light was shocking, and each hill looked poetic. Everything felt full of hope from that magic trick of a new day. Steve Miller escorted me to the side of the chute where the horses would be led in, and we knelt behind a long panel of orange netting. There? Really? It all seemed unwise— Steve Miller could lose his job, and I could lose my life in that spot, ground level with those pounding hooves. Still, Steve Miller knew those horses better than I did, and even though I was flushed with nerves, I could see how eager he was. I could feel the anticipation in the air.

I wondered where everyone was. It seemed like we were the only two people even awake. But then I looked closer. There was Lorraine on Cactus, waiting at a discreet distance; a few other BLM guys, too. Each was in place.

Steve checked his watch. "The helicopter should be coming any minute."

"Where is it now?"

"Not far, I'm guessing. The pilot floats around out there for a bit first, getting an idea of where the different bands are. By now he's probably moved them together, and they're likely heading in our direction."

"How does he move them together?"

"Positioning the helicopter, getting close, hanging back a little. Pretty much after that, they'll come forward on their own. When they get near the site, though, he'll close in—"

I heard it before I saw it. The helicopter rose over the hill, like the bad guy in a movie, or maybe like the hero, just before the world might end. And then I saw the horses themselves, cresting the hill and barreling down. They stampeded, manes flying, tails whipping behind them, their group a single mass as they surged forward. There was the *wup-wup-wup* of the helicopter, and the blows of hooves, and what it sounded like most was a cataclysmic storm, and what it looked like most was beauty and more unfathomable beauty. I gripped Steve Miller's arm as the helicopter swooped low as a hawk.

"Here's Kit," he said, and then I saw him. It was fast—all movement and muscle. Kit ran out, leading Jasper, and then he crouched at the ready beside him, right in the center of the open wings of the chute. I grabbed Steve Miller's arm again, looked at him for confirmation that this was the intended plan. It couldn't be, could it? He was sure to be trampled. But Steve Miller's gaze was fixed. His eyes were on Kit, and so I dared to watch.

The horses charged forward, and the very second before they reached him, Kit leaped out of the way and let Jasper go, and that pilot horse took over like the leader he was. Kit flung himself away and lay flat on the ground, as the mustangs followed Jasper in.

The horses galloped down the chute. They were right next to us, close enough that the dust spit toward our faces as the immense bodies stormed past. The noise was mammoth. So much noise that even their heavy breathing sounded mighty and mythical. I held my own breath. Their eyes were wild, and I forced my own frightened eyes open. They were a cyclone of nature, both primitive and evolved, and as I huddled there, I felt like a creature of the earth, the same as they were. They were dirty and rough, strangers to the shiny, well-bred animals you saw on a racetrack. I could smell them. These horses were worn and life-wise, and when they arrived at their shocking destination, they banged against the holding pen with mighty crashes; iron against iron as the gates clanged with the weight. They vocalized with their high-pitched brays: *Ee-e-ee-eee*. They were beautiful but not, suffering but saved, victims and perpetrators, defeated yet triumphant in the way they were *still there*, full of fury and will.

"Watch," Steve said, and I turned my attention to where he directed, back to the open rangeland. Two mustangs had broken from the pack, and they ran frenzied figure eights just beyond the entrance. Out of nowhere came a man I'd seen before at the site: the old guy with the big belly. He was on his horse and had a rope looped around his arm, which he spun in a circle in the air; then there was another familiar face doing the same, and they worked the two stray horses closer until they, too, veered in and headed past us.

The helicopter whipped up and then disappeared back over the hill. It was all, every bit of it, the most magnificent and unreal thing I had ever witnessed. It had gathered me up, too; I hadn't taken a single picture. It would all have to remain right there in my own changed heart and mind, same as the earthquake fault that day, same as a thousand other critical junctures that had no photographic proof.

In the corral, the mustangs twitched and settled themselves or else continued to bang their huge bodies against the gates in protest. Some looked afraid, just as I'd worried they would, yet some already seemed settled into the fate the day had brought. Mostly I saw their raw, intense energy, and that energy filled me, too. I felt euphoric.

A gloved hand gripped my arm where I stood, and I spun around. Kit was there beside me, and he lifted me off my feet. I could feel his own elation. He spun me around, midair.

And there, right then, was where we might have kissed. I felt the electric possibility of it. I would have put my mouth on his and he would have held me hard, and it would have been a mad and a passionate kiss, a kiss of the sun rising and setting, a kiss with all the frightening risk and glorious rewards of being alive. We would have knocked Kit's hat to the ground. We would have looked at each other and seen the future.

But that's not what happened. Something immeasurably more remarkable and important occurred instead. He set me on my feet, and my tricky, secret heart revealed itself, because there I was once again, wishing that my stupid, infuriating Thomas, my own husband, the one I loved, had been beside me to see what I just had. Oh, I was much, much more of a romantic than I ever knew. And that unknown part of me, the fact that it existed at all, well, it filled me with joy. Look at that. I believed in things that lasted.

Around us, around Kit and me, there was the scuff and scrubble of activity, the need for action. I could feel the raw, animal force, the vitality. Kit put his hands on the sides of my face, and our eyes locked. I looked at him for a long moment, and in that moment I gave him everything I was able to give. I could feel him do the same.

"Just this," he said. "Just for this one second."

"And I'll never forget it," I said.

That morning I'd thought that my story was insignificant, but once again I'd been proven wrong. No life was ever ordinary, and no story of love was, either, not even mine. Whether tragic or commonplace, each attempt at the damn thing, each shot at love and life itself, was brave. Every effort at it was flawed and messy, complicated, oh, yes, occasionally triumphant, often painful, because how else could it be? Look at the mission we were given, look at the stunning, impossible mission—imperfect love in the face of loss. Any sane person with the facts would turn their back on a mission like that. And yet we loved; of course we did. We kept at it; we added our thread to the design. The courage that took—there was nothing ordinary about that.

"Hit the gas a little," I said from the passenger side. "There's no need to be afraid."

"Yeah, just because you're an old lady doesn't mean you have to drive like one," Shaye said from the back. She seemed lighter since her visit to the lawyer. A decision could be deadweight lifted. I hadn't heard the details, only Shaye's complaint about writing a fat check.

"All right, all right," Nash said, adjusting her rear end in the seat. She was lighter, too. A revealed secret could also be a deadweight lifted. When I told her about the gather earlier, the well-orchestrated beauty of it, she'd only pressed her eyes closed for a moment before saying, *Get the keys*. Now we'd been on the dirt road leading to the Tamarosa arch for a good hour. After all the lessons regarding brakes and mirrors, we'd progressed only about a hundred feet.

"At this rate it'll take you six weeks to get to Los Angeles," I said.

"Step on it," Shaye said.

This is exactly what Amy said from the backseat when I was teaching Melissa to drive. My most beautiful daughters, my babies. They'd grown up so fast. Every parent heard this warning. People said it frequently enough that it ended up having no meaning whatsoever until one day it did. No matter what happened or hadn't happened my whole life long, them being in it had made it all worth it.

And then Nash did exactly what Melissa had also done. She gave it too much gas, and we lurched ahead, and the car went hurtling down that road. Shaye squealed in the back and even ducked a little.

"Take it down a notch, Nash." I tried to keep the alarm out of my voice.

"Whoo-ee!" Nash said.

We flew, hitting the ruts in the road hard enough to make my teeth clatter. "Ease up just a bit," I said.

"Nash, slow it down," Shaye cried. Up ahead, Rob, who'd been grazing peacefully by the roadside, made a lumbering run for it. "Apply the brakes, damn it!"

Nash came to a stop. She spun out a little. I swear, I smelled the heat of screaming brake pads and tires. "My, that felt good."

Shaye was laughing hard back there. "Oh, God, I'm going to wet my pants. You scared the shit out of both me and that buffalo."

"Who knew he could move that fast," I said. "How do you know if you've had a heart attack?" We were cracking ourselves up.

"Look at that. I haven't forgotten a thing," Nash said.

"Turn down the air conditioner," Shaye said. "It's like the arctic back here."

This cracked us up more—who even knows why. Nerves and the relief of being alive. Nash turned off the engine and we sat for a moment.

"Where is Jack, anyway?" I asked. "Did he leave the ranch after what happened?"

"Nah. He stayed for a long while. Then he got a job managing some rich rancher's property in Montana. Married the daughter, though she's gone now. He's still up there."

"Hey! Second-chance time?" Shaye said.

Nash scoffed. "Jack was always better as an idea."

"Why didn't you ever marry Harris? He's clearly devoted to you," I asked.

"It goes both ways. You know why? He can love a strong woman, and that's a rarity. But I like to live alone. I've always liked it," she said.

"You know what else you never told us?" Shaye said. "That director. How'd he end up in the river?"

"Reckless fury," Nash said. She looked downright smug after just burning rubber.

"I want to know why Grandma Alice had to go rescue our mother," I said.

"That's probably when she had that pregnancy scare," Shaye said.

"What are you talking about? What pregnancy scare?"

"She never told you? Some boy she met at a gas station."

"She never tells me anything."

"She tells me entirely too much," Shaye said.

"Well."

"She probably just forgot. Like the way she told you twice about her party at Anthony's Home Port and didn't tell me at all."

"I guess everyone has their secrets," I said.

chapter 23

Nash

"I guess everyone has their secrets," Nash's niece says, and she is right. Everyone lives just a little more and a little harder than they let on. That was no pregnancy scare Gloria had, but Nash is keeping her mouth shut. Sure, there is squabbling and envy and jabbing between sisters, but sisters don't tell. Besides, her nieces don't need to know everything about Gloria and that boy and how ugly abortion was in the old days, and they don't need to know everything about Stuart Marcel, either. Nor does Harris, even if they share everything else, including the folds and sags of their old, loving bodies.

As far as secrets go, Stuart Marcel and what really happened to him that day—it's Nash's last one. Jack's, too, if what he said in that letter is true. *I never told another living soul*, he wrote. *That day, and a certain night, too, belonged to only us.* Now, though, she's decided to finally reveal what happened, to one other person: Mr. Michael McKinley, otherwise known as Baby Edward Austen, now of McKinley and James Architects, Los Angeles.

Every person must come full circle to his or her rightful life, Nash knows. Sometimes, you have to make that same trip more than once.

She plays the memory again, of his first few hours: the way she and Ellen take the baby and wash him in the kitchen sink just after the wagon comes from the hospital to pick up Lilly's body. Doc Bolger holds the infant in his hands as if weighing a pot roast, takes his temperature, and measures his head with a tape. He pronounces him healthy and well. He is small but full-term, farther along than Lilly or her doctor thought, which happens with *placenta previa*, he tells them. Nash does not know what the term means, only that it sounds wrongly lyrical, like the Latin name for a flower. The baby is slippery in that warm water, and they wrap him tight in a blanket.

A shocked Cook returns; delayed in Reno while trying to find pastry snails and good veal for croquettes, she's now shaken and pale, trying to put a meal together that no one wants. Jack and Danny clean up blood in stunned silence, and Veronica stares out the window and smokes a cigarette. Alice will be back by morning, and they will figure out what to do then. The baby will stay with them for now, it's decided.

"The husband," Doc Bolger says. "He must be notified. The family."

"She has no family," Nash says.

"The husband, then. He has a son. He's lucky. They could have both died."

"He's not the father," Nash says.

"No?" Doc Bolger says.

Ellen stays silent. Doc Bolger shakes his head, and whether this is meant to convey disapproval of Lilly or of them, it is impossible to tell. "He needs to be notified," he says again.

The cook, Irma, waits until Doc Bolger leaves. She's seen plenty of life on the ranch, too. Her eyes are red, from cutting onions, from crying. She grips a kitchen towel in one hand.

"That man, the father," she says. "He called all morning. She didn't want to speak to him, so I made excuses. She went outside. Didn't want to hear the phone anymore."

"What'd he say?"

"Just that he was calling long distance from Los Angeles, and to get her on the phone, quick."

"He's in Los Angeles, at least," Nash says.

"Not for long, if you ask me."

Hadley returns with an entire shelf's worth of Vitaflo nursers and Carnation milk and antiseptic baby oil and diapers and pins and jars of food and cans of Heinz strained chicken for babies.

"He won't need these for quite a while," Ellen says, as Hadley unpacks more jars of strained peas and peaches and bananas and corn and beans.

"No?" Hadley looks lost.

"Just this." Ellen brings the milk to the kitchen, where Cook warms it for Edward Austen. This is what Nash names him, anyway. Edward, for the name Lilly chose when she left home, and Austen, for the author of her favorite book. Ellen rubs the bottom of the baby's pink, ridged feet with her thumb to get him to wake long enough to sip from the bottle. He is more interested in sleeping. It is late, but tiny Edward Austen is the only one who *can* sleep. Nash hears Jack vomit from trauma. Danny gathers the bloody towels and gets rid of them. Even Boo's eyes are wide open in Nash's room, where he's been locked away once more. He's taking advantage and lies on Nash's bed, where he's not supposed to be.

Hadley sits in stunned silence on the couch, and Veronica puts her arm around her. "I'll never see anything the same way again." Hadley speaks in a hush. "I swear to God, I won't."

Nash joins them. Ellen sets the baby in Nash's arms and kneels down in front of her. Nash adjusts the blanket around his beautiful, scrunched face. His hair is black like Lilly's and soft as satin. He is wearing the tiny gown and socks from Lilly's suitcase, which look huge on him. He smells like deep water. A feeling arises and overtakes her. Nash has never experienced anything like it before. It is love, but larger than love. It is devotion, but larger than devotion. Her whole heart belongs to this small being, with his tiny fingernails that are as translucent as shells. Every piece of her has just been handed over. As far as love goes, well, it's over for Nash now. This is love.

"I am sorry I ever carried on about Eddie. None of that even matters," Ellen says.

"I know," Veronica whispers.

This is all that matters; now and before now and after now, this is the reason—this rosebud mouth, and this smallest, new hand gripping her finger.

That is when the phone rings in the kitchen. It is past midnight. It can be only one person.

"It's him," Ellen says.

He knows the truth about the baby, Nash is sure of it. Somehow, he's found out. It's the way the phone sounds. A ring can sound like a question, a polite question, even, but this one sounds like a declaration of intent.

"Oh, Lilly," Hadley says.

She waits until Veronica has gone to bed, and Danny has gone home, and Hadley is asleep on the sofa, and Jack appears to be dozing in Alice's favorite chair. She hands the baby to Ellen, who is the only one awake with her. Nash kisses that small, delicate head and goes upstairs to change again. The still-

bloodied clothes she put on that morning to go to the courthouse are in a heap on the floor. Now she drops her jeans and
shirt with them, selects a practical, somber dress. She gathers a
few things. She finds You-Know-Who's wedding ring, the
abandoned gold band of Mrs. Fletcher, the ring that belongs to
her now, which she still has tucked in her underwear drawer.
She slips it on, just in case. She may need to stay somewhere
for a while.

It's time. Downstairs, Ellen hands her the bag of bottles and
nipples and milk. "It's important to sterilize these," she whispers. "At least, use very hot water from the tap. And keep him
warm. Keep his head warm. Are you sure you don't want me
to come with you?"

"I'm sure."

They make a bed of blankets on the front passenger seat of
the Styleline Deluxe. Ellen kisses the baby and then Nash's
cheek.

"Be safe," she says.

Jack is awake after all. Of course he is. He watches out for a
person. It's the best thing about him. He comes outside and
nods to Ellen on her way in, his hands shoved into his pockets.
He passes Nash a slip of paper with his own writing on it.
There's a name and an address. "You can't just run with nowhere to go," he says.

The paper reads, *Miller Adoption Services, 45 Stone Road,
Sacramento*. She looks at him with a question in her eyes.

"Something that happened when I was a kid. Back in high
school."

"Jesus, Jack," she says, but it hardly matters now. None of it
does.

"Nash, before you go. I want you to know, about the other
night—"

He takes her hand. He doesn't need to say anything more, and neither does she. They will always have great affection for each other. But passion, high drama, even love—they look entirely, irrevocably different to her now. She feels the fault line of before and after.

"I already do know," she says. He kisses her cheek, too. And then he looks in the car, sees the rifle on the floor of the backseat, the Savage Model 720, which Nash took from underneath Alice"s bed. He nods his approval. "Take I-80 from Reno, Nash. Follow the Truckee River." He isn't calling her Peanut anymore. No, that young girl is long gone, and good riddance to her.

She starts the engine and heads down the road. She isn't particularly scared. And she isn't one bit sorry about Stuart Marcel or this reckless thing she is about to do. Not right now, anyway. Not when there are crickets and millions of stars and miles and miles of open road. There is a thin yellow curve of moon in that big, big desert sky. The night air smells like dry grass and horse manure and summer. She is flying down that dirt road with her true love beside her, and she is filled with . . . well, she is mostly and most simply *filled*.

She is soaring. There is a rise in her whole body now, as they pick up speed and the ranch falls away behind them.

Edward Austen, the little bundle of him, begins to make fussing sounds just past the turnoff where she and Jack went to see the aerial show that time, where the tiny, faraway man stepped out into the sky and walked on that wing.

Nash pulls the car over. She unwraps Edward Austen and croons to him. She sings a song she's made up, and she puts Lilly's name in it. She hopes Lilly can hear her. Edward Austen's body is so tiny that the diaper looks as big as a turban on a man's head. Her hands shake; she puts her fingers against his skin so that the pin won't prick him. She wraps him back up, and she feeds him the bottle that Ellen has made, and she rubs his feet as Ellen did. She pats his back, with its tiny, bony spine, and she cups his head with her palm. She holds him against her chest, her jacket wrapped around them both.

She awakens. The sun is coming up. She has the sweet surprise of waking up in the Styleline Deluxe with a baby sleeping against her, just before that moment, that awful moment upon waking, where her story comes back to her. The horror of the day before descends. A sob comes up her throat as she remembers Lilly and that blood and her blank eyes and Lilly's body being taken away in that wagon. She thinks of Lilly's shiny hair, and her laugh, and her hand reaching out for Nash's as she stood on those rocks.

But then Nash remembers her vow. She changes Edward Austen and feeds him and then turns the key of that engine. She needs to get to Sacramento.

It is morning, and the rabbits are hopping around as if it's the first day of spring. She takes Old 395, just in case. It's not the main road, so no one will see her. She'll feel better once she's out of Reno.

She is just past Davis Creek when she thinks she sees a black Cadillac a long distance behind her, and then it is gone. She tells herself that this is nerves, that she is seeing things. At this distance, it could be any black car. But then, as she nears Virginia Street, she sees it again. It is black and low, as if it's creeping. It has a large chrome face, and on its hood it wears that silver flying goddess like a jewel in a crown.

"Dear God, dear God," Nash prays. She places her hand on

the bundle that is Edward Austen, to steady him, and then she steps on the gas.

It is there behind her, no doubt about it. Stuart Marcel's Cadillac, with Stuart Marcel himself behind the wheel. She sees his large head with the dark hair swooped back, and she can feel his eyes on her.

Her heart races. Stuart Marcel is caught at the new two-color signal on Fourth Street. The city is just waking. The judges and attorneys are still eating their poached eggs on toast and drinking their first cup of coffee. Stuart Marcel is not someone who stops at a signal. He speeds through. Nash flies toward Virginia Street. Here's what the Styleline Deluxe is capable of: sixty-five, seventy. More. She is a mustang fleeing a plane swooping low. Her body is fight and panic and bare determination.

He is right behind her, just on the other side of the bridge. And—wait. Is that Al Johns's truck behind him? She has no idea what might have happened at the ranch in her absence, but what she does know right now is that even the Styleline Deluxe will be no match for the shiny new mechanical mastery of that Cadillac. She must do something else, something rash, that will save them both.

She thinks of the day of the driving lesson, how Veronica stood right up to Stuart Marcel, her nose nearly touching his. Yes. Nash is also capable of that kind of strength, by God.

She pulls over. She grabs that rifle and steps out of the car. Here, this is what her anger truly looks like; this is the full force of it, and of her love, too. Stuart Marcel is going a hundred miles an hour over that bridge. Nothing matters to her except Edward Austen. Edward Austen and the others of his kind, the small, wrinkled newborns—they are what all the folly and passion and trips up and down the courthouse stairs are really about, and Nash understands this now. The drama and madness are a snickering trick of nature, an outlandish but irresistible hoax with one ongoing goal: tiny beings such as this one, wrapped up and sleeping peacefully, unaware of all the fuss that got them here.

This, Nash thinks, is for Lilly. And for the first Mrs. Marcel, falling down, down, down from the ledge of that Topanga Canyon road, a flesh-and-blood woman who banged against those rocks, who, somewhere along that fast trip to the ground, became merely a body, a body likely as mangled and bloody as those horses Nash had seen. Nash lifts the Savage Model 720, and how she loves its name right now. *Savage* is what she feels—fierce, furious. Nash takes aim.

There is a loud crack, and Nash flinches. There is something else, too—the fact that Nash has always been a lousy shot. She aims for one of those white-walled tires, hoping to do enough damage to slow him down, but instead she gets the winged goddess, who shoots off and soars, midair. She is gone, an ornament no more, heading for the roof of the Washoe Courthouse, where she'll land. Her sudden freedom causes Stuart Marcel to lose control of his speeding car. It is also airborne now; Nash can see its shiny underside as it takes flight and flips over the rail of the Truckee Bridge, like one of those hundreds upon hundreds of gold bands.

She hears it crash. There's the boom of weight hitting water. When she opens her eyes again from squeezing them shut, she sees that she was right—it *was* Al Johns's truck following behind that Cadillac. There's the store's H&J painted on the side, and Jack is rushing out of that truck, and he has his hand cupped around his mouth and he is running toward her and shouting, "Nash! Nash! Go! Go!"

Nash goes. There's no time for either guilt or gladness. That bullet is down at the bottom of the Truckee, and, soon, Stuart Marcel will be, as well. That's where he'll remain, the bastard, until his big, brutal body and the battered carcass of that Cadillac are finally fished out of that river filled with wedding rings.

chapter 24

Callie

Shaye had her hand cupped around her mouth and she was shouting. "Callie! Cal!" She had her cute little sundress on, the one decorated with cheerful fruits, oranges and strawberries and watermelon slices. "What are you doing? I was looking everywhere for you."

She dragged another old lounge chair out of the pool house and set it next to mine. What was I doing? Looking out over the abandoned hole, picturing it sparkling with water. Imagining women in formfitting maillots and high-waisted two-piece bathing suits, chatting and reading magazines. Seeing Shaye and me, diving for pennies as our mother sunned nearby, the fragrance of Sea & Ski in the air.

"Are you okay?" she asked.

"I don't know," I said.

"Talk to me."

"I'm just surprised to find myself here."

"Here, like the ranch here?"

"No, like *here* here. All of it. I don't know—" My voice caught.

"Oh, Cal." She came over to my chair and sat beside me.

"We're going to break this thing," I said. I wasn't sure how to convey what I was feeling or even if I wanted to.

"We're not going to break it." She put her arm around my shoulders. "You've been so sad, Cal, haven't you? Even before this, before coming here. The months before Amy's graduation? I could hear it on the phone."

"Sad?"

"Sad. Really sad."

Sad—I hadn't even called it that myself, but the word took me down like an arrow. My God, the truth slammed into my chest, and I folded my arms across it. The defense seemed necessary. There was a terrible avalanche in there, threatening to spill.

"Why wouldn't you be? I mean, think about it. The girls leaving home. Your job. Thomas's mother dying—"

"No. You know how I felt about her."

"Still, Cal. Still. Come on. That's a huge piece of your life that's over. And then Hugo."

Damn it. Damn her! At the sound of Hugo's name, I saw him, that big, innocent boy who was my friend, my sweet protector, so sick and then gone. The weight in my chest, it felt more than I could bear. My throat shut tight. "Silly," I whispered.

"Silly? Are you kidding? It's loss, Cal. It's *grief*. You keep talking about Thomas losing his mother, but, Cal—"

"No."

"Yes."

"I don't want to hear this." I could barely speak.

"You're grieving. You're grieving a lot of things."

Damn her, damn her, damn her, and damn the truth, and damn everything else that needed damning, *everything*. The heaviness in my chest was growing greater, pressing so hard that I started to cry, and I hate to cry. My sorry heart was breaking. It was breaking because shoulder pads were gone and so were bad perms, and the little pink potty chair the girls used, and so, too, was the car filled with soccer cleats and rainy, muddy clothes and snacks in foil packages. All of that was finished now, and so was the way Hugo turned in circles before lying down. I didn't know where the time had gone, and Shaye was right, and I heaved with grief, crying like an idiot for elementary school Valentine's Day parties and Hugo crunching his breakfast and swimming lessons, that moment—that delicious and perfect moment—of wrapping two small shivering bodies in their towels before heading home. Grief, yes, for the times Thomas and I would be in the front seat of the car with sleeping children in the back, for the quiet satisfaction of that life. The snug capsule of a family, speeding through darkness as rain fell, the windshield wipers going back and forth—how could one ever get over the loss of it.

"Oh, God. God." I sobbed like a fool, then gathered some last remaining bits of control. I wiped my eyes with the palm of my hand. My nose was running. I was a big damn brokenhearted mess.

Shaye put her other arm around me now, too. I was held in the circle she'd made for me. "Don't get mad."

"I'm already mad," I sniffed.

"Don't get more mad."

"What?"

"There's something else."

"If it starts with *don't get mad*, I'm not going to want to hear this, right?"

"You know how you also keep talking about Thomas going through a midlife crisis? Cal, I think *you* are having one."

"Oh, no."

"It's totally understandable, you know? That's what happ—"

"Tell me it's not true."

"I think it's true. I mean, the way you bolted down here in the first place . . . your camera, the forest-service guy—"

"You encouraged me!"

"I know I did, but Cal, I just think . . ."

I put my head in my hands. Shit. "You're right," I said, but my voice was muffled in my fingers.

"What did you say?"

"I said, *You're right*. You're right, okay?"

"I'm right? Can I record that on video or something?"

"I can't believe it." I was struck. I didn't know what to say. I felt so stupid. How could I have missed this? It was all more complicated and much more simple than I ever thought. "It's been *me*."

"Well, I'm no Dr. Love, but I'd say it's been both of you. Clearly, you've both been hit."

She held my hands. I was so grateful for this woman, my sister.

We sat in the quiet, while I took in the truth. Birds rattled the branches of a tree, had a conversation about something, maybe us. A lizard darted past as if embarrassed to be caught naked. Nature went on, ignoring our human crises. I felt exhausted, as if my center had been dug out with a spoon. But something new sat there, in that empty, excavated space—the small, slight glimmer of relief.

"Look who's back," Shaye said. I thought she meant me at first, but then she hooked her thumb in the direction of the pasture, just beyond the old riding ring.

"That old lug," I said. It was Rob, with his huge lumberjack shoulders and big dejected head.

"Have you ever noticed he has a beard?"

"It's a 7-Eleven-guy beard."

"You know what? I'm actually going to miss him when I go home."

I really looked at her, for the first time that morning. I turned my teary red eyes right on her. "You're going home. You decided."

"I paid that lawyer for his hour and got the hell out of there. Sometimes you need to do something to know you don't want to do something, right? I'm not ready to give up. I don't know what's going to happen. I mean, a stepfamily, God. Two people get married, it's hard enough, let alone when six people do."

"I'm glad, Shaye," I said. "I am. I like Eric. He's nothing like Mathew was, or Quentin. *Nothing* like. You *needed* to leave them, you really did. But in spite of his decisions right now . . ."

"In spite of his decisions right now, I made a good choice this time. I did. Before, I chose the lightning, hoping it'd save me from the thunder, you know? Does that sound like a country-western song?"

"Bring me your moody, your dark, your psycho masses . . ."

"Right. Hey, I know my mother when I see him."

I smiled. "But Eric's a good guy."

"He is. That's what gives me hope. That's the thing. Thomas, too. We're lucky."

"We are." She squeezed my hands.

"Cal, we've got to get out of here before our six weeks are up."

"I love you, Shamu," I said.

"Oh, sweetie. I love you, too."

"You know what we should do tonight? We should raise a glass and toast this damn place and everything that's happened here," I said.

"Better believe it. Moo!" Shaye yelled in Rob's direction.

"Careful. You might get him riled up."

"Does he look like he's capable of getting riled up?"

"That's not what you said when you were screaming your head off the other night."

"Oh, and you were the picture of bravery? Well, he's more scared of us than we are of him."

"Remember? Mom used to say that about the boys in junior high."

"Mooo!" Shaye yelled again. She did a pretty good cow.

Rob lifted his shaggy head and stared us down. When he took a few bored steps in our direction, Shaye squealed and grabbed my arm, and we jumped up, knocking the lounge chair sideways. We ran into the house as if he was after us, just for the thrill of it.

I knew there'd be no gather that day. Kit had told me they'd be on site, sorting horses by sex and age and temperament, deciding which animals got to stay on the rangelands and which would go on to the corral facility just outside Carson City. I was surprised how many different trucks were there. Many large, long trailers were parked in a row near the temporary pens. The first round of mustangs would be going on to their new lives.

"Cowboy, you got a visitor!" Lorraine yelled when she saw me.

"Looks like it's lunchtime, gang," Kit said. He hopped over a gate and came my way. His sky-blue T-shirt was half untucked from his jeans, and damn that man if he didn't nearly saunter.

Steve gave a catcall, whistling with two fingers. "Enough of that, fellas!" Kit called over his shoulder.

"Sorting looks like a horse audition. Him over here, her over there, yes, no . . ." I said.

"Can you tell? And all of those guys needing medical care." He gestured toward a small caravan already heading out.

I followed Kit around to the far side of the long line of trailers. A woman closed up the back doors of the last one, shaking the latch to make sure it was secure. I could hear the horses in there. One thrashed against the side, flinging his large body, making his outrage known.

Kit took my hands. "You came to say goodbye."

I couldn't answer that. My heart was in my throat. "He wants out." I nodded toward the truck.

"He only knows that he doesn't want to be where he is now. It'll all look different tomorrow."

"Promise?"

"I promise."

"Kit . . ."

"Come here." He pulled me close. "You don't have to say anything. I know. I understand."

"I'm sorry."

"Sorry? For what? If you're sorry, I should be, too. I'm not in any place to . . . There's no need for apologies, none at all."

He held me for a long time. I took in his smell and the feel of him. I took it way in, as if it were a whole lifetime. My heart felt crushed. I could cry again. I would miss this man. Still. I may have drifted like a seed to my life, but even seeds settled where they might best thrive.

Finally, we stepped apart. "I'm going to miss you," he said.

"I was just thinking the same thing."

"You've done more for me than you know," he said. "Thank you. Truly."

"No, thank *you*. So much."

"In here." He tapped his temple.

"Always."

The driver of that trailer had gotten in. She honked the horn long and loud to warn of her departure. One arm appeared out the window and she waved, and then the trailer lurched forward, with all its wild and complicated cargo.

When I got back to the ranch, only Shaye's big SUV and Nash's new Ford Fusion Hybrid were out front. So I was startled to see a third person on the porch, someone with Nash and Shaye. His hands were up over his head, and with those strong shoulders of his, he was lifting the last corner of that swing onto the shiny bolt now screwed into the recently reinforced beam. Shaye held up the other end, and Nash's arms were crossed, her bossy pose. Tex lay with his chin on his paws, watching, but when he heard my car, he scurried to all fours and sprinted to the driveway, barking his head off. I hadn't had a greeting like that in a long time.

Or a greeting like the next one.

He ran to the car, and when I got out, he took me into his arms. He held me hard. "God, Cal. You are a sight for sore eyes. I have been such an idiot."

"Thomas," I said.

"What have we been doing?"

"This is a surprise," I said.

"You haven't been answering your phone, so I called here. . . . I left a message."

"On the ranch machine? I think it's broken." Shaye and Nash still stood on the porch, those snoops, pretending to be busy but clearly trying to listen in. "We've got a lot to talk about, Thomas."

"We do."

"I've got twenty-two years' worth of things to say to you."

"We've got time, Cal."

"I am so angry with you."

"I know. We've both been angry. We've both been—"

"Lonely. I've felt so lonely."

"We're going to talk, Cal. As long as we need to. We'll talk our heads off."

"Thomas, jeez. We've got some stuff to fix. And our house . . ." I said. I didn't know where to start.

"It's too damn big for us."

"We have so much—"

"*Stuff*," he said. "I feel burdened by it."

"You do? I do, too."

"Really?"

"I don't know why suddenly, but I do." I felt choked up. I always worried that if I cried, I'd never stop, and now look. It was true. I was feeling too much. It seemed like I had been away on a long, long trip, and was once again packing for another.

"We can have a big huge bonfire on the lawn and really give Mrs. Radish something to gawk at."

I laughed. Stupid Mrs. Radish. Thomas hugged me again.

"I miss our girls so much," I said into his shoulder. My voice wobbled, near tears. "I don't even know what to do with myself I miss them so bad."

"Oh, man. I know. How could they just leave us? God damn them."

I laughed. So did he. But much passed between Thomas and me when we separated and looked at each other then. Tiny, wrinkled fingers and reading aloud and school plays with costumes made from T-shirts and glitter. Oh, we were pitiful, the way we loved our kids.

"This place. God, Cal, it's really changed."

"It's a *mess*. All I could see at first was the mess. And everything that needed to be *repaired*." At least the swing was up now. Thomas and I, we were so very much alike.

"It's still beautiful, though. I mean, *look*."

I did. I looked at the riding ring and the dirt-filled pool and the acres of dry yellow and orange land stretching out to yellow and orange hills, all still stunning. In spite of the fallen fences and the places where the mustangs stormed the grasses and the plain old passage of time, it took your breath away. It stood fast, against every storm and drought. I was glad he could see what I did.

"I think there's a rifle in the pool," Thomas said.

"There is."

"I was so worried," Thomas said. "I took the train down! It was fantastic, Cal. We should take the train! But when I got here, there was no one at the station, and I figured you didn't want to see me, and then they misplaced my bag, and I thought, shit, what else could go wrong."

Nash and Shaye had finally found their good manners. Nash called from the porch. "If you two will excuse us . . ."

"We're going to go start dinner!" Shaye yelled cheerfully.

They disappeared inside, but Tex just sat his little butt down to watch what might happen next.

Well, here's what happened next. I looked at Thomas, and I saw home.

"It is so good to see you, Mack," I said.

chapter 25

At the precise moment that Nash's heart is breaking, just as she stands in front of Mrs. Macy Milburn's agency, holding her true love in her arms, Jane Reynolds Fremont arrives at the train station in Carson City. Someone from Tamarosa Ranch was supposed to fetch her, but no one is there, not a single person, and now her bag seems to have gone missing. *What else could possibly go wrong?* she thinks. She throws up her hands in frustration, and then she collapses onto a bench, puts her head in her hands, and begins to cry.

As Nash holds that baby close against her and removes Mrs. Fletcher's wedding ring, she has no idea about Jane Reynolds Fremont. The newest problems, their latest guest—they are all things she'll learn the next day, when the exhausted and distraught Mrs. Fremont finally arrives by taxicab. Even if Nash did know, though, she would not have been able to think about anyone or anything else right then, certainly not about the way life just keeps going forward, as she prepares herself to hand over the bundle that is Edward Austen. It is the right and true thing to do, she understands. She is tempted to flee with him, to make a new life with him, but that is not what is meant for Edward Austen or even for her.

Now she fills out the paperwork—*Mother: Lilly Edwards,*

Los Angeles. Father: unknown—as Mrs. Macy Miller prattles on in a decisive voice. *We will find him a good home, Miss Edwards,* she says. *I have a list right here. A family in Montana, one in Idaho, several in Colorado* . . . Mrs. Miller's arms reach out.

It may be the right and true thing, but as Nash kisses that hard little nose one more time before saying goodbye, her heart feels destroyed. Nash buries her own nose in him, and she takes in his smell and the feel of his tiny gripping fingers as if it were a lifetime.

She can barely see through her tears on the way back to the ranch. But when she arrives home, all of the women are there to bring her back in, like a herd of cattle circling around its injured one. Veronica, who has long since missed her plane, is making drinks, and Hadley insists that Nash sit and tell them everything, and Ellen, who has Boo up on her lap, says how proud she is of Nash. The funny thing is, Nash is proud of Ellen, too. She was so strong. Strong enough that she looks different now.

Even Alice is there. Home, finally. She takes her daughter in her arms. "Oh, my girl," Alice says. "My darling girl."

It is not in celebration that they raise their glasses, their Moscow mules made of vodka and ginger beer and lime. It is in respect and awe of all they have seen and experienced together. The toast is a promise they all make to one another. The deepest and most unbreakable vow to a bond that needs no words. No one says anything as they raise their arms. There is only the clink of glass against glass.

Nash knows that Thomas is following a good distance behind her. He thinks she can't see him, but she can. No doubt those girls are in that car, too. Likely, niece Callie has given in and decided to bring Tex along. He is probably riding on his toes, with his nose out the window, catching all the smells he's been missing while stuck on the ranch so long. When Nash gets back, just before she sends them all home so she can begin to die, she'll make Callie promise to look after him. The little dog has taken a liking to her.

There are some trips a person needs to make alone, though, and she hopes the four of them will turn back after a few miles, when they are reassured that she is all right.

She is all right. It is all coming back to her. Not only the road and the feel of the wheels beneath her and the steering wheel under her hand, but his sweet scrunched face and wrinkled feet and his warm curved head with the thin, pulsing skin of his fontanel. That's what Ellen told her it was called, and Nash had thought it a very beautiful word, a gentle, delicate word for the way the small bony plates moved and shifted, the fault lines between them fusing and growing whole.

She cannot imagine whom this tiny baby she has loved her whole life long will have turned out to be. Before her search, the last she'd heard of him was when Stuart Marcel's sister tried to claim the infant shortly after he was born. Eve Ellings had stepped in on Lilly's behalf. The father was a quick fling when Stuart was out of town, and Eve—a true friend, as Lilly had said—made that clear. Now it seems he landed all right, into the loving home of Doris and Ned McKinley of Missoula, Montana. What the years brought the child, though, Nash can scarcely imagine. She only knows that on the phone, Michael McKinley's voice was deep and curious and kind, maybe kind enough to even forgive her. She knows that the time is right to ask, anyway. Time to forgive herself, too, for her part in the events of those days. The horses came back, and, just as Jack promised so long ago, she saw their beauty again, when she was up to her elbows in soapsuds. She has been changed, and been changed again. Her story, *the* story, is a perfect, perfectly tumultuous, intended circle.

On the seat beside Nash is the photo she will bring Michael McKinley, the only photo of his mother she could find, beautiful Lilly in her hotel scene in *The Changelings*. It's as if Lilly is riding with her. Nash turns on the radio but can't get any station out here in the desert, not even the one with that silly Dr. Yabba Yabba Love, who thinks she has answers to the human heart. If Nash knows anything, it's this: You could pile up every book and every article and every radio show by every know-it-all who claims to have love figured out, and you could dump them all in the Truckee River. No one knows how to do it, only that we must do it. Love has always been a mystery and it will always be a mystery. It is wild and thundering, a beast of nature. You could try to capture it and sort it and tame it, but it would just keep on being wild and thundering, a beast of nature, through each and every hard and glorious eon, until the very last one.

Nash decides the silence is fitting. The silence is reverence for that very fact.

Still, a person can take silence for only so long. And reverence, too, for that matter. Life is too beautiful and too terrible and too damn short not to celebrate every moment you can. As soon as she sees Thomas's car pull back and then turn away, going back down its own road, she pops in that CD, the one that poor Deke Donaldson didn't know was still in the player when he sold her this car. She chuckles at what she got away with. She turns it up. The bass thumps, and so does Nash's old heart, and the road goes on, and the story continues.

Acknowledgments

I owe a debt of gratitude to Bill and Sandra McGee's wonderful book *The Divorce Seekers*, which was an invaluable resource for information about the Nevada divorce ranches. Bill was the head dude wrangler at The Flying W, and his book is a treasure if only for the photos alone—images of cowboys, the ranch, old Reno, and mule-sipping socialites in the midst of their six-week cure. Steve Yurich, a regional forester and my father-in-law, also served as inspiration for the bureau men in the book. While he wasn't here to advise, I hope he would have appreciated their portrayal.

Much thanks and appreciation, too, to my long-time agent and friend, Ben Camardi, and to my editor, Shauna Summers—editor, ally, and lovely human being. Thank you, as well, to the fabulous Random House team, especially Jennifer Hershey, Marietta Anastassatos, Nancy Delia, Virginia Norey, Kristin Fassler, Maggie Oberrender, Michelle Jasmine, and Sarah Murphy.

Love and gratitude, as ever, to my family—my parents, and the larger clan. Special love, love, and love to my sweeties—my daughter, Sam Bannon; my son, Nick Bannon; and my husband, John Yurich. Thanks for bringing the joy, guys.

the secrets
she keeps

A Novel

Deb Caletti

A Reader's Guide

A Conversation with Deb Caletti

Random House Reader's Circle: What gave you the idea to write a story centered on the "Reno cure" and divorce ranches of the mid-twentieth century? Your portrayal of Tamarosa Ranch and the women who stayed there is so vivid, dazzling, and authentic. How did you go about bringing this place and this era to life, and from where did you draw your inspiration? Did you do anything specific to transport yourself into that world?

Deb Caletti: A few years ago, I came across a single line in a book that mentioned a "divorce ranch." I'd never heard the term before, and out of curiosity, I looked it up. When I learned what they were, and understood the transformative experiences that were had there, I was intrigued. But when I realized how little there was about them in the popular culture, I had one of those writer-moments where your heart beats fast and you think: *This.* Here was all of my favorite stuff in one beautiful, dusty, desert locale: marriage, heartbreak, women of varying ages supporting one another, and attempting to understand themselves and their relationships.

Bringing it to life, though, was trickier than I'd antici-pated because of exactly what I'd found so thrilling—how little there was out there about the ranches. Luckily, I dis-covered *The Divorce Seekers*, a stunning coffee table volume of photos and memories by a former dude wrangler at the famed Flying M. E. Ranch, Bill McGee. The images— with their smoky, black-and-white, retro allure—are what brought the time and place alive for me so that I could bring them to life in the novel. Not only was it an invaluable re-source for information on day-to-day life on a divorce ranch, it also set the mood. I'd open the book to an image of two sleepy roommates in the middle of their Reno cure, wearing silky chemises, drinks in hand, or to a photo of one of "the gals" in her party-night finery, and I'd be just where I needed to be. Music of the time occasionally helped, too. As well, I researched the bestsellers of those years written by women, so I could get a feel for the female voices of the time. Some-times I'd read a page or two in order to "get into character" so to speak.

RHRC: What's the most surprising thing you learned about life on a divorce ranch?

D.C.: I was surprised how wild it all got on the ranches. When you think of that time period, you imagine a (liter-ally) more buttoned-up experience, but no. The sex with cowboys, the drinking, the letting loose—it all sounds a bit film-version-cliché but was very much the truth. Each gen-eration thinks they've invented sex and rebellion, but we seem like over-sharing novices in comparison. Their experi-ences were not splayed out on every television and computer screen, and the language around it was discreet and even somewhat coy, but these were no trips to the convent.

What also surprised me—and what became extraordinarily important thematically to the book—was how timeless our struggles are in terms of love. I could see the story lines repeating over the generations. We battle the same old things they did—bad choices, infidelity, abuse, career-versus-marriage conflicts, intruding parents. We move on too fast after a breakup; they'd go from the courthouse to the marriage chapel. We're intrigued and tempted by a life not like ours; they'd buy ranch wear and try to bring home a cowboy. We've been taken (or we take); we're endlessly hopeful (or fed up and jaded); we fall for the wrong person (or, finally, the right one). And so it was then. It was this baseline that led me, in part, to using the mirror images that begin and end each chapter. Hopefully, those brief repetitions underscore the idea that here we are, all over again.

RHRC: *The Secrets She Keeps* stars a true ensemble cast of women, each startlingly unique but all equally real. Was it difficult to create so many different, dynamic personalities and have them all sharing space, or did they come to you and interact with one another naturally?

D.C.: Ensemble casts are something I like to do as a writer. It's a challenge, and I think the varying perspectives bring layers to a story. I had an ensemble cast in two of my young-adult novels, *Honey, Baby, Sweetheart* (in which a young girl and her mother go on a road trip with a group of old people to reunite a pair of geriatric lovers) and *The Secret Life of Prince Charming* (in which a young woman and her sisters return objects their father has stolen to every woman he's ever been in love with). So I've had experience managing those numbers before. Essentially, a character must sound like him- or herself, and this is true whether you're writing one or twenty. I don't find this to be particularly difficult. If you think about your extended family all sitting around a dinner table, you realize how different each individual sounds. In addition to what they say and how they say it, Mom and Aunt So-and-so dress like opposites, and while the uncles are both hardheaded, one still wears his class ring, and the other has that weird beard and bad habit of interrupting.

RHRC: Can you speak to the experience of writing a dual narrative that has one foot in the past and one in the present? What were the most challenging and rewarding aspects of that process? Was it ever hard to switch gears from one story line to the next?

D.C.: The switching itself was rewarding—going back and forth brings a freshness and energy to the work. It's similar to the experience of *reading* alternating chapters, where you're disappointed to leave the first set of characters but are eager to see what's happened with the others since you last left off. I write chronologically, so sometimes that means waiting to write a big scene I'm looking forward to, or, in this case, waiting to get back to that exciting event in the past or present. Switching can provide tension and momentum for a reader, but it can do the same for a writer. And natural momentum makes a book a joy to write.

In terms of challenge, the past/present switching made for a *ton* of research. It was akin to writing a research-heavy contemporary novel *and* a historical one. When you go back into the past, *every little thing* must be considered and checked—each item of clothing, every phrase, every piece of furniture and automobile. Kitchen supplies! Hair products! Restaurants in a city! Music! What kind of gun would they have had at the ranch then? When did cars first get radios? Was a certain slang expression used yet? Which hat did a man wear for work and which for dress? This brings us back to the rewards, though, because I learned about divorce laws through time, and obstetric practices, and the fact that ambulances were still not commonplace in rural areas then. I played virtual dress-up with the many beautiful outfits I discovered and drooled (or cringed) over the food of the time period. I am still seriously curious about those greengage plums packed in sugar-sweetened brandy.

RHRC: The mustangs play a huge role in the book, not only in terms of their sheer majesty but also their plight and the need to preserve and protect the land they inhabit. Are these larger issues something you already had a vested interest in exploring when you set out to write this book, or did that interest develop as you dug deeper into your research? Have you ever seen the mustangs running, yourself?

D.C.: This may sound hugely disappointing and unromantic, but like Callie, I have no experience with horses. I've never really ridden one and, prior to this book, knew little about them. I've never been to a ranch and have only been to Nevada once, in the backseat of the car with my parents when I was seven. As a writer, I often think about Lilly Tuck's speech at the National Book Awards the year she won (and the year I was a finalist for *Honey, Baby, Sweet-*

heart). Her book was *The News from Paraguay*, and she began her speech by saying that she had never been to Paraguay, didn't know much about Paraguay, and didn't even really care to visit Paraguay. While I'd love to spend time on a ranch and was fascinated by all I learned, I understand what she meant. The adage urges writers to "Write what you know," but if we did, there'd be many novels about us sitting home alone, pecking at the keyboard. Or else reading online reviews and becoming crippled with self-doubt.

That said, when searching for the story line, themes, and symbols that would bridge the two narratives, the mustangs were a natural choice. Campaigns to save the mustang began just before the book does, in 1950, when Velma Bronn Johnston (Wild Horse Annie) of Washoe County became involved in the campaign to save the wild horses after following a truck loaded with horses and dripping blood on its way to a slaughterhouse. (Yes, a certain scene in the book is a nod to her.) In 1951, photographer Gus Bundy also began shooting images that became instrumental in changing gathers by airplane. But in addition to lending historic accuracy, the horses are a physical representation of love itself: passionate, messy, unpredictable, and stunning. The complicated questions that surround them, the lack of clear answers, were also symbolically on the mark.

I may not have known anything about the mustangs before I began, but I developed a great respect for them and for the individuals on both sides of the question, particularly the land managers who must consider every corner of the issue. I was astounded at the care they take to balance the interests of the land (and the other living things on it) with the some fifty thousand wild horses and burros currently living in the western states.

RHRC: Callie is awed and humbled by her interactions with nature while exploring the Washoe Lake area, which lends such perspective to her life in Seattle. Living in Seattle yourself, do you find this reflects your own experience in any way? Do you prefer a city existence or the "of-the-land" lifestyle that Kit leads, or do you strive for more of a balance?

D.C.: Callie's observations are mostly part of her personal process, where she eventually learns that you sometimes need to get out of your daily existence to appreciate the beauty of your daily existence. Still, I think there's some truth to the differences she notices, in terms of the biking techies and hipster baristas and self-aware food versus "life like that—the one going on right here right now, with men in cowboy hats, men with silver belt buckles, men with horses and guns." We are very connected to nature and the outdoors here, too, but sometimes there's an affected quality to it, a persona that's worn along with all the right clothing from REI. Ranch life seems more straightforward, and the relationship to the land more pragmatic. That said, it's also true that you'll find some of the most stunning, breathtaking parts of this country in the Northwest, and we who live here do our best to appreciate that fact.

The city-or-not dilemma has always been large for me. The idea of sprawling acres of land and a small town has huge appeal. I used to live in a house on a salmon-running creek at the foot of a mountain before moving to the city when I remarried. I loved being near water, trees, and creatures. (Though I could've passed on the bear and the cougars.) I adored bumping my Jeep along the rugged dirt road, reveled in the awareness of seasons and the perspective nature brings. I still long for miles of windswept dunes, or a herd of cattle with room to roam, or a dock on a remote lake. But there is also the matter of little-black-dress literary parties, great restaurants, and the need for the nearness of a library. The perfect life would be a pair of old work boots next to the heels.

RHRC: Hadley keeps a saucer of foil-wrapped confections by her typewriter to "tempt the muse." As a writer, do you have any habits, processes, or, like Hadley, treats that get your creative juices flowing?

D.C.: Hmm. Wonder where I got *that*? I confess that I've gone beyond the saucer to an actual drawer. Occasionally, a little self-bribery is useful. I usually start the writing morning with strong coffee and a shortbread cookie, the kind in the red plaid box that are all butter, glorious butter. Other treats in the drawer—Red Vines, Hot Tamales, chewy butterscotch, a bit of good chocolate. Full disclosure: I considered lying when answering this question.

RHRC: Nash and Lilly bond through the trading of beloved books. In that moment, Lilly asks, "Don't you wish you could live inside a book sometimes?" What book(s) would you live inside if you could?

D.C.: *A Moveable Feast* would work nicely. Paris in the 1920s, with Ernest Hemingway and pals like James Joyce, Ford Madox Ford, Gertrude Stein ... F. Scott Fitzgerald reading Hemingway the first draft of *The Great Gatsby* at their neighborhood café, La Closerie des Lilas ... Ahh. I'm also drawn to books like *Under the Tuscan Sun*, where a woman goes to a foreign country, remodels some crumbling villa, makes friends with villagers while walking her charming dog, all the while eating fabulous food.

RHRC: Of all the women you've brought to life in this novel, which would you say most resembles yourself? Or who would you most like to resemble? Who would be your partner in crime if you were to spend time at the Tamarosa Ranch?

D.C.: Almost every character has a bit (or more) of the author in them, I think. Callie and Shaye reflect my own yin/yang: settled and restless, steady and unsteady, cautious and occasionally heedless. I have the aspirations of Hadley, and I've had (past tense) the naïveté of Ellen's and Lilly's unfortunate taste in men. I have Nash's leanings toward solitude and open air, her book love, and her appetite. I'd most like to take on her realistic, calm worldview, though, and the strength she's developed over her years. Veronica is least like me and, therefore, probably the one I'd want as a partner in crime. During a six-week cure, you'd need a Veronica to encourage a little mischief. And to push you toward the life that's truly yours.

Questions and Topics for Discussion

1. Imagine you were doing a six-week stint at one of the divorce ranches of yesteryear. If you could choose which women (past or present) you stayed on with, who would they be and why? Who's your favorite of the characters at Tamarosa Ranch under Nash's watch?

2. Of course, the divorce ranches weren't all fun and games for women seeking quickie divorces, but as in *The Secrets She Keeps*, there's a definite spirit of liberation, indulgence, spunk, and camaraderie underlying it all. What part of checking into a divorce ranch could you get used to, if you had to? What would be the hardest thing about it? How are these pros and cons addressed in the novel?

3. The notion of home plays a major role throughout the book. Callie loved her house so much that she'd "put up with almost anything if it meant not losing that brick pathway [she'd] planted with perennials." Veronica, on the other hand, doesn't know where she'll call home once she's officially divorced Gus. What does home mean or come to mean for each of the characters? Discuss the larger statement the novel might be making about home when human nature seeks both permanence and change.

4. At one point, Callie wonders, "What heedless actions would you change if you could read the future," going on to say, "I don't have the answer to that even now." By the end of the novel, do you think Callie should want to change any of her "heedless actions"? Would you wish for the opportunity to edit your own life in such a way, or like Callie and Nash, do you believe in fate instead?

5. Callie and Shaye find it hard to believe that Nash never got married. Why do *you* think Nash never joined the ranks of married women? Would it have changed your impression of her if she ever had?

6. Jack tells Nash that seeing the wild horses changes a person; that it's a message from nature that leaves you transformed. How does seeing the horses change Nash and Callie in fundamental ways? Can you describe a similar event in your own life that had the same effect on you?

7. Shaye's love life, with its many conquests and questionable "dark storm clouds," is completely at odds with Callie's enduring marriage and domesticity. But they've both ended up at a crossroad in their lives and relationships, where they seem to be searching for the same thing. What is that thing and have they each managed to find it by the end of the novel? What lessons did they learn from each other's disparate experiences and approaches to love that they might not have realized on their own?

8. How did it affect your read to have Callie's marital issues set against the interwoven stories of the divorcees at Tamarosa Ranch? Did you see her problems as more trivial in comparison to those experiences or tantamount? How might you have seen her and the book in general differently if this were Callie's story alone?

9. "Every person must come full circle to his or her rightful life, Nash knows. Sometimes, you have to make that same trip more than once." Discuss how this sentiment applies to the journeys undertaken by the central characters.

10. One of the major things Callie grapples with is the expansiveness of life and its endless possibilities. At one point, she remarks that being in the desert "was a whole slice of life I knew nothing about, which makes you realize just how many such slices there are." Later, she says, "There were so many possible lives to lead. Every day, you chose your life, even if you could forget that." Do you think Callie finds this position liberating or maddening? Does the limitlessness she sees before her actually stunt her in some ways? On the flip side, why did she have to step outside of her little slice in order to be satisfied with it, and what made her choose that life in the end?

11. Did you realize all along that Callie was undergoing a legitimate midlife crisis or did this come as much as a surprise to you as it did to her? Why do you think she was able to hide it from herself for so long? Was it easier to see Thomas's actions as more indicative of a midlife crisis for some reason?

12. Nash offers such comic relief to the story, even though she's the one facing her own mortality. Do you think her clear-eyed, straight-shooting nature is a result of her nearing the end of her life, or do you see glimmers of that personality from her earlier years? What was your favorite life lesson learned from Nash? Does she remind you of anyone you know?

13. What did you make of Jack as a character? Nash says she fancied the idea of him rather than the man himself. Did you get the sense while reading that he functions more as an idea for her than a man? Or as a means to some end?

14. "When it comes to sisters, it seems that one stays and one goes, one remains bound and the other is set free. [Nash] is who she is in good part because of who Gloria isn't. In order to be herself, in order to be different from her sister, she had to take what was left over, the opposite, unchosen road." Compare the sister relationships in the book. Does this statement hold true in all cases? Does it apply to your relationship with your own siblings?

15. Discuss how the past and present are contrasted in the book, both in terms of character foils and times, mind-sets, customs, etc., either changing or staying the same. Do you wish any of the old, forgotten ways as portrayed in this story were still preserved? Like Nash, do you think we've come light-years from the bygone era of divorce ranches, or like Shaye, do you think those days might not be as far in the past as we'd like to believe?

16. Nash and Lilly exchange books in an act that bonds them as friends. Have you spoken the love language of books with your friends, and which are the stories you've gifted? Which book would *you* have given Lilly if you were in Nash's place? Which would you have given Nash?

17. The opening chapter told from Nash's point of view establishes the expectation of "a doomed mission of the heart." Did you have any preconceived ideas about what Nash's mission entailed, and if so, were you surprised by the revelation of her actual secret in the end?

18. Nash says she doesn't know if she believes in happy endings but that the story goes on. Do you think this particular story has a happy ending, or that things are left open-ended? What do you hope for these characters if that's the case?

About the Author

DEB CALETTI is an award-winning author and National Book Award finalist. Her many books for young adults include *The Nature of Jade, Stay, The Last Forever,* and *Honey, Baby, Sweetheart,* winner of the Washington State Book Award, the PNBA Best Book Award, and a finalist for the California Young Reader Medal and the PEN USA Award. Her first book for adults, *He's Gone,* was released by Random House in 2013, followed by *The Secrets She Keeps.* Deb lives with her family in Seattle.

About the Type

This book was set in Berling. Designed in 1951 by Karl-Erik Forsberg (1914–95) for the type foundry Berlingska Stilgjuteri AB in Lund, Sweden, it was released the same year in foundry type by H. Berthold AG. A classic old-face design, its generous proportions and inclined serifs make it highly legible.